CAESAR, CICERO & CLEOPATRA

What really happened?

Arthur J. Paone

CAESAR, CICERO & CLEOPATRA

What really happened?

Copyright © 2014 by Arthur J. Paone

Revised February, 2015.
Minor corrections, name
simplifications and
an Index of Names added in the
Appendix.

ISBN 978-0-9746366-9-6 (Print)

ISBN 978-0-9746366-8-9 (Digital)

Library of Congress Control Number:
2014915374

All maps are the original work of cartographer
Julie Witmer: jewelcartografx@gmail.com
(found by way of freelancer.com).

The cover image was primarily created by Vook
through Bowker Identifier Services.

Back cover photo of author: Nick Pinto, Xavier
'57.Editing was by Kirkus Editorial.

CAESAR, CICERO & CLEOPATRA

What really happened?

CAESAR, CICERO & CLEOPATRA

What really happened?

CONTENTS

INTRODUCTION

I was not surprised when the Headmaster called me into his office and told me that the Latin Department was shutting down. By this time I was the Latin Department. It had shrunk from a roster of five teachers to one in just a few years. First, Xavier had made the third and fourth years of Latin elective subjects. Then it dropped the requirement of Latin entirely for the first two years. Thus this "alien and useless language" would be studied only if a gaming-crazed fourteen-year-old somehow miraculously chose to do so. Hence I was on my way out after thirty-five years of teaching. No more would the words of Cicero, Caesar, Horace, Juvenal, Levy, Seneca, Virgil, Suetonius, Plutarch and the others be heard in the corridors of Xavier High School. Taken together with the

What really happened?

disappearance of the cadet uniforms, it was no longer Xavier to me.

It was near the end of the school year so I did not have to endure the sympathy of my colleagues for very long. I decided to resign the day after my last class and go someplace where I could live comfortably on my pension and not have to think about the stupidity of modern educators.

It was easy to decide where to go. Having never married, and with most of my siblings gone, I was alone in making the decision. To Rome! Where Latin once ruled.

Hence I soon found myself in the Alban Hills, about twelve miles southwest of Rome, in a town called Frascati. This community was famous for the white wine named after it and for some scientific laboratories. But its real draw for me was the many old villas in the hills outside of town. One of them was called Tuscalana, after the beloved villa of Cicero, Tusculum, and was situated at the highest point of an ancient volcanic ridge. Of course it bore no resemblance to what Cicero may have had, nor did anybody even pretend that it sat where Cicero's did.

This villa, like many others in the Alban Hills, was built during the Renaissance and housed a succession of cardinals, popes and other notables over the centuries. These men vacationed here and in scores of other villas, just as the ancient Roman nobles and wealthy had, to escape the heat and humidity of Rome. Lucien Bonaparte, who did the first excavations of the area, once occupied it. It turns out he was not very organized and simply sold what antiquities he found on the auction market in Rome to pay for his expenses. Many of those objects are now scattered around the museums of the world. But in his defense he was one of the first to do historical excavation in the nineteenth century and the discipline had not yet been developed.

Today the Villa Tuscalana is owned by the Salesians of

CAESAR, CICERO & CLEOPATRA

What really happened?

Don Bosco and used principally as a retreat for aged priests and as a conference hotel. The Salesians, or the Order of St. Francis de Sales, had originally been founded by an Italian priest, Don Bosco, to help the poor that were being crushed in the Industrial Revolution. It still ministers to the poor around the world.

I could not resist the lure of the names "Tusculum" and "Don Bosco," nor the magnificent views from the garden of the villa. Cicero had written a famous philosophical discourse called Conversations at Tusculum (Tusculanae disputationes) and in it he incidentally describes, with loving care and affection, his own luxurious villa at Tusculum. As for "Don Bosco," two of my brothers as kids had gone to a summer camp called Camp Don Bosco and would often sing the Don Bosco camp song around the house: "Camp Don Bosco, Camp Don Bosco, Camp Don Bosco w…a…y…." I suspect many of our major decisions are based on even more flimsy grounds. At any rate I pestered the Fathers until they agreed to let me renovate a tiny ruined chapel far off in a corner of the gardens and live there at a modest rental.

Over the next few years I became accustomed to the leisurely pace of the other residents in the Alban Hills, often exploring the ancient ruins nearby, relying heavily on my walking stick and my inseparable companion, Gus. I had found Gus in a little cave, the lone surviving puppy of a mother who had apparently starved to death. I am not sure but I suspect he is a combination of a miniature dachshund and a corgi.

Sometimes we did our exploring with one or more of the retired Salesians who lived in the villa itself. I had become acquainted with some of them while using their wonderful library, which had an excellent collection of books in Latin. I eventually learned that some of the Salesians were as addicted as I was to the Latin language and we would often discuss the texts of the ancients.

What really happened?

I had resigned myself, without realizing it, to this kind of quiet but pleasant existence for the remainder of my years.

Then one day an accident suffered by Gus propelled me into a new life. We had been exploring some unremarkable ruins in an isolated and uninhabited wood a few miles east of the villa when I suddenly realized that Gus had disappeared. I called out for him repeatedly and must have searched around endless ancient columns and marble crevices for hours. Finally I decided to return to the spot where I last remembered seeing him. I sat down on the lower marble step of what must have been an entranceway to some building and just looked around. After some time I noticed a particularly dark space along a low stone wall only about twenty feet from me.

Sure enough, upon inspection, this dark area revealed an opening in the wall. I got down on my knees and tried to peer into the hole. I could not see anything but I felt a slight disturbance in the air to suggest that just inside the opening there must be a deep drop. I put my head into the opening and called out for Gus. I called out a few times and my heart took a leap of joy when finally I heard a responding bark echoing in the emptiness.

Fortunately I always carried with me some climbing rope, along with an ax, a pick, and a small flashlight. I sometimes used them to explore interesting caves that we would come across. Even though the area was famous for its villas, from ancient Roman days to today, there still was evidence of the caves that people inhabited in even earlier times. Though this deep opening presented more than the usual challenge, there was no way I was going to leave Gus. I first widened the opening by removing some adjacent stones. Then I tied one end of the rope securely around a nearby column and very slowly lowered myself into the dark opening. Though I could see nothing as I descended I could hear Gus's barking getting louder until I

What really happened?

was finally down on solid ground next to him. It turned out that the descent was no more than twenty or twenty-five feet down. We of course were delighted to see each other again, but I had to sit down and rest a while before trying to climb up with Gus.

I clicked on my little flashlight and looked around. I immediately noticed a number of large objects in what appeared to be a large room. I determined that they were trunks or chests of some kind. The trunks seemed to be made of very hard wood and each contained a lid that was tightly fastened by several metal rods. The chests were very heavy. I could not even budge one of them.

Naturally I was excited by the discovery. A host of possibilities about what I had found— or rather what Gus had found—in this ancient land ignited my imagination. But there was little I could do by myself with what tools I had at hand. I would have to go for help.

I was now anxious to be back up in the light of day with Gus and get back to the villa. With such energy that I did not know I had, I was able to scale up the wall with Gus under one arm and soon we were both seated on the ground outside the opening, me panting heavily and Gus running around in joy. That very afternoon when I got back to the villa I searched around for some help and soon found it in the library. Four of the Fathers that I had become close to were there.

I described to them what I had found, and we sat around and discussed the best way to proceed. The youngest among us was Giovanni, who was in his early fifties and strong as an ox. He was all for going after the "treasure" immediately. But it was our oldest companion, Leo, who got us to settle down and think through it all, step by step.

Being Italian and having headed some of the Salesian organizations in Italy for a number of years, he had a deep understanding of how things were done in Italy. He

What really happened?

pointed out that by law such a find would have to be reported immediately to the Ministry of Culture in Rome.

Even though none of us had had his experience, we all knew just enough about Italian government agencies to let out a chorus of groans. However, being priests and brothers, and used to obeying a higher authority, they all decided, and I readily agreed, that we could for the time being ignore the law. We all knew that once the government got involved, a cloak of secrecy would descend on the discovery while behind the scenes the different bureaucracies would battle over who would be "in charge," where the contents would be studied, who would make the announcement, where they would get the financing, and so forth and so on, for so long that we would all have been long been dead and buried before anything happened.

Once that was out of the way we similarly dismissed any idea of informing the head of the villa, much less the head of the Order. They were not as free as we were to be so cavalier about the law.

We also quickly put aside the question of what to do with our discovery until we could determine just what it was. Chests full of gold would mean one thing and require a certain course. If they contained objects of art, then another path. If they were ancient clothing and cooking utensils, then another. If documents, yet a different direction. So rather than waste time in speculative debate, we concentrated on the practical problem of getting the chests out of the cave to a location in the villa where we could study the contents. We easily agreed that we would tell no one else until we determined what we had, since even a whisper of such a find in this part of the world would have treasure-hunters, government officials, the police, and God knew who else coming down on us like an avalanche.

We visited the site the very next day, this time equipped

What really happened?

with ladders, some tools, and heavy flashlights. We had borrowed the gardener's pickup truck for our venture. We made the hole wider and descended to the floor.

It appeared that the chamber had been carved out of rock and was about the size of a modest living room. In it were five trunks made of solid wood, each one identical. The trunks had not been locked, but only tightly secured with iron bars. Around the rim of each trunk where the lid met the base someone had been glued very thick layers of two different types of substances, which we later identified as cork and asbestos, materials that the ancients often used for insulation. With some lubricants and a lot of chipping away we finally opened the first truck. Even before we could gaze on what it contained we were assaulted with a strange and very strong odor. At first we almost panicked, thinking it might have been a trap set by the ancients, and that we would all soon collapse from some strange poison.

When nothing else happened and no one fainted or died, we looked into the trunk and saw dozens and dozens of what appeared to be small and narrow canvas bags neatly piled up, one on top of the other, in orderly stacks. We needed to examine what the bags contained, but decided to do it in the privacy of my cottage. Since the trunks themselves were too large and too heavy for us to remove, we would have to carry the canvas bags in our arms up the ladder.

It took us about a week to retrieve, carefully and in secrecy, all the little bags from that extraordinary cave. There were several hundred of them. But on the very first day we learned that we had come upon the dream of a scholar's life.

Each of those bags, as we first called them, was in fact a heavy parchment in which was wrapped a roll of papyrus, or a scroll. Most of the scrolls, when fully unfolded, were about fifteen or twenty feet long, consisting of a series of nine by thirteen inch sheets glued

What really happened?

together one after another. We had all seen papyrus scrolls before, but no one could remember seeing papyrus of such fine quality. The scrolls were covered with columns of small but neat writing in Latin.

This was more than we could handle. Now, as they say, it was getting serious. So we meekly went up to the office of the villa's leader and told the good Father what we had found.

He quickly came over to my now very crowded cottage and examined some of the scrolls. Then he sat down heavily and seemed to lose himself in thought. We anxiously awaited his verdict.

"Well," he finally said, "get these precious things up to our library and let's start work on them."

The catch was duly transferred into the library and it became the center of our lives for the next few years. We determined that the parchment scrolls contained the notes and research of Gaius Asinius Pollio, a contemporary of Julius Caesar's, which he apparently had used to produce his seventeen-volume History of the Civil War, which covered the conflict in Rome from 60 to 42 BC.

Pollio had been a loyal supporter of Caesar's, serving as an officer in his army and fighting under him from the beginning to the end of the civil war. Thereafter he had kept his distance from Augustus, but was allowed to live in peace. He became famous as an orator and patron of the arts. Horace and Virgil were among his beneficiaries. He has come down to us as an often-quoted historian of the period, but an historian whose works, sadly including those seventeen volumes on the Roman civil war, have been lost to posterity. Much of his writing was done at his country villa in, yes, Tusculum. It seems that after Cicero's death Pollio somehow came into possession of the great orator's villa.

One of the Salesian Brothers was very experienced in carpentry. He made a careful examination of the trunks

What really happened?

and quietly consulted with some experts in Rome. He found that the trunks were ingenuously constructed storage containers, using some of the hardest woods known in the ancient world, probably imported from Africa. In combination with layers of densely packed cork and asbestos as well as a half-inch sheets of steel, the containers had for two thousand years kept insects, moisture, and even the air itself, away from the scrolls. That explained why the scrolls were as pliable and easy to handle as if they had just been written upon.

Another Brother spent much time examining the few gold coins we had found in each trunk, something that at first struck us as curious. After much research he came across pictures of them in a coin book at the Vatican Library, which explained the figures and cryptic letters on the coins. The coins bore the head and name of Emperor Flavius Honorius Augustus, who reigned as Emperor of the Western Roman Empire from 395 to 423 AD, residing mostly in Ravenna, where the Western capital of the empire had retreated under pressure from the invading barbarians.

We could only speculate what all this meant. But we eventually did come to a consensus, as amateur archeologists, that the descendants of Asinius Pollio decided sometime during the reign of Honorius to preserve their famous ancestor's works for prosperity, though their world was falling apart around them and they themselves might not survive much longer. So they constructed these special trunks and deposited Pollio's books and records in them. Since we had only his notes, and certainly not all of them, this meant that Gus and I had stumbled across only a fraction of the trunks they must have buried in the hills to escape the rampaging barbarians. The coins told us that these trunks were hidden here most probably around 410 AD, when Alaric I and the Visigoths sacked and burned Rome.

What really happened?

The Salesian Fathers are compiling a complete copy of Pollio's notes and will publish them with extensive commentary. It is a guaranteed blockbuster. All the proceeds beyond expenses will go to their work with the poor. The Salesians are confident that when the inevitable explosion occurs upon publication, they can escape any legal entanglements by simply claiming that the scrolls had been in the basement of the villa all this time. Such a claim would be transparently absurd to everybody. But the Church still had some power in Italy and the government of the day was as weak as usual and its leaders would be glad for any excuse to avoid a confrontation with the Church.

I myself am using Pollio's notes to write this story, focused primarily on Julius Caesar. My book will be published in conjunction with the work of the Salesian Fathers. As I am well beyond the September of my years, and am a bit weary after the long and difficult study of Pollio's notes, I readily agreed that the net proceeds, after funding a trust for Gus, will also go to the Salesians' work with Pope Francis's poor.

Arthur Paone

Villa Tuscalana in the Alban Hills.

CAESAR, CICERO & CLEOPATRA

What really happened?

MAPS

ITALY AND GREECE

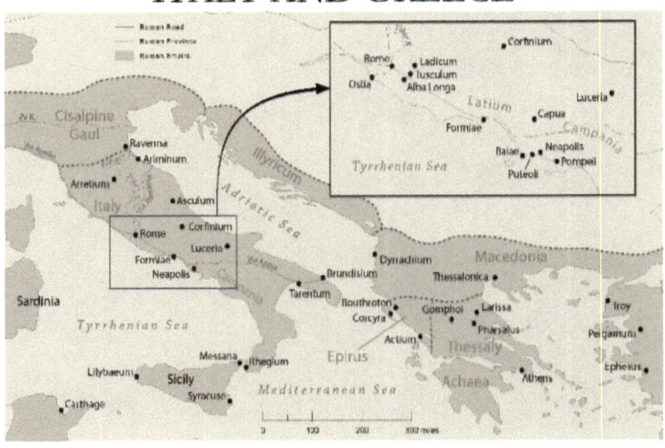

What really happened?

THE MEDITERRANEAN

ASIA

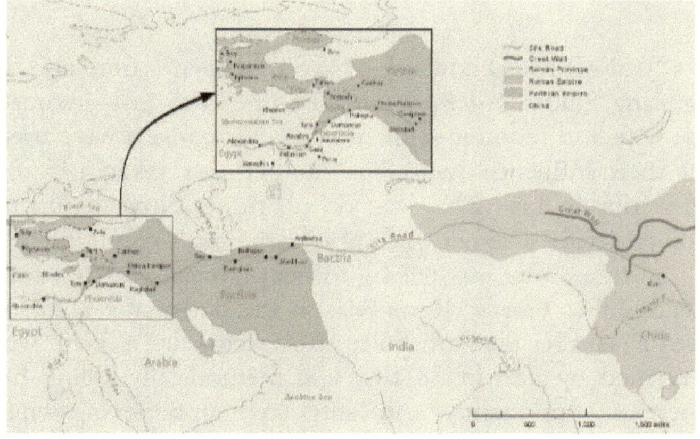

PART I
ROME
CAPITAL OF THE ROMAN REPUBLIC
82 – 57 BC

I
82 BC

"Gaius, you know, don't you, that no one else is refusing Sulla's orders. Young Pompey has just divorced his wife and renounced his friends. My cousins have used all their influence with Sulla to get you taken off the Proscription List. They can do no more. Now it's up to you to decide whether to comply with Sulla's conditions."

Aurelia Cotta was talking to her eighteen-year-old son, Gaius Julius Caesar. Rome was in the midst of a reign of terror as the dictator Sulla, the victor in a civil war launched by him in 88 BC, was methodically killing his enemies, opponents, and suspected opponents, while confiscating their properties. Championing the Senate and its nobles, the "Optimates," he had defeated the followers

What really happened?

of Gaius Marius and Cornelius Cinna, who were the favorites of the people, the "Populares."

Gaius Marius had been a great general who had stopped the threatening migration of hordes of Germans toward Italy and served as consul for several unprecedented terms. Cinna had taken up his policies of land distribution to the poor and the expansion of citizenship to the Italian allies, and they had joined forces. But Marius passed away in 86 BC, after his own reign of terror, and Cinna ruled by himself until he was killed in 84.

Caesar's relationship to these two men had landed him on the Proscription list. Marius had been his uncle, married to his paternal aunt, Julia. Cinna had been his father-in-law, his daughter Cornelia marrying Caesar at Cinna's behest just the year before, shortly before Cinna's own killing. What's more, this Caesar, though only eighteen, had already shown himself to be something extraordinary. Sulla was not going to ignore him just because of his tender age.

"Dear Mother," responded Caesar, "I know you fear for me, but I would not be true to myself if I put my wife Cornelia aside and renounced her father and my uncle as Sulla is demanding. I cannot even imagine doing such a thing. It will just not happen."

"Your uncle Marius and your father-in-law Cinna are both gone, Gaius. There is simply no one left who can protect you if you continue to defy Sulla."

"Then I will not stay here. Cornelia and I can quietly leave Rome and just disappear. There are many friends of Marius and Cinna in the Italian cities who will hide us."

"And they will have to feed you as well," Aurelia said, "as Sulla will confiscate everything you own, including Cornelia's dowry. He will also have me and my family watched so we will not be able to send you any help."

"Please, Mother, I would not want you to risk yourself or your family on my behalf. We will be able to survive in

What really happened?

the countryside. Sulla will never dare to touch you or the Cotta family if I just disappeared. He will send agents after me, surely, but I will deal with that."

Aurelia, though still fearful of the dangers her only son was placing himself in, was nevertheless quite proud of the young man that she had raised. He would rather face death than not be true to himself, at eighteen years of age! How could he know himself so well at this stage of his life?

"Do as your spirit directs you, Gaius," she said. "Whatever you decide you will always have my love and support."

The eighteen-year-old then went into hiding with his young wife. A year later Aurelia's connections and family obtained a position for him on the staff of a relative serving in Asia. There Caesar served brilliantly and only when Sulla died a few years later did he return to Rome.

In Rome the intelligent and charismatic Caesar immediately gained the support of the people with his advocating of liberal policies for land distribution to the poor and the expansion of citizenship to Rome's Romanized friends and allies, following the policies of Marius and Cinna.

His devoted wife, Cornelia, died in 69 BC in the fifteenth year of their marriage. In the same year his aunt Julia, Marius's widow, also died. He created a sensation with the funeral games he put on for them, the first ever for women, borrowing heavily to do so. During these proceedings he also boldly displayed the trophies and images of Marius and Cinna, much to the joy of the populace and the irritation of the Senate, most of whom were appointees of the late dictator, Sulla. His funeral oration was also extraordinary and was remembered for many years thereafter, particularly for his claim that his family was descended from the god Venus. This man was different in almost everything he did, defying tradition and the forces of power whenever he thought it necessary.

CAESAR, CICERO & CLEOPATRA

What really happened?

CAESAR, CICERO & CLEOPATRA

What really happened?

II
57 BC

"'Gallia est omnis divisa in partes tres . . .'"

"What kind or rubbish is that? What is Caesar trying to feed us?"

"Who the hell cares how many parts Gaul is divided into? Let it be divided into a thousand parts—or no parts. What does that high and mighty big shot think he is supposed to be doing up north—preparing geography lessons for the vulgar mobs of Rome? What a freak!"

The speaker, Bibulus, sat back on his couch while he allowed a slave to refill his cup with wine and water. Bibulus, a descendant of the ancient and still powerful Calpurnii family, was lounging in the expansive gardens of his home on the Palatine Hill, together with some friends. He was still smarting from his humiliation at Caesar's hands two years earlier when they both served as co-consuls, the highest political offices in the Roman Republic. Acting on behalf of the tiny group of conservative noble families who traditionally controlled the Senate, Rome's governing body, Bibulus had vigorously attacked every piece of liberal legislation that

What really happened?

Caesar, through his collaborative tribunes, had proposed.

This faction's instinctual hostility to Caesar even encompassed his initial and seemingly non-controversial bill which would require, for the first time, that minutes be kept of all Senate meetings as well as those of the people's assemblies and that those minutes be published daily. Upon passage, this law would for the first time open up to public scrutiny what had been the erstwhile opaque maneuverings of the nobles in the Senate. Now, thanks to Caesar's law, not only the people of Rome, but citizens throughout Rome's provinces would quickly learn what the nobles were up to. This seemed reason enough for oligarchs to hate him.

Facing such stubborn opposition by the Senate's controlling clique, including Bibulus' father-in-law, Cato, his most implacable foe, Caesar had promptly resorted to the practice of bypassing the Senate entirely by going directly to the populace, the people's assemblies. Under the Roman constitution, these assemblies possessed the sole power to pass legislation. However, the Senate had long controlled even this process with the development of a parallel or quasi-constitutional system that called for the prior approval by the Senate of any legislation proposed to the assemblies. Caesar blithely ignored this tradition, though not without serious risk. Previous efforts to use this totally legal route to overcome the adamantly "status quo" Senate, had ended a number of times in the assassinations of those men by the Senate, including the most famous of the reformers, the brothers Tiberius and Gaius Gracchus.

But Caesar had learned some lessons from the fate of the Gracchi, and that of several other murdered reformers in the past hundred years. In addition to his brilliant eloquence, his network of family, his friends and his purchased allies, Caesar was not averse to the threat or actual use of some strong physical measures to get his

What really happened?

legislation passed. This was one reformer who intended to live to see his legislation implemented.

In that memorable year 59 BC Caesar had simply ignored his colleague Bibulus. Bibulus attempted to thwart the reforms of Caesar by an assortment of devices, such as the reading of unfavorable signs from the heavens or negative omens from the entrails of sacrificed animals, which by yet another tradition fostered by the nobles, should have caused postponement of any legislative action by the populace. Caesar also was prepared for the use of armed thugs by the Senators at public meetings and during voting by the popular assemblies. He hired his own armed thugs and met violence with violence. Caesar insured that these stratagems did not work this time.

By the middle of their year's terms of office, a frustrated and frightened Bibulus had retreated to the safe confines of his home, refusing to participate in any official proceedings and attempting to forestall legislation by constantly issuing unfavorable signs from the heavens, as was his right as a co-consul—but all to no avail. In his spare time, of which he now had much, Bibulus would compose and publish all sorts of defamatory and inflammatory stories about Caesar's character and personal life.

Caesar disregarded these as well and was in fact quite content to run the government by himself. During that year Caesar was able to enact a number of "radical" measures, including an urgently needed distribution of public and government-purchased lands to landless veterans and to the poorest families of Rome, as well as adjustments to the financial system which brilliantly resolved, for the time being, the conflict between creditors and debtors that had frequently disrupted Roman life.

"I would not be so ready to mock him, Bibulus," his friend Scipio, scion of another ancient and powerful clan, the Metelli, warned.

What really happened?

"In passing the Forum this morning," Scipio continued, "I heard Caesar's Commentary from Gaul being read out loud to a very large group of attentive citizens. I understand this has been going on for weeks."

"Big deal, Scipio. That illiterate rabble hanging around the Forum has nothing better to do than consume free food and listen to fairy tales . . . More wine, Scipio?"

"These are no fairy tales, my good Bibulus," another friend, Brutus, remarked. Unlike the others, his cup was filled mostly with water. Brutus was sometimes called Brutus Caepio, after the wealthy Quintus Servilius Caepio, who had adopted him as an adult. In his own right a gifted orator and Stoic student, Brutus ironically was the natural son of the brilliant and influential Servilia, the half-sister of Cato, Caesar's implacable enemy. Servilia was also alleged to be a longtime romantic interest of Caesar's. The tiny group of families that had ruled Rome for centuries inevitably had tangled relationships.

"Our friends and relatives on his staff in Gaul," Brutus continued, "report everything to us. So we know that what he writes in his dispatches to the Senate as well as in his commentaries to the public are precisely what has happened in Gaul. In addition, the merchants who follow his army have confirmed his accounts. As far as I have heard, not a fact that he writes in his commentaries is out of place.

"Nor is it just the usual riffraff that is eating this up. Many freedmen and slaves of some of our friends have been seen copying these commentaries from those posted on the public billboards in the Forum. Many citizens just stand in line to read them and yet others would remain in the rain or under a hot sun to listen to these stories from Caesar. Even our friend Cicero, certainly no lover of this radical Caesar, has been heard to comment that he has never read Latin written with such clarity and brilliance, comprehensible to all yet still noble and elegant.

What really happened?

"I tell you," Scipio interjected, "the people love it. They are hearing about fascinating battles fought against hundreds of thousands; about how we are protecting our Celtic allies from the migration of hundreds of thousands of Helvetii moving across Gaul, driving the survivors back to where they came from, to again face off against the fierce Germanic tribes just across the Rhine; about enemy cities and towns being stormed; tens of thousands of the enemy killed and tens of thousands more sold into slavery—all to the glory of Rome, and much more to the point, to our safety.

"People have not forgotten the devastation caused to our allies and friends in Gaul, and the very serious threat to Italy half a century ago caused by the masses of just two Germanic tribes, the Cimbri and Teutones. They had poured over the Rhine and ran across Gaul, slaughtering several armies that we sent against them. Some even crossed the Alps into Italy."

"Scipio," another colleague, Casca, joined in. "While you are speaking I feel that history seems almost to be repeating itself. It was of course Caesar's uncle, Marius, who finally stopped and annihilated the Teutones at Aquae Sextiae on the far side of the Alps, and then later did the same to the Cimbri at Vercellae on our side of the Alps. Though this time in Gaul no Roman army had first to be destroyed before Rome acted decisively. We must admit that Caesar on his own has moved so resolutely and so quickly that it seems he has turned around this migrating multitude in a flash—long before they could become a threat to Italy itself."

"Yes, Casca," answered Scipio. "His victories have been swift and ingenious—almost as if he could see the enemy movements from the sky and read the intentions of their leaders. And his commentaries—this also has never happened before: a general not satisfied with just sending dispatches to the Senate, as he is obligated to do, but also

What really happened?

sending detailed and finely written reports to the people directly, with frank honesty, describing the good and the bad. It does not just flatter them; it makes them proud to be Romans and to have such a general on the frontiers."

"Hogwash to all of you!" Bibulus jeered.

Bibulus was forty-three years old, the same age as Caesar. That small happenstance was not a fortunate one for Bibulus. Being the same age, the two patricians were thus compelled repeatedly to compete against each other up the long ladder of political office, called the Course of Honor: from military tribune, to quaestor, aedile, praetor and finally the highest office, consul. Except for consul, where there were only two elected each year, there were multiple slots for the other offices. The law provided minimum ages for each office and there were required intervals between them. Some offices where not allowed to be repeated. Both men had dutifully stood for election to each office over the years, at the minimum age requirements—a matter of pride.

Unfortunately for the plodding and mediocre Bibulus, he inevitably found himself lost in the shadow of the larger-than-life, charismatic and free-spending Caesar as they served together at each stage. This only added to his bitterness, which lasted to the day he died some ten years later in the civil war, when, notwithstanding all his efforts, he again failed to put an end to Caesar. Caesar, for his part, in his commentaries at that time, found something to compliment him about, as was his wont even with his most diehard enemies.

"This man, though from an ancient patrician family," Bibulus earnestly insisted, "is intent on depriving us of our right to govern the Republic, something which our ancestors have justly earned for us with their great deeds and service to Rome over hundreds of years. He and his appeal to the populace and his radical agenda are all directed against us, and who we are. He must be stopped

What really happened?

at some point, before he gains too much power. As for the fickle rabble that adore him so much today, they will forget him tomorrow. What's more, they will turn on him at his first defeat."

Caesar, however, would never be defeated in the years and years of wars to come. Nor did the people ever forget or turn on him, but rather they loved him to the very end, and even thereafter.

CAESAR, CICERO & CLEOPATRA

What really happened?

PART II
ALEXANDRIA
CAPITAL OF EGYPT, 48 BC

III

Gaius Julius Caesar, fifty-two years old, stood alone just before dawn at the prow of his speeding three-banked flagship. He was now virtually the sole ruler of the Roman Republic. Two months earlier at Pharsalus in Greece he had decisively defeated the Senatorial forces led by Gnaeus Pompey, Rome's consul and general who had once been an ally of Caesar's and in fact also his son-in-law. It was now October.

"You asked to see me, Caesar?"

"Ah, Zeno, so good of you to come all the way up here. The cold and wind could hardly be a pleasant thing for you."

"On the contrary. I am very excited to be sailing again toward Alexandria. And we must be close to her now."

What really happened?

"Yes, that is why I wanted to talk to you. I understand you have often been to Alexandria."

Nearly two years previously, on January 11, 49 BC, determining that all chances of compromise with the controlling faction of nobles in the Senate were ended and feeling himself about to be cornered by his enemies, Caesar had crossed the Rubicon in a seemingly foolhardy action with a force of only 4,800 men. But he had then unexpectedly swept down Italy like a wind, with cities and towns opening their gates, providing food, money, troops, and otherwise flocking to his side.

His overwhelming popularity with the people throughout the Italian peninsula stemmed in part from his consistently liberal policies during his climb along the Course of Honor, the traditional Roman elite's route up the political ladder. From Quaestor in 69 BC at the age of thirty-one, with his automatic entry into the Senate, to his turbulent but fruitful one-year term as Consul in 59, he had argued for and sought to expand Roman citizenship to her allies, particularly the Italian towns, and to distribute land—public land or government-purchased land—to landless veterans and needy families in Rome.

But more immediately Caesar's widespread popularity was due to his remarkable nine-year military campaign in Gaul that permanently secured Rome's northern border and pacified those endlessly dangerous lands from which hordes of invaders had descended on Italy over the centuries.

"Yes, Caesar, you have heard correctly," answered Zeno. I have often been to Alexandria, but it is never enough. I go as frequently as my meager purse allows; and as often as my teaching and law duties in Cnidus and Rome permit. That is why I am so grateful that you have taken me along with you."

"Zeno, having you and your interesting conversation along with us on this voyage has been all my pleasure. I

What really happened?

owe you thanks. But you mention your duties in Rome. Will you still be returning there? I had heard that you were relinquishing most of your law cases and even your pupils."

"That is true, Caesar. I had intended to retire to Cnidus, the city of my birth, upon which you have just bestowed such honors. But I have changed my mind and will be returning to Rome. I am afraid that I actually miss the hustle and bustle of Rome, even the tumult in that city. Cnidus and the simple life among my many, many relatives are no longer so attractive."

Caesar noted Zeno's less than enthusiastic reference to his relatives. "Some do say, Zeno, that the only relative you can choose is your horse."

Zeno chuckled appreciatively.

"But," Caesar continued, "for the reason I sought you out tonight. Tell me about Alexandria."

After crossing the Rubicon, Caesar's race down the Italian peninsular with his ever-growing army threw Rome and the faction in control of the Senate into panicked confusion. As on many previous occasions Caesar's lightning speed had made up for his sparse forces. No one seemed to know exactly what Caesar was going to do or how large his forces were.

The Senate faction immediately turned to Pompey. The General was known as Pompey the Great for his conquests in the east. Six years Caesar's senior, Pompey had once been a political ally of Caesar and even had been married to, and deeply in love with, Caesar's daughter Julia. But he was not the man he once was. In addition, he had convinced himself that his expansion of the Roman Republic's territory in the east had earned him a permanent position as "The first man in Rome." He would bristle at the slightest suggestion that he was not such. Thus he was vulnerable to flattery, and this the Senate faction poured on in copious amounts.

What really happened?

But in the last few years the warrior had been less than healthy. Recently he had returned to Rome after a long convalescence from an almost fatal illness. It was in this condition that he had been cynically co-opted by the controlling faction of nobles in the Senate. They in truth had little more taste for the vain Pompey than they had for the amazingly popular and energetic Caesar. The controlling faction in the Senate would use Pompey only until he somehow managed to dispose of the much more dangerous Caesar. The faction truly detested Caesar. They believed he presented a real challenge to their status as the perennial rulers of Rome. Pompey up to then had been considered the greatest Roman general, and it was for this that the nobles recruited him. They felt confident that he could engineer Caesar's defeat. But Caesar's lightning race down to Rome after crossing the Rubicon panicked all of the leading citizens in Rome, including Pompey. So after some indecisiveness and hesitation, a quality that was to mark the rest of his role in the civil war, and perhaps reflected his now diminished capacities, he finally decided to evacuate Rome.

The military forces of the Senate greatly outnumbered the troops that Caesar could call upon, primarily the army he had developed in his nine years of warfare in Gaul. But those Senatorial forces at the moment were spread over the provinces of the Roman Republic, from Spain to Syria. It would take time to gather them together. Pompey did not want to confront Caesar with the troops he had in Italy, some of whom had earlier served with Caesar and whose loyalties might be in question. He therefore decided to evacuate Italy and consolidate the Senate's legions across the Adriatic in Illyricum before coming back to Italy and challenging Caesar. This was a route that had often enough been taken by others. So he ordered all senators and officials to evacuate Rome and accompany his army south to the port of Brundisium with the intention of

What really happened?

crossing the Adriatic to Illyricum. Once his forces in Illyricum were consolidated and any new recruits properly trained, he could then return to Italy and take care of Caesar with overwhelming military might. Pompey's great strength was in organization, so his evacuation proceeded smoothly. A huge fleet had already been prepared in Brundisium to take his army to sea, as well as the fleeing senators, their slaves, colleagues and families.

Caesar arrived in Brundisium before Pompey had taken ship. But his entreaties for a conference were rebuffed and Pompey left with his forces and Senate allies. Before leaving he destroyed any remaining ships that he did not need so as to deny transportation to Caesar. Caesar promptly ordered his army to start building ships he could use to pursue Pompey. Since that chore would take months, he returned to Rome and spent some days putting the affairs of state in order. Then he went to Spain and over several months succeeded, without much bloodshed, in capturing the legions left there by Pompey. Here he persistently evangelized among the Roman legions in enemy camps to come over to him or disband to avoid bloodshed. He did this throughout the civil war.

After settling matters in Spain and leaving one of his senatorial legates in charge of the province, he was back in Brundisium. He set sail with part of his army with what craft were ready and crossed to Illyricum, immediately sending back the transports for the rest of his army. Pompey by this time had had a year to recruit further legions and train his army. As it was now in the middle of winter, however, the Pompeians were totally surprised by Caesar's appearance on the coast. Caesar had caught the overwhelmingly superior fleet of Pompey, under the command of his old colleague Bibulus, napping. But that was not to happen again as Bibulus sprang into energetic vigilance and it took many months before the rest of Caesar's army was able to make it across to Illyricum.

What really happened?

Meanwhile numerous indecisive skirmishes ensued between him and Pompey. And there was endless moving about for fodder, with each side trying to wear the other out, both losing some men and supplies. But Pompey always made sure never to accept a pitched battle with Caesar, regardless of his numerical superiority. Finally forced by his overconfident colleagues and senators who were anxious to put an end to the outmanned Caesar and then divide up all the estates and offices of Caesar and his supporters, Pompey did commit at Pharsalus—and lost mightily. He and most of the leaders on his side had run off before the battle was even half over and escaped to different destinations. Pompey felt disgraced by his defeat so did not join his subordinate commanders or the senators, but raced for help to his allies in the east; while his angry and resentful colleagues, senators, and commanders—as well as his two sons—escaped to the west and eventually gathered themselves in Spain and Africa.

Caesar had left Rhodes less than four days earlier and with favorable winds was now approaching Alexandria, the fabled capital of Egypt, with a small force of thirteen warships, thirteen hundred legionaries and eight hundred cavalry and their horses. His warships were the faster three-banked and four-banked ships that were propelled by a combination of oars and sails, depending on the winds and the waters. He was in a rush to catch up with Pompey so he did not take any of the larger but slower transports with him. Instead he squeezed his small force onto the galleys.

Considering that the battle of Pharsalus had involved sixty thousand men on Pompey's side and thirty thousand on Caesar's side, counting horsemen and auxiliaries, his forces this day did seem meager. But he felt that after his great victory he would be safe anywhere in the Mediterranean world, with or without troops. In fact

What really happened?

towns and cities that had previously supported the defeated Pompey quickly sent officials to him pleading for forgiveness and pledging their loyalty, money and troops.

His confident belief that he would be safe anywhere after his emphatic victory over Pompey The Great had recently been reinforced. While crossing the Hellespont in a dingy with a few men (these boats were the only ones available for him and his men to make the crossing) he ran into a squadron of Pompeian warships. When the captain of the Pompeian fleet learned that it was Caesar himself standing in the small boat and glaring at him, he respectfully surrendered his entire fleet to the victor of Pharsalus, wisely counting on Caesar's reputation for generosity and clemency.

Caesar's judgment after Pharsalus was to pursue Gnaeus Pompey himself, who was fleeing eastward away from the remnants of his defeated army, which had scattered westward. The Great Pompey had years before brought into the expanding domination of Roman much of the east up to the borders of ancient Persia, now Parthia, including Syria and Palestine, either as Roman provinces or as vassal states. In addition Pompey had been a special patron and protector of King Ptolemy XII of Egypt whom he had restored to his thrown after being expelled by his riotous Alexandrian subjects. Pompey was therefore more dangerous than his defeated army, Caesar felt. He could easily raise more armies and fleets among his friends and clients in the east if given enough time. So time was of the essence as he approached Alexandria in pursuit of Pompey the Great.

"Alexandria is the dream destination for any educated Greek," Zeno stated in answer to Caesar's question. "Its marvelous boulevards and gleaming marble buildings are unrivaled in the world. It is the center of all Greek learning, with it fabulous library and academy where scholars from all over the world study, discuss everything,

What really happened?

and write books. Oh, how I shake with anticipation to be in the midst of that library, surrounded by tens of thousands of books—almost every book ever written in our world. I also have some friends in the academy whom I am hoping to meet up with.

"You will notice in the streets many ancient monuments and statues. This is because the Ptolemies over the centuries have wisely, for the sake of their acceptance by the Egyptians, been careful to recognize the great antiquity of Egypt, some believing it stretches back tens of thousands of years. One way they have done that is to bring to Alexandria from many parts of Egypt ancient monuments to decorate Alexandria's palaces, streets, and gardens."

"What of its citizens?" asked Caesar.

"An unruly mix, I would say," answered Zeno. "The Great Alexander founded this magnificent city nearly three hundred years ago and had it designed in the finest Hellenistic tradition, with grand boulevards and straight crossing streets, magnificent temples paying due respect to the local Egyptian gods as well as those of Greece, and grand palaces and public buildings. But he intended it primarily for Macedonians and Greeks—yes, pardon me, I do still make the distinction, though you Romans view us as one. He thought they could rule the vast ancient land of Egypt from this isolated post, facing the Mediterranean and with its back to the Nile, however much Egypt is the Nile.

"Over time every form of creature has drifted to this city, not to mention the native Egyptians, either as prisoners of war or as migrants seeking the better life. There are Syrians, Phoenicians, Romans, Parthians, Thracians, Jews, Arabs from Nabataea, and others. Then there are the runaway slaves, mostly from Roman and Greek masters from all over the Mediterranean, and criminals from other lands and military deserters. This

What really happened?

makes for a volatile and unpredictable populace.

"It is true," Zeno continued, "that many foreigners are traders or bankers, but most have settled in Alexandria to partake of this very sumptuous and prosperous city. Alexandria is a great center of trade, at a crossroads where the ships and caravans of many nations meet and exchange goods. The Ptolemies have been generous to the city's population and its many industries—the manufacture and exporting of glass, textiles, gems, dyes, herbs, and medicines as well as the processing of huge quantities of corn and other grains, and of course its famous shipbuilding and merchant marine. Then there is Egypt's lucrative monopoly on papyrus—one cannot write a book today without the scrolls produced in Alexandria from the papyrus plants grown only on the Nile. Thus Alexandrians and the inhabitants of the city's suburbs can, if they want, easily find dignified and gainful employment. That is why so many come here. They say the city itself has over five hundred thousand citizens."

"That is perhaps more than Rome," observed Caesar.

"And that is not the only difference with Rome. Roman buildings, except for some recent temples, theaters and forums—particularly those, excuse me, of Pompey and those being constructed by you, yourself—are made of wood and tiles. Alexandria, on the other hand, gleams as a city of marble, granite and limestone – dazzling compared to any other city except perhaps for Athens.

"Alexandria was a city planned for grandness as well as for the sake of efficiency, convenience and beauty. Hence, for example, here the streets are straight and intersect with other straight streets, so you can easily find out where you are going. They are not a hodgepodge of crisscrossing roadways as they are in Rome—excuse me for saying this, Caesar—where it is a mystery how people find their way home."

"I will readily admit," said Caesar, "that you are not far

What really happened?

off the mark. But I have planners and architects busy working on these matters. Give me ten or fifteen years and you will not recognize Rome. But what can you tell me of Egypt's rulers today? I understand that since Pompey's client, Ptolemy XII, died a few years ago, his two heirs have not been working well together."

"I myself, Caesar," replied Zeno, "do not have personal knowledge of what is happening as I have not been back here in some years. But it's no surprise that they are squabbling. It seems to be a curse of the Ptolemies to have endless family feuds, most of them dangerous and deadly! But I too have heard the same as you."

Zeno abruptly pointed out across the dark sea beyond the ship's prow. "Look, Caesar, there it is!"

"Yes, I see it," said Caesar. "The Pharos lighthouse. Indeed, it is as they say. The light is so intense, and yet we're nowhere in sight of land. They say that its light can be seen some thirty miles out to sea, perhaps about where we are now."

Others begin gathering on deck as word of the sighting spread. The beam became progressively stronger as the night was clear other than the mist through which the light easily pierced.

IV

As Caesar's small fleet continued to draw nearer to Alexandria, he and Zeno remained at the prow of the flagship discussing what each knew about Alexandria—Caesar from hearsay, as he had never been there. They were joined by Caesar's two secretaries, Julius Faberius, a son of one of his freedmen; and Pompeius Trogus; as well as Caesar's much younger second cousin, Sextus Julius Caesar, a valued and cherished member of Caesar's staff since his battles in Spain against the Pompeian forces. Sextus was a grandson of a Julii who had served as consul in 91 BC, so his family tree was more distinguished than Caesar's, at least of course until Caesar himself attained the position of consul.

Periodically Caesar would interrupt the conversation and turn to Faberius or Trogus to dictate something quickly—a letter to an official somewhere in the vast area under Roman control, an order to a military legate or an eastern king, or just notes for further thought. Special couriers were always in his entourage prepared to carry his tablets or scrolls on land or sea to their destinations.

Sextus had been greatly honored by Caesar the year before when the youth was sent in Caesar's stead to accept

What really happened?

the surrender of the Pompeian legions under Varro in Spain. Thereafter he had served on Caesar's staff throughout the campaign in Illyricum and Greece. Caesar always paid special attention to relatives of his, however distant, who came or were sent by their parents to serve with him. However, unlike many others who had come to him, he felt a special liking and attachment to this young man, whom he found wise for his age, energetic, daring, and brave in battle. Caesar had been giving him progressively more responsibilities and hoped to develop him further, if the young man's talents permitted.

The secretary Pompeius Trogus was the son of a Celtic chieftain in the northern Italian province of Narbonne. The chieftain had led cavalry for Pompey against the gifted and popular rebel general Sertorius in Spain. The aristocrat was awarded Roman citizenship by Pompey and took Pompey's name, as was often done, in gratitude. His son of the same name joined Caesar's staff at a very young age and because of his broad education and evident devotion to Caesar, eventually rose to become a confidential secretary.

Dawn had arrived at the same time as the fleet appeared outside the Great Harbor. Caesar ordered that signals be given to pause in a wide sweep and to weigh anchors. Small boats were immediately lowered from each galley as officers hurried to join Caesar on the flagship for the usual conference.

A reverential silence descended on the now crowded decks of the flagship as all eyes beheld what scholars had designated one of the Seven Wonders of the World: the Pharos lighthouse.

Zeno broke the silence as he, with obvious pride, pointed out that the unbelievable 350-foot lighthouse had been designed, financed and constructed by a fellow-citizen of his hometown, Cnidus. The Cnidian Sostratos, a fabulously wealthy merchant, Zeno explained, had become

What really happened?

a confidant of the first Ptolemy and undertook the task of building a lighthouse. The work was not finished until the middle of Ptolemy II Philadelphus' reign about 290 BC. He did concede, however, that the original tower has been modified over the last few centuries, but not by much, he insisted.

The lighthouse, seemingly gigantic from the view of the ships, appeared to be made of marble as it shimmered brilliantly with the sun rising in the east. There appeared to be at least three separate towers, each shaped differently and with different statues on its ledges, one structure on top of the other with a huge golden statue of some god at the very pinnacle standing over the forever shining light. Later Caesar himself saw the gigantic bronze mirrors that ingeniously concentrated the flames of a fire and cast its famous light out over the sea.

"Caesar, a word with you?" Sextus said as he glanced at the others, politely suggesting their withdrawal. Zeno bowed to Caesar as he left but not before noticing Sextus Caesar's unusual garb, more in keeping with a local merchant than a staff member of Caesar's.

When the others had gone, Caesar nodded as Sextus drew near so he could speak in a lower voice.

" I have strange news from the shore," he said, with a frown on his brow. Sextus, with a small crew, including two former residents of Alexandria, had disguised themselves as natives or merchants and gone ashore some little distance from Alexandria on a lonely beach, having been dispatched from the flagship on a fast galley two days earlier.

"I regret to report that word is the Great Pompey was murdered at Pelusium, a coast city some miles east of here. In addition, there is a civil war going on. Apparently the child-king is there with an army facing off against his sister, who has her own army across from his."

"Are you certain, Sextus?" Only his words indicated

What really happened?

Caesar's deep unhappiness at this news.

"Yes, sir," he said in reply, careful to lower his eyes to the ground so as to avoid seeing any show of emotion by Caesar.

The ruler kept looking at Sextus, but with his mind obviously elsewhere. After a while he asked: "What is happening in Alexandria?"

"It seems," reported Sextus, "that things are quiet there for now. The city has a small garrison which was left behind while the entire army and all of the king's ministers and advisors went with him to Pelusium. The people, who quite obviously favor the king over his sister, seem nervously awaiting the outcome of an expected battle."

Caesar seemed to think for a moment and then said: "Sextus, send a boat to Pelusium with a dozen senior centurions dressed as natives. Each should take his sword and daggers, but hidden in his garments. Make sure among the centurions you include either Cassius Scaeva or Titus Carfulenus as the squad's leader—they both speak Greek. However do not send both of them and do not include yourself. I need you here. Make clear that I do not want any disturbances in the shadow of the Egyptian army, and though they are to defend themselves if necessary, the first order is to get back to me with information."

Caesar paused, but Sextus remained quiet as he had become acquainted with Caesar's lightning-like decisions and knew there was more he would say.

"The centurions," Caesar continued, "are to find out what they can about Pompey's death. Who killed him and when, why, and how. And whether there are any remains. If there are any remains, bring them back to me with all due respect. Determine also if any others of Pompey's party are still on shore. Bring them back as well. Also, if possible, the centurions should find out what they can about the nature of the Egyptian army without exposing themselves. I want them to report to me in Alexandria as

What really happened?

soon as they feel they have discovered whatever they could. They are not to stay there more than a few days. Instruct them that if we ourselves are forced to pull out, we will send them notice and a place to rendezvous."

Caesar turned and walked quickly toward the center of the ship where his officers had gathered for the conference, his secretaries following close behind. Once among his officers Tiberius Nero, second in command of the fleet, reported that some sixty to eighty Egyptian warships were arrayed in the Great Harbor, but without rowers and at anchor. There were also many merchant ships busy with commerce and people were crowding the shore.

"It seems that we have been observed and there is some activity with small boats," Nero said, finishing his report.

After some discussion among his staff and officers, Caesar decided that he would enter the harbor with the flagship and one other vessel. Nero was to stay with the remainder of the fleet, but anchors were to be raised and all men prepared for battle.

Caesar continued to dictate the necessary orders to Trogus and Faberius, to be sent with the officers back to their ships: "I will draw slowly closer to shore while signaling our pacific intentions by hoisting the peace flag next to the admiral's pennant, and further requesting a conference with the authorities by use of our bronze signal shield at the prow. There can be no misunderstanding of our peaceful intentions. So if there is any hostile move on their part I will give orders for a quick retreat. Visibility is clear so we will use the flags for forwarding orders. It seems the Egyptians have not expected a visit from us, so they will be slow to weigh anchor. It also appears that they do not have the troops to man many ships and I therefore do not expect trouble. But let us be prepared for it. I will await inside the harbor for the reaction of the authorities."

What really happened?

And so Caesar's flagship and its escort, to the measured beating of mallets setting a stately pace for its 170 rowers and with cornets signaling the presence of the Commanding General, slowly passed the Pharos and entered the Great Harbor.

CAESAR, CICERO & CLEOPATRA

What really happened?

V

While a number of smaller boats had left shore and moved toward Caesar's two ships, they had stopped well short of the galleys and seemed to be full of civilians just gawking at the Romans. After some time, perhaps an hour or so, a larger boat left port and headed to the flagship. Again this vessel seemed to contain mostly civilians, but dressed more elaborately, and a few men were in military garments, though only with swords at their sides. As the small Egyptian vessel drew near it signaled a request to come aboard, which Caesar with a nod ordered his signaler to okay.

Soon boarding Caesar's ship was an individual in colorful robes and a hat indicating he was a scholar. With him was a dour and weathered soldier in a mixture of Roman military garb and perhaps Egyptian military dress. Two slaves brought up the rear, each carrying a small canvas bag. The slaves were as black as coal and reminded the Romans that Egypt was indeed in Africa. Caesar indicated to Sextus that only he, Sextus, and his two secretaries were to receive this delegation.

"Greetings great and victorious Caesar," proclaimed the scholar in fancy Greek. "Welcome to Alexandria on

What really happened?

behalf of King Ptolemy Theos Philopator, who is presently away from his city. I am Theodorus, tutor to the king and director of the library. With me is General Lucius Septimius, a legionary from the forces of Proconsul Aulus Gabinius who has been stationed in Egypt for seven years for the protection of the king."

"Greetings Director and . . . General" replied Caesar, glancing at the two men and trying to make out exactly what this "General" Septimius was wearing as a uniform. His voice had carried a very slight questioning inflection.

Sextus was not so subtle as he almost guffawed and was about to exclaim "General? General of what army?" but fortunately caught himself immediately as he noticed a barely perceptible frown appear on Caesar's brow. But the Egyptian delegation had noticed the look of disdain shown by Caesar's officers at the word "general." This was no type of general they had ever seen. An insult had been delivered, however unintentional, and Septimius' face tightened and colored.

Theodorus, quickly recovering after reading the reaction, continued smoothly: "Lucius Septimius was a valiant and much honored military tribune under Pompey and then under Gabinius. However he has been so helpful and loyal to the king all these years, especially in managing and training the army and integrating the disparate types of recruits we are compelled to utilize, that the king has bestowed upon him many rewards, including promotion to a General of our Egyptian Army.

"But great Caesar I have been remiss in failing immediately to give you the wonderful news. We are humbled and honored to announce the end of your long and dangerous quest—you now have the final victory you so earnestly sought, and we have given it to you not without great risk to ourselves—all out of loyalty and respect to Rome and to Caesar." He gestured to one of the slaves to come forward.

What really happened?

"In this bag is what remains of the head of your bitter enemy, Gnaeus Pompey, severed from its body by our General Septimius with the very sword that he carries now in his scabbard. I am honored to present . . . Pompey."

The slave withdrew a bloody and mangled head from the bag and offered it to Caesar.

Sextus of course was not surprised, but the two secretaries were startled. Caesar himself turned away from the spectacle in evident disgust, letting out a gasp. Sextus quickly came forward and took the head and bag, removing it some distance from Caesar.

Both Theodorus and Septimius showed their own surprise at this reaction—disgust instead of joy from Caesar and only repulsion and disdain instead of admiration and gratitude in the faces of his company.

Caesar turned back to Theodorus in short order with his composure fully recovered. "But Director, Septimius' blade must have been dull indeed. This bruised and chopped up specimen could be that of any poor soul."

Again Septimius felt the sting of insult. He instinctively moved ever so slightly closer to Caesar, only to be confronted by Sextus who had suddenly appeared in front of him as if by magic.

Theodorus raised his arms in a gesture of peace and called to the second slave who, though shaking with fright, proffered his bag. From it Theodorus extracted a gold signet ring and offered it to Caesar.

This offering Caesar did take, as he recognized it immediately. Nevertheless, he studied the ring carefully, turning it around several times in his hands. Tears begin to fall freely from his eyes as he handed the ring over to Sextus.

"Yes, indeed, it is Pompey's. . . ."

"I have long been accustomed," said Caesar, "to seeing his familiar imprint on scrolls and tablets, writing to me to give advice and encouragement, particularly in the early

What really happened?

days of my campaigns in Gaul – then his delight with being the husband of my dear Julia; then his anguish in writing as an enemy."

"I beg your pardon, Great Caesar," Theodorus said, not understanding the warning signals given out by Caesar's companions, "but we have, at great risk to ourselves, killed your most powerful enemy. Are you not gratified?"

"Caesar does not kill his enemies."

Now it was the time for the Egyptian delegation to snicker and raise their eyebrows, though they were wise enough to remain silent.

Caesar decided to change the course of the conversation. So he asked, "While your king may be out of the city on some type of business, as you say, where is your queen?"

Septimius and Theodorus looked at each other and it was again Theodorus who replied.

"She also has gone out of the city for her own reasons."

Caesar suddenly tired of the game. "We wish to come ashore and stay for a short period, Director. Will that be suitable?"

"Yes, of course. Your appearance was without prior notice but we have nevertheless prepared a magnificent wing of the palace for your use. It is the marvelous building which Ptolemy VIII added to the palaces of the Ptolemies. Your men can find bunks with our city garrison in the barracks a little distance away."

"Thank you, but my entire staff will stay with me in this wing which you describe. From what I have been told such an edifice would have a great many rooms, more than sufficient for me and my staff to set up a temporary base. My legionaries as well as my cavalry and their horses will camp outside my residence. They will construct the usual field camp, but perhaps utilizing some of the existing walls

What really happened?

of the palaces."

"Oh my god! Caesar! Impossible!" Theodorus blurted out. The king would be furious that one of the palace gardens had been turned into a camp and that common soldiers were making a home in the Palace of the Ptolemies. Never!"

Caesar ignored the response and said merely, "Good day, Director . . . and General. Thank you for your visit and your report. We have friends with us who are familiar with Alexandria, so you do not have to wait to guide us to our quarters. From what I have heard of your city's simple and elegant rectangular structure, we should have no problem finding our own way to Ptolemy VIII's wing."

Both Theodorus and Septimius seemed on the verge of objecting but thought better of it as several of Caesar's officers, who had joined them on a signal from Sextus, stepped in front of Caesar and moved toward them. They would promptly get off the flagship on their own, they both clearly understood, or they would otherwise be thrown overboard. They quickly exited.

It was not a meeting heralding friendly relations.

"Sextus," said Caesar. "Signal the fleet to stand down and move into the harbor. We will disembark beginning with the last ship to enter the harbor and finish with ourselves. Assemble the men on shore in parade formation with their standards and musicians as usual. I intend to enter the city as Consul of Rome, so prepare my dress and entourage."

"Yes, sir, I will see to it immediately."

"Trogus," he continued. "Take that cursed bag and see to it that the finest embalmers in Alexandria clean and repair as best they can the head of Pompey the Great, making it as suitable as possible for burial. Then requisition in my name a pure gold case, dignified in design, from one of the palaces—I am sure there are many—and place the head in it. Seal the case and prepare

What really happened?

it for transport to Pompey's family in Rome with whatever else of his remains that may come our way in the next few days. I will dictate a letter to his wife Cornelia. Likewise, take this signet ring, prepare it in a suitable case and have it sent to the Senate in Rome by the fastest confidential and trusted couriers available. I will also give you a letter to accompany it.

Faberius, have you been taking notes?"

"Yes, sir."

"Do not put away your tablets just yet. I will want to set down some of my thoughts on these curious events. But first, Sextus, please fetch young Balbus, Postumus, and Zeno."

The three soon arrived and received a briefing from Caesar about what they had just learned from the Egyptian delegation. Then Caesar asked: "Postumus, as a banker you have been in and out of Alexandria. What do you think we are facing?"

"In short, Caesar," Postumus replied immediately, "the usual deceit and treachery of the Egyptians, accompanied by insolence and shouting. As you know," Postumus continued, "after Gabinius put Ptolemy Auletes back on the throne, I endured a fruitless year living among these ungrateful, fickle and treacherous people trying to collect the debt that Auletes owed our bankers, money he spent to recover his kingdom."

"By the way, Postumus," said Caesar. "How much is the Auletes debt now? And please don't confuse and compound it with your infernal banker's interest upon interest."

"Caesar," responded Postumus with a hurt look. "The use of money for a period of time is as important as the money itself. If we did not—"

Caesar smiled and playfully tapped Postumus' shoulder. "I understand, banker. I meant no offence. But what remains of the principle, as Auletes would have

What really happened?

understood it?"

"About seventeen million denarii," Postumus promptly replied.

"Thank you. But I interrupted you," said Caesar. "What else were you about to say?"

"It does not surprise me," Postumus continued, "that these 'envoys,' if they were such, really told us very little. These Egyptians are forever either lying outright or deceiving, subtly and not so subtly. For instance: what mission is the king on? And where is the queen, his sister? And where are the handlers of this boy-king? I understand he is barely fourteen years old."

"Yes, they told us very little," Zeno interjected. "Nevertheless, Caesar, I assure you that their silly efforts at secrecy will all be for naught. You will understand what I mean once you encounter the garrulous Alexandrians. Without asking a question we will soon learn everything we want to know."

"Young Balbus, my friend, what did you make of our visitors?"

"I was taken aback by what you said of this Septimius," answered Balbus. "A Roman soldier who kills, apparently with no remorse, a great Roman general on the orders of a fourteen- year-old Egyptian king? And this erstwhile tribune is now a 'general'? Caesar, Will you let this all stand?"

"Time and circumstance, my good Balbus, are important elements in our lives. There will be an accounting, I promise you all, but only when the time and circumstances are different. Now, do go on."

"It did not take long," continued Balbus, "for this Septimius to go native, and a seasoned Roman soldier at that. What? Five or six years since Gabinius brought him here? Imagine what the rest of the Gabinians look like, as most of them were not even Romans but mostly mercenaries from Gaul and Germany, as I am told. The

What really happened?

breakdown of discipline and order must be complete with them. We will have to watch our backs, Caesar. "

"Yes, I would think so," Caesar replied. "Something the two sons of Bibulus apparently failed to do."

"What is that, Caesar?" asked Zeno.

"A few years ago," Caesar explained, "when Bibulus was governor of Syria the Parthians were threatening our borders after their defeat of Crassus. Rome felt it should build up its forces in Syria but was unwilling to raise more soldiers in Italy. So Bibulus remembered the two legions that Gabinius had left in Alexandria to protect Ptolemy Auletes but were now doing nothing. Bibulus sent his two sons to reclaim them. The Gabinians, however, rather than give up the good life in Alexandria—most of them had married local women and begun families—actually murdered these two noble Romans, sons of a consul and governor."

"For Jupiter's sake!" exclaimed Balbus.

"Now, Faberius, some dictation," said Caesar. "The rest of you, prepare to disembark and meet the Alexandrians."

VI

The procession started out okay. Caesar in his purple-edged toga sat on his magnificent white stallion with his lieutenants on their own horses by his side, followed by the eight hundred cavalry and the Sixteenth and Twenty-seventh Legions' remaining 3,200-man force dressed in clean uniforms, standing crisply at attention with their javelins and swords by their sides. Each legion stood directly behind its familiar standard, bearing the insignia of its many campaigns, the Sixteenth far more than the Twenty-seventh, and with the centurions proudly carrying their own campaign medals on their chests. The standards were raised at the sound of the trumpets and the commanding general's presence was duly announced by the loud blare of the cornets.

But that was the beginning and the end of the parade. Tens of thousands of Alexandrians had by now gathered on the docks and for whatever reason were obviously not happy with Roman soldiers tramping down their streets. They had deeply resented the forceful restoration of Ptolemy XII by Gabinius and the crippling exactions of Postumus when he was imposed on them as Egypt's "treasurer." They further resented Cleopatra's punishment

What really happened?

of the murderers of the two sons of Marcus Bibulus and then her sending sixty warships and five hundred Gabinians off to Asia to help Pompey in the civil war. They did not know or care who this new small group of Romans represented, but they were not going to let them march into the city like they owned it.

Stones, bottles and garbage reined down on the surprised Romans, who had to raise their shields over their heads to avoid injury. Caesar's officers surrounded him and likewise raised their shields. Soon a small group of Egyptian soldiers worked their way over to Caesar. The Romans had stopped in their tracks and the mob relented momentarily while they watched the confrontation between the garrison and the head of this new Roman party.

"We have been invited by Theodorus the director of the library on behalf of the king to take up residence in the palace," Caesar, who had to shout to be heard above the roar of the crowd, said to the leader of the Egyptians.

"I care little for whatever that bookworm may have said. You are not, I repeat, not, to parade Roman lictors with their fasces in the King of Egypt's capital or blow your infernal trumpets on our streets."

His officers looked at Caesar for direction, but found none, only a suddenly composed and quiet countenance, as if he had just made a decision and was quite satisfied with it. They themselves were familiar with this reaction, or apparent non-reaction, by Caesar, and so they immediately relaxed, now waiting for what they knew would be decisive action.

At that moment both Aldric and Waldo, Caesar's German cavalry officers, came rushing up with their swords drawn, but were stopped by a wave from Caesar.

"My men are clamoring to attack," Aldric shouted. "Do we have your permission?"

No," Caesar replied, and glancing at the Egyptians,

What really happened?

"not just yet, Aldric."

Sextus demanded of the Egyptian officers that they prepare a safe passage for them.

"We are civilized people, Romans," the Egyptians replied. "What do your fear? Forget this military display. Put down your arms and you can each find your own way through our grand city to wherever you wish to go."

Caesar cut off any further absurd discussion and motioned his officers to gather for a conference. "Get Zeno up here immediately," ordered Caesar to an officer. "Zeno knows his way around this magnificent and friendly city. He will lead us to our home away from home," Caesar's tone and amused look immediately erased the tension that had appeared on the faces of his staff and lieutenants.

Zeno hurriedly joined the conference. It soon ended, Caesar gave his orders and the officers scattered to different locations. Within minutes trumpets sounded, signaling changes in formation. Standards and pennants waved this way and that way, suddenly and with such precision that the at first bewildering maneuver of the troops seemed to have been practiced hundreds of times before. Thousands of legionaries and cavalrymen moved in an elaborate dance establishing a huge square.

A solid phalanx of legionaries interspersed with the eight hundred German horsemen, with each man's javelin thrusting forward, now faced the mobs on all four sides of the square, each legionary with his shield forward and with another shield held over his head by a comrade. The remaining legionaries formed up smartly and in order under their standards behind Caesar and his staff.

At the trumpets' signals, the solid phalanx on all sides step by step began slowly to expand the space around the Roman forces. With javelins protruding from their shields, the outside line of legionaries and horsemen rhythmically jabbed their javelins back and forth out toward the crowds.

What really happened?

The Alexandrians for their part had suddenly fell silent at the magical movements of the Romans, but soon returned to what seemed to be their customary riotous mode. The Roman soldiers on the phalanx were thrusting their javelins in such manner as to avoid actually hitting anyone in the crowds, but necessarily they did wound those foolish enough to refuse to back up. The howls of those thereby wounded helped in moving the angry mob back, step by step.

Eventually the soldiers on the sides had worked the crowds all the way back so as to push them off the road entirely, leaving them little space to maneuver between the slashing javelins and the walls of buildings. Up front and in the rear the soldiers had cleared a path fifty yards in depth. The entire formation then stepped forward, one short step at a time, each foot sounding a uniform stamp as if they were oars following the beat of the mallets on a ship. The march, with trumpets and cornets blaring, standards and pennants waving, finally began moving forward, but no more than at a slow walk.

The Egyptians officers who had so arrogantly conferred with Caesar, found themselves caught within the Roman formation when it magically formed. At first they tried to break out but their frantic efforts to escape through the impenetrable surrounding walls of soldiers proved futile. After a while the Egyptians settled quietly behind the legionaries and for all intents and purposes became part of the parade.

During the slow walk, everyone had occasion to reflect upon his situation, including Caesar, who seemed to indicate by his countenance that he would like to be left alone.

He berated himself for being such a fool. Fortune could not do it all alone. There was no magic in the world. He had been given numerous warnings. While he was still in Rome he had known there was some kind of trouble in

What really happened?

Alexandria. He had heard it from the soldiers and officers returning from Syria. The Roman traders had warned their bankers in Rome of impending unrest. Yet he chose to sweep all those hard facts aside when he learned of young Sextus Pompey's success in obtaining sixty ships and the services of five hundred Gabinians from the Egyptian queen. He arbitrarily and for no good reason took those few facts as a sign of stability in the kingdom and its continued allegiance to at least Rome itself, even if not to him.

But what other way was there to interpret the utterly outrageous murders of Bibulus two sons? Any rational man would have concluded that there was obviously something seriously wrong here, and potentially dangerous for a Roman—not a place to walk in helpless, as Pompey had done and as he himself was now foolishly doing. At least Pompey had had much greater and more justifiable expectations for a friendly welcome. He had restored this great and ancient family to its throne. Yet, they showed their gratitude by murdering him. What could they have in mind for me? Caesar wondered. Someone here was being extremely shortsighted and apparently had adopted treachery as a governmental policy.

Caesar continued to berate himself: Pompey had the wisdom to test his fate by himself, as he had heard no report of any massacre. But what had the brilliant General Caesar done! He had placed the lives of four thousand good, loyal and faithful veterans at great risk, unnecessarily. Every soldier's death, he thought, would be his fault. It would be as if he had murdered them himself.

Though, as he looked now at their determined faces, they no more than he would wish to turn back now and escape to their ships. This mob had challenged them, and Romans did not turn away from challenges. As usual, his loyal men were expecting him to find a way to retrieve their dignity. And this he pledged to do, at any cost.

What really happened?

It was true that he did not expect the Alexandrians to greet their Roman occupiers, for certainly that was what they were, on bended knees. But he swore to himself that they would be on their knees in tears by the time he and his army left.

Fortunately, Zeno was of another mind as he went up and down the line assuring everyone who would listen that the Alexandrians were not really all that bad, notwithstanding their horrid howling, screaming and cursing which could still be heard in the distance, though none of their projectiles could reach them now. In any event, the gated and walled palace area was only a short distance away.

This especially small and slow parade soon became a legend in Alexandria, retold again and again by an impossible number of people who swore that they had been there personally, with almost each retelling including new details and embellishments. By the fourth century of the Common Era an Alexandrian scholar attempted to gather all the extant versions of the tale and reconcile them. The resulting work, which thereafter was accepted as the authoritative description of Caesar's parade, consumed fifteen large volumes.

VII

The enormous gates of the palace quarter opened upon their approach. The angry Alexandrian populace seemed to have disappeared somewhere along the way, either losing interest in their fruitless protests or kept at bay by Egyptian soldiers.

As they rode through the portal they encountered no official delegation, just curious residents coming out to see what the noise was about. They could see that the quarter contained numerous palaces and other great residences. Caesar's men by this time had reorganized themselves into their original marching formation. They passed luxurious dwellings surrounded by great gardens as Zeno directed them along a certain road.

Soon they came upon a monumental building, one of the largest most of them had ever seen, with its own walls surrounding three sides and its imposing entrance at the end of an elegant marble stairway. The building itself seemed to be encased in either marble or polished limestone, like most of the buildings in the royal quarter. Various statues and monuments were scattered about, as were trees and grassy pathways.

"And that, Great Caesar, is the fabled Library of

What really happened?

Alexandria," announced Zeno. Caesar glanced that way and could not help being startled by its grand magnificence, but he knew his tired and hungry men would not be interested in a tour right now. Again as they approached the equally enormous gates of the inner palace they opened quietly and seemingly without effort, as if on air.

This time, however, there was a small welcoming delegation, with Theodorus and Septimius in the midst of about a dozen men in obviously expensive and colorful robes.

"Welcome, Caesar," Theodorus called out as he smiled and outstretched his arms in a mocking greeting. "I hope you enjoyed your short trip. You did tell us you knew your way."

Caesar had slowed his horse to a slow walk and for a few seconds glanced at the delegation, but then quickened his pace as his entourage, following his example, knocked into and roughly brushed aside the welcoming committee. Its members bristled at such extraordinary rudeness as they struggled to keep from falling. They were angry and were about to say so but quickly understood from the looks of Caesar's men that they would risk life and limb if they protested. Only Theodorus and Septimius among the greeting committee understood what had happened.

"Caesar looks very angry," Theodorus whispered to Septimus. "He understands that we intended the mob to kill him. I am going to disappear from the city. I do not intend to cross that man's path again. Let Pothinus, as advisor, or should I say, keeper, of the king, deal with this. He is now on his way here from Pelusium."

"If only he had come ashore first, like Pompey did," Septimus said in return. "We could have easily dispatched him. But he came ashore only after all his forces had. But so what? We may have missed our two best opportunities, but there will be others. I killed that giant of a general

What really happened?

Pompey with my own hands, this puny creature will be non challenge."

"Be wary, Septimus, your deed may be going to your head. This man is different."

Zeno guided the Caesarians easily to a great palace to the left of the inner palace's entrance, again with its own walls, and adjacent to yet another huge building, seemingly some public building rather than a residence.

"There is Ptolemy VII's palace," said Zeno, "and next to it the theater he erected. They both back up over the road to the docks. I have never been here in the inner palace but I know the layout well from plans in the library."

Caesar and his staff rode around this palace and then the palace grounds while his army rested in place. He dismounted and entered the building with several of his men. He was met by a host of slaves who apparently had been assigned to take care of his needs. After examining some of the rooms, he emerged and called his staff and officers together for a conference.

"Sextus, the legions and cavalry will encamp in the gardens facing the rear of the palace. They can utilize some of the existing walls as part of their fortifications, but the rest of the camp can follow the usual lines of our field camps. Set up a fortified barrier around the front of our residence and post guards, so at least this building and its grounds will be secure. Post more guards and lookouts on the roof.

"Inform Young Balbus," Caesar said, "that he has been requisitioned as our temporary quartermaster. His first task is to choose, arrange and provision such rooms in this building as he thinks necessary for the staff and those officers as choose to stay here rather than in the camp. Tell them that under the circumstances it is their choice.

"Have someone get Vibullius over here as I want him to start thinking about further fortifications. And ask my

What really happened?

friend Mithridates to join me after he has bathed and settled in.

"In addition, Sextus, send me four trusted senior centurions. I will have secret orders prepared for them to take to our forces in Rhodes and to in Greece. I will need more legions, cavalry, ships, corn, ballistic, and other siege equipment—all the material we did not take with us in our rush.

"Finally, dismiss every single person you find in this building and on the grounds. Thank them but tell them we will care for ourselves. We do not need the services of Ptolemy's slaves, agents, or anyone else, whatever they claim to be—cooks, waiters, gardeners, whatever. Then do a sweep of the building and the grounds to make sure we are rid of them all.

"Then you can get yourself a bath and some rest. Our host Ptolemy VII, whoever he was, seems to have loved his baths. I saw an unusually large series of rooms dedicated just to that. You and the others will enjoy them. I will join you later.

"But first Faberius and Trogus, sit with me as I have some letters to dictate."

CAESAR, CICERO & CLEOPATRA

What really happened?

VIII

"Mithridates, my friend. Thank you so much for coming. I hope you enjoyed your bath."

"I certainly did. What a facility. It paid to be a Ptolemy!"

"I am afraid I am going to have to ask you to go on the road again, and as soon as possible. As you can see we are in an intolerable situation here."

"I don't understand, Caesar. These Alexandrians are obviously not happy with you Romans and they are also famous for their unruliness. But it does not seem to be any more than that. You and your men are safe and secure here, and the dock is so close with your warships for departing whenever you wish. Both the king and queen I am sure will be overjoyed to see you when they come back from wherever they are. They owe so much to you and to Rome. I feel confident that they will put an end to this unruliness and give you all the assistance you need to continue our pursuit of Pompey."

Caesar then filled in Mithridates and made a note that the officers needed to be briefed on Pompey's death and the fact that Egypt was in the middle of a civil war. The officers would then see that the news got down to every

What really happened?

man.

"So my dear Mithridates, if this boy-king, or whoever is advising him, has shown himself to be so perfidious as to murder Pompey, his family's greatest benefactor, I have to assume he is capable of any treachery."

"He would be insane to move against you, Caesar. You are now Rome itself."

"Mithridates, I do not know the mind of whoever is running this country, or at least whoever is in charge of its army. Whether they are rational and logical or greatly uninformed and maybe even hallucinatory, I cannot read what their intentions are. But I am determined not to be caught unprepared again. That is where your services come in. You have some of the same friends in Arabia, Palestine and Cilicia as I do. I am sending you to my allies seeking horsemen, troops, archers, ships, corn and money. I have letters for you to deliver to Malchus, King of the Nabateans in Arabia; to Hyrcanus, the high priest of the Jews in Judea; and to the other leaders in these regions. Gather what forces you can from them and return to me as quickly as possible."

Mithridates stood still for some time, trying to absorb this unexpected turn of events. Then he made his mind up and said: "Absolutely, Caesar, I will immediately take a few men with me and travel night and day. But I wonder about one of your instructions. Why should I approach Hyrcannus on your behalf when the Jews had sided with Pompey?"

"I know, Mithridates, but they will have heard of Pompey's defeat by now and will be anxious for an opportunity to return to my favor. Enemies today are so often friends tomorrow."

"And the reverse as well, Caesar. Would you not say?"

Caesar chuckled and they hugged their farewells at the very moment that Sextus was entering with several other officers.

What really happened?

"Caesar, the King's chief minister, Pothinus, and his assistants or aides have arrived, they say, from the king at Pelusium and wish an interview with you."

"Finally, the hand behind all of this. Show him in my dear Sextus, but do stay with us, with your men. Everyone is to understand that he is not to turn his back on these people for a minute."

"Indeed, Caesar."

"Ah, the great and victorious Caesar!" exclaimed the richly and elaborately dressed Pothinus upon entering the room. "It is such an honor to be in your presence."

"Greetings, Pothinus, Chief Minister to King Ptolemy XIII. Do we have you to thank for our warm welcome to the city founded by Alexander the Great?"

Pothinus hesitated for a second in his reply, not sure whether Caesar meant what he was saying. Then he quickly decided to be positive.

"Yes, Caesar. As you know the king's father owed his throne to Pompey and there was great love and support for Pompey in the kingdom. Thus for us to put an end to your quest and finally hand you the head of Pompey took a great deal of courage on the part of the king, and of course, us, his advisers. You understand of course that the king still is only fourteen. He relies on us a great deal. But we took that risk out of our great respect for you and for Rome, as you are its true leader."

Caesar chose not to acknowledge that comment. Instead he said: "I am deeply disturbed by this war between brother and sister. Rome counts on a steady source of corn and grain from Egypt, and its stability is of vital concern to us. A civil war cannot aid in its stability. What is the cause of this war?"

"There are many causes, Caesar. Did not the queen when she was effectively in control of the throne by herself send with Sextus Pompey almost our entire fleet, sixty great warships, in his father's war against you?"

What really happened?

"Was that the cause of the conflict between brother and sister?"

"One of many, as I said. But I will not bother you with these Egyptian affairs. Certainly Caesar has many other important matters to attend to and the affairs of Egypt should be the least of them."

"But I have just mentioned, Pothinus," Caesar said with a certain edge, "that the stability of Egypt is a primary strategic concern of Rome's. Trade and commerce from the East come through Alexandria to Greece and to Rome. We rely heavily on Egypt's consistent supply of corn. No, very much contrary to what you say, the affairs of Egypt are very much a matter of concern to Rome, and consequently of concern to me, as its consul.

"In addition, I have a personal interest in these matters of inheritance and ruling as well. It was while I was consul that Ptolemy Auletes was confirmed in his position and Egypt granted the status of friend and ally of Rome. These are not minor matters, Pothinus, nor matters that are of no concern to Rome or to me personally. In addition, there is the matter of Ptolemy Auletes's will in which he asked Rome to ensure the safe transfer of power upon his death to two of his children as equal rulers, his eldest boy and his eldest daughter, who would in the Ptolemaic and Egyptian tradition rule as husband and wife."

"Will? What 'will' do you speak of Caesar?"

"I have not seen it, Pothinus, but I have long heard of it. Certainly you must be familiar with it, or how else would these two youths be ruling jointly after their father's death?"

"I do not know," Pothinus answered. "But at any rate that business is over. Their joint rule has ended. This girl brazenly attempted to usurp the throne for herself but her efforts have failed. She has been deposed for her crimes. When we capture her she will no longer live."

"And by what authority was the lawful queen of Egypt

What really happened?

supposedly deposed?" Caesar asked.

"Heavens, great Caesar, you have such weighty matters to attend to across the Mediterranean world. I even have heard that there is unrest in Rome. I suggest you not waste your precious time on these trifling matters."

Sextus flinched at this blatant arrogance and disrespect. But Caesar himself fell silent. Here indeed, he thought to himself, was the mind behind these recent events. A eunuch minister who has deluded himself into thinking he was actually the ruler. Under his fantasy rule the comities of diplomacy, treaties and friendships have no part to play, and treachery becomes governmental policy. A shortsighted but nevertheless a dangerous man.

"Minister Pothinus, you must forgive me," Caesar said. "We have had a long and difficult journey. I wish now to bathe and rest. I have to admit that I am tired. Would you excuse us, please?"

This would seem to have been a final order to leave, but Pothinus did not understand it, or pretended not to. So he continued: "Caesar, on the way here I noticed that your army was in the process of destroying the royal gardens to this palace to set up a camp. My king will be extremely disturbed by this. I must ask you to remove your troops immediately from the gardens. They can find places in the upper city with the Egyptians or the Jews or in the barracks with the garrison."

Caesar's only reply was to bow his head ever so slightly, signaling the end of the interview, prompting Sextus quickly to move forward and as politely as possible escort the scowling Pothinus and his party of puzzled comrades out of the residence.

Upon Sextus's return Caesar greeted his smiling cousin by instructing him to have all the palaces in the inner quarter searched; determine where the rulers kept their documents and find the copy of Ptolemy Auletes's will that must be with the State's papers.

What really happened?

Finally, Caesar left to take his bath.

IX

"Zeno, I expected to see our friend Theodorus, the director."

"His assistant, Dionysus, reports that Theodorus has left the city to visit relatives but that you were to be shown all courtesies, and allowed entry into any of the rooms of the library as you may wish to go."

"Curious, but no more than many other things around here. Tell me, Zeno, with such a vast array of rooms and niches, which ones should I seek to enter?"

"There are said to be four hundred to five hundred thousand mixed and single scrolls in Alexandria's library, collected over the centuries. The Ptolemies were determined to make Alexandria the center of Greek and Hellenistic culture. They commissioned the acquisition of every known Greek book; the acquisition indeed of every existing book in the civilized world—from the great Babylonian libraries, Athens, Sparta, the cities of Iran and those of Arabia, Palestine, Judaea and as far as India. What was not already written in Greek they had translated into Greek. Even the very library of Aristotle himself found its way here. There is said to be at least two hundred works of that great philosopher and teacher on these shelves,

What really happened?

though many are emendations of his works.

"The Ptolemies placed a higher priority on their library than their commerce. It was known that any ship that passed through Alexandria would be searched for original scrolls. The scrolls would be "borrowed" and copied by scribblers at the library. Often the heads of the library decided to keep the originals themselves and send copies back to the unfortunate owners.; other times they were satisfied with the copies and sent the originals back to the more fortunate owners. So anything you imagine resides here in this library. But here comes Dionysus, an old friend of mine. He, I am sure, will help you decide where to start."

"Welcome, great Caesar, I had heard that you would be coming. I am at your service."

"Dionysus," asked Caesar, who apparently had already decided where to start, "where are the annals of Alexander's travels and the accounts of Alexander's wars by the first Ptolemy which I have heard exist here?"

"They are among the most sacred and secret scrolls we have. We have all of the great Ptolemy's books. For Alexander's annals themselves, he did not write that much but we have them all—in his own hand. Only his dear companion Ptolemy took the necessary care to preserve the Great Alexander's writings. But I am afraid that it's not frequent that we permit viewing—"

Zeno abruptly interrupted him: "Dionysus, please just take us there, now!"

Caesar soon settled himself into a comfortable chair and began reading through the annals, exciting and fascinating even to this veteran traveler. The Greek was very ancient and what he could not decipher Dionysus helpfully found scholars who assisted. For hours Caesar sat, entranced by the hand of Alexander and his comrades. Alexander's famous bematists, with their odometers, would measure his travels with remarkable precision, so

What really happened?

his locations were never in doubt. The lengths of Alexander's journeys were absolute marvels. No wonder, Caesar thought, that his troops often rebelled at moving forward another step. Alexander traveled with the same men that he had started with, often for many years at a time, while picking up recruits along the way. But the Macedonians were always the core of his armies.

It was finally at the Acesines River in India, beyond the Indus River and beyond the Punjab plain where he had beaten King Porus, where his men finally and absolutely refused to advance, even on the threat of death. None of Alexander's pleading to them—that they were only twelve days' march from the great Ganges and then to the outer ocean and the end of the world, could move them, as they had often heard similar entreaties.

The Roman read with much interest the speech of Coenus, Alexander's greatest general and his closest companion, representing the rank and file of Alexander's exhausted foot soldiers, though he himself was a privileged officer. Caesar heard something familiar in Coenus' poignant plead to Alexander to allow these men, those who had survived years of battles and diseases, to finally return home. They know, Coenus pointed out, that they would be rich upon returning home with the spoils collected over the years, but unless they returned soon there would be none of them left. They did not begrudge Alexander's quest to reach the ends of the earth, but they pleaded that he do it with younger men; he could recruit enthusiastic youths back in Macedonia who would follow him to those ends. But these men were utterly exhausted. They had lost so many of their comrades to battle and disease. Soon they would succumb themselves.

As it was, Alexander did have to stop at that point. And he himself did not make it back to Macedonia, but died in Babylon, perhaps with a spirit broken by his men's refusal to join him in seeking the edge of the world. Perhaps he

What really happened?

intended it that way, having planned to make Babylon the center of his new empire.

Caesar thought of the mutinies in his own army, when his men felt they were being asked to go beyond what they could endure, beyond their agreed enlistment periods or farther into unknown regions than they thought reasonable. He had talked some of them back; others he had disbanded. He understood that armies had to be recycled. The same men could only go a certain distance. Then recruits with enthusiasm and fresh blood would obey orders to go further.

On the other hand, he knew that only veterans could serve as the heart of any army. Without veterans there was no army. Only they could call up deep reserves or unknown wisdom or vaguely remembered experience when all else had failed and miraculously come up with the unexpected maneuver or unimaginable extra effort to snatch a victory from defeat. He remembered how often in his long career a handful of veterans in the right place, at the right time and inspired as only he could do were able to turn certain defeat into victory, transform a defeatist army into heroic fighters and lead whole armies over enemies many times their number. He had seen it happen so often. He would do anything to keep his veterans.

But these words of Coenus did remind him that there were limits, and he must keep them in mind. This story of Alexander's final stop just before the Ganges reminded him of that lesson again. He tried very hard to stay close to his men's heartbeats.

Caesar had already started to disband some of his more veteran legions, those who had served their sixteen years or sixteen campaigns, and he planned to continue to do so in a systematic way, so long as he had enough veterans for any expected confrontation. He still had under arms over the Mediterranean world veterans who had well exceeded their sixteen years. He would need to disband many of

What really happened?

them before they became as rebellious as Alexander's men had become in India. But, still, only veterans could turn a battle.

A few days later he had asked Dionysus to show him what the Greeks felt were their most advanced studies of the geography of the earth. He then became engrossed in the scrolls of some writers, Greeks again, who were speculating on the size of the earth. Some of their opinions greatly conflicted with his Roman concept of space, and he was trying to reconcile them when Sextus gently nudged him. Caesar's bodyguards had warned Sextus that when Caesar was so absorbed in his readings, it was wise to approach quietly.

"Ah, Sextus, you return me to the present. What is it?"

"Caesar, Centurion Scaeva has returned."

Caesar rose abruptly and followed Sextus back to his own private room at the residence.

"Welcome back, Scaeva. Thank you and the other centurions for undertaking this dangerous mission."

Scaeva was in the midst of the men he had traveled with. Each, though weary and disheveled, wanted to be a part of this important report to Caesar, and Scaeva gave each of his colleagues a position about him.

"We are honored, General. But we have only disturbing news to report."

"Go ahead."

"The king as you know is at war with the queen. He controls the fortifications at Pelusium where Pompey's agents had first made contact. Somehow Pompey's people knew he was there and not at Alexandria. Pompey's emissaries asked for an interview, reminding the king of Pompey's services to the king's father. Apparently it was the king's adviser, the eunuch Pothinus who spoke for the king. Word is that between Pothinus, Theodorus, and their chief military minister, Achillas, the decision was made that Pompey was a loser and there was no upside in helping

What really happened?

him. They could turn him away, imprison him for Caesar, or kill him. They say that Theodorus convinced the others that 'Dead men don't bite.'

"Pompey consequently was treacherously invited to come ashore for a visit with the king. Fortunately he did not bring his wife or children with him, but just two centurions and a freedman by the name of Philip. Sent to greet him were their general Achillas and a Roman officer by the name of Septimius, along with some other soldiers. Just before reaching shore, as Pompey was rising to disembark, he was run through from the back by Septimius, and then immediately again by Achillas. The two centurions were likewise dispatched before they could draw their swords.

"Pompey's wife and friends could see from where they were what had happened, but then the Egyptian ships began moving toward them. Prudently the Roman ships turned and fled. It was Septimius who separated the head of Pompey from its body, and then dumped Pompey's body into the water along with the dead centurions.

"We found Pompey's freedman Phillip on the shore next to a small mound of stones. He told us what had happened. He and some passersby had retrieved Pompey's body from the water, cleaned it and dressed it as best they could. They then set up a pyre from scattered branches and other wood and cremated the Great Pompey's remains. His ashes were buried and marked by this mound of stones that we looked upon.

"We searched for and finally found the bloated remains of his two centurions. We likewise cremated their bodies and buried their ashes next to Pompey's." Scaeva paused at this point.

Caesar and the others remained quiet for some time, absorbing the grim and treacherous scene. Finally, Caesar urged Scaeva to continue.

"We then found some men hidden in the bushes who

What really happened?

turned out to be Roman officers who were hiding on the beach and dressed in rags. They reported that they too had been surprised by the treachery of the Egyptians when they arrived soon after Pompey under the command of Pompey's legate, Lentulus. Some of Lentulus' men had been killed and he himself was 'arrested' by the Egyptians and brought to the king. Others of Lentulus' party escaped and apparently tried to make their way to the Roman colony in Alexandria. We have brought back with us the survivors from Pelusium."

"Make sure, Sextus, that they are cared for as if they were our own. Anything about the Egyptian army?" Caesar asked Scaeva.

"Just above the shore where Pompey was assassinated, there is a small mountain called Mount Casius where the king's army was encamped. Across from them and a number of rivers of the delta we understood from the locals that the Queen of Egypt had encamped her own army, having raised it from the Greeks, Phoenicians, Jews and Arabs of Ascalon and the surrounding cities.

Apparently Cleopatra was much favored by the Greeks outside of Alexandria and by the native Egyptians, whose gods she had studiously respected during her short reign. It is said that she speaks the native Egyptian language— actually the very first Ptolemy in all these centuries to do so. At any rate they say her army is formidable and that any battle will not be one-sided. In addition, we heard that except for the Roman Gabinians, the rest of the Egyptian army consisted of recruits from pirates and criminals from Cilicia and Syria, bandits who have decided to settle for regular meals, slaves who had escaped from their Roman and Greek masters throughout the Mediterranean, and deserters from various armies, including those of Rome—a motley group that the Gabinians have been trying to form into a fighting force."

"Did you learn how many there were and what

What really happened?

equipment they may have?"

"Everyone we talked to had a different estimate, often depending on where they were when they saw the army as it passed. We ourselves approached as close as we dared. Their scouts and lookouts were scarce and lazy, so we were able to get somewhat close. From the reports we already had plus our observations of their fires in camp and the size of their fortifications, we estimate an army of twenty to twenty-five thousand men. That's the best we could come up with."

"Splendid Scaeva, splendid. Not only could your shield hold off a horde of the enemy, but your eyes and mind have pieced together a complete picture for us. Good work. Anything else before I let you and your men get a well deserved bath and rest?"

"Just one more thing, Caesar, we would like you to meet Pompey's freedman, Philip."

Caesar rose and embraced an old and fragile Greek.

"Thank you, Philip. You have served your master well and by that you have served Rome well. Stay with us in the palace. I will have a room prepared for you. After you have rested and recovered from your ordeal, determine where you would like to go. I will see to it that you arrive there safely and with sufficient resources for a life suitable to a noble, which you are."

"Thank you great Caesar. May I say, sir, that Pompey always spoke of you with respect and affection, particularly when he was husband to your beloved daughter Julia, whom he loved more than life itself. He regretted only that you wanted to be the first man in Rome when he had assumed that he would be such for the rest of his life. But I must say that he loved you."

"And I loved him, too, dear Philip."

They embraced again and stood still for a moment. Then Caesar asked that Philip be seen to his room and that his every need be attended to.

What really happened?

Caesar ordered Trogus to bring Vibullius. The engineer had been assigned one of the larger rooms in the palace.

Upon Vibullius' arrival Caesar said: "Vibullius, while you were Pompey's Prefect of Engineers did you ever have to construct a monument?"

"Yes, Caesar," Vibullius replied. "The Great Pompey liked to leave something in each town or city he conquered to remind the populace of Roman might. So we constructed many a monument."

"Get together with some of the sculptors and other artists among my legions—Sextus will identify them for you—and prepare something special so that these people also will remember Pompey."

Vibullius was surprised by this order. Had the shoe been on the other foot, he thought, Pompey would certainly have paid no attention to the memory of Caesar. Yet here was Caesar paying honor to Pompey. "What kind of a monument, Caesar?"

"First," replied Caesar, "I want it situated at the very top of Mount Casius so that it could be seen not only from the beach where he was murdered and from nearby Pelusium and the surrounding country, but also far out into the sea. I want it lighted at night. Perhaps you can visit the Pharos tower to get some ideas on lighting."

"Caesar," said the now confused Vibullius, "you are describing a monument that would be greater than any I have seen in the east. You have only a small force here, and I do not know what your finances are, but the cost will be immense."

"Thank you, Vibullius," Caesar said with some annoyance. "But tell me something, did your commander Pompey tolerate this kind of questioning?"

Vibullius shrank back, realizing his mistake. But he took heart when he saw Caesar's frown quickly disappear and be replaced by a smile.

"My apologies, Vibullius," said Caesar. "There is good

What really happened?

reason to question the logistics of such a project. I understand. But that's what you and I have dealt with for many years. Please be assured that I will find the people and the other resources necessary. Any other questions?"

Vibullius was hesitant for a moment, but then asked what he felt he had to know to start his commission. "Caesar, what do you have in mind for this monument? A statue? A series of figures or columns? A huge inscription?"

"Rather than tell you what the monument should consist of, let me tell you what I want it to say to the world. Today and for many generators to come," Caesar said with unexpected heat, "when the Alexandrians and Egyptians look up at the mountain top, Vibullius, I want them to think they hear the angry voice of Pompey, like thunder from the clouds. I want them to regret that monstrous murder. I want them to live in fear of the spirit of Pompey, and the very real might of Rome."

Vibullius and the others looked on in stunned silence. Something had obviously touched Caesar deeply. Vibullius finally recovered enough to say: "We will prepare ideas and sketches for your review."

"No, no. Vibullius," Caesar said with some edge. "You now know what I want. You and the artists are fully capable of producing it on your own. Just put it up on that damned mountain, yesterday, rather than today. I want the murderers to be the first to cower before it. And it must be done quickly as I plan to dispatch each and every one of them to Hades as soon as I am in a position to do so."

Few in his presence had witnessed Caesar's anger before, so no one dared to be the first to speak. Vibullius was the most astounded and thought that only now was he beginning to understand this phenomenon called Caesar.

It was Caesar who broke the silence, his tone suggesting that his anger had not abated. Turning to Sextus, who immediately stiffened and then nodded,

CAESAR, CICERO & CLEOPATRA

What really happened?

Caesar said: "Bring me Lucius Septimius."

CAESAR, CICERO & CLEOPATRA

What really happened?

.

X

"I protest the force being used to drag me here, Caesar. And I insist that my sword be returned to me. I am a General in the Army of Egypt and should not be in your presence without the king or his advisors. I demand to be released, immediately." Septimus spoke with some anger. He was not without courage.

"You are a military tribune in the Roman Army, not any kind of general that we would recognize. That is how our records indicated your status when you were stationed here by General Aulus Gabinius."

"You have been grossly misinformed, sir. The king has . . ."

"But Tribune, let us not discuss your rank. Tell me, instead, about your recent encounter with Proconsul Gnaeus Pompey."

"You heard everything you need to know from Theodorus upon your arrival. Recall, sir, that I was there when he related to you the events of Pompey's end."

"But I wish to know more circumstances. For instance, by whose order did you murder Pompey?"

"It was not a 'murder,' as you say. In any event all of our actions were on the king's orders."

What really happened?

"But the king is a child of fourteen. Where did this momentous idea come from?"

"I understand that it was from his senior advisors."

"And they are?"

"You have met two of them, Theodorus and Pothinus. The third is his military advisor, Achillas."

"Tell me about the killing itself."

"What is there to tell?"

When Caesar did not respond, Septimius reluctantly continued. "Achillas and I drew our swords and executed Pompey on the king's orders and for your benefit."

"You drew your swords? Then certainly Pompey must have drawn his. I know for a fact that as a Roman officer he always wore his sword by his side. He also was always a quick soldier, and he would not have allowed himself to be dispatched without offering a stout defense. Well, Septimius, you do not answer."

After an uncomfortable minute passed, Septimius answered:

"He did not see."

"What do you mean: 'he did not see'? Was he blindfolded?"

After another brief silence, Septimius spoke haltingly. "As it happened in the small boat . . . we were behind him."

"Ah, I see it now. You ran your sword into Pompey's back!"

A very long silence ensued. Finally, Caesar rose and stood still for a moment. "Military Tribune Lucius Septimius, by the evidence of your own testimony, I, Gaius Julius Caesar, Consul of Rome and on behalf of the Roman People and the Senate, find you guilty of the murder of Proconsul and General Gnaeus Pompey. You are sentenced to death. You will be removed from here immediately to your execution."

Septimius' cries of protest were eventually muffled by

What really happened?

Caesar's German bodyguards who had been given the task of removing him from the building and performing the execution under Sextus' direction.

Upon Sextus return Caesar asked him to summon Pothinus and whatever other Egyptian ministers were available for a conference in the building's study. Meanwhile he would take a quick tour of the city to check the mood of the people.

Caesar had already paid his respects to Alexander the Great whose grand tomb was located near his residence in the palace quarter. He remembered when he was a young man how he had loved to study Alexander's exploits, thus he had expected to be moved upon viewing Alexander's embalmed features. But he had felt nothing. I guess, he mused to himself, I am already too old and have had too many of my own battles to be touched by those of others. Though, he thought, the Great Pompey must have felt differently as he had worn, almost as a talisman, a red robe supposedly owned by Alexander, which Pompey had taken from a temple somewhere in the east.

Caesar was more impressed by the regular streets of the capital, neatly crossing one another at right angles; the noble and grand breadth of the two main Avenues, the Canopic Way, running east to west, and the Street of the Soma, north to south, which intersected in the middle of town. Each was a wide processional boulevard, wide enough for twenty chariots side by side. The avenues for their entire length were bordered by colonnaded walkways with awnings, gardens, giant palm trees and shops interspersed at regular intervals.

Many temples and public buildings, all in marble or polished limestone, lined much of the grand avenues. There were magnificent temples to the ancient Egyptian gods as well as to the gods of Greece. Caesar noted the large number of very old Egyptian statues and monuments that the Ptolemies must have had transported to

What really happened?

Alexandria from the rest of Egypt at great cost and expense. It appeared the Ptolemies were wisely intent on cultivating the Egyptian population by connecting themselves to events and individuals in the long history of Egypt.

Caesar was dressed in plain garments while touring the city, and was accompanied by only a few of his bodyguards and some aides, including his ever-present secretaries who would jot down his observations from time to time. But they were recognized as part of the newly arrived Romans and were met with sneers and insults from the townspeople along the way, forcing him to remind his bodyguards from time to time to keep their restraint.

Just in case this hostility he was witnessing graduated into armed conflict, he used his touring to imagine what fighting in these streets would entail. He took careful note of the buildings and streets in each quarter of town, envisioning how best to manage and move men and equipment around if necessary; what defenses he could devise if fighting broke out and where he would set up his lines. Indeed he would have to come up with some novel approaches that his legions would need to learn quickly. He must discuss this at length with the engineer Vibullius and some of his lieutenants when he got back to his residence. So far during their stay in Alexandria there had been much unpleasant mumbling from the populace toward his soldiers, but not much violence, except he did lose several men who made the mistake of being caught alone in some alley at night. Orders now were for no one to travel alone.

Upon returning to his palace Caesar found Pothinus, looking annoyed, in the midst of a group of Egyptian officials in Caesar's study, having been gathered there by Sextus. "You have asked to see us, Caesar? I would think by now you would be on your way home, as I hear there is much happening in Rome."

What really happened?

Caesar felt himself becoming increasingly displeased at the presumptuousness and arrogance of this eunuch. True, Pothinus was the chief minister to the king and he needed to respect that, but still there was much ostentatiously lacking in this man's respect for Rome and its leader.

"Pothinus, I hear the ex-consul Lentulus has been arrested by the king's soldiers. Do you know of his whereabouts?"

"A Lentulus? Should I know this individual? I am not sure I have ever heard of him. Is he an adherent of Pompey and what would he be doing in Alexandria?"

"Pothinus I doubt your people would fail to recognize a former consul of Rome. Please find out where he is and have him escorted to me. Would you please do that?"

"Of course, Caesar. A small request which I shall happily carry out," he said as he turned to leave.

"But the main reason," Caesar stopped him in his tracks, "I have asked to see you and the other ministers that are here in Alexandria, is that I have decided as representative of Rome to arbitrate the dispute between the king and queen."

"Caesar, you are very kind, but I assure you that we can take care of this ourselves."

"It does not seem that you are doing a good job of it, as brother and sister are facing each other with opposing armies at this point. In any event, I wish you to be quiet for a few moments and listen to what I have to say. It was during my first consulship some years ago that Rome and Egypt entered into a treaty of friendship. In any such situation it is the duty of Rome, and its consul, to assist any ally when difficulties arise. The good health, prosperity, and stability of Egypt are very important to Rome, particularly when there is trouble on our borders, as there is now. On behalf of Rome I as consul will mediate between Ptolemy and Cleopatra. You are immediately to send emissaries to both of them and ask them to disband

What really happened?

their armies and to come here for a conference."

"Caesar, I do not think this is wise, and I hesitate to follow your request."

"Be as it may, Pothinus, but my orders will be obeyed. To assure that the king and queen receive my instructions, I will send my own messages to them as well. Please, Pothinus, no more protests. In addition there is the debt of Ptolemy Auletes that remains outstanding. I understand from the Roman bankers that seventeen million denarii are still outstanding."

"Absolutely not. I have never heard of such an amount."

"Well, fortunately I have with me Postumus, whom you recall served as treasurer here for a while."

"Only until we ran that detested extortionist out of town. Don't tell me he has had the nerve to return?"

"Greetings, Pothinus, we do meet again," said Postumus as he emerged from the group about Caesar. "I see you have not changed at all, and in fact have grown in your arrogance."

Caesar interrupted the men. "The only reason I mention Postumus is so you understand that I have complete records of the Ptolemy debts, payments made and its entire history. Those books are available for your inspection at any time. But I have decided as part of my effort to reconcile the king and queen, that I will make a gift of part of that debt to the Egyptian people. Your government, Pothinus, will only have to repay ten million denarii. The balance I make as a gift to the young monarchs. I would expect you to begin making payments immediately with what you have on hand and to raise the rest as soon as possible. You will deal with Postumus in this matter. That is all I wish to hear on it for now. Please see to it that the emissaries to the king and queen are sent out immediately."

With that Caesar turned to leave the study with his

What really happened?

lieutenants, leaving the fuming Pothinus and his aides to be let out by the soldiers.

XI

Caesar was making it his regular habit after exercises and a review of his men to retreat to the great library and its adjacent academy. To a Roman these facilities were a marvel. Libraries in the Roman world were confined to the homes of the rich and only their friends were allowed entry. Here the Ptolemies had opened the greatest library in the world to all scholars, many of them invited to Alexandria and living at the court's expense in the academy. Then throughout the city there were smaller libraries for use by anyone.

Caesar now could often be found in the academy where the scholars were housed and where they discoursed in splendid gardens and baths. In the middle of the academy building was a round communal dining room where all the scholars could eat and continue their conversations. Small rooms around the interior were reserved for scholars doing special projects. In one large room were many tables filled with scribblers translating or copying texts.

Today he had been joined by Zeno, who was much enjoying the free access he now had to almost anything in the library so long as he accompanied Caesar. They were seated at a table engrossed in conversations with some

What really happened?

Greek geographers and mathematicians, debating the works of Archimedes and Eratosthenes. The latter's work was of particular interest to Caesar. One of the great directors of the library in an earlier age, the Stoic geographer and mathematician had come up with what he claimed was the most accurate measurement of the earth. He had written his most famous works just before 200 BC. Caesar was attempting to reconcile the figures of Eratosthenes with what he had learned in his studies as a Roman, primarily from the writings of Aristotle. But even Alexander the Great's bematists had found Aristotle way off the mark.

Eratosthenes had the novel idea that all the oceans were connected; that Africa could be circumnavigated and that India could be reached by sailing westward from Spain. Further, he had established a more exact calculation for the length of the year and created a new calendar consistent with his calculations. His successors were still working on that calendar. Caesar made a note to request some of the Eratosthenes followers to review the Roman calendar, now way out of date with seasons falling at the wrong time of year.

But it was Eratosthenes's calculation of the circumference of the earth that was most fascinating to Caesar. If that Greek geographer was right, then the world was much larger than the Romans had been taught. And what did those unknown areas consist of? Water? Land? Or both? It was at one of these sessions that an unusual looking young man had joined them and merely sat and listened. Caesar was told quietly that this new attendee was Bao Yang, a man from the other side of the world, a place called China, and that he was an aide to a great Chinese scholar in residence by the name of Liang Wei.

During the third or fourth time that Bao Yang had joined the discussion, speaking perfect Greek, he revealed a detailed knowledge of parts of the earth that Caesar had

What really happened?

never heard of. Upon further inquiry Bao spoke of great landmasses to the east of the Parthian Empire and India. Caesar asked Bao if he could meet his master, the scholar Liang Wei. Arrangements were made, but Bao made it clear that Caesar should come alone.

XII

Pothinus simply ignored Caesar's request to send an emissary to Cleopatra informing her of Caesar's wishes for a conference. So it was Caesar's men who delivered the invitation to her. Gaining entry to her camp under the customary signals for a meeting, the trusted equestrian Publius Rufio and two centurions conveyed Caesar's invitation. Cleopatra was delighted that the Roman had decided to intervene. When she had learned of Pompey's murder by her brother's men on the beach she had given up hope that Rome would help. Her father had always been a faithful friend of Rome, and in particular, of Pompey. She herself during the brief time she was on the throne had followed her father's policies toward Rome. It was quite clear to her father and to her that Egypt could maintain its position in the east only with the assistance and forbearance of the now all-powerful Romans. This Caesar, while still a question mark, but still a Roman.

Cleopatra immediately accepted the invitation and advised Rufio that she would come to Alexandria as Caesar wished. After the Romans left, Cleopatra conversed with her close advisors, including her chief lady, Agatha and her long time teacher and aide, Apollonios. Everyone

What really happened?

agreed that any mediation conducted by a Roman would be favorable to her, as her father had always counted on Rome to ensure that his wish for succession be fulfilled. By her father's expressed wish both she and her young brother, Ptolemy, were to be joint rulers. Once on the throne again, Cleopatra was sure she could deal with her brother. But the only question was how she would get to Caesar.

Her military leaders suggested that she would need at least a cohort of cavalry to get through her brother's lines and reach Alexandria. If they moved quickly at night they had a chance of evading detection or at least catching them so much by surprise that they could fight their way through.

"I am not sure that it is such a good idea," said Agatha. "Any kind of fighting is a gamble and we should not be gambling with the queen's life."

"I agree," echoed Apollonios.

"Any large movement from our camp will draw the attention of my brother's men," Cleopatra said. "So if we leave with troops, there will be a battle. I too would like to avoid bloodshed at this point; I do not want Caesar to receive me with blood on my hands. Let us think about this."

Eventually it was Cleopatra who made the final decision to go to Alexandria without any armed men at all but only with her aide Apollonios. "I know the roads from our camp to Alexandria better than anyone here, and only I know the various secret passages in and out of the palaces. A young woman and an old man, excuse me Apollonios, would draw no attention anywhere."

Notwithstanding the protests of almost her entire staff, in the middle of the night Cleopatra and Apollonios slipped out of camp on two nondescript horses and headed for the main road between Pelusium and Alexandria. Only her staff knew of her leaving, as it was

What really happened?

certain that Ptolemy had spies among her troops. Word was put out that the queen had come down with a minor illness and would be in her tent for a few days.

As Cleopatra had predicted, their journey attracted no attention and they were soon at the gates of Alexandria. This would be the most dangerous part as they were sure that Pothinus had troops watching for her. Without hesitation Cleopatra guided Apollonios down to the shore where they hired a small boat to take them to the royal harbor inside the great harbor. The boatman had no questions when Apollonios handed him a hefty purse. Once inside the royal harbor where she had frequently played as a child, Cleopatra had no trouble finding a small boat and directing Apollonios into the royal palace grounds.

XIII

By this time King Ptolemy had reluctantly left Pelusium. The petulant youth was angrily complaining that he had to leave his army just when it was about to move against his sister's army. Nevertheless Pothinus convinced him to comply with Caesar's request, at least for the time being. Ptolemy became further enraged when Pothinus informed him about the gold in the treasury being transferred to Caesar in partial payment of his father's debts to the Romans. Again, Pothinus convinced the king that for now they should just bide their time.

Now everyone awaited Cleopatra's response to Caesar's call for a peace conference.

Days later Caesar, as had become his habit in the afternoon, was in the academy reading some scrolls when Sextus approached with some news.

"Caesar, you have a visitor."

"Not the king again? I have explained to him that there are to be no hostilities between him and his sister and that their dispute must be resolved."

"No, sir, it is the queen, Cleopatra. She arrived at your residence unannounced. "

"Peculiar, but then what is not peculiar around here.

What really happened?

Let's meet the young lady."

"In addition Caesar, we have learned the fate of proconsul Lentulus."

"His 'fate'?"

"He was imprisoned by the king. After you made inquiry of Pothinus about his whereabouts, we were told that Lentulus was executed in his prison cell. I am sorry, Caesar."

"Yet another gift from this perfidious Pothinus. Why kill a proconsul of Rome at this point? Utterly gratuitous and stupid! My patience with this fool is coming to an end. Sextus, put a careful watch on this perfidious creature. His time may be running out."

"Yes sir."

Caesar with his two secretaries and bodyguards followed Sextus back to the palace and to his study, where stood a youth and an old man.

"Forgive me, Caesar, for my abrupt entrance."

"Welcome, Queen Cleopatra. We were wondering where you were. The king arrived several days earlier. But now that you are here, all is well. Where is your entourage?"

"Caesar, this is Apollonios of Sicily. He is my 'entourage.'"

Caesar could only raise an eyebrow and look over at Sextus with a question on his face.

"Caesar," Sextus answered, "the queen did not feel safe in entering Alexandria openly. She knows that the king's advisors have sent assassins to kill her and would do so on sight. Her army is encamped on the other side of the Delta in the Pelusium area. So she entered last night on a small boat only with Apollonios, and even with that, she was hidden in a laundry bag. Our sentries did stop Apollonios as he came onto the grounds, but let him go to deliver his 'laundry'."

"Well, well," was Caesar's only comment.

What really happened?

"Yes, sir, I understand. The guards will receive some further training."

"In any event, Sextus, please escort the queen and her solitary aide to a couple of empty rooms in a separate section of this building so that they may be self-sufficient. But make sure her area has very limited access so we can guard it carefully. She has some enemies in the palace compound."

Turning to Cleopatra, Caesar said: "My Queen, when you are ready please send word to me. I wish to see both you and the king to resolve this dispute. Meanwhile, if you will permit me, I will send some of my men to your camp to bring back your court. After all," he said with a smile, "what is a Queen without her court?"

"So kind of you Caesar, but we will need more than a couple of rooms. I have over fifty ladies and eunuchs in my court."

Caesar showed no expression but thought for a moment. "Sextus, determine how to house the queen and her court in one of the wings of this palace. Clean the place out as you did this wing so we do not have any of Pothinus spies around and then set up a guard around it. Make sure there is a separate kitchen, baths and dining room in that wing."

"Yes, sir."

"Thank you Caesar." Bowing slightly she followed Sextus to her new quarters.

These Ptolemies, Caesar thought, are something else. I would not have been able tell the difference between the queen and the king if I met them alone on a street. They look almost identical and I would have guessed that the king was the female of the two, if told they were brother and sister. So much for the Egyptian tradition of brother and sister marriages.

"Faberius, make note that the Queen speaks perfect Latin as well as her own Greek. Also, I will be interested in

What really happened?

learning how this young lady—what is she now, twenty-three or twenty-four?—was able to gather an army not only to confront her brother's army, but also all the powers that be in Alexandria."

"That is no mystery, Caesar," Faberius quickly responded. "While you have been spending time with the scholars in the library, Trogus and I have felt we were of no use to you there. So we dressed ourselves as best we could as natives and have been wandering the city, talking with these very talkative people. It turns out that the queen is very much more popular outside of Alexandria than she is in the city. There seems to be many reasons for this. One reason is that the rest of Egypt does not share the extreme antagonism to Rome held by the Alexandrians. Cleopatra, as her father was, is known to be loyal to Rome. In addition, she speaks the language of the Egyptians, the very first Ptolemy to do so, as well as the languages of many adjacent nations, including the Iranians or Parthians, the Arabians, the Hebrews and others. Further, she has often traveled around to the temples of Egypt and supported their priests and the local Egyptian gods, making her very popular indeed. The temple priests in Egypt wield a great deal of influence in their towns, and are also the wealthiest residents of those towns.

"When Pothinus and Achillas succeeded in forcing her and her court to flee Alexandria for their safety, they found ready support and refuge among the Greek and Egyptian cities along the coast. She established herself at Ascalon, where the Greek, Jewish and ancient Phoenician presence is great. With the gold she was able to take with her from Alexandria she raised a willing army from the local population and the surrounding areas."

"So all this information, Faberius, which is quite interesting, you were going to tell me at some point?"

"Caesar, this was the first opportunity we've had since we learned of these things."

What really happened?

"Relax, Faberius, you and Trogus have done very well. Let us prepare for this conference with the royal couple. You have Ptolemy Auletes's will? I understand it was not difficult to find."

"No, Caesar, it was among his personal papers which the court maintains among the state papers in the main palace. The sentries were not at all happy about our intrusion but Sextus and his men paid no heed to them. Fortunately, the guards left behind by the king to guard the palaces are even less military than Trogus and me. But I am afraid Pothinus now knows you have the will."

"Let me review the will," Caesar said, "and then we will make some notes in preparation for the conference."

CAESAR, CICERO & CLEOPATRA

What really happened?

XIV

Once settled in Caesar's study later that day, Caesar read Auletes's will to King Ptolemy and Queen Cleopatra.

"So you see, my king and queen, your father wanted you both to share the throne as equal rulers. In addition, he specifically asked that the Roman government insure that his wishes be carried out. He had much experience in how difficult it is to maintain the throne in Egypt, and he did not want either of you to endure the same trouble.

I therefore want you both to dismantle your military camps and agree to set up one small royal military force. Rome will guarantee your safety against foreign enemies. Then you are both to rule together, husband and wife and as equals, making each decision jointly. That is what your father wished, and that is what Rome insists upon."

Pothinus was about to speak when Ptolemy jumped up from his chair.

"No! No! We tried that and it did not work. She," pointing repeatedly at Cleopatra, "pushed me aside and made all the decisions herself. My friends and advisers were ignored in her court and I was treated as a child. I won't go through that again. I refuse to abide by your decision."

What really happened?

"Young man, . . . "

"No! No! You see, right away you yourself are putting me down 'Young man' indeed! Just because I am fourteen years old it does not mean I cannot lead Egypt. That has happened time and again in Egyptian history. Perhaps you are not familiar with our history, sir?"

There was perhaps a smile forming on Cleopatra's lips. Pothinus dropped his head into his hands. Sextus frowned as he glanced at the other Romans. Caesar spoke, however, without any trace of anger or even annoyance, and in fact more like a father than the Dictator.

"You are right, your majesty. I am sorry I used that term. I was being careless. But you will admit that I am much older than you and that I have much experience in the world. I can tell you that even if a program did not work at one time, it can very well work a second time if enough intelligent changes are made.

"You both also must consider the health and prosperity of Egypt. You cannot drain her of her resources in a civil war. While you are both at war your neighbors will find it easy to encroach on your borders. While you are at war you cannot harvest, gather and sell to Rome the wheat and other products that we depend on you for. Egypt would suffer greatly. You must put aside your disappointment and join your sister in ruling Egypt."

As a reply the young Ptolemy tore off some of the gold chains around his neck, threw them to the floor and stormed out of the palace. He raced through the outer gate of the palace quarter itself, then, when a crowd had gathered about him, cast his crown into the street and screamed for the Alexandrians to save him from the Romans. As could be predicted it took a very short time for thousands of Alexandrians to stream through the palace gates, aided and abetted by the Egyptian guards, and surround Caesar's residence. The Romans immediately threw up a two-line deep line of legionaries all around

What really happened?

Caesar's building and easily held off the Alexandrians with their shields.

Nevertheless Caesar thought it wise to address the Alexandrians himself. He appeared by himself on the portico and raised his arms for quiet. He then spoke to them at length. He read the entire will of Ptolemy XII to them and in particular the request of Ptolemy to Rome to ensure that the provisions of his will, granting joint and equal authority to his eldest surviving daughter and his eldest son as co-rulers, were followed.

The Alexandrians continued to mumble in a show of discontent until Caesar unexpectedly announced that on behalf of Rome he was returning Cyprus to Egyptian rule and was naming Ptolemy's younger daughter, Arsinoe, and another younger brother, as co-rulers. This seemed to do the trick. At this surprising news the mob quieted down. The annexation of Cyprus by Rome, though in accordance with the wishes of its last ruler upon his death, Ptolemy XII's brother, had been bitterly resented by the Alexandrians and was the immediate reason years earlier for deposing Ptolemy XII, who they believed did not sufficiently resist the Romans.

Eventually the mob dispersed and Caesar ordered that a banquet be held in his dining hall in two days time to celebrate the reestablishment of Cleopatra and Ptolemy as co-rulers.

But Pothinus and the king had no intention of abiding by Caesar's decision. They were sure that the Egyptian army, which greatly outnumbered the Romans, together with the Alexandrian population, could put a quick end to Caesar. So Pothinus sent a secret message to Achillas that the king wanted him to march his army to Alexandria and free him from the Romans.

Thus two days later during the celebratory banquet Caesar learned that the Egyptian Army and fleet had left Pelusium and under Achillas were approaching Alexandria.

What really happened?

Twenty thousand troops were nearing the city and the port was about to be blockaded by Egyptian warships. Caesar withdrew from the banquet to consult with his officers in the camp outside, but not before ordering that both the king and queen be escorted to separate parts of his own residence, there to be guarded and kept as his "guests" until he could determine the intentions of the Egyptian army.

Unaware that Achillas was marching on Alexandria at the secret orders of Ptolemy, Caesar had two eminent emissaries sent in the king's name to the approaching army to demand that it stop and explain its actions. But Achillas, leading the army, killed one of them and severely wounded the other, who escaped with some aides and reported back to Caesar. Caesar called a council of his officers together.

"Well, Vibullius," said Caesar, "your engineering skills will be put to the test. Will your fortifications be sufficient so that our four-thousand man force can hold off the twenty-five thousand Egyptians until reinforcements arrive?"

"Caesar," replied Vibullius, "I have not been idle. We will need to draw in a bit, but we can easily hold them off."

Caesar had to pull his men back to a fortified enclosure that included only his wing of the inner palace complex, the theater, which served as a natural citadel and which had access to the harbor and the docks, the library and the academy. The walls of these various buildings were used by Vibullius as part of the fortifications, amplified by quickly constructed towers placed regularly along the walls. The Egyptian army had no ability to scale those walls or even threaten them in any serious way. They lacked siege equipment or in fact any knowledge of siege warfare.

In addition, the only approach to Caesar's residence was through the streets of the royal quarter facing the front, which allowed him to prevent Achillas' army from approaching his building by setting up barriers and posting

What really happened?

relatively few men behind them.

A stalemate soon ensued which lasted for the next four months, intersped with small battles. In one of them Caesar gained control of the Pharos lighthouse and the harbor. Having insufficient men to guard the Egyptian fleet anchored in the harbor and wanting to keep it out of the hands of the enemy, he set fire to it, using flaming pitched balls catapulted from the top of the theater adjacent to his building and overlooking the docks. Nearly a hundred Egyptian ships were thus set afire. His own fleet he had kept safely in the smaller royal harbor, which at one point had to beat back a hastily rebuilt Egyptian fleet. During the four months of minor skirmishes in the streets there were also a number of small naval engagements.

During this back and forth, reinforcements from Calvinus arrived in the form of an additional legion, the Thirty-seventh, composed of volunteers from the former Pompeian army. The Thirty-seventh Legion doubled his forces, and brought military equipment, siege equipment, additional horses, and corn supplies. Even at that Caesar judged that his forces were still insufficient to take on the Egyptian army directly.

Caesar at one point released the king in response to the pleas of a delegation from Achillas and the leading men of Alexandria. Ptolemy, though promising to end the Egyptian army's hostilities, immediately joined Achillas and urged him to go on the offensive. Meanwhile, Arsinoe had slipped out of the palace with her eunuch tutor Ganymede also to join Achillas. An attempt by Pothinus to poison Caesar at a banquet was stymied by an alert slave of Caesar's. This turned out to be Pothinus' last act of treachery. Caesar had him executed immediately. Thus Caesar awaited the arrival of Mithridates of Pergamum and his allies.

XV

It was during this four-month stalemate that Caesar and Cleopatra came to know, and then to love, each other. It began in the library and the gardens of the academy where they would debate history, geography, science and art with the scholars. Each was surprised by the other's universal curiosity and keen intelligence. Cleopatra gradually stopped thinking of Caesar only as a powerful Roman General. Caesar ceased viewing her only as a tomboy who was oddly married to her brother.

Perhaps the most frequent topic of these discussions was about Alexander the Great. What did he accomplish? How did he do it? What if he had been allowed to go to the Ganges and then beyond? Did he die from malaria or a broken heart?

"Caesar, you can travel from what you call Farther Spain to Antioch in Syria, and use just one language: Greek. That is because of Alexander."

"It is true, Latin will get you only so far. But with Greek, one can travel the known world."

"Alexander," Cleopatra continued, "did not just create colonies, he made sure that the core was Greek or Macedonian and that the city was established along Greek

What really happened?

civic lines; that there would be academies and libraries and that scholars, architects and engineers would come from Greece and Macedonia to live there as well. He was as much interested in spreading Greek culture as he was in conquering territory for his Macedonian empire."

"He also was in the habit of naming these cities after himself. How many Alexandria's are there?"

"Fifteen, I believe."

What," Caesar asked, "do you think of his Orientalizing program?"

"You mean his marrying and having children by all these different princesses along his campaign trail?"

"Yes, but also about the time he required the mass marriage of over eighty of his closest Companions to Iranian women and then the marriage of ten thousand of his ordinary troops to oriental women. He believed it was impossible to rule his empire with just Greeks or Macedonians, or even in partnership with Persians or other Orientals. Rather he wanted to produce a new class of rulers of mixed races."

"Is that shocking to you, Caesar?"

"It certainly would be to my colleagues in the Roman Senate."

"From what I know of the Roman Senate – remember that my father had taken me to Rome when he went to seek Rome's help. Anyway, from that experience as well as my reading and conversing with bankers, traders and ambassadors, I think it does not take much to shock the Roman Senate, except when it comes to greed. It seems your Senators have a thick skin when one of their own is charged with fleecing a province or a colony. I hope I do not offend you Caesar."

"No, not at all. That is one of the flaws I have been trying to eliminate. Most senators seem to think that an appointment as governor to one of our provinces is a license to steal. I have been trying to change that. It is no

What really happened?

good for Rome if our provinces are denuded or made angry. Rome will prosper only if its provinces, allies and friends prosper."

"Caesar, what do you think if Alexander's men had not mutinied on him in India? What if Coenus had not argued on behalf of the army to stop his never-ending quest?"

"My guess, from what Alexander wrote and your own ancestor Ptolemy has written, that this mysterious empire in the east that we hear about now and then would not be so mysterious and that the Greek language would have traveled much farther east."

Such were their conversations and during each one they revealed more of themselves to one another. Soon it was as if they had grown up together. And had been good friends for a long time.

But it was during the battle on the between Pharos and the mainland when Caesar was trying to capture the mainland end of the causeway that Cleopatra realized that Caesar meant more to her than she had realized.

Cleopatra had been in the habit of sneaking out of the palace with Agatha and Apollonios to watch some of the battles between Caesar's men and the Egyptians. So it was that she and Agatha were on a ship under the nervous but careful eye of Tiberius Nero when Caesar almost lost his life in the battle on the causeway.

"Why do those foolish Roman generals," asked Agatha, "insist on wearing their purple cloaks in battle? And then further to signal to all the world that the general is there with their stupid trumpets? They are begging to be killed. Look how the Egyptian marines are focusing their javelins at the figure in purple, our Caesar."

"Caesar says," replied Cleopatra, "that fighting among his men, and that they know he is doing so, is essential to their morale and an important reason for his successes. He knows he draws the special attention of the enemy, but he is more interested in the attention of his men."

What really happened?

They both then held their breadth as they saw Caesar leap into the water and swim to a nearby Roman galley, only to see that galley itself tip over from the huge number of men trying to board. They searched about frantically with their eyes over the hundreds of men swilling in the water and finally saw Caesar calmly swimming to their own galley with his purple cloak held up in the air with one hand. Cleopatra felt her heart jump and tears welled in her eyes. Caesar now meant so much to her. It took all of her willpower not to rush to the soaking Caesar and crush him in her arms. But that did happen later that night in the privacy of Caesar's quarters.

XVI

The Roman bankers, traders and their families resident in Alexandria had taken refuge with Caesar, along with some Roman soldiers who had survived the attack on Lentulus and made their way to Alexandria. Their numbers were spread out in the palace and in the camp. It was from some of the traders that Postumus learned that the Parthians had transported the ten thousand Roman soldiers captured in the defeat of Crassus at Carrhae to the far end of the Parthian Empire.

"See if you can find out, Postumus, exactly where they are and what their condition is," Caesar asked. "Never have so many Roman legionaries fallen into slavery. Rome must do all it can to bring them back."

"Our Roman traders," said Postumus, "cannot safely go back into Alexandria right now, but they do have many slaves and freedmen, some of them Alexandrians. I will ask that they be sent to the port and mingle among the traders, especially those who have had contact with traders from an empire in the east. I am sure we can find out much more if we supply them with enough money to loosen some tongues."

"Do that, Postumus," Caesar said, "and no cost is to be

What really happened?

spared. But tell me more about this 'empire' in the east."

"Alexandria is a crossroads of many nations," explained Postumus, who himself had spent much time in Alexandria. "Goods arrive here from the farthest corners of the earth for use by the Egyptians or for transportation further west, including Rome. In recent years they say an ancient empire far to the east sent its armies out to contact the civilized nations of the west. They were followed by traders from that ancient land and a regular route for caravans was established. Much information travels that route, I am sure we will learn what we need from them."

"Crassus had talked about pushing through Parthia and Bactria and into India. He spoke to me of his dream of going as far as Alexander and maybe even farther, to the Outer Ocean. But he never mentioned anything further east. That young man at the academy, Bao, spoke of his homeland, something he called China. Can this be the empire the traders talk about?"

"It could very well be, Caesar. But you seem to know more about it than I do."

"Which is not much," replied Caesar. "But thank you, Postumus." He turned to Sextus. "Sextus, would you have the queen join me. I want her to come with me to the library today. I have a special project in mind and she may be of help."

Since Cleopatra's arrival Caesar had not only learned about the secret passages from his residence to the library, but also discovered how very popular she was with the scholars at the academy. In fact it turned out that she had recruited many of them during the few years she was still ruling. With her at his side he was amused how much more easily and quickly accessible to him were even the most ancient and jealously guarded scrolls. He looked forward to telling Cicero, who would be green with envy, how many books in Aristotle's own hand he had already read.

What really happened?

Presently Cleopatra arrived with her constant companion and first lady, Agatha. Agatha was a Greek lady descended from an early Alexandrian family, reaching back to the first Ptolemy's settlement in the city. She was very attractive, though much older than Cleopatra. It occurred to Caesar that she must have had a role in Cleopatra's upbringing, as she herself was highly educated and spoke almost as many languages as Cleopatra. Except for her other constant companion—Apollonios, a combined bodyguard, counselor and man of many talents, again much older than her—Agatha was Cleopatra's closest confidant. Apollonios was originally from the Greek town of Syracuse in Sicily but along the way he had been integrated into the Ptolemy family by Cleopatra's father, Ptolemy XII. Apparently his ministrations to Cleopatra again suggested to Caesar that he dated back to her childhood.

"So, Gaius, you now send for me like a servant," Cleopatra stated with feigned hurt upon her arrival.

"My apologies dear Cleo, but I am in a hurry to get to the library before I am taken away by some other crisis. I am anxious to get some of your scholars to begin work on a special project. Please come with me." He turned to Faberius, his ever-present secretary. "Faberius, have the slaves take those bundles that Sextus just brought along with us to the library."

"Ah, yet another of Caesar's secret projects," remarked the queen as they left for the library.

As they entered the library through the secret passageway from the palace, Dionysius greeted them. "Welcome great Queen Cleopatra and Consul Caesar. It is always a joy to see you two. Queen, it is as if you were born here. You have grown up among these scrolls."

"Yes, Dionysius, many a wonderful day have I spent here. But we need to see two of your scholars, the two men famous for their knowledge of metals."

What really happened?

"Ah, the 'metal men,' as we call them. Make the mistake of mentioning a mineral in the presence of Agape or Eusebios, and you will not be able to extract yourself from an avalanche of arcana that they will cause to fall upon you."

"Yes, they are the two I had in mind. Where are they?"

"I am sure they are in their little hideaway in the academy. It will be faster if I just take my illustrious guests there than try to describe where they are. It seems that the longer a scholar resides here the more secret niches he can find to hide out, if that is what he wishes, to read and discuss his theories with only a few selected others. This way."

The splendor and grandiose proportions of the library were matched by those of the academy. Up and down marble stairs they walked, passing rooms where several men could be heard debating and then past gardens with long pathways. Down one of those pathways they came to a sitting area where they found the metal specialists, Agape and Eusebios, engrossed in a debate and unaware of their approach.

"Please do not be startled my friends," Dionysius said, attempting to sooth the men as they approached, though startled they were. "I have brought you some guests who are anxious to seek your knowledge."

Both men jumped to their feet on seeing Queen Cleopatra and Caesar and bowed nervously.

"Be of good cheer, gentlemen," the queen assured them. "My colleague here wishes to test your expertise. Good to see you both again. You look well."

"Dear Queen," said Agape, speaking for them both. "We were so happy to hear that you were back again. What treacherous people the king's advisors are. He would do well to be rid of them."

"No politics, here, Agape," Dionysius interjected. "You know the rules."

What really happened?

"Forgive me, Queen. I forgot my place."

"Good men," Caesar interrupted. "It is an honor to meet such distinguished scholars. We have read some of your works even in Rome."

"You flatter us, great Caesar," the scholar Agape replied. "But there are those in Rome who can read Greek?"

"Agape, I have already admonished you," Dionysius frowned while waving his finger at Agape. "Enough of that tongue, you are in the presence of the First Roman among Romans. He does not have to hear your little jibes."

But Caesar waved his hand and said lightly, "We have often heard of the great liberty the Ptolemies have traditionally granted their scholars. Let me not hinder your style. Please speak your mind as you see fit. But I have come here specifically to ask your assistance."

The two men raised their eyebrows in surprise. "We indeed are the 'metal men,'" said Agape, "but in a library. What kind of help can we give a warrior?"

Caesar went on: "You of course have heard of the great defeat of the Roman armies five years ago under Marcus Licinius Crassus, where his son also perished."

"Yes, we have, Caesar." This time Eusebios replied. "We are sorry for your loss, as it seems these were men dear to you."

Caesar hesitated only a second, enough to register the depth and empathy of Eusebios' statement.

"Thank you. But I mention that battle because of some unusual things we learned from the survivors. They uniformly testified that the arrows of the Parthians, though launched from some distance by their mounted archers, were able to penetrate any defenses we had: shields, armor, helmets, and every other device we were using for protection. In addition, once the arrows pierced something, they were impossible to extract as they were

What really happened?

finely barbed. No arrow entering a leg or arm could be extracted. The men died from loss of blood or eventually poisoning.

"The survivors brought back many of these arrows, some of them still embedded in shields or helmets. I have had the arrows examined by our metallurgists in Rome and in Syria, as well as in Rhodes. None of them could identify the metal used by the Parthians. Needless to say I do not want a Roman army to face the Parthian again unless it is equipped not only with arrows made of the same metal, but with shields and helmets that could blunt them and prevent any penetration."

While Caesar was speaking Sextus had taken a number of arrows from the bundles carried by the slaves and handed them to the Greek scholars. The scholars looked carefully at the arrows and felt them carefully.

"My, my, my. Someone has developed a new form of metal," mused Agape as he turned one of the arrows over and over in his hands, even biting the end of one.

"These are very different from the normal metals used for weapons," Eusebios said. "There is an unusual feel to them, as well as a strange coloring. At first sight I cannot imagine what the metal consists of."

"I need to know," Caesar said, "and as soon as possible, what this metal is composed of. In addition, can you locate for me a source where I can gather this ore in great quantities? That is why I have come to you."

Agape looked at Caesar and then at the queen.

"Agape and Eusebios," the queen said, understanding their question. "Caesar represents Rome. It is Rome that protects us from our enemies. And today it is Caesar who demands that the Queen of Egypt retain her throne. What you do for Caesar, you do for me."

"Great Queen," Agape answered after a short pause. "We love you and we, all of us here and all those who have come before us, owe you and your ancestors the fact that

What really happened?

Greek culture has not only flourished but has spread over all the world. For you, we will do anything. We will determine what this metal is made of and discover the sources for the ore from which it is made. This I guarantee to you, your Majesty."

Everyone was silent for a while, no doubt impressed by such great devotion. Then Caesar got up, clasped the scholars' hands and left with Cleopatra and the others, leaving the bundles of arrows for the specialists to examine.

On their way back to the library, Bao Yang, the aide to the Chinese scholar, Liang Wei, approached the group.

"Caesar," Bao greeted Caesar with a bow, "and great Queen."

"Greetings, Bao. I hope you are well today," Caesar responded with a smile.

"If it pleases Caesar, my master is available now and asked if you would join him for a glass of wine and some fruit."

Caesar recalled that Bao had requested that Caesar meet with Liang by himself and without companions. So he addressed Cleopatra and the others.

"Queen, I am about to engage in what you and the others will find to be an extremely tedious discussion with scholar Liang Wei. So, please go on. I will see you all back at the palace. Sextus, I will be safe here and will need only Trogus and his tablets with me."

Unknown to Caesar there had been an ongoing heated argument between Liang Wei and his military aide, Cheng Sun. The later had vehemently objected to Liang's meeting alone with Caesar. "Only evil could come of your conversations with the master of Rome," Cheng had argued. "There is nothing that we can learn from him, but there is much he wants from us. The emperor would be displeased to hear of this."

"You threaten me, Cheng Sun," said the aged Liang

What really happened?

Wei, "with the displeasure of the Emperor? You have never set eyes on the Emperor Xuandi, while I am well known in his corridors. Please don't be so presumptuous."

Liang would not allow himself to get into a debate with a lowly soldier about the intentions of the emperor. Of course there was much to learn from the Romans. They had rode through their world like the wind. That could not be done without special qualities and resources —things his people should know about and study.

Years ago why would Emperor Wudi have sent Zhang Qiam all over the world to learn about other nations, their customs and their commerce? Why did he also send General Li Guangli out to conquer and subdue China's western borders? Not just to bring those splendid horses of Dayuan into the empire. He wanted them to find out what the rest of the world was doing. He sent traders and caravans into Parthia for the first time ever to bring them our silk and magnificent lacquer items and receive in return things then unknown in China.

In addition, Liang's Confucian master, Liu, personally instructed him to study all he could of the west in its own great center of learning, Alexandria, in addition to searching for ancient and unknown Chinese scrolls that may have found their way here. Finally, he was here at Emperor Xuandi's orders, not only to learn about the west, but also to teach the west their ways so as to make trade between them easier. Many caravans have followed him at the orders of the Emperor, bringing their silk and other expensive goods here and all along the way.

Caesar and Liang did have their wine together that day, and then lunches and dinners in the many days to follow. Caesar's bodyguards gradually got accustomed to the trio of Chinese coming over from the library to see Caesar in the palace that they no longer stopped and searched them before entering to sit and talk with Caesar. Liang had preferred not to take the soldier Cheng with him all the

What really happened?

time, but the soldier insisted that his orders were to always accompany the scholars.

Caesar was particularly interested in the vast unknown areas of the earth that Liang was describing to him, along with their exotic names and unfamiliar customs.

He also inquired about the luxurious cloth called "silk" that the Egyptian elite seemed to wear as commonly as Romans wore wool. For that reason at one of their meetings he had brought with him some of the Parthian war banners whose extraordinary cloth had so startled Crassus's soldiers during their battle at Carrhae. He thought the cloth was rare, only to find it used as everyday dress, at least by the very wealthy. He wondered how soon Rome would be engulfed in this new luxury, something he would have to curtail, he was sure, as Rome's wealth should not be passed so easily east to this China. On the other hand, if this silk found its way to Rome in much quantity, he was sure Roman traders would return the favor with shipments of olives, olive oil, wool, gold and whatever else they had to offer all the way back to where the silk originated, enriching themselves and every city along the way. He must make sure that his bankers and traders in Rome read at least summaries of what his secretaries Trogus and Faberius were recording.

This would change much in our world, he thought. Crassus had wanted to follow Alexander to Bactria, India and even to go beyond to the Outer Ocean. His dear friend would be as surprised as he has been to learn that the Outer Ocean was indeed not properly named at all. He was anxious to see Cicero's face when he told him of this. He could not fault his own scholars by their ignorance of China. Liang has made it clear that prior emperors had insisted on keeping their world isolated. Only recently has the policy of that vast land been changed. Well, there was much to learn.

CAESAR, CICERO & CLEOPATRA

What really happened?

.

XVII

"My dear Cleo, by the time any child of ours can wear a toga I will be over seventy years old—hardly any Roman lives that long; certainly I will not."

"Do women wear togas in Rome?"

"Okay. You make a valid point. But be it male or female," Caesar replied, easily absorbing the barb, "any child of ours will have little chance of living beyond my death. My host of enemies will see to that."

"Again, my Roman is being presumptuous, and so very Roman—that only a man could provide protection for a child. Do you not remember your studies, or have they been deficient? Have you never heard of the great queens Hatshepsut or Nefertiti? Whether it was a king or a queen, the Ptolemies, and indeed the Pharaohs before us for many centuries, have been quite capable of protecting their own.

What could be more fortuitous, Gaius? You yourself speak of how much larger the world is than you had thought. How could a single man, even you, or even a group of senators in Rome, rule over the vast territories of a conquered Parthia, and an India and maybe even a China? You will need Alexandria. My city of Alexandria

What really happened?

would be a natural location for a ruler allied to Rome. Or maybe even a joint ruler. Both you and I are descended from the gods. Our children would be the perfect combination of east and west, and can rule it all."

"Good Jupiter!" Caesar exclaimed with feigned shock. "Now we are 'gods.' And our children will be ruling the world, including the still unknown land of China! My dear Queen, perhaps you forget that at this moment we are prisoners of your own army. Our lives are at risk. So first we must survive this crisis before we can dream about creating a world empire. Don't you think?"

"Ah, Gaius, you may have other reasons not to want a child with me, but please don't tell me that you are in danger. You are as safe here as if you were in your mother's womb.

"You have further fortified already strong fortresses—this portion of the palace; the library and the academy, the theater. You have insured that we are almost a separate city from Alexandria. In addition you have an underground passage to the royal harbor where your ships lay in wait in case you need a speedy getaway. Your lines of supply via your ships remain open. You have the walls guarded with the most veteran and disciplined troops that exist in the world—each one ready, indeed anxious, to lay down his life for you - not only your Roman legionaries, but even your German horsemen. On the other hand, I would guess that there is not one soldier on the other side who has such loyalty—either to my brother the king, to their general or to my sister and her eunuch. Each of your men is thus worth a hundred, or even a thousand, of my brother's troops. You can choose when and where to fight. "So please, do not use the possibility of danger as an excuse. You have to decide: do you want to create a Roman-Egyptian child who may one day rule the world? But now, please, enough of this endless chatter of yours, and let us get to more important things."

CAESAR, CICERO & CLEOPATRA

What really happened?

XVIII

"Caesar, Postumus reports that he has heard back from agents of the traders sent to find out more about Crassus's men. He says he has some very interesting information."

"Thank you, Sextus, let him in but stay with us, as well as you Trogus. Make note of what he has to say."

"Caesar," Postumus said as he sat himself down at Caesar's request. "I have not brought in any of the traders, either Roman or Egyptian, because I assume you do not want them to know how interested you are in this information. But I believe I can relate all that they have found out."

"Fine. Go ahead, good Postumus."

"The Parthian leader at Carrhae, one called Surenas, after treacherously killing Crassus, overwhelmed our forces. He chased a number of them back to Syria, but his King Orodes immediately ordered him back as he did not want Surenas to get the Parthian army bogged down in Syria. There seemed to have been other problems he was dealing with in the east. The Parthians did, however, capture about ten thousand Roman officers and soldiers.

They were at a loss at first as what to do with their huge number of prisoners. Surenas wanted to execute

What really happened?

them all but King Orodes saw much value in a mass of disciplined, trained and young Roman legionaries. The problem was where to locate them. Anywhere in the west of Parthia would only invite rescue attempts by the Romans from Antioch or even tempt the prisoners themselves to make a break for it. Orodes decided that they should be transported to the most eastern portion of the Parthian Empire, and at a location very difficult to access so that even the bravest and most audacious of them would give up any hope of escape."

"And where would that be, Postumus?"

"There is a very large oasis in the middle of a great desert at the far northeastern Parthian frontier. It is called either Alexandria Margiana, or Antiochia or something along those lines. None of my informants knew just exactly where it was or how far it was. But they are sure from all they heard that the Roman prisoners have been taken there and have been employed in agricultural work, building roads and the construction of grand projects, such as aqueducts and dams, as only the Romans know how."

"Another city with Alexander's name," Caesar commented wryly. "He did like the sound of his own name. I recall reading in Ptolemy's annals that Alexander sought to anchor his victories by frequently founding colonies with his Greek and Macedonian followers, particularly the old, sick, and weary—or just the rebellious who could or would not travel on any longer— and called many of the settlements after himself. I think I even recall the name Margiana, far to the east on some river. I must consult my scholar friends at the academy. But do you feel, Postumus, that this information is accurate? I want very much to retrieve those men, but I must not be mistaken as to where they are."

"Yes, sir, I understand," answered Postumus. "But I can say to you that I feel very confident about the location of the prisoners. Several different traders told the same

What really happened?

general story to our agents. These traders were from various cities along what people are calling the 'Silk Road'. Indeed this oasis city of Alexandria Margiana, or whatever it may be called, seems to be an important transit point on one of the various routes along this Silk Road so many traders know of it. It is said to be wealthy and resplendent, primarily based on its trade with India and other locations to the east with the Egyptians, Arabs, and Greeks going to the west. It is said that the city is constantly growing and becoming wealthier. That may be why King Orodes decided to send the legionaries there, as everyone knows that much varied talent exists among them."

After warmly thanking Postumus, Caesar said to Sextus: "These conversations of course are to be kept to ourselves. I will be at scholar Liang Wei's place in the academy for a while if I am needed. We can dispense with the bodyguards for this short outing but Trogus, please accompany me."

Once Trogus confirmed with Bao that the soldier Cheng would not be in attendance, Caesar met with Liang in the latter's room at the academy. Caesar had been in and out of the library and the academy so often, that no one any longer made any fuss upon his appearance.

"Well Caesar," said Liang after being told about the Roman prisoners. "While we have talked about the trading route to China often enough, I don't recall mentioning Antiochia, or Alexandria Margiana as it is often called. There are several roads that the caravans use and many cities along the way. But this Antiochia is a very important stop along one of the major routes."

"The so-called 'Silk Road', Liang?"

"Yes, indeed. But it is not just one road, there are several routes going east and west, some more favored by certain caravans than others. Also some routes may fall out of use periodically because of some local disturbance. Thanks to the ever-increasing quantity of our precious

What really happened?

cloth that the west has been demanding, people tend to call the whole complex of roads the Silk Road.

"But please, dear friend, do not ask me about the process of making silk. Almost every child in certain parts of China grows up with this knowledge, but also with the knowledge that it would mean death if he or she ever revealed our secret to the rest of the world. But most of us do not need that kind of persuasion, as effective as it might be in many cases. We are proud of the unique things that come from our civilization, and would not want to see others take them from us."

"No, Liang," Caesar said with a smile, "you are not speaking to my banker Postumus, or a Roman trader or a manufacturer. I use money; I do not make it. Besides, I understand from the queen that as much can be made on this fabric by trading and transporting it as by manufacturing it."

"Hmm," was Liang's only response.

"Be that as it may," Caesar continued, "what I am interested in is this city called Antiochia. How far it is from here? How does one get there? Are there watchtowers or military checkpoints along the way? and things of that nature."

"Ah, those are easy questions, and the Egyptian scholars or even their traders here would be able to tell you all you want to know."

"Yes, I assume so. But I trust your people's grasp of geography and distances, and even more your own discretion."

"I understand, and I am honored. Bao, please bring me my maps."

Liang continued: "It is said that this oasis has been inhabited since the beginning of time, or at least from the earliest days of men. . . ."

"My dear Liang," Caesar softly interrupted, "could we skip over the earliest days of men and get a little closer to

What really happened?

our time?"

"Oh my, please excuse me Caesar. We old teachers do like to immerse ourselves, don't we? But here is something you would find interesting and more recent. In ancient times the oasis was called by many different names, one of them by the name of Merv, for a very long time. But when Alexander finally made it through a vast desert, he was so delighted at its fruitfulness and its strategic possibilities, that he settled many Macedonians and Greeks there and called it Alexandria. Yes, again, Alexandria. He did have that penchant. He wanted Greek culture and learning to flourish here, far to the east of his native land. But fortune was not kind to the city. It was often overrun by barbarians from the north.

"Things were put back together again after a while and Greek culture was re-established by Antiochus, a son of one of Alexander's companions. Not surprisingly, he renamed the city 'Antiochia,' though some still call it Alexandria or Alexandria Margiana. He rebuilt the fortifications and many splendid buildings. The city prospered in agriculture and then in trade as travelers and goods increased from east to west and the other way. When the Parthians conquered it they respected the local culture and did not destroy anything. In fact, Antiochia maintains a certain amount of independence that few other cities under Parthian control enjoy. The Parthians found the place prosperous and were wise enough not to kill the golden goose."

Liang nodded to Bao who now laid out some maps on the table between Caesar and Liang. "You will see, Caesar," the scholar started up again as he pointed to a location on the map, "that Antiochia is surrounded by a great desert. However there is a route along the southern part of the desert that comes north as it passes the city and at that point it is just a three day's journey by caravan to the city itself."

What really happened?

Caesar studied the map and all the strange-sounding cities along the routes going east and west. At length he asked, "The distance between Alexandria and Antiochia?"

Everyone looked down at the map, with Bao making measurements with some instrument Caesar did not recognize. "I would say," Bao responded, "using the established land routes that it would be about seventeen hundred to seventeen hundred and fifty miles."

Caesar sat for a while in silence. Then he bent over the map and studied it very carefully, running his finger along certain routes. Finally he asked, "What is the distance between the free city of Tyre and Antiochia?"

Again Bao made some measurements. "About twelve-hundred and fifty to thirteen hundred miles."

Again Caesar sat in silence, as if thinking something through. "What would one find along the route?" he asked, finally. "Any fortifications or military checkpoints?"

"No, not at all," Liang said, smiling. "These are commercial routes that are very valuable to the cities and kingdoms through which they pass. The only military or police activity is against bandits and the like, all intended to protect the very profitable caravans that pass through. Each city and kingdom extracts its tolls, of course; the local merchants profit by selling lodging, food, other supplies, camels, horses and the like; goods are exchanged or purchased, with further taxes levied on those transactions. With such easy income for the cities along the route, they make every effort to facilitate the passage of commerce. All obstructions to its free flow are eliminated or minimized by the authorities. Merchants and caravans are the kings of the highway along these routes of gold, as far as the communities along the way are concerned."

The men continued to discuss what a traveler could expect along the Silk Road for some time. Caesar seemed to be pleased with what he had learned and thanked Liang

What really happened?

and Bao generously when he finally got up to leave.

"One other thing, Caesar," Liang added. "I have come to cherish our friendship and I feel that I have met a truly rare individual . . . No, please do not protest. You know best what I mean. At any rate, I feel that I wish to give you a gift.

"I have learned how heavily the defeat of your friend Crassus has weighed on you. I also have heard that young Publius Crassus was as dear to you as this young Sextus is. Word in the academy is that you are planning to avenge that defeat. Next time you visit me, I will have a gift for you, something that will help in your avenging the deaths of all those Romans."

Caesar looked at the Chinese scholar and could not fathom his meaning. What secret gift could this slight, elderly scholar offer a soldier about to engage in brutal warfare? But he had learned to respect the wisdom and discretion of this gentleman. He thanked Liang and said he looked forward to their next visit.

After Caesar left, Liang said to Bao, "That confounded Cheng never seems to leave his room unlocked. We need to redouble our efforts."

"Yes, Master," Bao responded. "Perhaps he is more negligent after his final meal of the day and his walk in the gardens. I will endeavor to watch more intently during that hour."

"Good idea. Before Caesar disappears on some mission or other, I want him to have that crossbow. It will send five times as many arrows and travel ten times as far as those Parthian bows that the Romans so dread. Our warriors are also forever praising its accuracy, once the archer leans how to manipulate the secret mechanism on the crossbow developed by our experts. I want the great Caesar to have this weapon when he next meets the Parthians."

XIX

As Caesar and Trogus left Liang's quarters, two slaves who said that they had come from the scholar Agape, greeted them. Would Caesar accompany them to Agape's room?

Caesar recalled that Agape and Eusebios had been tasked with the mystery of the Parthian barbed arrows. Though he was anxious to get back to the palace so he could discuss what he had just learned with some of his staff, he nevertheless also wanted to know about that metal. So he nodded to the slaves and fell in behind them and mirrored their quick pace through the now familiar halls of the academy. Again as they passed rooms and gardens with men reading or debating, hardly anyone took special note of the comings and goings of Caesar, whom they began to think would have been a scholar like them in another life.

"Forgive me Caesar for chasing after you," Agape said in greeting. "But we knew that you considered what we learned to be important."

"Not at all, gentlemen. I am most grateful that you have pursued this project."

Caesar took a seat at a table across from Agape and

What really happened?

Eusebios, with Trogus seated just behind him.

"It is good news and bad news," Eusebios began.

"What other kind of news is there, my friend," Caesar replied.

"The good news is that we have analyzed the arrows and determined precisely their metal composition. What makes this metal so formidable and special is the inclusion of three ingredients. These three ingredients added to the steel make the metal so light yet so much stronger than steel alone that an arrow made from it would be able to pierce all the known shields. I will give Trogus their names but they will be meaningless to you."

"And the bad?" Caesar obligingly asked.

"The ores with thee three ingredients are very rare and are not found anywhere in the west. As far as we can determine, they can be found only somewhere along the Ganges in India or even farther away. It seems that the Parthians have learned of the qualities of the ores from which these ingredients are derived, and for years they have been importing and stockpiling them from India for use in their armories. Of course they guard these ores and the whole manufacturing process with great care."

"We're not concerned about the manufacturing process," Agape added. "There are no secrets for us or the metallurgists of Egypt when it comes to processing metals. We can easily work that out. But obtaining the ore is a matter beyond our ability."

"Any idea where the Parthians are stockpiling these ores?" asked Caesar.

"Nothing definite," Agape answered. "But I would wager that they would keep the ore close to their famous metal factories in the mountain area just outside a city they call Doura-Europos."

Caesar recalled the maps shown to him by Liang and Bao, and he saw this city in his mind. It was one of those along the Silk Road. If Trogus had not copied the maps

What really happened?

while they were there, he would see if he and Trogus could draw them from memory that night. He could of course always send Trogus back to make more careful copies later, but he needed to piece together all this information quickly. He felt that he was close to something very important for his future plans.

"Is that all, gentlemen?" he asked.

"Yes, great Caesar, though we will continue our attempts to find out other locations where the ores may be located."

"And where the Parthians store those that they have already acquired," Caesar added as he rose to leave.

XX

It was not until early March, seven months after Caesar had arrived in Alexandria, that Mithridates of Pergamum finally arrived in Ascalon, a four-day march south to Pelusium where a strong Egyptian garrison guarded the eastern coastal entrance to Alexandria. He had traveled overland along the coast from Syria with a large army from the various states of Cilicia, Syria and Palestine. At Ascalon they joined up with what remained of the army which Cleopatra had raised a year before, a mixture of Philistines, Greeks, Egyptians and Jews, devoted to the restoration of their queen. There they waited a short period for an Arab contingent of cavalry coming from Petra under King Malchus of Nabataea. Malchus had been unhappy with the treaty requiring an annual tribute to Rome, which Pompey had forced on Malchus' predecessor and was hoping that this gesture to Caesar would find enough favor to redo the terms of that treaty.

The combined army swept south and overwhelmed the Egyptian garrison in Pelusium in fierce fighting. Then, after leaving a garrison of their own, Mithridates moved west along the coast to the delta, where they again defeated an advance force sent by King Ptolemy's court to stop

What really happened?

them. Rather than crossing the numerous rivers that lay between him and Alexandria, Mithridates marched south, accepting the obeisance of the communities along the way who were anxious to be found on the winning side when this war was over. At Memphis, where the various rivers joined the Nile and afforded the first opportunity to cross that river, Mithridates went across and began immediately heading north to relieve Caesar in Alexandria.

Mithridates sent word to Caesar, describing his advance and the likely course of his march, giving Caesar the opportunity to meet him at some point before Alexandria if he so wished. At the same time King Ptolemy also received word of Mithridates' approach. The king was the first to leave Alexandria, his council deciding that they should engage and defeat the army lead by Mithridates before it could join Caesar. Counting on a faster journey he decided to board his entire army on his fleet and sail up the Nile to confront Mithridates.

Caesar entered the queen's rooms. "I will be sailing out with my men tonight, Cleo. I should be back in a week or two. Once we join up with Mithridates I will finally have enough troops to meet Ptolemy's army head-on and put an end to this mess. Then your position on the throne will be secure."

"I am preparing to accompany you. I should be ready shortly."

"Absolutely not, Cleo. Are you mad? We are going into battle and you cannot risk our child by the vigors of a march," Caesar insisted.

"How dare you tell the Queen of Egypt where or where not she could go?"

"For the sake of Jupiter, Cleo, it was you who insisted on begetting a child. Now that you have had my heir in your womb these months, you needlessly put it in jeopardy. Remember, please, I have had some experience as a general. I do not need your assistance."

What really happened?

"But the people of Egypt will not take kindly to a Roman killing their king and yet again setting someone on the throne. I have learned that lesson sadly while watching how hated my father was after Pompey and Gabinius restored him. They will scorn me if it is perceived that you alone secured the throne for me. No, I must be seen to be with the armies that defeat my brother. Else I will have no legitimacy."

Caesar could not deny the strength of her arguments. Nor would he allow her to abort his child, which marching down to Memphis certainly would. He thought about this a moment and then made a decision.

Cleopatra watched his face carefully. Though she was a queen and a descendant of the great Ptolemies, and though she had never felt fear in any confrontation with a man, Cleopatra was taken aback when before her eyes this man called Caesar suddenly seemed transformed. There was something very eerie about the aura now emanating from him; his tone of voice, the darkness in the depths of his eyes, his very countenance all seemed not only to demand but also to expect absolute obedience. Nay, Caesar, she thought, you may deny that you have the blood of gods in your veins, but there is something other than human about you.

"Perhaps, Queen Cleopatra," he finally said, in a formal tone, "we can settle upon a reasonable compromise. One that will have you with the army when we defeat Ptolemy, but at the same time avoid the hardships and perils of a march."

"I am at your command, Caesar," she responded, just as formally. "But I thought you were sailing after the king. Your men and horses have been boarding your ships all night. A sail on the Nile will not be disruptive to me and would not harm our child. Now you speak of a march?"

"Notwithstanding our readying to sail," Caesar explained, "I do not intend to risk a sea battle with the

What really happened?

Egyptian fleet. I want to join forces with Mithridates on land and only then meet and defeat the Egyptian army. My army and I are best on land. The fleet movement we are making is merely a deception. But it can be part of our compromise. Have your ladies and eunuchs pack in preparation for a voyage on the Nile and then join me on the flagship."

That night Caesar's fleet left the Great Harbor and headed west, away from the mouth of the Nile. His movements, as expected, where being carefully watched by the King's agents and duly reported to him on his journey up the Nile. Ptolemy, his sister Arsinoe, and her eunuch Ganymede, who was now in effect leading the army, could not fathom what Caesar was up to. They were satisfied, however, that whatever he was doing they would reach Mithridates' relief army first and demolish it before facing Caesar again.

It was only after a short distance from the Alexandria area but well beyond the view of any observers in Alexandria that his ships turned inward back to the coast and entered a small harbor. His troops quickly disembarked in disciplined order. The Queen and her entourage, however, remained on board. The plan was for her later to sail up the Nile, keeping a safe distance from Ptolemy's ships, and then meet Caesar somewhere near Memphis.

On the flagship before he himself disembarked, Caesar had conferred with Sextus. "I am concerned about this odd army we are about to face."

"Yes, I know. Many of them are Roman soldiers. They will fight like us and will know our tactics."

"It is not their fighting ability, nor their knowledge of Roman military practices that concern me, Sextus. It is true that once they were soldiers in the legions of Rome, fighting honorably under Pompey and then under Gabinius. But in my mind they are no longer Roman. In

What really happened?

the past seven years they have somehow lost all their best officers and their most honorable centurions. They have degenerated into nothing more than bands of marauders. Whatever the cause, they are no more than undisciplined bandits now. So it is not them that I worry about, but rather it is the attitude of our own legions—the Sixth, the Twenty-seventh, and the Thirty-seventh— that concerns me.

"Our men," Caesar continued, "are very familiar with my policy of clemency during this calamitous civil war between Romans. They know of my many efforts to avoid Roman blood, on either side, and sometimes this has frustrated them. I don't blame them, for they are soldiers up against other soldiers who are trying to kill them. But as I see it in the world that comes after this civil war, we will need every Roman to help in managing our Republic, and to keep it growing. At any rate, I suspect that our men will have my policy of clemency in the back of their minds as they fight the Gabinians. But that is not what I want them thinking during this coming battle. It will hamper them.

"So, Sextus, pass my orders to the generals and the legates, who will pass them on to the tribunes, then to the centurions until every single man has heard and acknowledged it. The Gabinians are not to be given any quarter, under any circumstances."

Sextus was surprised, and his expression showed it.

"I know," said Caesar. "This is a hard and rare order from me, so many, like you, may be surprised. That is why you must make my orders clear and include an explanation of my reasons for it. I know that most of them were originally Gauls or Germans, but still they were trained as Roman soldiers and normally would be treated the same as Roman soldiers from Italy, Sicily or any of our provinces. But their behavior has forfeited whatever we might have owed them as comrades. Living like Egyptians or actually like renegades for seven years has robbed the Gabinians of

What really happened?

anything that was Roman about them. They also are complicit in the murders of Bibulus' two sons and that of Pompey and Lentulus…. No surrender is to be accepted. Not one of them is to escape death. No quarter whatsoever."

"Yes, Caesar, I will have Faberius and Trogus immediately prepare the appropriate orders and I will talk to the generals and legates myself."

"Thank you, Sextus."

This is the least I could do for you, my old friend Gnaeus Pompey, Caesar thought. And for you, Lentulus, and for the two young sons of my noble enemy Bibulus and the others whose blood those treacherous Gabinians have shed in this land.

XXI

In four days of forced marches Caesar joined up with Mithridates at his camp along the Nile. Previously Mithridates had seen signs of the king's fleet putting into a harbor north of them. In taking command of the joint forces, Caesar was introduced by Mithridates to the kings, chieftains and other leaders who had brought men and horses to his rescue. The first leader to be introduced was Antipater, the chief minister of Judea.

"My lord," Antipater said, "the high priest of Judea, Hyrcanus, has sent us and pleads with you to forgive his having given assistance to Pompey in his war with you. At that time it was only Pompey, the great conqueror of the east, including Judea, who alone represented Rome to us. I hope the blood and valor of my fifteen hundred men in these recent battles with Ptolemy's forces have removed any stain on our relationship."

"My noble Antipater," Caesar responded. "I have heard from Mithridates all about the outstanding daring and courage not only of your men, but of you yourself in these recent battles. I understand the reasons for your people's past support for Pompey, but now it is I who owe you, chief minister, as well as the high priest and the people of

What really happened?

Judea my great gratitude. I am in your debt."

"Our happiness and joy," replied a smiling Antipater, "in being able to help you, great Caesar, much exceeds whatever obligation you may feel. It has been an honor and I know that when we face King Ptolemy we will measure up to our reputation."

"I am sure you will," Caesar replied as he looked to the next leader being brought forward by Mithridates.

"Ah, I recognize this king. My thanks to you, King Malchus. I have also heard from Mithridates that your valiant Arab horsemen excelled all his expectations in their swiftness and boldness in battle. Thank you and to you also I am in great debt."

They hugged, giving Malchus the opportunity to whisper to Caesar that the Nabateans were suffering greatly from the impositions of Pompey.

"We will make amends, King Malchus," Caesar assured him. "Sit down immediately with Sextus and talk to him as you would to me. He is my right hand. Before our armies part, he and I will have conferred and you will get a new treaty, which I guarantee will be to your liking."

Some more time was spent in greetings, including the governor of Ascalon, who was personally leading Cleopatra's old army. Finally then all the leaders sat down to discuss the forthcoming battle. After a while, however, their conference was interrupted by the sounds of jubilant cheering coming from outside their tent.

As the leaders emerged to see the cause of this uproar, Caesar could only smile as he saw men on their knees before a very regal looking Queen Cleopatra, accompanied by the ever-present Agatha and Apollonios. Nor was he surprised at either her sudden appearance or her obvious triumph. From this unique lady, he thought, anything could be expected.

Later she would explain how, coming upon Ptolemy's fleet, the ship she was on and its escorts had stopped out

What really happened?

of sight. At her insistence she and a small group of her servants were lowered into a boat. Tiberius Nero, who was in charge of the ship, persuaded her also to take along a senior centurion and three legionaries, if nothing else to deal with Caesar's sentries, as they would be approaching the army at night. With Agatha, Apollonios, a few of her familiar female slaves, and two oarsmen, plus the centurion and three legionaries, her small party slipped by Ptolemy's fleet unnoticed. Caesar silently observed that notwithstanding such a modest arrival, the queen had succeeded in having herself prepared and dressed so that her appearance in the camp could only be described as spectacular and majestic.

Ptolemy established his camp some distance north of Mithridates' camp, building it along Roman lines, thanks to the Gabinians who formed the core of his army. It was situated on a very favorable piece of land, elevated above the Nile. The camp appeared to have only two approaches, one on its west side which faced an open plain and the other on its east side where a steep road led from the harbor on the Nile up to the back of the fort. Its northern side looked out over an impassable marsh and its southern side sat atop a steep cliff.

Early the next morning Caesar led the combined army out of camp and marched north to seek a battle. His legions and his German bodyguard were anxious finally to do battle like the soldiers they were trained to be, and to put behind them those endless skirmishes in the streets and alleys of Alexandria and those months of defending their walls and fortifications. Now they were marching again, in familiar formations and were eager to put an end to their stay in Egypt with a swift and total victory.

Caesar's forces encountered annoying Egyptian horsemen as they were trying to cross a narrow but steep canal just some miles below the king's camp. His German cavalry, as frustrated as the legionaries were by their

What really happened?

months of defense, scattered up their side of the canal until they found easy fording areas and swam across with their horses. Upon reaching the other side they quickly regrouped and raced back south to surprise the Egyptian horsemen from the rear.

Between their own surprise and the ferocity of the Germans' attack, the Egyptians quickly panicked and attempted to flee, only to be chased and cut down to the last man.

Caesar's armies on the other side of the canal, watching the battle, let up such a cheer and roar and the Roman trumpets so loudly announced the small victory that the Egyptian soldiers miles away took the distant sounds as an ominous sign.

Caesar set up camp that night just below the King's fortifications. He then galloped with Sextus, Mithridates, Malchus, Antipater, and his German horsemen, Aldric and Waldo, to inspect what they would be facing the next day. Each man kept his own thoughts as they looked up at the enemy's camp: high walls in the front, a steep road in the back, the impenetrable marsh to the north and the cliff in front of them, the southern part of their camp. Ptolemy or his advisers had selected a strong position. Caesar and his host noticed that Ptolemy's people had created a number of large ditches in front of the fort, some filled with water and others presumably with spikes and other traps. It would take some time and much effort to traverse those ditches, but it was eminently doable. Caesar's men were experts at working under improvised protective roofs made of metal or hides while filling in ditches in front of them with the spades that each man always carried in his kit.

But absent the usual siege equipment that Caesar had to leave in Alexandria in order to travel quickly, it would take some time to subdue this camp. Yet Caesar quickly knew from this first tour that the enemy camp was his for

What really happened?

the taking. It was only a question of how long and what efforts would be required. How many times in Gaul and in Spain had he encountered such seemingly 'impregnable' fortifications? The very things that gave confidence to the defenders he would turn into their undoing. If no one could get in, he would make sure that no one could get out. Did that vast multitude behind those fearsome walls not have to eat or drink? He would assure that neither food nor water could get to them. Sooner or later they would attempt a breakout, only to be slaughtered by his ready forces.

In a way this setup reminded him of the great battle of Alesia five years earlier in Gaul. The brave and brilliant Gallic warrior Vercingetorix had gathered a great army and immense amounts of food and supplies into his impregnable fortress at Alesia. In time Caesar surrounded him with an eleven-mile series of walls and forts. No one could get out. When a vast army of Gauls arrived to attempt Vercingetorix' relief, Caesar build yet a second circuit, an outside line of walls, ramparts and forts, this time fourteen miles in length. Now, no one could get in.

Here in Egypt his task would be much easier. He assumed that Ptolemy considered his fleet in the harbor to be his escape route if necessary, and meanwhile it served as his line for supplies of food and material. Caesar saw his plan as cutting off the fleet from Ptolemy's camp by the construction of two twenty-foot wide and twenty-foot deep ditches running from the marshes, across the road between the camp and the fleet, and then down to the harbor. Using the dirt from the ditches his men would raise ramparts high enough to protect them from missiles thrown from the camp on one side, and high enough for them to rain missiles on any relief contingent from the fleet.

As for the front of the fort, it would be a matter of time for his men, working under mantelets and sheds with

What really happened?

their picks and spades, to fill in those ditches and advance to the walls. Then siege equipment, towers and catapult would be built and the walls surmounted. But his talented legionaries could construct all that.

He judged that this plan would take Ptolemy's camp in a few weeks at most. But even that was too long a time for Caesar. So first he would try other methods.

Thus at dawn he brought out his legions and cavalry, having integrated the much larger forces of the allies into his formations, and divided them into two contingents. The larger contingent he had march around to the front of the fort and deploy in battle formation, inviting Ptolemy to come out of the fort and engage them. The smaller contingent he kept in reserve in case of an advance from the rear of the fort or from the harbor.

Ptolemy, however, on the advice of the Gabinians, did not accept the invitation and so did not stir from the camp the entire day. Eventually Caesar withdrew his army and had them return to camp.

The next morning at dawn he decided not to await the enemy's acceptance of battle on an open plain, his best option, but would try to storm the fortified camp. He sent his major forces against the front of the camp in the west as the open plain allowed the easier access. But Ptolemy's military leaders had expected this and they had built unusually stout and high fortifications, preceded by ditches and other deadly traps. This attack soon slowed down to a crawl as the men had to form into testudos, small squares of men with protection afforded overhead, in front, rear and on the sides by their shields held in front or over their comrades in tight fcormation so that there were no openings. Others worked under sheds and mantelets to begin filling in the ditches.

Against the opposite or eastern side of Ptolemy's camp Caesar sent a lesser force to attack the rear wall. But these troops came under double fire as they attempted to

What really happened?

ascend the steep road to the back of the fort: missiles, stones and other projectiles were hurled from the high walls of the camp in front, and in the rear slingers and archers on the fleet in the Nile kept up a constant hail of arrows and stones. Hence the men here made even slower progress. They had practically to craw along with their shields positioned not only in front and overhead, as they had often done in battle, but now also to the rear, each small squad making up a separate unit inching its way up the road.

Caesar rode from the western front to the eastern rear, observing the two battles, giving new orders and at the same time continuing to reconnoiter Ptolemy's fortifications. Then what so often happened in his battles suddenly occurred again. Caesar had another of those almost superhuman perceptions that had defined so many of his victories. He saw something that no one else had seen. He stopped with his bodyguards and ordered Sextus to find Senior Centurion Carfulenus among the Sixth Legion and bring him up immediately.

"Carfulenus," he said to the centurion. "Look up there and tell me what you see."

"I see the side of the enemy's camp atop a steep precipice, my General."

"A steep precipice, good Carfulenus?"

Carfulenus immediately understood what Caesar was thinking. He then sat quietly on his horse and carefully studied the side of the cliff. He looked intently at its bottom and then allowed his eyes to traverse to the very top.

"The answer to your unspoken question, Caesar, is 'yes.' With the right men we can do it, climbing with no armor and carrying only our swords and daggers."

"I leave it to you, then. Take three of the younger cohorts, probably from the Twenty-seventh, and go up very quietly. But take two trumpeters with you so you can

What really happened?

make the loudest clamor at the right time. Much depends on the secrecy of the ascent."

"Yes sir," answered the centurion, and he marched off to where the Twenty-seventh was stationed in reserve.

What Caesar had noticed was that the battles on the east and west sides of the camp had drawn off nearly all of the enemy troops, either to engage in the battles or to observe. There was hardly anyone to be seen on the ramparts in the middle of the camp. Everyone had assumed that the cliff itself would be as impassable as the marshes to the north, so no attention had been paid to its defense.

It took nearly four hours for the nearly 1,500 men to inch their way up the side of the cliff. Upon reaching the top they encountered no one at first, and then only a few stragglers which they quickly dispatched. Once gathered together and rested, they formed themselves into two formations, each with a trumpeter at front and the rear. Then to the accompaniment of the familiar blare of the trumpet signaling attack, they launched themselves with screams and war cries upon the rear of Ptolemy's astonished troops, one formation attacking the defenders at the front of the camp and the other at the back of the camp.

Soon total panic overtook the defenders. As many fled the Romans picked up their abandoned shields and moved forward. The defenders had no idea how the enemy had gained entry into the fort. Most assumed that Caesar's entire army was among them. All resistance seemed to have vanished in the panic and confusion. The Egyptian army in the camp disintegrated in minutes. It officers opened the gates and everyone attempted to flee at once.

Caesar's armies in the front and rear of the camp, which only moments before had been inching ahead under heavy fire, now were facing not missiles, but panicked enemy soldiers racing toward them through the open gates

What really happened?

trying to escape.

Between those who drowned on reaching the Nile and those cut down in a futile attempt to flee along the plain, almost none survived. It was later determined that the king and his ministers had managed to board a vessel only to sink with it and drown as the ship was weighed down with fleeing soldiers.

Caesar's forces and those of his allies continued to pursue the remnants of the Egyptian Army while he met with the leaders in his tent. He again thanked each of them and promised them recognition and rewards from the Roman government.

"King Malchus, I would ask to borrow your cavalry. I intend immediately to ride to Alexandria with my own German horsemen. Together we will be able to deal with any difficulties that may arrise there. I owe those Alexandrians a visit.

"King Malchus; Mithridates; Governor of Ascalon; Antipater . . ." Caesar went down the line to name each leader. "I ask you and your staffs to accompany Queen Cleopatra back to Alexandria aboard my flagship. She at this moment is being carried in a litter down to the harbor under an escort lead by Vibullius. I wish you a good journey and will see you in Alexandria.

"Sextus, you remain here to clean things up and then march our forces at an easy pace back to Alexandria for a well-deserved rest and celebration."

With that Caesar moved swiftly out of his tent and to his horse. Quickly the contingent of eight hundred German horsemen and a thousand Arab cavalry started on the road up to Alexandria.

As they approached the outskirts of Alexandria Caesar rode over to Waldo's side and conferred with him.

"Waldo, there are several gates into Alexandria. If we find one blocked, we will try the others until we can get in. The king left only a token garrison here so I do not expect

What really happened?

all the gates to be guarded. Now if these fools put up the slightest resistance, you need not exercise any restraint."

"Yes, Caesar. I understand."

XXII

If Caesar was half hoping that the Alexandrians would engage in their usual riotous behavior so that his cavalry would have an excuse to teach them a long overdue lesson, he was disappointed as he neared the Canopic gate. Word of his total victory over Ptolemy had flown up to Alexandria even faster than his swift horses. Thousands of citizens, led by the city council, were on their knees screaming out pleas for mercy and forgiveness. These were the very people who had tormented him and his men from the first day they had laid foot in Alexandria. If he may have had a desire to slaughter them all he was now stymied. They were on their knees begging forgiveness. As insincere as he was sure they were, his avenging sword had to be lowered.

But not for all of them. Caesar's face remained set as he slowed down to inspect these suddenly repentant crowds. He stopped with Waldo and the leader of the Nabatean cavalry, and considered the scene.

Finally, he turned to Waldo. "Round up the entire city council. I believe there are fifty of them. You spent months here with me and I think you will recognize them. Most of them are dressed in elaborately decorated robes

What really happened?

with fringes of gold, so they should be easy to spot. I want each of them crucified, nailed to crosses spread out along the main intersection of the Canopic Way and Soma Street. Their bodies are to be left exposed until the vultures have picked them clean.

"I know that our men are as angry at these people as I am, but make sure that no harm comes to any other citizen and that there is absolutely no looting or misbehavior. Have them ride forward through the city in good formation to our camp in the inner palace and then stand down. Let them know that they will not go empty-handed, as I will reward them generously for their good behavior."

"Yes, Caesar."

A relieved and joyous Zeno and a large number of scholars from the academy, including his friend Liang, greeted Caesar at his residence. All of them had been waiting with much concern for their own safety. They had no idea how they might have been treated by a vengeful Ptolemy and his court. But word of Caesar's victory had also reached them and their happiness now showed in their faces. Caesar was pleased at the sight.

Next day Cleopatra arrived on the flagship in the company of the kings, chief ministers and other leaders of the allies. The fickle Alexandrians put on a clamorous and seemingly joyous welcome for their Queen. Every street was packed with celebrants. The Queen entered the city in a triumphant procession, though she frowned at the sight of fifty of her subjects hanging from crosses as she passed Alexandria's most majestic intersection. Later that day Caesar, though protesting mildly, had the bodies taken down and returned to their families.

The following few days were taken up with many festivities, with Cleopatra revealing yet another talent—the ability to satiate kings and leaders of state with exquisite and varied entertainment, food, and games.

Soon Sextus arrived with the army.

What really happened?

Caesar rode out to greet them. Sextus gave him a summary of his mopping-up operation.

"Caesar, word of your orders to give the Gabinians no quarter must have somehow spread to them. Not one of them sought to surrender. Not that they put up much of a fight after Carfulenus started his miraculous attack. The Gabinians threw down their weapons and spent most of their energy trying to escape. None of them did, I assure you. Nevertheless among the other forces of Ptolemy we accepted the surrender of approximately five thousand men. They have been encamped outside the city."

"I have no use for them, Sextus. Nor can they be trusted to be disbanded among the Alexandrians. They are no more than bandits. Sell them to the Roman slave merchants in our camp and distribute the proceeds to our troops. But please also see to it that our soldiers don't take out the frustrations of the past months on the Queen's subjects here. She will have to gain their loyalty in the days to come. Assure my men that they will be rewarded for their restraint. Now go get yourself a long bath and meet me in my rooms for a private dinner with the Queen."

XXIII

"Liang, thank you for the lunch."

"You are welcome, Caesar. But I suspect you did not come here just to share some victuals with me."

"When is only food sufficient? But you are correct; I am here to ask you for something very special."

"Special?" said Liang.

"Yes, may I borrow my friend Bao here for a couple of months?"

"My heavens! I would have expected anything but that. What do you intend to do with my poor Bao? And does he have anything to say about it?"

Looking at Bao, Caesar could only smile at his astonishment.

"Well, of course he does. Either of you can veto my idea, but let me explain it to you first. I plan to travel to Antiochia on the far side of Parthia."

Caesar waited until the Chinese men could get over their surprise and settle down again to listen.

"Of course I will have to go through a territory where a Roman soldier could not enter without a battle. But I will not go as Caesar, nor even as a Roman. I will be part of an Egyptian mercenary bodyguard for a great Chinese

151

What really happened?

merchant on a special mission to the emperor."

Liang frowned, as he quickly understood what Caesar was about to propose: "And our little Bao will be this great Chinese merchant?"

Caesar nodded.

"Please, Caesar," Liang continued, "he is a young scholar, familiar with scrolls and debates, not with horses, swords and the exchange of merchandise. In addition, you would be putting my assistant in great danger, something I have never asked him to do."

They all sat silent for a while. Caesar did not want to press the men, and he well understood that Bao would be facing a perilous journey. They would, he thought, have to fully embrace and accept the idea of their own free will, and with enthusiasm, before he would take Bao with him.

"May I ask, Caesar," Bao said, breaking the silence, "for what purpose you would be going to Antiochia?"

"The ten thousand Legionaries."

The scholars looked at each other and then seemed to recede into thought. They of course knew about the Roman disaster at Carrhae and the huge number of prisoners taken by the Parthians and how deeply Caesar had been affected.

Caesar rose to leave. "I apologize for placing you gentlemen in this awkward position. I did not intend to embarrass you or make you feel that you are letting a friend down. I am asking much more than any friend has a right to ask and I fully understand your refusal. Thank you for listening to me and of course our conversation must be kept absolutely secret."

Liang looked at Bao as the young man also rose.

"Caesar," Bao said in a soft voice. "I have vowed my loyalty and service to Master Liang Wei. I am not free to give such to another. But if I were free, I would gladly accompany you, whatever the dangers."

With little hesitation, Liang rose and embraced Bao and

What really happened?

spoke what he knew both Bao and Caesar wanted to hear. "You are free, my dear Bao, though I will have great difficulty in explaining to your mother what happened to you if you were not to return. She would not understand that I sent you off in the entourage of a foreign man-god."

Caesar and Trogus left the Chinese men after some further discussion. Then they made their way to that garden in the academy where they often had seen the scholars Agape and Eusebios conversing.

"Greetings my great metal scientists."

"I can feel," Agape said to his companion Eusebios with feigned fright, "that Caesar is about to take something from us."

Later that day Caesar and Cleopatra finalized their plans.

"I will take with me Vibullius. As you know he used to be Pompey's chief engineer but is still young and vigorous enough to be able to ride hard and long with me to Antiochia. I want him to see as much of Parthia as possible so he could incorporate that knowledge into our plans for the campaign. I will also take ten seasoned tribunes and centurions under the leadership of Young Balbus. That man has shown the same talent for discrete negotiating as his uncle. I may have to leave Balbus and the others in Antiochia to locate and buy the freedom of the soldier-slaves if I cannot quickly do so myself. Fifteen of my German bodyguard, including Waldo, will also serve as escorts for Bao. Aldric will have the rest of the horsemen with him for the protection of your caravan."

"You are also taking most of the gold from our treasury. I hope you understand that you can't leave me in poverty."

"The Egyptian Court in 'poverty!' You are beginning to sound like old Pothinus. But seriously, I promise I will make it up to you as soon as I return to my Asian province. It is unfortunate that gold is the only universal

What really happened?

currency. I cannot be weighed down with goods to trade or spend any time haggling. Gold is gold. Each of my twenty-five horsemen will have with him another horse loaded with as much gold as the horse can carry and still trot at a decent speed. I understand that your caravan is being fitted with a comfortable traveling tent for you and your ladies. I don't have to remind you that you are coming near to the end of your term."

"No, you don't," Cleopatra retorted with some heat, holding her swollen belly with both her hands. "We also will be carrying some gold, but most of our payments will be in exchanged goods; Egyptian things that the Parthians will be happy to take in place of gold—gems, glass items, papyrus, refined cottons, medicines, spices, as well as a good number of exotic and beautiful female slaves. By the way, I love your clever idea to have me travel as one of King Juba of Numidia's wives. At least I can act as a queen, and my ladies will immensely enjoy dressing me and themselves in the fashion of Berber women."

"The Parthians," Caesar noted, "will be very reluctant to part with those precious ores. But I am sure you can convince them. So long as they believe that the material is going far off into Africa and indeed into the hands of one of the allies of the defeated Pompey. Nothing like 'divide and conquer'. So it will just be a matter of price. But the problem, again, will be time. I hope Agape is correct about where those warehouses are located. You will have just enough time to get to Doura-Europos, exchange the merchandise and then get back to Alexandria at the same time as I do. You will not have much occasion to search around for the warehouses."

"If he says he has learned where they are," Cleopatra responded, "then they are where he says. By the way, how in the world did you get those two old men to agree to accompany me?"

"I told them it would be a comfortable little diversion

What really happened?

from their studies. I assured them that if arrangements have been made so that a pregnant queen could travel comfortably, those same arrangements should be suitable for them. But I think the real impetus is the excitement of seeing all those rare ores. Also, they are truly devoted and grateful to you and would do anything for you. They understand that their expertise is essential in completing your task successfully, otherwise the Parthians could give you any material and call it what they wish. Our scholars are taking with them a whole assortment of chemicals to test the ores. I have complete faith in their abilities, as well as their discretion. Only they and you will know the real purpose of your caravan. And even they will not know where I have gone."

"I am sure," Cleopatra added, "that I can put on a very convincing show for any observers. We will look like just another caravan, but this one from the far away African land of Numidia. I will do a lot of trading along the way. I will be taking some of our most valued products, pretending that I traded for them in Alexandria for the usual ivory and other goods from Numidia. We will leave here with a host of packed camels and will return with camels hopefully packed with your rare ores.

"But Gaius. I have a favor to ask of you. I believe you have effectively silenced the unruly Alexandrians. But Egypt is much greater than this city from which we rule it. I am a new queen and my journey to the throne this time has been soiled with much blood. There is sure to be resentment, or at least unease, in the rest of Egypt about my position. It will take much effort to convince them to remain loyal to the throne in Alexandria. In the years to come I will need to recruit soldiers from the masses of Egyptians, and I can only do that if I have the support of the priest class in the cities. Similarly, I need their cooperation to grow, harvest and send to Alexandria the wheat that feeds your Italy. Gaius, I have an idea which

What really happened?

could help give me in those efforts."

"Go ahead, Cleo, what are you thinking?"

"While we are on our journeys into Parthia, could your troops and as many of your allied armies as you can convince to delay from departing make a show of strength throughout Egypt on my behalf? I would like the armies led by someone like your lieutenant Sextus, representing you, together with Agatha and Apollonios in the commanding circle as my personal representatives.

"The armies thus organized should visit the great cities of Egypt and spend some time in each with the ruling priests in their temples. Most of these towns and cities are run by the priests from their temples where the wealth of the community is usually stored. Let them know that Cleopatra has not only Rome but the entire world supporting her. Your Sextus Caesar, Mithridates, Malchus, Antipater and the other kings and chieftains with their different armies appearing in the great cities would do much to stabilize my rule. Your grand armies have already been in Memphis, but I suggest they return to Memphis as it is such an important center of religion and culture for the Egyptians. Let the leaders there know that my friends are here to stay. Then there is Thebes, but also Abusir, Aketaten, Hierakonpolis, Amana, Abydos, Mendes, Avris, Sais, Qus, Naqada and as many others as they can visit with some measure and dignity."

"Cleo, a brilliant idea," Caesar replied immediately. "I cannot think of a more useful task for the armies during our absence. I will get Sextus to organize that immediately. I am sure our allies, provided we feed and reward their soldiers, will be happy to accommodate you. After all, it is also to their benefit that Egypt remains stable and friendly."

Caesar later described the plan to Sextus: "I am leaving you in charge of the army and Egypt while the Queen and I are gone. Most of the time you will be on the road in the

What really happened?

show of strength; but do not leave our friends in Alexandria without a monitor, perhaps Tiberius Nero. I also suggest that you have my freedman Scribonius's son, the knight Rufio, at your side for the entire time. I want him trained and ready to take command of the legions I will be leaving here to keep Cleopatra not only on the throne but loyal to us. Rufio has shown himself very competent in battle and is well respected by the men. Fortunately he has no ambition to rule the world and will be delighted with the honor shown by this assignment. But you need to take his measure yourself in the next three months or so and at the same time get him ready for his assignment.

In addition, you are to take with you Agatha and Apollonios and make it clear to the high priests in each city that they are the personal representatives of the Queen. She intends to utilize Agatha and Apollonios in the future in her task of governing this huge land. You yourself, by the way, will not be staying in Egypt after our return, because I have an important role for you to play in Syria. But more of that upon my return."

Sextus was not surprised by his cousin's decision to place a person of the knightly or equestrian order at the head of legions, a position usually filled by a noble at least of the senatorial rank. He had long ago ceased to wonder at Caesar's novel moves, and knew that each was carefully considered by him and had good reasons supporting them. As it happened he too was much impressed by Rufio and thought he was a natural leader. Nor did it hurt that Rufio and Agatha had shown special interest in each other, notwithstanding their difference in ages.

XXIV

It took only a week to complete preparations for the
secret journeys. Just after darkness on April 2, in the year
47 BC, Caesar and twenty-five men on horses and each
man tethering another horse loaded with packages, made
their way through the secret passages in the theater and
down to the royal docks where a swift four-banked ship
waited for them. Bao was dressed in glorious and
resplendent garments, which Caesar could only assume
were the insignia of the Chinese emperor's royal courtiers.

Caesar, Vibullius, Waldo and young Balbus were alone
on deck as the warship made good time traveling east
along the Egyptian coast.

"Gentlemen, forgive me for being so secretive about
our journey. While I have the upmost trust in each of you,
you all have servants, slaves, aides, and friends in
Alexandria—too many people watching your every move
and listening to your every word. It could be fatal for us if
any rumor of our mission began to circulate in Alexandria.
The city is filled with spies from all over the world, and in
particular with agents from Parthia. So I decided it best to
tell no one about the purpose of our trip until we had
boarded."

What really happened?

"You embarrass us with this totally unnecessary apology, Caesar," Vibullius said, speaking for all of them. "You should know by this time that each of us has absolute faith in you and would not question any decision by you to keep us in the dark. We assume always that you have good reasons."

"Thank you, Vibullius. We will be sailing east along the coast of Egypt and then up the Phoenician coast, past Ascalon, Gaza, and Judea, until we reach the island city of Tyre., a very busy and prosperous commercial city.

"I have chosen Tyre to began our land journey because our caravan there will draw no special attention. In addition, we will have a neutral territory in which to practice our 'caravan' skills. Tyre, as you know, is an old and independent Phoenician city where Greek is now the main language. Though a part of the Roman province of Syria it has retained its special status as an independent city—a status that it has maintained for centuries under various foreign empires. There is no Roman garrison located there and the city officials are used to the passage of every sort of traveler from all over the world. So long as the customs duties are paid no questions are asked.

"We will then travel east at a very quick pace, along what people are calling the Silk Road. Officials in the cities along the Silk Road are likewise familiar with a wide variety of missions and caravans that emanate from Tyre. We will not be conspicuous in any way, so long as we pay our customs duties.

"Prior to disembarking in Tyre we will change into what some of you may considerer strange garments. Everyone is to carry his sword and daggers as usual, but we will be dressed as Syrian mercenaries. Our story is that we are traveling as bodyguards to the Emperor of China's special courier, Bao Yang, who is taking a quantity of ordered herbs and medicines to China to combat some kind of plague in the capital city. I am hoping that the very

What really happened?

mention of a 'plague' will keep the curious away from us and speed us on our way."

"That explains," said a smiling Vibullius, "those elaborate clothes on the scholar Bao. I must say, though, he does project the image of some kind of haughty court courier."

"Yes," answered Caesar, with some amusement. "He has taken his new role very seriously and is trying to fit himself into it as much as he possibly could. I am afraid we are going to have to live with this new Bao for a few months. In public we are his servants."

"But our true mission, Caesar?" asked Waldo.

"We will travel as fast as we can east along the caravan route to a city called Antiochia. It is approximately thirteen hundred miles from Tyre. My goal is to travel about thirty to forty miles a day so that we will get there within forty-five days. We will exchange our horses as necessary for fresh ones along the way and each night will raise a tent wherever lodging is not readily convenient and secure. Guard duty will be rotated among all of us, except for Bao. Also except for Bao—remember, he is a scholar and not a soldier—we will sleep in our clothes and take baths in streams along the route. Whenever we meet customs officials or any soldiers, Bao will speak for us. I am told that Greek is universal along the route but if need be he also speaks a variety of other languages, including Parthian."

"Our pack horses are carrying heavy bundles," Waldo commented. "May I ask if our mysterious cargo has anything to do with our real mission?"

"We are carrying gold in those bundles," Caesar answered, "hidden under various herbs. Once in Antiochia, hopefully we will be exchanging that gold."

"Exchanging the gold, Caesar?" queried a puzzled Waldo.

"Yes, comrades," Caesar stated. "I intend to purchase the

What really happened?

freedom of Crassus's enslaved legionaries."

XXV

As Cleopatra's Numidian caravan made its way out of the ancient port city of Gaza, a busy trading center boasting of its Hellenistic culture, it ran across Nabatean caravans from Petra making their way to the port which once was theirs. Having recently been restored by the consul Aulus Gabinius under orders from Pompey the Great, it was now a Roman client city but there were yet few signs of Rome. Greek temples, statues and other Hellenic buildings lined the streets.

Cleopatra was not surprised that her caravan raised no special interest, as she passed even more exotic parties from other parts of the world. She had become familiar with Gaza and the Palestinian cities that they were now traveling through during her youthful visits as a royal tourist. The prosperous independent city of Tyre was likewise familiar to her, its freedom made obvious by the total absence of any foreign soldiers and the confidence of the local customs authorities.

The great metropolis of Damascus, fought over by descendants of Alexander the Great's generals for centuries, still bore the character of a Greek city. Roman rule here however was more obvious. Pompey had

What really happened?

installed a large garrison and its presence was felt throughout the city.

It was only at the sight of what seemed a forest of giant tents that made up the nomad city of Palmyra that she and her entourage first felt they were in strange lands. The sun-darkened warriors on horseback might have been frightening were it not obvious that they were there for the protection of the caravans from desert bandits. The warriors had first been seen far on the outskirts of Palmyra but kept some distance from any of the groups moving on the road. Everybody soon became used to their presence and once in Palmyra itself they seemed to have disappeared. There the "Numidians" mingled easily with the nomads as well as with the sophisticated traders also encamping in Palmyra. Though in the shadow of the Parthian Empire, the fiercely independent tribes that made up Palmyra had learned that it was much more profitable to grant hospitality to the traders that passed through their city than to pillage them. Food, water, slaves, women, lodging in luxurious tents with their baths and gardens would all come at a cost, most happily paid by the weary travelers, in addition to the custom duties.

The "Numidians" soon gained the reputation of bringing great wealth and beauty from that far-off land. Other traders eagerly sought out their goods. Cleopatra, however, had instructed her people that the best merchandise, including the exotically beautiful female slaves, were to be kept for their next important destination, the great Parthian fortress-city of Doura-Europos.

During the week that the Numidians lodged themselves in one of the most expensive and luxurious tents in Palmyra, every caravan leader and dignitary of Palmyra visited King Juba's wife. The woman dazzled her visitors with her knowledge of languages and the sumptuousness of her surroundings. A prince of Palmyra's king arrived

What really happened?

one day with an invitation for the queen to visit him in his royal tent.

During a sumptuous dinner, before which many expensive gifts had been exchanged, she explained to the king how desirous her party was to obtain some special ores, which did not exist in Africa. The Berber King Juba's experts had made it a high priority to search for these ores so the Africans could built the farming implements and other tools that could withstand their climate.

The King of Palmyra and his sons listened carefully and finally assured her that they would make enquiries of all the traders coming through their city and would even speak to their friends in Parthia about Juba's needs. The King adroitly made it clear, with the upmost courtesy, that his kingdom's prosperity rested on the generosity of the traders that traveled his roads and that he expected any help in locating these ores would be rewarded. King Juba's queen just as adroitly made it clear that she would leave him much richer if he did help her.

So it was no surprise that when the Numidian caravan arrived in the outskirts of Doura-Europos under the escort of Palmyra princes and a hundred of their warriors, that the highest authorities of that city cordially met them. Again Cleopatra and her entourage established themselves in the most expensive lodgings that the great city could offer and began a series of lavish entertainments.

It was during one such evening that a Parthian official regaled the queen with a story of an exotic Chinese prince with his Syrian escorts who had recently sped through their city on an urgent mission to bring medicines to the capital city of China, then suffering under a terrible plague. The Parthians, though not superstitious, were relieved when the Chinese prince paid the customs duties and promptly left the city. The less connection one had with any plague, he explained to the sympathetic queen, the better.

What really happened?

As it turned out the information which Agape and Eusebios had acquired concerning the location of the warehouses was unnecessary. No searching the countryside was necessary, as the ores came to them, or at least their owners did. A week of negotiations brought to a hurried end by the unexpected indisposition of the queen, a bargain was reached which emptied the Numidian caravan of its goods, including the rare purple dyes it had acquired in Tyre and all its beautiful female slaves, and in return the hundreds of camels in the Numidian caravan were packed with enormous amounts of ore. Agape and Eusebios were kept busy for days ascertaining the authenticity of the ores, but in the end they were totally satisfied. In addition, it was agreed that Agape and Eusebios would return from time to time to obtain further shipments of this ore as might be needed by King Juba in Africa.

It was not clear to Cleopatra how much of her payments went to the princes of Palmyra and how much to the Parthian officials of Doura-Europos, or whether anyone in the Parthian government in Ctesiphon knew of the exchange. Nor did she care.

XXVI

Bao grew in confidence and stature with each successful encounter with custom agents, random checkpoints and mounted soldiers. Caesar and the others no longer smiled at his grandiose antics, but seemed to accept them as what the usual behavior of a great Chinese official must be.

Vibullius and Caesar had taken careful note of the fortifications around Doura-Europos and Baghdad, as well as the Parthian troop displays in the capital city of Ctesiphon. The ruins of the ancient city of Rey made them wonder about the glorious past of the Persian Empire. As they traveled through the prosperous and busy city of Damghan they noticed a dramatic change in the features of the natives and their costumes.

They deliberately slowed down when they got closer to their destination, hoping to see evidence of the ten thousand Roman prisoners. Caesar surmised that if the Parthians had taken the soldiers because of their skills, they would have put them to road building, the construction of bridges, and the like, and not have scattered them over the landscape in agricultural labors. So it might be possible to find traces of their work and then

What really happened?

the slaves themselves. But there was no trace of anything Roman when they went through Nishapur or Mashhad. The road then skirted a vast desert and finally turned south toward the city of Antiochia.

This city, as all of Alexander's cities, had been laid out in the best Hellenic tradition, with broad avenues crossing at right angles to each other. There were the familiar Greek temples and monuments, but also various bazaars indicating the importance of the city as a trading crossroad. Bao exceeded his usual flamboyant display with the customs officials when, upon paying the usual tariffs, he haughtily inquired about where he could find the most luxurious lodgings. Caesar had told him earlier that they would not stay in tents in Antiochia, but make an ostentatious display of their wealth and thereby try to gather information.

"Bao," Caesar had said to him as they neared Antiochia. "I am going to have you change your story."

"Ah, Caesar," he replied. "But I have become a prince and even in my sleep I can recite the terrible sicknesses in China that we are racing to eradicate."

"You can still play the role of a prince, dear Bao," Caesar assured him. "But now your goal has changed. You are no longer carrying medicines to China. Rather, you are on a mission for the emperor to fetch those Roman prisoners that even the court in China has heard about. The emperor, you will inform one and all, is intently interested in the knowledge the Romans have about how roads, bridges, aqueducts and buildings are built in the west. He has heard that there were scores and scores of great craftsmen and engineers among the captured legionaries."

"We are coming out in the open," Bao said in wonder. "Just like that?"

"Yes," Caesar replied. "We do not have much time. Once we are settled in, I intend to send Balbus, Vibullius,

What really happened?

and the centurions out into the city to see what common information there may be on the street about the Roman slaves. People talk, especially in a large trading town like this. The presence of ten thousand Romans could not go unnoticed. But eventually we have to disclose a desire to purchase these slaves. Might as well start as soon as we get into the city. Make sure you invite as many traders as you can to dine with you at your lodgings."

"Yes, Caesar. I find that I am not, after all, disappointed by our changing drama. This also sounds like an enjoyable role. I will not fail you."

Caesar could not be but surprised again as how Bao was leaping to this new challenge. Thank you, Fortune, for this man.

Once the party was comfortably ensconced in the palace that Bao had rented, and all finally had extensive baths and massages, to their utter delight, they dined in the palace's banquet hall. Along the way Bao had generously invited other traders and some city officials to dine with him.

Late in the afternoon of their third day in Antiochia, while Bao was explaining the emperor's need for the Roman slaves to some of his invited guests, Vibullius took Caesar aside.

"Some important information, Caesar. Perhaps we can talk in your room?" he said.

"Yes, of course" said Caesar as they made they way out of the banquet hall. Once they were alone Vibullius made his remarkable report.

"While in one of the inns I heard three men at a table speaking Latin. I looked over and was astonished to recognize one of the three as having been a young engineer some time ago under my tutelage, a man by the name of Cinna. Fortunately my Syrian outfit prevented him from immediately recognizing me, as others would have noticed his shock. I was with two centurions and

What really happened?

asked them to go outside and make sure that when the Romans left that they accost them quietly. Once they had left I would join them, but they were not to say that another Roman was there. Their task was to pretend to be Syrians with a Chinese trader and to determine what state of mind the Romans were in. I did not want to disclose myself to people who had been corrupted by the Parthians and had become so close to them that they would betray me. Meanwhile I hoped to listen to their conversation as they were speaking freely, feeling sure that no one in the tavern understood Latin.

"Unfortunately they were talking about some women they had met recently and about their exploits with them. Finally, they seemed to have exhausted that subject and got up to leave. When I followed them out of the tavern I saw our centurions wave to them and then they gathered to speak. After some ten minutes or so the centurions led the Romans down the street and at the same time beckoned to me to follow. Once they had come to a quiet street they stopped and turned toward me, at which time I joined them.

"Indeed it turned out that they were still true and loyal Roman soldiers. It took some time for them to get over their shock when I told them who we were and that you, Caesar, was also here and that you were hoping to purchase their freedom.

"Eventually Cinna explained that of the ten thousand original prisoners, three thousand had died from diseases or had been executed while trying to escape during the long journey from Carrhae. Another thousand had succeeded in escaping just before they reached Antiochia and had become mercenaries or bandits under a former officer, operating, he understood, further east along the Silk Road, well beyond the border of Parthia. Yet another thousand ironically had just been purchased by some trader and were being taken away somewhere to the east.

What really happened?

He further explained that the remaining five thousand legionaries were kept in a camp just outside Antiochia and were presently engaged in building roads for some Parthian contractor. Most of them were allowed to go into town from the camp since no one any longer had any hope of escape, particularly since each of them had been branded by the removal of his right ear and the burning of a Parthian letter, meaning 'slave,' on his forehead."

"Where are these men now, Vibullius?" Caesar asked, frowning at the thought of Roman soldiers being so branded.

"They had to go back immediately to the camp or they would be missed. We agreed that one of us would be at the same tavern every day around the same hour to keep them informed of how you and Bao were proceeding with your attempt to purchase them."

"Good work, Vibullius," a delighted Caesar said. "We have found them! Sad to see that their number has been so reduced, but still a lot of Romans to retrieve. Now it is even more imperative that we move with great speed. We cannot expect these poor souls to keep this astonishing news to themselves for very long. We are in great jeopardy."

"Forgive me, Caesar, if I have made a grave mistake," Vibullius quickly stated.

"No, no, Vibullius. Sooner or later we would have had to reach this point. We always knew that there would be that risk. Well, we are there now and we must act. Let's get back to Bao and his guests and see if he has gotten anywhere."

As they were returning to the banquet hall they met Bao coming their way.

"Caesar," Bao almost shouted, "I have found the way!"

"Go ahead, Bao, but carefully," Caesar said in a soothing tone, trying to get Bao to calm down.

"I have just learned that a great Parthian lord is the sole

What really happened?

owner of some five thousand Roman slaves; that he has them encamped just outside Antiochia and he is using them to build roads. With your permission, sir, I wish to go to that camp immediately and speak to this lord about purchasing his slaves."

Caesar stared at Bao and took a few seconds to process this astonishing news. Then he said:

"By Jupiter, comrades I believe Fortune may be smiling on our mission! Vibullius, find Balbus and Waldo. We will all escort our blessed master Bao to this camp."

The Parthian contractor was offered so much gold that he began to think he could just retire and go someplace more hospitable to live, now having enough money to build a palace and stock it with servants. He was sure the Parthian government would have no trouble with these slaves now going to China. After all it raised no objection the month previously when he had sold the thousand slaves to another Chinese lord, and incidentally, at a quarter of the fabulous price being offered by Bao. When the government learned of this transaction, it would of course demand its share of the purchase price, but it would never know the fantastic amounts he had gotten for the slaves.

Arrangements were quickly made to hire five hundred of the contractor's other workers who were free men. They would be armed and given horses to act as guards over the Roman slaves for part of the journey. Bao explained that he had already hired guides and armed escorts from the east who would meet them outside of Antiochia and take them all the way to China. The prisoners would now be shackled and prepared for the long journey to China. Departure would be in three days, as sufficient food and other supplies had to be purchased and packed upon the camels.

Caesar explained to Vibullius what his plan was and asked him to convey it to Cinna tomorrow at the tavern. It

What really happened?

was most urgent that the prisoners remain quiet and continue to appear to be resigned to their fate. Nothing must delay their departure, as every minute increased the risk of exposure.

The people in Antiochia as well as those in the other cities along the Silk Road were used not only to the traders and their caravans, but also to the sight of shackled slaves being transported to new destinations. Thus the Roman slaves walked out of the camp in orderly fashion and began the long journey under guard.

But as soon as this mass of men was well beyond the environs of Antiochia, Bao had the convoy turn off the road and travel a little distance into a quiet valley where they could not be seen by any travelers. Bao then convinced the guards from Antiochia that his small but heavily armed escort would be sufficient to watch the shackled prisoners until his hired guards from the east arrived. He said he expected them momentarily. With each man receiving more than a year's pay as a bonus, they were more than happy to abandon their task and return to Antiochia and their normal lives, having made a small fortune for almost no work at all.

The Roman prisoners sensed that something special was happening as the guards melted away. They were now in a small valley surrounded by desert hills, unobserved by anyone. Caesar and his men, including Bao, quickly went up and down the line unlocking the chains. As they moved from man to man, some men began weeping, others shouted with joy, others just crumpled to the ground, sobbing, many insisting on kissing their liberators.

When Vibullius came upon Cinna himself among the shackled soldiers, he called out to Caesar to join them. Cinna fell on his knees and kissed Caesar's feet when they were introduced.

"Get up soldier, enough of this. I am as overjoyed as you are to be able to do this. You are brave and loyal

What really happened?

soldiers of my dear friend Marcus Licinius Crassus."

At the mention of their former commander's name, Cinna and the others nearby let out a gasp.

"Heavens," said Cinna, "it was the most awful sight I have even seen. General Crassus was forced by his own men to go alone to negotiate terms of surrender with the Parthian General Surenas. The general's most senior and loyal legates, Octavius and Petronius, accompanied him, refusing to let him go alone. As soon as they reached the bottom of the hill where the rest of us had stopped, the treacherous Parthians attacked them. The three fought bravely, but were overwhelmed by dozens of soldiers and that creature Surenas."

"You mention," Caesar said, "that his own legions forced Crassus to negotiate. But Cassius has reported that Crassus had been duped by an Arab guide in the pay of the Parthians who led him into a trap."

"That coward and traitor Cassius!" Cinna exclaimed. "It was he who had demanded that Crassus go down and negotiate surrender with Surenas. And it was he who kept demanding that Crassus listen to the Arab guides. But worse of all, when we realized that it was a trap we still had sufficient forces to do battle with the Parthians. But all hope for battle disappeared when Cassius turned his cavalry around and made a mad dash for the safety of Syria. He left us to our fate. We of course were in a hopeless condition without cavalry, as the Parthian cavalry was what had been beating us."

"Interesting, Cinna, very interesting," was Caesar's only commend as he looked into the distance over the heads of the rejoicing men.

Eventually everyone was free of his chains and each heard the familiar but now heartbreaking trumpet signal to get into formation, as well as the peculiar sound of the cornet announcing the presence of the commanding general.

What really happened?

Caesar had witnessed many a battle, many a victory, and many a battlefield celebration. But never had he ever witnessed the utter joy of these endless cheering and crying men. A platform was erected and Caesar mounted it. He removed his Syrian headdress and looked out at the legionaries. Soon word had reached every astonished man: it was the General Gaius Julius Caesar! They knew he wanted to speak, so total silence suddenly fell over the formation.

"Brave legions of Rome, I salute you!"

Again, a thundering cheer arose from the five thousand weeping men. Balbus and Waldo nervously looked about for fear that they were going to be noticed by the Parthians. But Bao had instructed the puzzled guards from Antiochia to march everyone so far from the road and out into the desert, that there was not a soul anywhere nearby.

"Comrades, you are now free. But we are thousands of miles away from any Roman territory, and it will be impossible for us to fight our way back. Each of you will be given sufficient gold so that once you get beyond the Parthian border, which is not far from here at all, you can make your own way to wherever you wish. Some of you may want to purchase property around the cities east of here and begin a family. Others may rather band together, purchase arms and offer yourselves as mercenaries to the many tribes and kingdoms to the east who I understand are forever in need of men to fight their battles. Some of you might even seek out and join your former comrades who escaped and are already operating some distance from here. I assure you, that whatever choice you make, it will not be considered dishonorable in Rome. But it would be hopeless for you to seek to go back through Parthia to Roman territory. If any word of your presence in Parthia reached its government, you would be hunted down and killed. Go east along this route they call the Silk Road, and I promise you: if Fortune allows, in a few years I will

What really happened?

return with an army to take you back home."

Again, this promise was greeted with prolonged cries and cheers. When the soldiers quieted down, Caesar made his final farewell, speaking with such evident sorrow that some thought they saw tears running down his face.

"Forgive me, comrades, for not being able to take you back to Rome with me, but if we attempt that, we will all soon be dead. So now we must part. You will move on; the gold must be disbursed to each of you and the food we carry divided. Then I must leave you."

XXVII

"Welcome back, Caesar," cried Sextus when he saw his cousin and the others galloping toward him. They all dismounted and embraced one another. With Sextus were Publius Rufio, Postumus, Tiberius Nero, Mithridates, Zeno, and a host of other officers, as well as Caesar's two secretaries, Faberius and Trogus, both of them openly crying with joy.

"Thank you comrades. The Queen? Has she arrived back yet?"

"Yes, Caesar. Her caravan returned a few days ago. She is well, and is now at the palace awaiting you."

"The tour through Egypt?" Caesar asked as he got back onto his horse.

"We were greeted at every stop with respect," reported Sextus. "Each city now knows the strength behind their Queen. I doubt there will be any trouble from them."

"How did the populace in Alexandria behave in our absence?" Caesar asked.

"Seems to me," Rufio responded, "that perhaps you have modified their habitual riotous nature. No protesting mobs; no clamor for this or that; just a busy and prosperous but orderly city—nothing like the Alexandria

What really happened?

that we knew for so many months."

"Ha," Waldo commented. "Perhaps the memory of their fifty crucified leaders dying in agony helped subdue the bastards."

"I will join the Queen at the palace," Caesar said. "Sextus and Rufio, please be in my room at the Palace after I see the Queen - we need to make preparations as quickly as possible for my departure. Alert everyone who needs the information that I will shortly be leaving by forced march for Syria with just the Sixth Legion and my German bodyguard. Send messages ahead to Mark Antony in Rome, Cornificus in Illyricum, Vatinius in Brundisium, Calenus in Achaea, and our governor or legion commander in Antioch. Also prepare a public meeting in front of the palace quarter for me to address the court and the Alexandrians. For the meeting erect a suitable stage for the Queen and her entourage, with two thrones on it.

"Come with me now to the palace, Trogus and Faberius, I have much to record."

"Congratulations, Caesar," Sextus shouted as Caesar galloped to the palace.

"Why . . . yes, of course. Thank you. The men are at least free," called out Caesar, taking the congratulations to refer to his having reached Crassus's soldiers.

As Caesar and his two secretaries entered the palace, he noticed the presence of Egyptian doctors and wet nurses, and also their beaming faces. The smiles seemed to be celebrating more than just his arrival. Congratulations indeed, my dear Sextus, he thought.

The doctors and others bowed and made way for Caesar and his secretaries as they strode to the bedroom door. Could he not hear the cries of a baby, or was that just his over-anxious mind?

Later, when the hugging and kissing were done, and Caesar cradled his son in his arms, he asked the Queen, "Cleo, when did this happen?"

What really happened?

"Dear Gaius, at the most inopportune time—while we were in Doura-Europos!"

"In Doura-Europos! By Jupiter. I must consult with the jurists—is my son Parthian? Egyptian? Roman? Perhaps Cicero's friend Servius Sulpicius Rufus can give me an opinion on my son's status. Or if the laws of the east govern, then perhaps our own Zeno can advise me."

"Gaius," Cleopatra said quietly. "Can I get you to refer to young Caesar as 'our' son?"

The next day Caesar again read at a public assembly the will of Ptolemy XII Auletes, which bequeathed the throne jointly to Cleopatra and her brother, the now deceased Ptolemy XIII, who were to be married and rule as co-equals. In place of the deceased Ptolemy XIII Caesar decreed that the twelve-year old Ptolemy XIV, Auletes's youngest son, take his place, and join Cleopatra as co-rulers. Again Caesar also read the appeal by Ptolemy Auletes to Rome that it assure enforcement of his will. Caesar further announced that Rome intended to secure the throne for this brother and sister by stationing three legions in Egypt under the command of the equestrian Publius Rufio.

Cleopatra immediately ordered Dionysius to have an announcement of her and her brother's ascension prepared to be sent throughout Egypt. Cleopatra explained to Caesar and Sextus that the carefully and elaborately worded text, in the three scripts of the Kingdom—hieroglyphics, Egyptian demotic and Greek—would then be sent to all the chief priests in each Egyptian town. The priests, who would also receive gifts of gold, would be instructed to have their best craftsmen carve the announcement on basalt stone and then display it prominently in the towns at an appropriate location.

Only the priests were still able to read and write hieroglyphics, but since they represented such a powerful class and their temples were such important centers of

What really happened?

wealth and culture, the script was still an essential part of all communications. The demotic script, on the other hand, would be read by all educated Egyptians and was used in the ordinary business and commerce of Egypt. Greek, however, remained the language of the Ptolemies and of the court.

As Caesar, together with the remaining thousand legionaries of the Sixth Legion and his eight hundred strong German bodyguard were about to march out, Bao came running up to him.

"Great Caesar, Master Liang did not want you to leave without the present he had promised you. Here it is, and a note from Master Liang is enclosed explaining the gift."

Bao then lifted up a large package carefully wrapped in cotton and silk cloths.

"Thank you Bao, and thank the Master. I will examine the gift this evening when we make camp after today's march. Balbus, please have this package placed with our baggage."

"Please, Caesar, do not neglect to inspect the gift. My Master says you will find it immensely useful."

"Bao, you can tell your Master Liang that I will examine it carefully when we stop to camp tonight. And thank you again for your courageous and infinitely competent leadership on our journey to Antiochia."

"And I will treasure those days the rest of my life," replied Bao, bowing deeply as Caesar rode through the Canopic Gate with his small army.

The last image that Caesar had of Egypt as he marched through Pelusium was the towering monument of Pompey on Mount Casius.

PART III
THE REPUBLIC AND BEYOND

XXVIII

"The hand of the emperor must not be seen, suspected . . . or even imagined."

The emperor's confidential operative, often employed to bypass the official ministries, was speaking. Peng Tao's physical appearance seemed to mimic his obscure role in the government in Xi'an, China's capital city – a whiff of a man, speaking in a whisper.

"Yes, your Highness," responded Li Long, one of Peng Tao's most brilliant, versatile, and cruelest agents.

"The emperor's opening to the west," Tao explained, "has brought us great wealth and he does not wish this to be jeopardized. Any suggestion that he is intervening in the affairs of an empire on the other end of the earth will frighten every nation along the Silk Road and may threaten our prosperity. Only with the wealth brought in by our silk have we been able to sustain our armies and navies. The

What really happened?

emperor must be utterly invisible."

"I pledge my life, your Highness, that it will be so," promised Long.

Even the first reports from Cheng Sun concerning the conversations between the scholar Liang Wei and the mighty warrior of the west, Julius Caesar, had unsettled Tao. Certainly the ancient principles of isolation and detachment from the rest of the world had faded under the Han Dynasty, but to discuss in detail the geography of China and the routes to the east with such a warrior had made Tao uneasy. As far-fetched as the notion was that a nation on the other side of the world would present a threat to China, it was always the wisest policy to eradicate even the first faltering signs of any danger.

It remained only an unspoken worry in the back of Tao's mind until Cheng's astonishing report that Bao Yang was going to guide this Julius Caesar and some Roman soldiers east along the Silk Road. Why would Roman soldiers explore the commercial route of the caravans, the first steps to Xi'an? But the last straw was the theft of Cheng's crossbow with its secret mechanism. Tao at that point felt compelled to seek an audience with the emperor. The emperor, as was his wont, did not make clear what he was thinking. But his broad delegation of authority to Tao to deal with the matter as he thought best, provided it was done with great subtlety and opaqueness, together with the emperor's wish that it not be disclosed to any of the official ministers, was all Tao needed to understand what the emperor wanted. This Caesar must be destroyed.

XXIX

Now that Rome's vital breadbasket had been secured with a particularly loyal queen firmly on the throne, buttressed by three Roman legions and, perhaps just as significant to Caesar, now that the chronically obstreperous Alexandrians had been force-fed with some degree of respect for Roman authority, Caesar was restless to deal with the numerous other crises that had arisen while he was in Alexandria.

Mark Antony in Rome had turned out to be a great disappointment as Master of the Horse, that is, the Dictator's second in command and therefore in charge of Rome while Caesar was away. Caesar had sent him back to Rome after the victory at Pharsalus with most of the army, many of whose legions had already gone beyond their sixteen-year military commitment and were clamoring to be discharged and given the rewards Caesar had promised them—land for farms and additional bonuses. Caesar had expected quickly to catch up with the fleeing Pompey, put an end to the civil war and then return to Rome to settle matters. That did not happen so that Antony found himself in charge of Rome for much longer than expected. And in this he failed.

What really happened?

Now that he was master of Rome and with the restraining presence of Caesar being absent, Antony quickly settled into a lazy life of licentious living with his friends. Thus he watched almost as a disinterested bystander while personal feuds between Caesar's appointed officials in Rome festered and grew into violence. Only when the Senate forced him to act did he bestir himself, and then so clumsily and roughly that scores of Roman citizens were unnecessarily killed before ended the dispute was ended. Even that resulted in resentment and anger among the Roman populace as Antony had come down violently against the more popular side of the debt-relief quarrel that was at the base of the conflict. At the same time, the unsettled legions, which had been parked in Campania awaiting Caesar's return, turned riotous and ravaged the countryside, with Antony finding himself helpless to quiet them down.

Meanwhile, the bloody victory at Pharsalus, while considered definitive and final by the states of the east, which quickly moved to subject themselves to Caesar's will, and which also convinced many of Caesar's senatorial opponents, like Cicero, to admit that they had lost, was yet not enough to persuade the bitter hardcore Senatorial faction to end the conflict. The civil war now became even more clearly one between the old nobility, which feared losing its ancestral privileges of power, and the revolutionary Caesar, who intended to reform the system from top to bottom so as to make it an effective instrument to rule the ever-growing territory under control of the Republic. Now that Pompey, their chosen tool, had been defeated, they still would not admit defeat and stubbornly regrouped with the remnants of the Republican army in Africa and Spain to prolong the civil war. They would rather die than allow Caesar to form any kind of government system that replaced their families as rulers of Rome.

What really happened?

Then there were others among the defeated nobles, such as Cassius and Brutus, who took the safer, though perhaps less honorable path, of feigning submission to Caesar, but biding their time when perhaps they might corner an unarmed Caesar in a dark alley.

Many of the leaders of Pompey's defeated army, including Pompey himself, had survived the fighting at Pharsalus, thanks primarily to their early exit from the battlefield. At first they scattered in all directions but eventually many of them, with the remnants of their armies, had found their way to Africa and Spain. While Caesar was in Alexandria, Scipio, Cato and other senators were recruiting additional armies in Africa among the Romans in the Roman and Greek colonies. They were also courting native leaders, in particular King Juba of Numidia. Juba was an easy convert because he held an old grudge against Caesar arising from a legal matter at Rome many years earlier.

In Spain the two sons of Pompey, Gnaeus and Sextus, had found fertile soil where Caesar's choice for governor had proven a bad pick, causing widespread discontent from his brutal greed. The governor was expelled by the citizens and then called back to Rome by Caesar, dying on the voyage back. But he left behind much bitterness, which the Pompey sons capitalized on in recruiting their army from the Spaniards as well as the Romans settled there.

In addition to those difficulties, a minor client king in what the Romans called Asia, Pharnaces of Bosporus, had taken Caesar's long absence in Egypt as an opportunity to unsettle the arrangements made among the states in Asia Minor by Pompey twenty years earlier. These were the settlements that Pompey, after his conquests and as Rome's representative, had worked out among those states, as well as the relative status of the various states in relation to Rome, including the amount of tribute to be paid to Rome each year. These settlements had been

What really happened?

approved in 59 BC by a very reluctant Senate under pressure from Pompey's ally, Caesar, who was then serving as consul. Caesar was the junior partner of what later came to be called the First Triumvirate, with Pompey and the wealthy Crassus being the senior partners.

Pharnaces, whose father had ruled over a much larger territory before being defeated by Pompey, was now attempting to regain his father's domains. His armies easily conquered his neighbors, all of whom were client kings of Rome, as he was, pursuant to treaties worked out by Pompey twenty years earlier. Such activity was clearly a challenge to Rome which had pledged protection to its client kings.

Shockingly, in the process of these conquests, Pharnaces had gratuitously mutilated whatever Romans, usually bankers and traders, that he found in these kingdoms with the most humiliating punishment for a Roman: castration. Thus this was again emphatically a war against Rome, which Pharnaces now assumed was without a leader.

Calvinus, Caesar's loyal and experienced legate in Asia, set out to stop Pharnaces. But in his anxiety to end the matter quickly so he could get down to relieve Caesar in Alexandria, Calvinus had unwisely engaged Pharnaces on unfavorable ground. He was badly defeated, retreating to safety with only fragments of his army. Pharnaces had thereupon taken back his father's kingdom of Pontus and was now invading neighboring Armenia to the east and Cappadocia to the south, again, both client kingdoms of Rome and even beyond the territory that had been ruled by his father..

Each of these crises was weighing on Caesar's mind, but with almost unnatural composure and focus, he determined that he would take the time first to reward those states in the region that had come to his aid in Alexandria and punish those who had supported Pompey.

What really happened?

Then there were also disputes between various leaders in the region, which required his attention as Rome's consul.

Thus he took the longer land route up the Phoenician coast. In Ascalon he showered the governor with gifts and praises. In Judea he formally thanked Antipater and Hyrcanus for their important help in his rescue and among other favors allowed the walls of Jerusalem, destroyed by Pompey, to be rebuilt. He further lowered their obligation of tribute to Rome and in other ways improved the status of Jews throughout the roman world. Mithridates and his entourage continued to travel with Caesar and, once Caesar had defeated the usurping King Pharnaces, the loyal and courageous Mithridates, a solid ally in a very sensitive area of Roman rule, was granted the kingdom of the Bosporus. Along the way Caesar pardoned all those cities and states that had supported Pompey, including the wealthy free city of Tyre, but at the same time he emptied their treasuries to finance his armies, repay Cleopatra and reward his officers.

Upon finally arriving in the Syrian province's capital city of Antioch, he reluctantly parted ways with his cousin and friend, Sextus Julius Caesar, who had been at his side for so many months and through many tumultuous episodes. He made Sextus commander of the legions in Syria and governor of that unsettled province.

"Sextus, I am truly sorry, but as much as I wish to have you by my side in the years to come, I must ask you to remain here as my legate. I need you, my dear cousin, here. This is an important station and it will become even more important when I undertake the Parthian campaign. You will be on a dangerous frontier with an unstable provincial Roman administration, thanks to the poor choices of the province's past governors, including Cassius. But it will be enough if you just keep the Parthians in check until I come back with my army.

"I can only leave you with the legions that are already

What really happened?

stationed here, which I think will need some training and rehabilitation, as it seems that no one has been paying much attention to them. Else we might have a situation here similar to the Gabinians in Alexandria. I am not sure, so be careful."

"Caesar," Sextus replied. "It is an honor to serve you wherever you wish. But I do have a favor to ask. When you get back to Rome and find it convenient, would you send word to my wife, Cassandra, and my children, about what I am doing. It has been a very long time since I have seen them."

"I understand, Sextus. In addition, you can rest assured that your family will not want in any way. They will be richly rewarded on your behalf, as I owe you so much."

"Thank you, Caesar. But there is no need for further generosity. You have already made me a wealthy man and my family is well situated.

"But you mention again your campaign to Parthia. May I be bold enough to ask you about your plans? I know I have no right to know, but I will be facing off against these people for a few years."

"Yes, of course you can ask. You, more than anyone, deserve to know what I am thinking as you will be on the front line.

"There are two areas I have to deal with in the east. The first, and I believe the much easier, is to push the Dacians back over the Danube and make that our northern border in Asia.

"Then I will come in and deal with Parthia, and perhaps areas further east. I have heard so much about the east while we were in Alexandria, that I am anxious to see what there is out there.

"Now, of course, my plans are only in a formative stage and they keep changing as circumstances do. But I can tell you that I will be sending legions for training and preparation to some location in Macedonia. I have chosen

What really happened?

Greece for congregating my army for the Parthian campaign because it is not only safe and secure, but also the area has plenty of resources to sustain the many tens of thousands of men and horses that I will be gathering.

"Crassus, when he entered Parthia, had thirty-four thousand legionaries in seven legions and four thousand horsemen. Yet he was soundly defeated. Hence I will prepare a greater army. I plan to have at least double that number of legionaries, and perhaps five or six times that number of horsemen. Remember, it was the Parthian horsemen and their miraculous arrows that bedeviled and ultimately defeated Crassus."

"You will be using your German allies again as horsemen?" asked Sextus.

"As many as I can get. The Germans are the fiercest and most versatile, though closely followed by the Gallic cavalry that have fought with me over the years. But for this expedition I will also need additionally to recruit among the experienced cavalry of Spain and Cilicia."

"Caesar, forgive me for saying this, but I am dumbfounded that you are able to look into and plan so far in the future, while we still have a senatorial army in Africa and in Spain appears to falling under the sway of Pompey's angry sons. Nor can it be ignored that the Senate faction still controls a huge fleet. Yet you are looking beyond all of that."

"Sextus, in my judgment I have already won this war. I consider these remnants only a nuisance that I will shortly deal with.

"The future of Rome lies in the east, and that is where I will concentrate my attention as soon I neutralize these delusional fools, in one way or another."

"Will you be going to Africa and Spain, Caesar?"

"I am not planning to do that. I will be sending legates with enough legions to deal with Cato, Scipio, and the others in Africa. I have no real concern about those

What really happened?

people; they have lost once and will lose again. It is in their nature always to lose in a military contest with me, but they still do not see that. It is again their usual blind obstinacy, now having its destructive effects in the military field, which prevents them from seeing the obvious: that it is all over for them. Their only possible strength is their alliance with King Juba. He might be something of a problem. We will see.

"As for Spain, the impetuous and poorly organized sons of Pompey have nothing of their father's greatness. They are petty and cruel individuals and will not be able even to hold on to their own men. I do not see them as any real threat. And the fabled fleet of the senators? As we speak now it is disintegrating. Its commanders are either abandoning their positions or reporting to me and asking for pardon."

"It is ironic," Sextus commented, "how such formidable forces just seem to have disintegrated."

"That is always what happens in great conflicts, my dear Sextus. Everyone tries to be on the winner's side before it is too late.

"I do not intend to get bogged down with these relics who continue to oppose me. I am looking to the future of the Roman Republic. And don't forget, Sextus, we also need to avenge the dishonorable murder of my dear friend Crassus and the death of his son Publius, as well as the tens of thousands who either died or were captured at Carrhae. Rome cannot allow that great defeat to go unanswered, or our entire eastern border will always be in jeopardy from ambitious rulers. Finally, I have promised to return to Antiochia to retrieve those Carrhae survivors— that alone would justify a march through the entire Parthian kingdom.

"But getting back to my tentative plans. Once I determine our precise location in Macedonia, Queen Cleopatra will begin shipping the swords, arrows, shields

What really happened?

and helmets that she is having made from the Parthian metal.

"Also, I have sent instructions to Balbus in Rome to meet me in Epirus on my way to Italy. A mutual friend of ours, Atticus, a wealthy merchant, has a fine estate in Buthrotum on the coast, and we can conveniently meet near there before I sail to Italy. I will be giving him Liang's amazing crossbow and he will make arrangements, through his business contacts in Epirus, to have it replicated and secretly produced in sufficient numbers for my forces."

"I find this fascinating, Caesar," Sextus could not help saying. "I am honored that you have shared your plans with me. It sounds like the Parthians are in store for a real surprise."

"Yes, indeed, Sextus, I certainly hope so." But then Caesar stopped. Turning slightly away from Sextus, he seemed suddenly to be absorbed in thought. Then, as if he had come to some conclusion, he turned back to Sextus.

"Perhaps, on second thought, my dear Sextus," he said, "we often deceive ourselves when we make plans with such confidence. It is often a foolish endeavor to place trust in elaborate plans. We sometimes fail to remember that in the end we are only human beings. We are dependent on what Fortune has prepared for us. Fortune has a large role to play in everything, but it looms even larger in the rush, mayhem, and violence of military affairs, where even the smallest thing could have great consequences. While we must do all we can to influence events, we also must be willing to accept our fortune."

Caesar paused, looked out over the city of Antioch, and then continued. "As for your role right now in Antioch, Sextus, you are to keep this place secure. When I join you with my army in one, two, or three years, I expect you will have these legions, and whatever other legions you can raise, well-trained and ready for our campaign into Parthia, and perhaps beyond."

What really happened?

The Antioch that Caesar and Sextus had found was still a very prosperous trading city. It had been the center of Roman administration for that area since Pompey had established the province twenty years earlier. But Caesar still did not feel it was either secure or safe enough for two reasons: first, it was on the front line with the hostile state of Parthia; secondly, the Roman legions stationed there had originally been recruited by Pompey and there was lingering sentiment among the troops for their old general. Caesar also did not have confidence that they had maintained the usual Roman regimen of training and discipline, particularly since they had been led for a while by that rotten apple Cassius.

Cassius, after running away from the slaughter at Carrhae, had commanded the legions in Antioch. Caesar recalled hearing that his dispatches to Rome while in Antioch were always filled with stories of his great deeds in defending the frontier of Rome and the ever-imminent invasion of Roman territory by Parthia. But these dispatches were at the same time disputed by none other than Cassius's good friend Cicero, who was then serving as governor in nearby Cilicia. Cicero's agents and informants in the east had flatly contradicted Cassius and told Cicero that there was no impending Parthian invasion. In fact the agents had reported that the Parthian king had recalled his forces from the frontier to deal with some internal disputes. In addition, what Caesar heard in Antiochia from Titus Cinna of Cassius' cowardice and treachery at Carrhae had set forever in his mind his opinion of Casius. He would have to keep this friend of Cicero's at a distance, though at the same time because of his powerful family connections, somewhat placated. Caesar was sure that Cassius, if he followed type, would show up at some point seeking pardon for fighting on Pompey's side. Pardon he would be granted, but trust, never.

XXX

"Veni, vidi, vici,"—three words that have echoed down the centuries; historic words which King Pharnaces of Pontus unwittingly bequeathed to Caesar at the battle of Zela, in August, 47 BC.

After leaving his cousin Sextus in Antioch as governor of Syria, Caesar moved rapidly north with his faithful veteran Sixth Legion, still at around a thousand men, only a fifth of its original strength, and his eight hundred German horsemen, into Pontus.

Pharnaces was amazed to learn that Caesar was already in his region so quickly. At first he tried to delay the Roman with a pretense of negotiations. Having kept close track of Roman affairs, he knew that Caesar was in a hurry to return to Rome to deal with the mess there. But Caesar had no intention of leaving this part of the world without first dealing with this gratuitous emasculator of Roman men.

Caesar was greatly outnumbered as he entered Pontus and approached the heavily fortified city of Zela, loyal to Pharnaces. Being outnumbered for Caesar was a frequent enough circumstance, but it was never definitive. So many other factors, of which Fortune was a large one, played

What really happened?

roles in battles. He had declined to augment his forces with the remains of Calvinus' two legions, which had recently been defeated by Pharnaces. Caesar judged that he did not have enough time to rehabilitate these downtrodden men. It was a fundamental principle of his never to fight, if he had a choice, with dispirited men. The spirit of his men was always of the upmost importance to Caesar. He stayed as close as possible to their moods and feelings. A spirited legionary was worth ten average soldiers on the enemy's side. However he did pick up some fresh Roman-trained troops from an ally along the way to Pontus.

At their very first encounter the overconfident Pharnaces foolishly tried to surprise and overwhelm Caesar. There was some basis for his confidence. He was the leader of a veteran army that had seen only victories over his neighbors and even over a Roman army. Further, he had many more soldiers than Caesar. But there was one thing that he apparently did not understand: Gaius Julius Caesar.

Pharnaces had camped his larger army just north of Zela. Caesar, upon his later arrival, had initially camped about five miles away and south of Zela. To "camp" was a big deal when it involved tens of thousands of men, horses, war material, slaves, servants, bankers, traders and other followers, including the usual group of women, friends, and children of the foregoing that followed a Roman army. The camp was a virtual city with streets, entrances and exits, ramparts, towers, and fortified gates. Each night on the march a Roman Army would set up such a field camp and then dismantle it in the morning.

While his camp was being constructed, Caesar went out with some of his bodyguard and staff to survey the potential field of battle. Again that eerie capacity to see what others could not came into play. He saw a substantial unoccupied hill on the north side of Zela, close to

What really happened?

Pharnaces' camp, but separated from it by a steep ravine. Caesar determined that gaining control of its heights with its strong natural defenses and just across from Pharnaces, would give him an advantage.

So during the night of the very day he had set up his camp south of Zela, Caesar sent out selected cohorts who quietly stole across the Zela plain, past the city of Zela, then onto that unoccupied hill and seized its heights. These men immediately began entrenchments in preparation for building the usual fortifications for a camp. The rest of Caesar's legionaries and horsemen soon followed them and joined in constructing the entrenchments during the night. While every single man was busy building the fortifications, the noncombatants were bringing up the baggage from the first camp.

In the early morning Pharnaces noticed the long trail of baggage being moved onto the hill just in front of him. He took them to be Caesar's legionaries moving to the hill, when in fact they were servants, slaves and other noncombatants carrying the camp's baggage. He decided that this would be an opportune time to surprise Caesar's busy men. He therefore launched his chariots and foot soldiers down from his own well-fortified camp into the ravine and then up the hill on the other side of the ravine to attack Caesar's men in the midst of their labors.

Caesar at first could not believe that anyone would be foolish enough to charge even a partially encamped army uphill. But when he finally realized that it was an actual attack, he quickly gave the order to his staff to regroup the army into battle formation. At the familiar sounds of numerous trumpets, every man, wherever he might be buried in digging around back of the hill or elsewhere, instinctively dropped his pick and shovel, put his helmet on and after grabbing his sword and javelins rushed in the direction that the trumpets were ordering. Once reaching the front of their unfinished camp the legionaries quickly

What really happened?

gathered behind their respective standards in the usual three-line battle formation: the least experienced and youngest in the first line with the oldest veterans in the third.

At first the rushing chariots of the enemy stunned the young men of Caesar's front line, but soon the lines stabilized as the more seasoned second line and then the third line took over at the front. Eventually both lines stabilized and the armies joined in a close and brutal hand-to-hand battle that went on for hours. At times those sections of the line being manned by Caesar's newly recruited allies would falter, requiring Caesar to gallop to that point with his horsemen and restore order. But the thousand veterans of the Sixth Legion on his right wing never wavered and stood steady as a rock, methodically repulsing wave after wave of enemy attacks. Then the Sixth Legion moved forward, and the entire Roman line in imitation also advanced. The enemy line, already at a disadvantage fighting uphill, buckled.

The ensuing slaughter of Pharnaces' army would be credited mostly to the ferocious and relentless swordsmanship of the frighteningly disciplined Sixth Legion. Caesar's army then marched up the other side of the ravine and swamped Pharnaces' camp. Caesar allowed the troops to loot the well-supplied camp and to keep whatever they wanted.

The city of Zela immediately opened its gates and submitted to Caesar, who then spared it from any destruction or looting. He did, however, extract a financial penalty, which consumed most of the treasury in Zela's temple.

This total victory in a short day made Caesar wonder about the justification for Pompey's title: "The Great," which he had earned twenty years earlier for defeating these same people. Pharnaces himself had managed to escape, only to be assassinated a few months later by a

What really happened?

rebelling relative in his hometown.

Thus: "veni, vidi, vici," in letters to his friends in Rome, including Matius and the elder Balbus.

Lucius Cornelius Balbus, the uncle of the young Balbus on his staff, had longed served with Caesar and he was trusted implicitly. Balbus was not just Caesar's friend, but was his confidential agent and financial adviser. When Caesar first met Balbus while serving in Further Spain as Quaestor in 69, Balbus was already a wealthy and cultured chieftain of Gades. Some years earlier he had led a very successful cavalry unit, which he himself had raised among his people, for Pompey in his campaign against the rebellious Roman General Sertorius. As a reward he was granted Roman citizenship by one of Pompey's lieutenants, Lucius Cornelius Lentulus Crus, the same Lentulus who after Pharsalus had faithfully followed his leader Pompey to Egypt and there suffered the same fate at the hands of the treacherous Pothinus.

Caesar as noted had met Balbus in 69 BC while serving in Spain as Quaestor to a family friend, the praetor Vetus. Caesar had earlier served in Asia as military tribune to another family friend. It was in these posts that Caesar had his first experiences in military affairs and he seemed to take naturally to the occupation. Likewise, as Caesar rose in his military stations abroad, he would take the sons and nephews of friends and relatives onto his staff for training and experience, and often also for their financial enrichment. Thus young Balbus, carrying the same name as his uncle, served under Caesar to receive training, experience and wealth. Caesar had a reputation for great generosity with his staff as well as with any soldier who distinguished himself. The practice of emptying the temple treasuries of captured towns and cities during his wars, particularly in Gaul, served as the source of his fabulous wealth—wealth which he shared with his men, the treasury in Rome and with the Roman people in the form of great

What really happened?

public buildings, temples and forums which he had erected for them.

After the victory at Zela Caesar decided to settle several disputes among sovereigns and vassal kings in the province of Asia and Rome's protectorates. In addition he wanted again to reward friends and extract fines from former enemies, whom he as usual also pardoned. Since he was urgently needed in Rome he curtailed visits to the various kingdoms and instead called all the chieftains to a conference in Taurus, the capital city of the province of Cilicia.

The announcement of the conference had been widely circulated, so he found on his arrival a good number of Roman senators and other nobles who had traveled from Rome and other parts to pay respects to the victor.

As it happened Marcus Brutus was also in Taurus at the same time, but on private business. Brutus over the years had become one of Rome's largest and most uncompromising moneylenders in this part of the world. He usually worked through agents who kept his involvement secret, since it was technically illegal, at least in Roman tradition, for a senator to lend money at interest, though many did so, and openly. More importantly, the use of agents who kept his involvement secret helped protect his carefully crafted reputation as an honest, austere and honorable follower of his somber uncle Cato.

Kings and tyrants in areas controlled or influenced by Rome often needed money to finance their overly ambitious plans. Sometimes it was to recruit an army, or to obtain money to pay the required tribute to Rome, or to build lavish public buildings to impress their subjects. Often it was the Roman bankers, who seemed to be everywhere, to whom they turned. Brutus obliged them, often at ruinous interest rates.

Caesar, however, was delighted to see again the cherished son of his old lover Servilia. He had watched

What really happened?

this handsome boy grow up during the years he had visited Servilia. He had played with him and had been pleased by his talents and manners. During the battle at Pharsalus a year earlier Caesar had instructed his commanders to be on the watch for Brutus and to spare his life if at all possible. Brutus had taken up with Pompey's side, claiming that it was Caesar who wished to restore in Rome the type of kingdom which Brutus's ancestors allegedly had vanquished. Brutus must have been forced to make a painful decision to join with Pompey, since it was on Pompey's orders that Brutus's father had been executed for joining some insurrection a good number of years earlier.

But Brutus's choice was not so much for Pompey as it was for the faction of senators whose families had long governed Rome and were now trying to keep Caesar from diminishing their power. He understood that it was a necessary evil for the oligarchs to employ the great general Pompey in their war against Caesar. After their agent Pompey had beaten Caesar, then his own turn would come—the great families did not want any one man to be powerful enough to upset their traditional system of governance.

Curiously, like Cicero, though he had publicly joined the senatorial party under Pompey and crossed the Adriatic to be with Pompey's army, he also found a way to avoid the physical hazards of a military role in the showdown between Caesar and Pompey. Cicero had claimed sickness and stayed in Dyrrhachium on the coast when Pompey made the fatal mistake, under pressure from the senators who tasted blood, of moving inland, away from his overwhelmingly superior fleet, to "chase" Caesar.

Brutus on the other hand did travel east with Pompey's army, but apparently was reading philosophy or something back in the camp while the battle at Pharsalus raged. After the defeat and before Caesar's troops overran the camp, he

What really happened?

had fled to a nearby town. From the safety of that town he had sent emissaries to Caesar to ask for pardon. Caesar was happy to see the young man safe and sound and embraced him as a lost relative. Brutus readily disclosed to Caesar all that he had heard of Pompey's plans and was of the opinion, which turned out to be correct, that Pompey would head to his royal clients in Alexandria. Then Brutus had departed for Rome while Caesar pursued Pompey to Alexandria.

So it was pleasant again, a year later, to behold the handsome, though somber, Brutus. He asked Brutus to stay by his side as a member of his inner circle, an honor that in Caesar's mind he was paying to Servilia. Then with his staff, now including Brutus, he began the process of receiving each king and chieftain.

During one of the conferences that he held over the next few days he was not surprised to receive a message that another of Pompey's generals, Cassius, would like an audience with him. Caesar granted Cassius the audience and duly forgave him for having fought for Pompey, though in the process he had killed many of Caesar's soldiers and sailors, some of them unnecessarily after a battle had been concluded. Caesar did not like or trust this vicious man. But again, Caesar was also mindful of Cassius's distinguished family and its powerful connections. He immediately bestowed upon Cassius the title of legate, that is, one of his lieutenants, but also quietly saw to it that it remained an empty title. Never would Cassius be allowed to travel in Caesar's entourage nor engage beside him in the battles to come. Once Cassius had received Caesar's pardon and returned to his place among the suppliants, Caesar turned to his German cavalry bodyguard Waldo and softly spoke to him.

"Waldo, do you see that individual?"

"Who, Caesar?" Waldo asked, looking in the direction Caesar had glanced at.

What really happened?

"That lean and hungry fellow. His face is sallow and he seems to be looking about for imaginary demons who might be haunting him."

"Ah, Caesar, indeed." Waldo recognized Cassius by Caesar's description. "What a sinister looking fellow. What do you wish, Caesar?" Waldo's hand moved to his hidden dagger.

"For the sake of Jupiter, Waldo, put that dagger away. I only want you to take note of him. He is from an illustrious family whom I do not wish to antagonize unnecessarily. I have just made him a legate, but it is to remain meaningless and he himself is to be kept away from me. I have also heard that he has an interest in killing me."

At that point Waldo again went for his dagger and was about to rush in the direction of Cassius.

"No, Waldo, please stay. Things are complicated in Roman society. In time, you will get to understand us. In fact, when we get to Rome the first thing I will do is to make both you and Aldric members of the Roman Senate. Then, as you sit among your new colleagues and listen to their chatter, you will begin to understand the complexities of Roman life. One of the more important things you will learn is the need to respect the powerful families. With their connections and money they could do much to undermine any of my programs—so their opinion must always be considered in any matter. For now, however, just understand that while I know he wishes to kill me, I must pretend not only that I do not know, but that I consider him a friend."

"Caesar, I beg your pardon, but I do not understand."

"Of no moment, Waldo. It is not any failing of yours, but of ours. At any rate, all I want you to do is to keep an eye on him and any of those people that seem always to surround him. They are not to get anywhere close to me. No violence—just keep that crowd at bay until we have moved on."

What really happened?

"Then that would include that other mean-looking fellow, Marcus Brutus, who even now is whispering in Cassius's ear."

"Ah, some more complexity. No, Waldo, the case of Marcus Brutus is different."

"How so, Caesar? They seem to be on very cordial terms. If one is dangerous, then so is the other."

"Normally, that would be the case," Caesar responded with what seemed like amused patience. "But here we have an exception to the rule. Young Brutus is the son of an old and dear friend of mine named Servilia. Many a pleasant day have I shared with that brilliant, witty and beautiful woman. I owe her for those days. What's more, I have been witness to this young man's life, from when he was a baby, to childhood and then to manhood. True, he is not the spiritual son of Servilia, unfortunately, but he is her flesh and blood. Perhaps his uncle Cato, a strange and bitter man who hates me with all his heart, has disfigured his soul. Cato, by the way, had stayed behind in Dyrrachium in command of the forces there when Pompey came after me. I understand that after Pharsalus he took most of those forces to Africa and is even now recruiting allies there to continue this futile war against me. Nor, I am sure, has the influence of Brutus's new wife, Portia, been beneficial, at least regarding his attitude toward me. Dear and beautiful Portia is as intelligent as her father, the very same Cato we are speaking of, and as hopelessly dedicated to my destruction as her former husband, Bibulus. You recall Bibulus, Waldo?"

"Yes, Caesar. That naval commander who refused to abandon his post as head of the Pompeian fleet even though he was very sick."

"That is the man, brave and dedicated. But the irrational hatred of me that caused his death I am afraid is shared by his widow, who now also shares the bed of Brutus as his wife. So there are many poisons that have

What really happened?

entered Brutus's bloodstream."

"Caesar, I beg your pardon," interjected Waldo. "But if I were to use the cold logic and reasoning that you have often advocated, I would say that this man Brutus might be even more dangerous than yonder Cassius."

"Now, Waldo, do not quibble with me. It is enough that I am indebted to Servilia. So I owe her son every advantage. Let it be."

"As you wish, Caesar." Waldo's words were compliant, but not his countenance as he glared with anger toward the two men, still conferring with each other.

During the interviews at Taurus Caesar had a number of the area's kings or chieftains before him who had supported Pompey. Each gave his elaborate excuses as to why he had, against his better judgment and feelings of love for Caesar, nevertheless been compelled by circumstances either to give troops or money, or both, to Pompey.

Caesar would pardon all of them, but each pardon was crafted for the person involved. Some he would allow to keep all their territory but with the payment of a hefty annual tribute to Rome. Others whom he had better reason to be annoyed with, would be pardoned and fined, but also would have their territories cut down and given to their competing neighbors.

Caesar was surprised during two of these interviews that young Brutus suddenly seemed to awaken and intrude himself into the proceedings. In both cases Brutus, somewhat incoherently, pleaded for the supplicant and begged Caesar to reduce the proposed fines in one case and in the other even to eliminate them.

Caesar's feelings on all of these cases were not strong to begin with, though he was trying to mete out equal justice. But in a show of respect to Servilia's son, in each of these cases he accepted Brutus's curiously passionate plea and reduced the fine he was about to impose in one

What really happened?

case and actually eliminated it in the other, precisely as requested by Brutus.

Later, when Caesar was chatting with Zeno, who was still travelling with Caesar, he remarked to him that Zeno's old pupil Brutus did not seem to have learned his rhetoric lessons well. Caesar related the episodes of the two kings on behalf of whom Brutus had intervened.

"I could not understand exactly what Brutus was saying; he seemed to be talking in riddles, but he certainly was exclaiming his cause with a great deal of passion. So, though not comprehending his reasons or the urgency of it all, I just granted him his requests."

Zeno sat quiet for some time. Caesar looked at him as if to say, well, what do you make of it?

Finally, as if coming to a conclusion after weighing the pros and cons of being frank on this matter with Caesar, Zeno said, "It seems that my dear erstwhile pupil Brutus has changed much from the days when I was his tutor, and from the days you knew him as a child or youth. Since then he has come to admire some of the less pleasant qualities of his fellow senators—things not learned when I instructed him in Servilia's house. I am afraid he discovered long ago that his nature was more in harmony with that of his uncle Cato's, which includes a conviction of his own haughty superiority over other men and, most unfortunately, a mean lust for money, and its endless accumulation.

"My good friend Cicero," Zeno continued, "told me that while he was governor of these parts a few years ago that he had been importuned endlessly by Brutus and his agents to help them in collecting on large loans that Brutus had made to some of these sovereigns. Cicero of course is no stranger to borrowing and lending. Most of his many estates in Italy he acquired with borrowed money. In turn when he was flush he would lend out money to friends at respectable interest rates.

What really happened?

"But Cicero sensed that here in the province there may have been some serious overreaching. At first he tried to be accommodating to Brutus's agents, as he wanted to gain some trust with his new friend. Thus he told me that he did persuade a certain king to dig deep into his already impoverished kingdom to raise a large amount of money and hand it over to Brutus's agents to pay part of his debt—only to receive bitter complaints from Brutus that Cicero had failed to force the king to pay off the whole debt.

"Eventually Cicero became alarmed at Brutus's importuning. Brutus, for example, at one point had simply demanded of Cicero that he appoint Brutus's agents as official Roman prefects of his in the province so they could use our troops to collect Brutus's debts with force. This Cicero finally refused. He learned later that a governor before him had acquiesced in this abusive behavior, and that the governor after him did as well. But he would not. On one occasion Brutus and his people wanted Cicero to arrest all the city magistrates of a town that owed Brutus a large amount of money that was earning interest at the astounding rate of 48 percent per annum, four times the legal rate set by the Senate and by Cicero's own governing edicts issued by him upon taking up his position. Cicero told me that he could not wait for his one-year term of office to end and hand over Brutus's unseemly demands to the next governor.

"I would guess," Zeno finally concluded, "from all I have heard that those two kings, to whom you just granted such generous relief, were deeply in debt to Brutus. I am also told that the interest rates on his loans to them were horrendous. In any event, whatever money you spared them, will soon find its way into Brutus's pockets."

"By Jupiter . . . !" Caesar began, but then abruptly stopped. He seemed to be playing over scenes in his mind. Then suddenly many things he had wondered about began

What really happened?

falling into place.

Zeno said nothing, knowing how these revelations must have hurt Caesar. So he just shrugged his shoulders.

Zeno's words wore heavily on Caesar during that day. He could only recall the happy and chubby boy bouncing around his mother's house when Caesar would call on Servilia.

As he took his leave of Taurus the next day to return to Rome, he noticed Brutus in the group of senators bidding him farewell. It had been determined that Brutus would take a different route back to Italy. Caesar had asked him as his representative to visit some of the more prominent Pompeians who had sought exile in Greece after their defeat at Pharsalus, and try to convince them to return to Rome and join Caesar in governing their Republic.

While thus studying Brutus Caesar had to admit to himself that his dear Brutus undeniably had changed from that happy and friendly little boy of the old days. Now his countenance resembled something else, something far different, yet still familiar to Caesar. He tried to place it but could not. Then he glanced among the other senators bidding him farewell, and noticed Cassius. Ah, yes, he thought, that lean and hungry look. My dear Brutus has nested with an unhealthy lot. I must do something about that when I get back to Rome.

XXXI

Caesar's entourage, now swelled by senators, their families, and a host of well-wishers, formed a long column as it approached Buthrotum in Epirus on the Adriatic coast. From there the plan was to board some boats already made ready for him and sail to Brundisium or Tarentum in Italy, depending on the winds, and then march up to Rome. Though he was in a hurry he did not want to miss the opportunity to visit a number of the Italian cities on the way to Rome and assure the population that all was well. He had been gone for so long.

At Buthrotum he was met by a crowd of locals, but also including his friends Atticus and Balbus. They had gathered as a group at the entrance of Buthrotum together with the city fathers.

"Caesar, welcome to our little city," Atticus said. Atticus had long had a huge estate in Buthrotum and felt he could speak for the city.

Caesar had visited Atticus's estate in Buthrotum previously and had wondered where both he and Cicero could have found the huge resources necessary to obtain and run such fine villas in so many places. He remembered that his loan to Cicero had helped Cicero acquire the one

What really happened?

in Pompeii, but what of Cicero's other eight or ten villas he had heard about? Those folks do love to own properties, he thought. But Atticus was a good-natured person, always willing to bend with the wind. The wind was now behind Caesar's back and so Atticus was most attentive.

"Great Caesar, congratulations on your many victories," Atticus continued, somewhat to the annoyance of the town fathers whose welcoming speeches were thus being usurped.

"We have been awaiting your arrival," Atticus continued, "and provisions have been made for your stay. My estate is at your service. Balbus has been here with me for several days already."

"Thank you so much, my dear Atticus. It has been a long journey. Greetings to you, one and all, good citizens of Buthrotum," he added, thus finally giving the city fathers their opportunity to speak.

And speak they did. This might be their one and only chance to talk to the leader of the known world. Caesar went from person to person and exchanged greetings and information with each one. When he finally got back to Atticus the equestrian turned the conversation to his good friend Cicero.

"Cicero," he told Caesar, "is worrying himself sick in Brundisium. He has been told that you have given permission for him to go back up to Rome but he is afraid to do so. He fears some of your followers. Yet he is miserable in Brundisium, bored to death. He is looking for a clear and public signal from you that he is in your favor."

"Atticus, it is puzzling to me why Cicero is still so worried," Caesar replied. "I have already written and told him he has nothing to be concerned about, that my feelings toward him have not changed. Have I not pardoned every Roman who has asked for it? It is not simply that it is in my nature to do so, but I need all the

What really happened?

help I can get to govern our Republic. I cannot do it alone. Our task requires the talents and support of all the good and honorable men of Rome, as Cicero would describe them. So feel free to tell him that he is safe and will be given full immunity—with none of his properties touched."

"Can I therefore assure him," said Atticus, "that you will write those instructions to Antony, in so many words."

Caesar hid his annoyance and said only, "I will be delighted to do so."

Atticus smiled: "I am sure he will finally be satisfied that he is safe. This should be enough for him to regain his composure."

Caesar smiled. "It should be, but I'm sure it will not be enough. It is not in Cicero's nature to feel secure for long about anything, except perhaps his literary and oratorical powers, which, incidentally, we all respect and admire. Cicero would continue to worry even if I wrote his pardon in my own blood! Just tell him, again, that all will be well.

"But I am anxious, Atticus, to continue my journey to Italy. Thank you for your offer of hospitality, but I will not be staying overnight at your lovely estate. I plan to sail in a few hours. But for now let us spend some time together in the town center with the others."

Eventually Caesar was able to extract himself from the greeting party and, getting Balbus to accompany him, left for the harbor. They galloped toward the waiting boats that would take him and his group to Italy. Most of his entourage, including his bodyguards with their horses, had already boarded ship.

"Balbus, how are you my drear friend?"

"Good, Caesar, and so extremely happy to see you. I have missed you, but more importantly Rome has slipped into disorder in your absence. Your Antony has been less than effective and perhaps even disruptive. But more of that later. Your message to me was that you had something

What really happened?

of some urgency to discuss with me."

"Yes," replied Caesar, "let us retreat to some place private where we can talk in peace."

Balbus was an extremely successful businessman and had contacts in nearly all the trading cities under Roman influence. So they rode over to a nearby villa owned by a business associate and were finally able to dine and talk in private. Caesar had with him several of his bodyguards and his two secretaries, as he was constantly composing letters and instructions.

"Balbus, this is why I asked you to meet me here," Caesar said as he took a package from one of his secretaries and unwrapped it. From the cloth wrapping he withdrew the crossbow gift that he had received from Liang.

Balbus looked at it with some puzzlement.

"I know," said Caesar. "It is a crossbow and you must be asking yourself : 'We are meeting here in secrecy, far from Rome, to examine a crossbow?' But bear with me. This is a very unusual crossbow. It was given to me by a Chinese scholar in Alexandria at great personal risk to himself. This crossbow is very special. The scholar stole it from a Chinese officer who had been assigned to watch him in Alexandria—not so much for my friend's safety as for keeping him in line. But my friend was much distressed by my description of how our Crassus and his army had been decimated by the Parthian arrows. He knew that I planned to seek vengeance and he wanted to help."

"So this crossbow?" Balbus asked, with raised eyebrows.

"I know what you are thinking Balbus. And I do not blame you. But the short and long of it is that this is a fantastic weapon that might alone help me defeat the Parthians. It has a secret mechanism that allows one to shoot many more arrows than any other crossbow but also at much greater distances and with greater force. Take my

What really happened?

word for it. I have had it tested extensively. It is a wonder-weapon and we will be the only ones in our part of the world to possess it—at least for the time being."

"Okay Caesar. I understand what you are saying and I can see the importance of this weapon. But still, why are we here talking about it?"

"Balbus, you have never failed me. You tell me why I have you here?"

Balbus thought for a few minutes, and then relaxed and smiled. "We are in Epirus," he said. "Far from Rome and far from Parthia. You have a crossbow, a 'wonder-weapon', as you call it, with a secret mechanism that could in itself defeat a nation. But you have only one crossbow."

"Ah, I knew you would understand," Caesar said with some laughter. "Where are there better craftsmen than in this part of the world? And who has all the right business connections to find us a discrete manufacturer to produce thousands of these crossbows in total secrecy? You, my dear friend Balbus, and only you."

"Indeed," Balbus responded, "indeed! An interesting assignment." Balbus closed his eyes and seemed to be lost in thought for a while. "Thousands you say, Caesar? And in secrecy?"

"Yes," was Caesar's response, delivered now with pleasure as he saw that Balbus was already solving the problem.

"How much time do I have?" he asked.

"I need first to settle things down in Rome and then get people started on some important projects that I hope will change the face of Rome and the welfare of the people in Italy and in all of our provinces," Caesar said. "Then it seems that the faction in the senate, or at least some diehard elements in it, have put together some forces in Africa and maybe also in Spain. I have to reconcile with them, hopefully. If not, then force may be necessary to put an end to their obstinate but futile opposition. That all has

What really happened?

to be done before I head to Parthia. So, good Balbus, I would say you have two years, at the most, three years. But the sooner you get it done, the better."

"It will be done, Caesar."

"Thank you."

XXXII

Caesar and Zeno found themselves together again at the prow of a sailing ship in the night, this time moving across the Adriatic to Italy in September of 47 BC.

Caesar had taken himself to the front of the ship, indicating to his staff that he wished to be alone, except for Zeno, whom he had summoned to join him. He was tired and his mood was somber. It was clear from all he had heard that Pharsalus had not settled the civil war as he had hoped. So many Romans from distinguished families lay buried under the dirt at Pharsalus, and yet the end was not in sight. Obdurate enemies were building forces in Africa and Spain. He would have to battle his fellow Romans again, and kill many of them. What a waste! In addition, the cities in Italy had learned of the chaos in Rome under Antony and wondered if Caesar's rule would bring that kind of disorder to the rest of Italy.

What's more, his veterans seem to have exhausted their patience in waiting for him to fulfill his promises made before Pharsalus. They apparently were through with just standing by and waiting for their bonuses and land grants. Nor did they like the rumors of more wars to be waged in Africa and Spain. Fir many of them their enlistments of

What really happened?

sixteen years were up. They were finished with wars. They wanted a piece of land and some money to start a family and live normal lives. Mutinies were rampant among the legions waiting in Campania, even among his beloved Tenth Legion, and Antony had been helpless in calming them.

Finally, he had obviously not succeeded in turning the Optimates around. Many had offered their allegiance and been pardoned, though some he suspected would turn on him in an instant if the circumstances permitted. But many others had taken off to Africa or Spain to prepare for further futile battles. Yet others had exiled themselves voluntarily to Greece or Rhodes and refused to take part in anything.

"Caesar," said Zeno as he approached the lone figure at the prow. "You seem pensive, if I may be allowed to say."

Caesar broke out of his reverie and turned, with a smile, to Zeno, ignoring his comment.

"We seem to be in the habit of conferring at the head of ships at night, Zeno. Does your scholarship tell you if that means anything?"

"Indeed, Caesar," Zeno replied. "I hope it means that we are friends and can converse anywhere."

"Ah, well put. I am sure that it does. But this time we do not have the excitement of approaching the great tower of Pharos or the glittering and sumptuous city of Alexandria. Instead we will soon set foot on the dreary port of Tarentum or Brundisium, and hopefully leave it as soon as possible."

"Nevertheless, Caesar," Zeno countered with a chuckle, "neither will we be greeted with riots and mayhem by the populace as we were in Alexandria."

"Ah, that much is so. But Zeno, I have a favor to ask of you."

"At your service, Caesar."

"Please don't be so obsequious, Zeno, it does not suit

What really happened?

you."

"Forgive me," Zeno said. "But I am concerned about the seriousness of your demeanor. I truly would like to be of service to you and help you, in some small way, carry these burdens that seem to press upon you."

"That is so gracious of you. In fact there is one serious concern of mine that I think you can help me with. It has to do with the education of my son, Caesarion. I want him to be under the care of intelligent and sensitive people. So I thought of you. You have been a tutor, among other things, and a great tutor if my information is correct. This is the favor I have to ask of you: I would like you to return immediately to Alexandria, with whomever you wish to take with you, and arrange for his education."

"Caesar," said a startled Zeno, "we have just returned from a very long and definitely unpleasant stay in Alexandria. You now ask that an old man like me return across this angry sea?

"When I left Rome some time ago I had thought I would retire peacefully in my birthplace of Cnidus. But that place defied desolation. I was getting utterly depressed, surrounded by family members and people I had not seen in forty years, and for good reason. So I was so happy when you arrived in our city in your pursuit of Pompey and then asked me to travel with you to Alexandria. I saw an eventual return to Rome. Now you ask me to go back?"

"Zeno, I am sorry. It is much that I ask of you, I understand that. But I do not ask it lightly. I need my son to be educated by the best there is in our world. You represent the best that there is.

"I want you to transfer to him your spirit and wisdom. Talk to him each day in that perfect Greek and Latin of yours. I want him speaking Latin without a trace of a Greek or Egyptian accent, and Greek without a trace of a Latin or Egyptian accent. His mother will take care of his

What really happened?

Egyptian. Read him philosophy and poetry. Make him smile and pay attention to your face. Infuse him with what it takes to be a great person. You, Zeno, can do that."

Zeno stood as if stunned for some time. What is it that Caesar is saying?

"Caesar," said a confused Zeno, "your son is an infant, he will not understand anything I say. He will not be able to respond. He cannot speak at this tender age. There is nothing I could teach him."

"My dear Zeno," Caesar responded in a reassuring tone, "let us think about a person. We know people who as youths were rotten to the core and, to no one's surprise, they grew up to be scoundrels. Likewise other children seem to have a composed and balanced disposition. Those children become compassionate and good men, some even strong leaders.

"My point is that people do not change their basic characters from the time they are babies to the time they die. The teachers they have when they begin to speak it seems to me have absolutely no influence on their basic character. It is too late by then to be of any effect. So the question is, are these children born that way and their destiny has been set by Fortune, or do they pick something up while they are babbling infants? If they are born that way, then there is nothing you or I could do. But if there is a chance that they may be learning from the moment they leave their mother's womb, then I want to do what I can to make my Caesarion a rational, balanced, strong, and compassionate man with a strong will and great confidence in himself.

"So I want you to reason with my babbling son. I want you to read him Sophocles and Plato and even the works of our dear Cicero. I want you to comment to him about the events of the day and express your loves and hates.

"Of course his mother will be doing that as well, but she cannot be with him all the time. The queen has much

What really happened?

to do both in Alexandria and when she comes to Rome next year. So you must fill in the gap."

"Caesar," an amazed Zeno almost whispered, "you indeed are a miracle of nature."

After a while he asked:

"And what does the Queen say of this?"

In response Caesar said: "You and she became friends during the time we were all in Alexandria. I have already spoken to her about this favor I am asking of you and she is wholeheartedly in agreement. I know that you were looking forward to your return to Rome. And I can imagine what you must think of going back over half the world to Alexandria again. It is not an easy thing I ask of you, nevertheless it is something I am asking.

"You told me in Alexandria, did you not, that you had released all your students in Rome and had passed your cases on to others. You had not expected to return. But now you are here— a great teacher, orator, and scholar totally free of obligations."

"Do you ever forget anything anyone ever said to you?"

Ignoring Zeno's plaintive comment, Caesar went on:

"You will have a suite of rooms for yourself at the Queen's palace— enough for your assistants, slaves, and freedmen. She will also supplement your staff as you wish, perhaps even with other scholars from the academy who could make your job less tedious. In return you will have my gratitude and, incidentally, I will fill your bank account to guarantee you a very comfortable old age, when you get to it."

"Caesar, would you believe I will do it just in return for your gratitude, and still feel richly rewarded. You are making me believe with all my heart things I have never even dreamed. Yes, yes, I will return immediately to Alexandria and convey to your son whatever I have."

"Thank you, Zeno."

What really happened?

The two men remained in silent contemplation of their surprising conversation as they looked out at the night. After a while Zeno ventured a question. "You mention Tarentum and Brundisium. May I ask why we are landing at the foot of Italy instead of outside Rome at Ostia?"

"I need to travel throughout the length Italy. Italy has become unsettled in the past couple of years. I want as many towns and cities as possible to see me. I want to reassure them in person that there will be order in Rome, in Italy and in the provinces; that all treaties will be respected; that citizenship will be generously extended as in the old days and that the wars will soon come to an end.

"I also, incidentally, intend to visit my friend Cicero, who is in Brundisium. If it happens because of the winds that we land at Tarentum, I plan to detour to Brundisium before going up the peninsular.

"My old friend Cicero I am told has become paralyzed with fear and refuses to leave Brundisium without my personal approval. That great man should not suffer such, so I intend to see him and reassure him. Those are the reasons we are heading to the heel of Italy."

Zeno stood and thought for a while. "What you say about the affairs of Italy of course are beyond any observation I can make. But as for Cicero, I do know him well. Forgive me if I offend you with what I say. But you seem to misunderstand Cicero. From everything I have heard, from him and others, he hates you with an intestinal fierceness and would be happy to see you dead. Why are you catering to him?"

"We will be arriving soon," Caesar responded in a mild voice. "So perhaps we should go down and prepare ourselves. Again, Zeno, I am greatly appreciative of your taking on the task of educating Caesarion."

Zeno immediately regretted what he had said. He should have known that Caesar was fully aware of what Cicero really felt. Caesar's people were everywhere, some very

What really happened?

close to Cicero. Obviously Caesar knew what Cicero felt but for his own reasons has chosen to pretend ignorance. Yet I only hope, Zeno thought to himself as he and Caesar made their way down to their cabins, that Cicero's treachery does not present any danger to Caesar. Just before reaching their destination, Caesar smiled and put his arm around Zeno to let him know, without words, that all was well between them.

XXXIII

After the civil war erupted in January of 49 BC, Pompey, as well as Caesar, made overtures to Marcus Tullius Cicero to join him. Because of his fame as an orator, his many friends and contacts and his literary genius, the two sides had sought Cicero's support. Cicero's politics were much closer to the conservative Senate class, which had recruited Pompey as its military leader, than to Caesar's. Nevertheless Cicero was attracted to Caesar's personality while at the same time fearful of his power and popularity. He knew that Caesar would never let the Senate faction rule Rome again. This was a concern to him as he favored the Senate faction.

To the annoyance of both sides Cicero hesitated endlessly, even after Caesar had made a personal visit to him at his villa in Formiae on March 28, 49 BC, to convince him to join his side, or at least to remain neutral and go to Greece or Rhodes for the duration of the conflict.

After much back and forth, including endless consultations with friends and relatives, Cicero finally chose to sail from Italy and join Pompey's forces. This coincidentally was at the same time that Caesar's fortunes

What really happened?

seemed unsettled as he had gone to Spain to deal with Pompey's lieutenants and not much was being heard about him back in Rome.

Thus, though he finally joined Pompey, who had crossed the Adriatic with his forces and most of the governmental officials to concentrate his armies and train recruits, his half-hearted and late support, along with his evident repulsion at the language of the bloodthirsty and revenge-seeking senators encamped with Pompey, made him unpopular even with the side he ultimately chose.

Though Cicero had lent Pompey a great sum of money for his war effort, he was religious in avoiding any military activities. He wanted nothing to do with pain and hardship, much less the danger of being wounded or killed.

Thus he offered excuses to remain in the Dyrrachium camp first established by Pompey on the coast and did not follow Pompey when he fatefully pursued Caesar inland to the eventual disaster at Pharsalus.

After the calamitous defeat at Pharsalus, Cicero concluded the war to be over and it was time to make an accommodation with Caesar. This opinion he unwisely announced in the Dyrrachium camp to the Senate faction and Pompey's sons who had survived the battle at Pharsalus. What he thought were reasonable opinions enraged the Pompeians and thereby inadvertently put him at the very risk of physical danger that he had spent so much effort to avoid. But with Cato holding back the others, Cicero hurried out of the camp and eventually found his way back to the port of Brundisium on the heel of Italy.

Antony, sent back by Caesar to be in charge of Rome after Pharsalus, conveyed the instructions to Cicero that Caesar intended on his return to review the case of each of the leaders supporting Pompey before that person would be allowed back in Rome. He explained that Caesar did not want an enemy faction developing in Rome itself while

What really happened?

he was settling matters in the east.

Cicero, however, insisted to Antony through various mutual friends close to both Caesar and Cicero, that Caesar had indicated that Cicero was an exception to his general instructions and that he could return to Italy and even to Rome. Antony thereafter backed off somewhat, but Cicero was still fearful to travel to Rome because he did not trust the followers of Caesar to be as forgiving as Caesar himself. So he stayed at the port city of Brundisium upon his return to Italy to await Caesar's arrival from the east.

And there he fretted during all the months that Caesar would spend in pursuit of Pompey after Pharsalus and then the long stay in Egypt. Cicero sent innumerable letters to everyone he knew who might be friendly with Caesar, complaining about his situation, the boredom of living in Brundisium, away from the excitements of Rome and the pleasures of his many villas, and begged them to intercede on his behalf. Cicero was well liked by many men close to Caesar, so his pleas were favorably received and passed on to Caesar as he dealt with matters in the east and in Egypt.

After the conference in Taurus, the recently pardoned Cassius took a more direct route back to Italy and arrived at Brundisium just ahead of Caesar's return. He was a friend of Cicero, sharing with him a passionate belief in the rightness of their "Optimate" cause; or as Cicero often insisted on phrasing it, the policies of all good and honorable men, as opposed to those of the vulgar laboring classes and even more to those of the masses of the poor. Being in frequent correspondence with Cicero, Cassius headed directly to Cicero's lodgings when he arrived in Brundisium.

They warmly greeted each other and celebrated their mutual survival. Eventually the conversation turned to their common situation.

What really happened?

"I don't know," Cassius remarked, "which would be worse. Living under the sole rule of Caesar, who has shown himself to be forgiving and humane, or under Pompey's son, Gnaeus. During the year we were preparing to do battle with Caesar, he would endlessly tell one and all that once he beat Caesar there would be nothing but violence and bloodshed in Rome for everyone who had not supported him and his father. If given only that choice, I must say I would prefer the benevolent tyranny of Caesar."

"But tyranny it will always be," Cicero heatedly replied, "something anathema to all good and honorable men in Rome. We are descended from the slayers of tyrants and the enemies of kings. Did our ancestors not chase the kings out of Rome? Did they not murder the tyrants?"

"Yes, yes, I agree, Cicero, please don't misunderstand me. He is still the enemy. I was just saying the Gnaeus Pompey might even be worse."

"So you have given up on our plans?"

"No, not at all. In fact three times while Caesar was in Cilicia conferring with the chieftains in Asia I approached his dwelling with a dagger in my belt. Out there I felt that his murder in the middle of the night would have been no surprise, since the place was crawling with ambitious and violent factions. Assassination seems to have become a normal process of governmental change in that area. No suspicion would have fallen on us.

"But it was the most curious thing. Each time I got anywhere near where he was sleeping for the night, out of nowhere would appear one of Caesar's bodyguards, particularly this brutal German, Waldo. It was as if they had been following me. Each time I was able to give them some plausible excuse for my presence, but soon I determined that it was my life that was in danger, not Caesar's. So I gave it up. We will have to try again in Italy, and this time it will have to be very public, with all the

What really happened?

risks involved."

"There will be no risks if we do it right," replied Cicero. "The people hate Caesar, both the decent men as well as the vulgar masses. He has no support in Italy other than his own army. Away from his army, which is in Campania and in a bad mood anyway, he would be an easy target. Then upon his death the people of Rome and Italy will rise to embrace the brave tyrannicides."

"You make it sound very safe and easy. I hope you are right, Cicero," Cassius said, with little enthusiasm. "But if I may say so to you, my dear friend, that you have not been very right in your predictions as of late."

Cicero swallowed hard to absorb the insult, as he could not afford to offend one of the few friends he had left. It puzzled him that he had managed to make himself disliked by both sides in this civil war. Yet he knew he was right; and if given the chance by Fortune it was he, Cicero, and only he, who could solve the Republic's ills and return power and governance to the class of decent and honorable men.

Was it not I, Cicero recalled to himself, who as consul single-handedly saved the Republic from the conspiracy of Catiline? Was it not I who, without hesitation, had put to death those traitors—notwithstanding the vigorous opposition of Caesar in the Senate who foolhardily insisted, against the overwhelming and angry passions of most senators, that the conspirators be spared for a trial according to Roman custom? Back then Caesar was just another senator and had not yet forged an army through nine years of fighting in Gaul, Britain and Germany. If it were not for my restraint, Caesar's reckless opposition that day would have led to his being hacked to death. It was I, as consul, who held back my eager guards.

And now here I am. Sitting for almost a year waiting for this man whose life I saved to return and decide my fate. By Jupiter I am angry. But I must bite my tongue. For

What really happened?

the time being I must be patient and not antagonize any more of my friends, like Cassius here, and just swim with the present current. I am sure my time will come again.

Presently Cicero brought himself out of this reverie and turned to Cassius.

"What of Brutus?" Cicero asked. "Is he still with us? He has been so inconsistent in this matter and yet it was his ancestors who chased the kings out of Rome and slayed the tyrants."

"Brutus," replied Cassius, "is first for Brutus and everything else comes afterward. You should have seen him currying favor with Caesar. But it was easy for him. Apparently Caesar has a soft spot for him."

"Yes, Cassius. You need to remember his relationship with Brutus's mother, Servilia. For years Caesar was in and out of his mistress's house and along the way watched Brutus grow up. In addition, Brutus did not engage in any military activities. Unlike you, he did not kill thousands of Caesar's soldiers. True, Caesar did also pardon you, primarily because he would like you and the others to help him govern. But never think that a man like Caesar will forget. You will never get close to him."

"Be that as it may," Cassius replied, "but when we met Caesar at Taurus he just took Brutus onto his staff as if he were an old ally. Later it was amusing to see Brutus actually using Caesar to help collect on the loans Brutus had made to some of the kings of the region, but Caesar had no suspicion as to what the scoundrel was doing. Our Brutus is not ready to do the deed himself. He's too busy collecting his debts, some at the most outrageous interest rates I have ever heard of. He had all the opportunity in the world to put an end to Caesar, not only because he was on his staff and had unlimited access to Caesar, but he also frequently dined alone with him and engaged, he told me, in conversations about literature. But Brutus would never risk his life to eliminate Caesar—he would prefer that

What really happened?

someone else do it."

"Yes, I do remember Brutus's peculiar streak of greed," Cicero said. "While in Cilicia as governor I had promised Brutus that I would help him in certain affairs which he seemed to have in the area, but I was actually shocked to learn how brutal and uncompromising his financial dealings were. I did my best to distance myself from them, even against his arrogant and condescending demands that I help him collect with Roman soldiers. I left matters for the next governor to deal with; someone whom I have heard was more helpful to Brutus. On the other hand, perhaps we are asking too much of our dear Brutus. I am not sure that any one of us is willing actually to die for the cause. What is the point of achieving our goal if we are not around to enjoy the benefits?"

"I think I am," Cassius replied.

"Do you think so?" Cicero asked skeptically. But to change the subject and lighten the atmosphere, he asked Cassius: "What is the word about Caesar's arrival?"

"They say that he will soon arrive in Italy, either here in Brundisium or nearby over in Tarentum, depending on the winds."

"I have asked my friend Gaius Matius to join me here, I expect his arrival any day now. Matius as you know is also a longtime friend of Caesar's."

"Yes, I know Matius. A wealthy man from our class, indeed from a distinguished ancient family—yet devoted to Caesar like a lap dog. There are so many of them and I simply fail to understand this phenomenon."

"That discussion is for another day, my dear Cassius. But now I must ask you, my friend, to be on your way. I do not want Matius seeing you here. These Caesarians are all very suspicious."

"Yes, I understand. And they have good reason to be. Caesar has many enemies—and each is well deserved."

XXXIV

A few days later Matius arrived, having made the journey from Rome at Cicero's request. Matius would have preferred to stay on in Rome as Caesar had given him a number of tasks to perform in preparation for his return. But he loved Cicero and knew how fragile and insecure he could be at times. Cicero in his letter to him had insisted that he could not face Caesar alone and urgently requested that he be with him on Caesar's return to Italy. Cicero was certain that Caesar was still angry with him for having run off to join Pompey just after Caesar and he had met at Formiae. Cicero did not understand how the misunderstanding had occurred, but apparently Caesar had developed the impression that Cicero had promised at that meeting at the very least to remain neutral in the civil war.

Matius thought this concern was exaggerated, as he knew how much Caesar respected Cicero's many talents. Caesar would rather lose his right arm than do any harm to one of Rome's great institutions. Nevertheless Matius thought it best to come to Brundisium to help sustain Cicero in his meeting with Caesar.

"Thank you so much, Matius," said Cicero upon embracing Matius. "I know what an imposition this trip

What really happened?

must have been upon you. I had hoped that my letter would reach you at your villa in Campania so that the trip would not be so long. But I understand from my slave that he delivered it to you in Rome."

"Cicero, I am ready to be of service to you wherever I might be. I am pleased that you think just my presence would be of comfort. It is flattering."

"Caesar cannot very well have my head cut off if you are standing next to me," Cicero tried unsuccessfully to joke but elicited only a frown from Matius.

"But more seriously, Matius," Cicero continued. "He must be gotten to understand that I left to join Pompey only reluctantly. Everyone around me, including my family, all insisted that I owed Pompey a great obligation because it was he who had convinced the Senate to allow me to return from exile. An exile ironically I would have avoided had I only listened to Caesar at the time. He had advised me most wisely when I was consul not to have the Catilinian conspirators executed. He said that killing them without trial, especially as they were from such prominent families, would establish a very bad precedent and indeed would come to haunt me. Was he ever so right! In just a couple of years after my term as consul I was forced into exile for those very executions. If only had I listened to his wise counsel I would not have needed Pompey's or anyone else's help to return to Rome.

"As I said, if it were up to me alone I would have joined Caesar, to whom I also owe a great many favors. Did he not take on my brother Quintus as a legate in Gaul, and in the process restored Quintus's finances? Did he not lend me a great sum of money, and at a very modest interest rate, when I needed cash urgently at the time I bid for that villa in Pompeii? To this day he has not ever mentioned repayment.

"So you see, Matius, my feelings for Caesar have always been warm and friendly; as was his toward me. But I feel I

What really happened?

have alienated him by my acts. That is why I want you, one of his best friends, at my side when he first sees me. Without a word on my part, which I fear I may be unable to utter, he will understand my friendly appeal to him."

Matius tried to move away from this embarrassing confession. "On the way down I received a letter from Caesar," Matius said. "He hopes to be at Tarentum what would now be within a day or two, ride over to Brundisium and then up to Rome. He is anxious to take in hand the mess in Rome and the mutiny of the soldiers in Campania. He is sending agents to the soldiers but he has to deal with the unrest in Rome himself."

"Yes," said Cicero, glad for the opportunity to bash one of Caesar's favorites to another of his favorites. "I have heard of the disarray Antony has managed to put Rome into. If he did not spend so much time drinking and partying, perhaps he could manage things better for Caesar. But, excuse me, have I already said too much?"

"That's okay, Cicero. You know you can speak frankly to me. Further, I cannot disagree with you. Antony has not been an effective Master of the Horse for Caesar. I don't know how he managed to allow this to happen, particularly when Caesar had also appointed all the officials in Rome. He let the factions in Rome continue their petty personal squabbles for so long that they degenerated into unnecessary violence, with each side claiming to be acting in Caesar's interest. Caesar will not be happy with this."

"But back to the reason I have brought you here," Cicero said. "When do you think we should start out to meet Caesar? I have seen a horde of senators, other officials, knights and veterans who are here to greet Caesar also. I really hesitate to have to get on my knees to beg Caesar's forgiveness in front of all these people."

"You do imagine the worse, do you not Cicero? First of all," Matius explained as patiently as he could, "you would not be doing yourself any favors by getting on your

What really happened?

knees, especially at your age. You know Caesar dislikes such obeisance from a Roman. In addition, I have been told that Caesar has already written to you to tell you that all is forgiven; that you have nothing to be concerned about and that none of your property will be confiscated. That hardly suggests that you need to go begging to him. What's more, none of these senators or knights should be looking down their noses at your paying your respects to Caesar. After all, what are they themselves doing down here from Rome?"

"Matius," Cicero protested while grabbing Matius robe. "A mere letter from Caesar is one thing. But to look me in the eye and to say it in the presence of a witness like you is something else."

"By Jupiter, Cicero, you are testing my patience."

"Nevertheless, Matius, what do you think of our taking the road to Tarentum in the early morning tomorrow before these others have awakened? If we are lucky we could meet Caesar on the road or in Tarentum before the others catch up."

Matius could only sigh in resignation. This man is hopeless, he thought. But he had come all the way down from Rome to calm Cicero down. He might as well humor him with another small journey.

So it was that late the next morning, after several hours on the road, Cicero and Matius, together with a small party of slaves and freedmen, saw the clouds of dust in the distance signaling Caesar's entourage coming their way. Cicero immediately sent his secretary Tiro on ahead to announce to Caesar that he was awaiting him.

After some time he and Matius were amazed to see galloping toward them the magical figure of Caesar, like a god descending to the earth atop a great white stallion, purple cape fluttering in the wind, the sun reflecting brilliantly off his resplendent helmet and breastplate, and suffused in the sounds of cornets announcing the presence

What really happened?

of the commanding general, trailed by dozens of his German bodyguard.

What a sight! Cicero almost cowered at the image of such power and for a brief moment he unwillingly understood why this man's veterans were so fiercely devoted to him. He had heard that Caesar would sometimes ride into battles just like that, ahead of his men, who would compete to risk their lives to protect him.

As Caesar drew nearer Cicero was relieved to see the broad smile on his face. Caesar drew to a stop a short distance from them, dismounted and walked to the group.

Embracing Matius and then Cicero, he said, "My friends, what in the world are you two doing out on this hot road? At your age you should be beside some cool pool, discussing philosophy."

"You should talk," replied Matius. "Still conquering worlds while you should be in your gardens watching over your grandchildren."

"But Matius, I have no grandchildren to mind. So I must travel for my amusement."

With that he took Cicero by the arm, indicating to the others that he wished to walk alone with Cicero for a while.

Cicero wisely had not gotten on his knees, nevertheless as soon as they were beyond the hearing of the others he said: "Caesar, if it were up to me solely, I would never have left to join Pompey. I know I promised you that I would at least stay out of it. But all those around me kept insisting that I had some kind of duty to accompany Pompey's armies; that I owed him some special obligation for his help in ending my exile. Even my family insisted on it. Oh, how I now wish I had other and wiser advisers about me."

Caesar made sure that the ironic smile that was trying to form on his lips was quickly suppressed, as he nodded knowingly in response to Cicero's laments. Two years ago,

What really happened?

he thought, Cicero might have helped him save the lives of hundreds of Roman noblemen if he had just used his great skills to convince them to stay neutral. But he just wavered forever in trying to determine what was the most profitable, and safest, course -- for himself alone.

Now most of the people on both sides simply despised him for his weakness, selfishness and insincerity. He no longer had any influence even with his 'decent and honorable men,' as he liked to put it. At this point he could no longer be of any service to Caesar in governing the Republic. But his great literary and oratorical achievements, Caesar thought, still commanded his respect and the great orator certainly deserved, despite himself, to retire in peace and quiet. Caesar needed to assure him of this or poor Cicero would fret himself to death.

"Cicero," Caesar said in a bright voice. "You should have heard what the Greek scholars in the Alexandrian Academy said of you. You would blush with embarrassment by their praise. They constantly referred to you as 'The greatest man of Latin Letters.' 'The only one who understands fully the ancient Greek thinkers,' and things of a similar nature. They greatly love and appreciate your bringing to the Latin world all that was best in the Greek world."

Cicero was taken aback by this unexpected compliment. The Greek scholars in the Academy! He could not help himself in responding sincerely. "Caesar, I am overjoyed to hear this. It is not often that I learn anything about how my works are faring among the Greek scholars. Do they so appreciate what I am doing?"

"Absolutely," Caesar replied. "They wanted me to tell you that you should continue to tell the world everything that the Greeks had discovered in literature as well as in science, the study of the gods and of humans. I assured them that in my Rome you would have all the freedom and comfort to continue your studies and writings."

What really happened?

Cicero was extremely pleased to hear this, and told Caesar so. Now he regretted that all the senators and other supplicants in Brundisium were not here to witness this scene: Caesar dismounting and walking alone with him like an old and good friend. There was only a slight flicker of a shadow that crossed his mind: the absence of any reference to a role for him in politics or the governance of the Republic. But he was too relieved by the generosity and warmth of Caesar's comments to allow this shadow to take shape. There would be time enough to explore those questions, now that he knew he was not only safe but was also in Caesar's favor.

XXXV

Peng Tao, the emperor's confidential operative, had called in Li Long to give a current report on his plans to eliminate this man Caesar.

"Your Highness, we are making progress, though I don't know how much longer it may take. These men are not as easy to manipulate as I had expected. Though only soldiers, they have been so well trained and disciplined, with many of them experts in different trades and occupations, from architects to doctors to musicians, that it will take more time than anticipated to accomplish my goal."

"I am unhappy to hear about this. I do not expect you to fail me."

"No, no, your Highness. You can tell the emperor that—. "

Tao abruptly interrupted. "The emperor knows nothing of your plans and he is not to be mentioned again! This project is just between you and me."

"Yes, my Lord, of course. I apologize. What I meant to say is that I am sure my idea will work, but not in the time frame I had originally given you. I had envisioned that it would take a year to strip their minds and fill them with

What really happened?

our own thoughts, as if they were their own. Now I am thinking, from the amount of progress we have been able to make, that it will take more than that, perhaps up to two years. But I am sure it will ultimately work and also that it will take no longer that two years."

"Do any of them suspect what is being done to them?"

"Whenever our doctors notice that a Roman is questioning our program for any reason, not only is that Roman immediately executed but so is his entire squadron. The Romans group their legionaries into squadrons of eight men who from the start of their military careers train and fight together, live in the same tents in their camps and in effect over the years become very close to each other, like a family. So if we see that one man begins to question what we are doing, we must assume that he has talked this over with his comrades in the squad. So all of them must be quickly but secretly executed."

"Doesn't the sudden disappearance of eight men at a time raise any issues with the remaining soldiers?"

"Not that we can see. They have become so used to the idea of a squad being a unit, that they would be surprised if anything happened that did not affect everyone in the squad at the same time. We just explain that the squad was sent to another project of ours. They do appreciate the reality that though they are being treated very well, they still are slaves. So the movement of any of them to other locations comes as no surprise to anyone."

"Would you review for me again exactly what you are doing?" Tao asked.

"As you know, we brought the original thousand slaves to one of our military camps just inside China. They are quartered in comfortable barracks in the center of the camp and their daily needs are attended to by other slaves who do not speak their language, though in effect they are surrounded by thousands of our troops in the rest of the camp.

What really happened?

"We have convinced them that we are very anxious to learn what those in the west know of military practices, road and bridge building and anything else they may have been trained to do. They have not seen any of our cities and have no idea just who we are, other than we are a mighty military power. Their days are spent rather leisurely in detailing what information they may have to our men who are in fact experienced doctors trained in the specialty of the mind.

"Each day they are individually engaged in conversation with some of our most clever men, all to convincing them that they deeply believe certain things. Their efforts are aided by the careful administration of certain herbs which we know relaxes the mind and opens it to suggestions. We try to get everyone in each squad to the same level. If we see one person is falling behind, we increase our attention to him. Eventually we expect that they will have absolutely no ability to resist whatever suggestions we put into their minds. As far as they are concerned, they will earnestly believe that these thoughts and conclusions are their own."

Peng Tao asked: "How many of the original thousand are there left?"

Li Long hesitated and looked uncomfortable.

"Well, Long, what is the matter?" Tao irritably prompted.

"There are about three hundred left," Long finally replied, but added quickly, "That will be more than enough for our purposes, I assure you, your Majesty."
"I hope you are right, Long, for all our sakes."

PART IV
ROME
47 – 44 BC

XXXVI

"Thank you so much for coming, Varro," Caesar said while extending his hand to the famous scholar. "I was hoping to be able to talk to you before heading down to Africa to deal with your friends Scipio and Cato. I will be leaving in a few days."

Varro, a native of the Sabine town of Reate some distance southeast of Rome, was sixty-nine years old, sixteen years Caesar's senior. This was a very advanced age in the Rome of that day. He thought to himself that this was a very strange scene. The Senate had just obsequiously granted Caesar even more powers as a Dictator. The man is in absolute control of our world. Yet he pretends that he simply 'requested' that I come here and then he actually thanks me. What would happen to me if I did not come? Perhaps the same fate that I fear awaits the misguided

What really happened?

Scipio and Cato in Africa.

"Caesar, I am delighted to be here," he replied. "I was so flattered that you sent your own freedman to fetch me. How long has it been?"

Then he suddenly realized even that pro-forma comment had been a blunder, as it might remind Caesar of the actual last time they had seen each other. That had occurred in Cordoba, Spain, two years earlier when as a defeated Pompeian general he cowered before Caesar. Varro had been Pompey's ineffectual military commander in Further Spain, but being of no great political or personal convictions he had been waiting to see where the wind was blowing between Pompey and Caesar. Though a long-time follower and admirer of Pompey, he was always willing to change sides if the circumstances required. In his defense it should be said that he was a man of letters and his friends should not have thrust him into military affairs. He always felt awkward with a military assignment.

Thus as Pompey's commander in Further Spain when the civil war broke out in 49, he just stayed quiet and waited for events to unfold. Unfortunately for him he had wrongly interpreted a few skirmishes in Spain at the start of the war to conclude that Caesar would lose. Thus he went all out, at least in his speeches, in his collection of supplies and raising of recruits, in support of Pompey. Then when Caesar quickly defeated the other Pompeian forces in Spain and even the cities that Varro had been given by Pompey to govern showed solid support for Caesar, he chose the course of wisdom and submitted his surrender. To this day he still could not decide whether Caesar's sending his young cousin Sextus Caesar to accept his surrender was an insult to him or a tribute to Sextus.

Caesar, gracious as ever, pretended not to notice Varro's unease. "Varro, you have been very successful here in Rome. Everyone is reading one or other of the works you have produced. I have at least half a dozen of your

What really happened?

books on my shelves. I congratulate you. Is there any subject that you are not knowledgeable about?"

"In truth, Caesar," Varo replied, opting to be frank and honest as he was too old to pretend any more, "I only seem so knowledgeable because our fellow citizens know so little. I feel compelled to remind them about things like what Rome was and what our ancestors had accomplished. So few people know today about our past. Then there is widespread ignorance about how to grow crops, or keep a decent kitchen, or how to prepare for a feast. I study these things and then share what I have learned with my fellow citizens. An easy enough task, and for that I am called a scholar. But I do demur."

"You are being too modest, my dear Varro. You are one of the most learned men of our day. Your desire to share with your fellow Romans what you have learned is the reason I have asked to see you."

Now, thought Varro, this meeting was not going where he assumed it would. What did the Dictator have in mind?

"How," Caesar asked, "can a citizen of Rome obtain one of your books, or at least be able to read it?"

Varro was puzzled by Caesar's unexpected question. Didn't the Dictator have anything else to do?

"Well, since you ask, I suppose any citizen could find my books in the libraries that our great men have in their homes."

"Varro, please!" Caesar promptly replied with enough emphasize to startle Varro. "Be serious. How many citizens could approach a home of the Metelli or the Claudii, knock on their door and ask to peruse their library?"

Varro did agree that such would be absurd. He chuckled to himself at the image of a tradesman trying to get into Cicero's library. But what was Caesar's point? Varro's books were already widely read by the nobles and many of his volumes were in the libraries of the best

What really happened?

citizens of Rome. He was more than satisfied with that achievement. So he did not understand this strange curiosity Caesar had about the ability of an ordinary citizen to find and read one of his books.

"But then, Caesar, I must admit that I am at a loss. The only places where books are kept are in the libraries of our better citizens. Further, I agree as you suggest that the average citizen of Rome would not have access to these libraries. Of course they could buy them in the market, but then you would rightly ask how many people could afford that? Nonetheless that is the way things are here in Rome. So, if I may ask, what is it that you are saying?"

"Varro," Caesar said. "Were you ever in Alexandria?"

"Yes, but many years ago. I was a student and part of our required course was to spend some time in the intellectual capitals of the world, Athens and Alexandria."

"Did you visit the great Library while you were there?" Caesar asked. "Or the Academy?"

"As mere Roman students the closest we were ever allowed to get," answered Varro, thinking wistfully of that long ago time, "was to wander about the gardens of these great buildings. Sometimes we would come across a scholar who would speak to us, but that was not often. We were just another group of young Romans doing an obligatory pilgrimage to the world's center of learning. We were not taken seriously and given no special privileges. We had more success in gaining access to the various small libraries in Alexandria. These were opened to all."

"You," said Caesar, "are recalling just what I was hoping you would remember. As you know I have just spent a great deal of time in Alexandria. I must admit that Alexandria has captured my imagination, as they say. I plan to remake Rome into a more magnificent city than Alexandria, something worthy of our capital city. Even the splendid temple and forum I am having constructed now would appear ordinary in the Rome of the future. There

What really happened?

will be more marble and stone, less wood; there will be wider streets, fewer alleys; public gardens will abound. Finally, there will be libraries where anybody, senator or slave, scholar or butcher, Roman or foreigner, could walk into and find a book to read."

Even the sixty-nine year old and cynical Varro could not help but be transfixed by this image. He was hoping that his astonishment was not showing on his face.

"That is where you come in, my learned and distinguished friend" said Caesar.

"Me, Caesar? What would an old scribbler do in the midst of all this rising marble and stone?"

Caesar replied with his arms flung wide. "The libraries, Varro, the libraries! There are things about libraries that are much more important than marble and stone."

Caesar allowed that to sit for a while in Varro's mind. Somebody as wise as Varro he hoped would be quick to understand.

"Yes, the things in the library are so much more valuable than the building," Varro finally replied. "It is true that I would be at home among those shelves of scrolls and reading tablets. I do know something about books. Is this where you are leading, Caesar?"

"Yes, of course. Someone needs to fill the libraries of Rome with the books of the world."

"Caesar, I think you are suggesting a very congenial task for this old man. I am amazed by the magnitude of your vision."

Varro seemed to think for a while, then smiled and shook his head. Then said: "I will use whatever I have left in me to help you make it a reality."

"I knew you would feel that way, my good Varro," Caesar said with a smile. "I want you to travel to Alexandria, this time as my special representative. Take with you other scholars, dozens of scribblers, architects and the like. Travel slowly and carefully in our best ships

What really happened?

and only in the right season. Then when you get there study the Library - how the scrolls are arranged; the hallways; the gardens; the statues. Then go over to the Academy and do the same. Put the scribblers to work to copy whatever you think we should have. Then visit the smaller libraries that the Alexandrians have in their different quarters and study them. Finally, come back to Rome and supervise the construction, staffing, and stocking of even a greater system than exists in Alexandria."
Varro stared in wonder at the calm face of Caesar for a few moments. Their eyes met and then both of them smiled. Varro wondered why he had never before understood this marvel of a man.

XXXVII

After Caesar had left Cicero in Brundisium in September of 47 he took the Appian Way for the most part up to Rome, with several detours to visit important cities not on that road and in one case to confront his mutinying legions in Campania.

All along the route he was greeted by throngs of people welcoming his return, but also beseeching him for one thing or another. Thus he promised the town fathers in Venusia that he would have experts in Rome prepare a template for a constitution for their town. In fact he would later send the template to most of the other towns in Italy and the provinces, which would use them to write their own constitutions, thus insuring uniformity of government at the local level. In Luceria he promised to send engineers from Rome to reconstruct their viaducts damaged by a recent earthquake.

Upon approaching the rebellious veterans near Capua he told his bodyguards and the rest of his entourage to remain behind. His staff was concerned because the mutineers had already killed two tribunes who had been sent by Antony to negotiate with them. But he insisted. Thus he entered their camp alone on his white stallion and

What really happened?

was immediately recognized by the astounded soldiers. He slowly trotted through their midst, greeting by name many of the officers and centurions, until every soldier learned that their commander had arrived and that he was alone. Instinctively many dozens of veteran centurions drew a protective circle around him and moved with him to a high spot in the camp.

Facing many thousands of soldiers, he remained silent for a long time. Then he spoke to them. In every previous speech to such a gathering of soldiers, before every battle and afterwards, he would start by addressing them as "Comrades."

Now his first word of address was: "Citizens," after which he paused for a long time. Instantly the veterans understood. They were no longer considered as comrades by their great and beloved commander. He was dismissing them from the army—something they had been clamoring for. Yet now that one word: "citizens" struck them like a thunderbolt. From every quarter shouts began to ring out until it became a great clamor: "We are not citizens. We are your soldiers!"

They begged to be forgiven and asked Caesar to discipline them for their mutinies and disturbances if he wanted by employing the ancient practice of executing every tenth man. Caesar declined this ancient draconian measure. He had never in his many years ever used it on his troops.

But he did demote the ringleaders that he had been informed about and those men soon found themselves discharged from the army. He again promised the veterans their bonuses and land to farm on, but only after he and they together finished off the enemy army that had gathered in Africa. One more battle, he swore, and then you will be rich and free. The soldiers, who an hour earlier had been deeply angry and resentful, the same soldiers who had killed two tribunes sent to them by Antony,

What really happened?

cheered Caesar and professed their continuing loyalty and willingness to serve.

With that he returned to his entourage and continued to Rome.

In Rome the Senate again voted him dictatorial powers and many other honors, more than he cared for. He sacked Antony as Master of the Horse and several others of his appointees who had allowed matters in Rome to fall into such disorder while he was away. Antony would not regain Caesar's favor for two years.

Caesar immediately embarked on a multitude of visionary reforms, which he continued to the day he died, intended to achieve a number of goals. He wanted physically to remake Rome itself into a grander, more refined and resplendent city fitting to be the capital of a world power; the large number of landless and poor veterans had to be put to profitable work or given land in Italy or the provinces to begin new lives; the poor had to be put to work at wages that could support growing families; the base from which military recruits would come had to be expanded by the granting of citizenship to more localities and the establishment of colonies in Italy and in the provinces; and he wanted to rationalize the relationship of the provinces to Rome and end the rapacious practices of the Roman governors assigned to the provinces.

So he had laws passed providing for land distributions to the poor; special incentives in money and land were given to larger families; work was begun on draining nearby marshes to produce more farmland; scholars were put to the task of codifying the multitude of conflicting Roman laws; massive road and building projects were begun; the Senate was expanded to nine hundred members and new senators appointed from the equestrian class, freedmen, the army and the provinces. He introduced a new calendar that finally correlated the seasons with the traditional holidays and eliminated the need to add days

What really happened?

arbitrarily to the year every so often. Another example of his legislation to benefit the poor was the bill that required the great landowners to employ free man for at least one third of their workforce, as most of the big landowners by this time had come to rely exclusively on slave labor.

Even his enemies did not criticize many of his administrative activities, though they did grumble that he was doing it without their participation. Further, many of the more conservative senators, including Cicero, resented mightily the generous grants of citizenship to the rest of Italy and Sicily and the induction into the Senate of freedmen and provincials, particularly Gauls, Britons, and Germans.

Notwithstanding the urgency of these tasks, he still had to deal with the remnants of the military opposition to his rule. He had sent generals with armies to Africa and Spain, but one after another failed to put an end to the stubborn resistance in those theaters. So eventually he himself went, first to Africa and then later to Spain.

XXXVIII

While Caesar was in Africa in April of 46 BC, where he would defeat Scipio and Juba at Thapsus and where Cato would later commit suicide in Utica, a small fleet carrying Cleopatra, her son Caesarion, and her court had arrived and disembarked at Ostia, the port serving Rome.

After settling in at one of Caesar's more secluded and expansive villas across the Tiber from Rome as he had advised her, she left Caesarion under the charge of Zeno and took a number of her ladies on a pilgrimage to the giant temple in Praeneste some miles east of Rome. Antony had reintroduced himself to the queen upon her arrival, reminding her that he was a cavalry officer with the forces of Gabinius when they restored her father to the throne in Alexandria.

Of course she was only a child then and would not remember one officer among many. Antony was still on the outs with Caesar and hoped that by catering to Cleopatra he could get himself into Caesar's good graces. Except his insistence in providing her with a large cavalry bodyguard, paid for by himself, was not the way to please her. His presumption that she needed his protection only irritated her.

What really happened?

Though she would have preferred to travel quietly, she acquiesced to this vain but magnificent looking man's wishes that he accompany them. She was more interested in avoiding delay and unnecessary conflict at this stage. After all, though the Queen of Egypt, she was still their guest as were many of the other visiting sovereigns she noticed in Rome.

Praeneste was home to the largest temple in Italy, a sanctuary for the followers of Fortuna Primigenia, an ancient Italian god. Over the centuries the sanctuary grew to resemble more a Hellenistic edifice in the east than anything Roman. It occupied a series of five vast terraces, built into the rock of a hill, which were connected by grand staircases, on the top of which stood the magnificent Fortuna temple itself. This temple could be seen from great distances away, even from Rome. Just east of the Fortuna temple was an associated but clearly subject building, a substantial oblong hall, which was Cleopatra's ultimate destination on this day. This hall was decidedly more Hellenistic than the other buildings and even had a large mosaic of the Nile running along its entire length. In the far end of the hall stood the deity being worshipped here, the Egyptian goddess Isis.

"When I came to Rome with my father," Cleopatra whispered to her two favorite ladies, Kassandra and Sophia, "I was eleven years old and my governess took me here. My father was engrossed in dealings to convince the Romans to help him get his kingdom back and I was left alone most of the time with my guardians. We would often come here, especially to visit that building over there. It is dedicated to our own goddess Isis."

"My Queen," Kassandra said. "I notice that there are mostly women here. Is Fortuna a special god for women?"

"Yes," answered Cleopatra, "and the priestesses often exhort the worshipers to remember that they are equal to men, if not better."

What really happened?

"Equality for women! In Rome?" whispered Sophia with a laugh. "The men here strut about like stallions and are so dismissive of their women."

"The women of Rome," answered Cleopatra, "do wield some power, but only over their husbands and only in their homes. They cannot control any major decisions, but they are respected in their homes by their husbands, brothers, and sons, who do by force of circumstances take their opinions into consideration, though they would never admit that to their Senate colleagues. Notwithstanding such domestic influence, I agree that Roman society is very much a man's world. In fact the Senate, all men of course, has often tried to suppress the cult of Fortuna Primigenia, but without success. You will begin to feel the oppressive nature of this culture the longer you are in Rome."

"Then I hope," Kassandra interjected, "that our stay will be short, if I may be allowed to say, my Queen."

"Of course, Kassandra," Cleopatra answered midly. "You know I want you to speak freely to me. But I am afraid our stay here will not be as short as you may wish. Caesar wants Caesarion and me by his side until he can complete his preparations for a Parthian campaign. He has some notion that Caesarion will be more Roman, and acceptable as such by the Romans, if he suckles on his milk in Rome rather than in Alexandria.

"At some point," she continued, "probably depending on the Parthian preparations, we will travel east again, with him, and return home while he journeys on with his armies to Parthia.

"But that will not be for some time. He still has to deal with his diehard enemies in Africa and Spain, and he says he also has much more to do in Rome."
Her two ladies could only look at each other and sigh.

XXXIX

"My Queen," announced Kassandra, "you have visitors. It is the Senator Cicero, his friend Atticus and Cicero's secretary Tiro. Are you available for them?"

Cleopatra's eyes rolled up, as this must be Cicero's tenth visit. Always seeking some favor or other. "Yes, I am, Kassandra. But give me a few minutes to bring Ammonius up to date and then show them in."

Ammonius was considered an ancient man in age and had been Egypt's long-time ambassador to Rome. He had served in that capacity for Cleopatra's father, Ptolemy XII, and now for her.

"It seems to me, Ammonius," she said to her senior diplomat, "that I have already seen every one of the Senate's nine hundred members, and their families as well. I find it amusing how these Romans, who brag about being so independent and powerful, simply crawl over here and throw themselves down before me in the most embarrassing way, just in the hope that Caesar would learn of it. This Cicero has not been an exception, though he arrives with a chip on his shoulder and a touch of arrogance, which I attribute to his looking down on the eastern sovereigns in general."

What really happened?

"Yes," said Ammonius. "He's a most curious case. Caesar respects him greatly for his oratory skills and his literary works and certainly Cicero also wants to be seen as friendly to Caesar, flattering him in public oftentimes. But I sense something dishonest about this man. From what I have heard about his private conversations from our Greek friends in the households of the Roman nobles, his hatred of Caesar is deep-seated. However, notwithstanding that, I would suggest that you continue to treat him courteously as you have all the others. But beware. He might be troublesome, no matter what you do."

"For the sake of Jupiter! You are being so melodramatic, Ammonius. I trust you and rely on you, but this old man does seem harmless, though a bit of a nuisance. I know that he is no friend of Caesar. I have also been able to put ears into many of the great houses here in Rome, so I hear much of what they say to each other. Of course I have not been able to penetrate their deepest conferences, but I do get reports back on what they generally say to each other over wine or meals. They seem to be forever pining over the glories and freedoms of the 'Old Republic.' What they really mean is that they miss the absolute stranglehold they used to have on Rome before Caesar."

"Cicero's latest obsession," remarked Ammonius, "is to mock Varro's work in Alexandria. He tries out different forms of mockery, all intended to put down Caesar's idea of public libraries. 'So now,' he would say, 'slaves will be able to read books on how to rebel,' and things of that sort. He says that 'the decent and honorable men' of Rome already have full access to any book they may want in the private libraries of their friends. It is, according to him, a shameful waste of public funds, and perhaps destabilizing, to provide books to the vulgar and working class, much less to freedmen and slaves."

"That may be," replied Cleopatra, "but once here he

What really happened?

has nothing but praise for Caesar. And along with that praise he seems never to run out of favors to request for himself or his friends. What a grubber. One day he asks that a certain student of his be given special privileges in the Library at Alexandria; then on another day he asks for some unusual treatment for his son and friends visiting Alexandria; then on another day he would like me to appoint one of his Greek slaves to a position in my court, someone who he has not even freed yet! Once he almost came close to demanding that I mobilize the entire Egyptian Army to track down and return some poor slave of his who had escaped.

"It seems this poor slave, Dionysius," Cleopatra continued with some amusement, "had been in charge of Cicero's library at Tusculum, so Cicero was particularly incensed. I heard from Ruffio in Alexandria that he had also been asked by Cicero to use the Roman troops there to search throughout the city and surrounding districts for his Dionysius. Imagine searching in Alexandria for a 'Dionysius'! You'd soon collect warehouses of them. Ruffio writes that he has just ignored these presumptuous requests.

"All of these efforts by Cicero just to bring that poor soul back to read aloud some Horace or Homer for Cicero and his friends in his garden. Now he is here again today, and I dread to hear what he wants from me. He certainly must feel confident about Caesar's feelings toward him. Ah, here they come now."

"Greetings, great Queen of Egypt," Cicero almost shouted as he drew near. Sometimes he forgot that he was in a private house and not on the rostrum. "It is a distinguished honor," he went on in the same loud voice, "to be in your presence again. Greetings also to you, my good friend Ammonius."

Cicero's companion, Atticus, had known the queen for some time and was actually more conversant with her than

What really happened?

Cicero. In Rome she sometimes called on him for some financial or trading information that he always seemed to have. His commercial contacts around the world, she had found, were unmatched. More importantly, he seemed to have some magical way of being on good terms with every faction in Rome.

"It is always good to see you, Senator Cicero," Cleopatra responded.

They then all engaged in some talk about the weather, the progress on the building of Caesar's new forum and temple, structures whose magnificence had never before been seen in Rome, not even matched by Pompey's great theater. They shared some wine, grapes and olives. Eventually Cicero got to his reason for coming.

"While conversing with the great Caesar in Brundisium last year he happened to mention his astonishment to have found a hundred and fifty original works of Aristotle in your library."

"Yes," Cleopatra said neutrally, suspecting what was to come. "We have been fortunate in our inheritance of Aristotle's personal library and works."

Atticus and Ammonius looked at each other with a bit of trepidation, as they both also suspected what Cicero was about to request. Tiro, who must have known his master's plans, merely looked down at the floor.

"As you of course know," Cicero went on, "I have been a great admirer and student of Greek literature and philosophy."

"You are often mentioned and praised in the Academy," Cleopatra commented.

"Yes, Caesar has told me. That is very flattering. Yet I envy those scholars at the Academy who can walk just a few steps and be in the midst of all the manuscripts of the ancients. But at my age it is not easy to travel, particularly to far away places like Alexandria. My Queen, I must confess that I have a burning desire to see and feel the

What really happened?

original scrolls of Aristotle and Plato. Not copies, some of which I have, but the original manuscripts in their own hands. How much more one can tell about a person when you can gaze at his actual handwriting and contemplate its curves and contours. It is almost like having him in your own gardens."

Everyone else in the room closed his eyes and took a deep breath, except for Cleopatra who kept her eyes on Cicero with what appeared to be a pleasant expression on her face.

"This, dear and mighty Queen, brings me to a modest favor that I ask of you. I would like to borrow those one hundred and fifty original manuscripts of Aristotle. I can wait a while for Plato's works. Doing this little thing for me will be of no extra cost to you, thanks to the wise and wonderful commission that Caesar has given Varro. Some of Varro's people are always coming back and forth. I understand that Caesar is having them all travel first class, on the best and safest ships. On one of the voyages back to Rome they can add a couple of extra trunks to their baggage and have Aristotle's scrolls delivered to my house on the Palatine."

There ensued such a palpable silence in the room that it almost shattered the ears of everyone, except for Cicero, who kept smiling at the queen.

Finally Cleopatra replied in a voice without any inflection: "We will see what can be done about that, my dear Cicero. I will have to speak to the director of the library about the logistics when I get back to Alexandria."

Only Cicero among those gathered in the room failed to understand what she was saying. So he plunged deeper into the abyss. "Oh, my Queen. No need to go to all that trouble. You have enough on your mind and I am sure you will also have hundreds of other things to do when you return to Alexandria. Just give me a letter of instructions to the Director and I will give it to one of Varro's people

What really happened?

returning to Alexandria."

Anyone but Cleopatra would have found herself backed into a corner and compelled to make clear to Cicero that his request was absurd. But instead she quickly rejoined. "Well Cicero, you make an excellent point. Since Ammonius here prepares all my letters of instruction to Alexandria, I will confer with him later today on this matter. Will you be staying for lunch in the garden with the other visitors?"

Cicero hesitated. He was not sure what her answer had been, confusing him with an offer of lunch with the crowd that was visiting her that day. He was about to ask her to clarify her answer when something in her eyes made him stop. Finally, he chose to accept her words as a promise to send those instructions.

"Thank you, my dear Queen. But Tiro and I have much to do. Perhaps Atticus may wish to stay for lunch. Again, thank you for your generosity."

XL

"Welcome back home," Calpurnia whispered into his ear as they embraced each other. "No matter how often you leave for a war, I can never get used to it. What a relief to see you home again, safe and sound, my dear Gaius."

"This matter in Africa took longer than I expected, my dear Callie," Caesar replied. "But it was not particularly dangerous. We have put an end to those sorry and obstinate people, though again at a heavy cost to the first families of Rome. I wish it had not been so.

"In Africa I finally questioned the long-term wisdom of my policy of clemency. I do not wish to kill these noble Romans, I love them and need them. But it seems that I pardon the same men over and over again, only to find them later arrayed in battle against me in some other place.

"So this time they went down almost to the last man. They fought bravely and honorably, perhaps knowing that there would be no more pardons."

"It seems," Calpurnia said as they released each other, "that Rome is full of your pardoned enemies who are falling over themselves to honor you. I find it difficult to trust these people."

"There is no need to trust them," Caesar replied. "We

What really happened?

can make good use of them without having to trust them. I will appoint them as governors of provinces or as praetors or even consuls so long as they work earnestly for Rome. Our Republic keeps growing, and it will grow much greater once I return to the east. I need these people and their families; I cannot do it with just my friends. Look at what my friends did for me in Rome while I was in Alexandria. What a mess I found upon my return."

"Speaking of your friends," Calpurnia said, "the Queen and her son have settled nicely into your villa across the river. I have been over there several times and I must say that her Caesarion is a charmer, and so precocious. The only difficulty with her days, she told me, has been the coming and going of your sculptors who she feels are making too many demands on her time. She cannot understand why she must sit still for so long and have them gaze at her. She told me that an Egyptian artist would just need to glance once at his subject and then he could produce a perfect replica in stone, metal, marble or wood. She says your artists keep reminding her that these were your orders, so she grits her teeth and bears with it."

Caesar could only smile at this. "When I see her tomorrow, I will make it a point to get her better adjusted to her task. After all, that is one of the reasons she is in Rome."

"As soon as she arrived in April," Calpurnia continued, "she and a few of her ladies went to the temple at Praeneste. I understand she has a special devotion to her goddess Isis."

"Yes," Caesar commented. "Some in Egypt even believe she is the incarnation of Isis. The people in the east tend to do things like that."

"Another of your friends," Calpurnia continued, "your Antony, I hear, was waiting at your villa for her arrival. Apparently he then insisted that she needed him and a cavalry group he had recruited to escort her to Praeneste.

What really happened?

He supposedly told her that Caesar would have it no other way and that the Queen of Egypt was never to be left unprotected."

"By Jupiter," Caesar said in exasperation at his troublesome friend Antony. "Sometimes he behaves like a fool. I did not give him any such instructions. In fact I have not talked to him since I removed him as Master of the Horse back in October. I wish he would use his money to pay for that house of Pompey that he took during the auction of Pompey's possessions. When I was told that he was not making any payments on it, I wrote him with instructions that he must follow all the auction rules, just like everyone else. At any rate, the Queen knows how to take care of herself and would look poorly on these masculine bravado theatrics. But what is done, is done.

"If it is okay with you, dear Callie, I will now go for a bath and take some exercises in the gym. I am stiff with all this riding. Then we can have a leisurely meal together. Have the cooks put together whatever you think best. I will have an appetite tonight."

XLI

The next day at his villa across the Tiber Caesar asked the queen. "Have you seen your sister since you're been here?"

"No, I don't think either Arsinoe or her Ganymede would appreciate any visit from me in their present circumstances. What do you intend to do with them? I understand that you Romans strangle your leading captives after parading them around in some circus-like celebration of a victory."

"You do like to mock our traditions," he said without any trace of irritation. "Be that as it may, the people look forward to these events. They get plenty of wine and food, wonderful spectacles that often display unique things from foreign lands and of course can thereby participate proudly in the triumph of Roman might over her enemies. In addition the troops look forward to them eagerly. Much of the booty will be distributed to them and many will finally get their discharge and grants of land. My wars, from Gaul, Germany, and Britain down to Alexandria, Zela, and the most recent in Thapsus over Scipio in Africa, are probably the grandest in the history of Rome. The celebrations next month will reflect that. As for your sister, she will be

What really happened?

featured in one of the four triumphs, along with other mementoes from my Egyptian campaign."

"Will she die at the end of the parade?" Cleopatra asked, "along with that giant Gaul, Vercingetorix?

"By the way I did visit Vercingetorix. What a fine specimen of a man! The house you have him imprisoned in looks like the villa of a wealthy Roman and has all its comforts, with gardens, a library, a bath, and numerous slaves, except that it is surrounded by high walls and guarded by soldiers twenty-four hours a day. Nor, of course, is he allowed ever to venture forth. His house is even more sumptuous than the one you have provided for my sister and Ganymede. It seems you respect him highly. But must he really die?"

"Who is this 'he' you refer to?" asked Caesar teasingly. "Are you so concerned about the eunuch Ganymede?"

"Ha, ha," Cleopatra replied sardonically, "don't play with me. You know whom I mean. The Gaul seems like such a noble creature. It is sad that he is to die. He has already suffered much from being imprisoned all these years."

"That is our custom," Caesar commented, showing no emotion on his face. "But it is different with your sister. I do not think the Roman people celebrating my victories next month will want to see a beautiful woman executed. They could not imagine that she actually was such a vicious enemy and a military leader.

"So after the celebrations I will probably send her and her entourage into exile on one of the Greek islands. I cannot risk having her continue to live in the villa she has occupied here in Rome. Crowds of Greeks and Egyptians would soon gather around her and make her a symbol of one thing or another. Nor can she be trusted in Alexandria. Your little sister is a born troublemaker."

Cleopatra coldly commented: "Do what you want with her, but she must be nowhere near Egypt or I will not be

What really happened?

as merciful as you to that witch."

At that moment Zeno arrived in the garden followed by little Caesarion, excitedly tottering along with his arms flaying about. Caesar got up and stood there awaiting the child's arrival.

"Greetings Zeno," he said, embracing the multi-talented man who was now in his guise as tutor. "Your little charge certainly is making progress."

Caesarion finally reached Caesar, who picked him up and kissed him.

"Well, son," he said, "what have you learned today?"

Responding for the laughing child, Zeno interjected, "Give me a few more days, Caesar, and he will be reciting one of Horace's odes."

"I did not expect it should take so long, my good Zeno. But seriously, have you been satisfied with his progress?"

"Yes, Caesar, he seems to understand more things every day, much more than his playmates."

"His playmates?" asked Caesar.

"Only the most precocious and advanced little ones that I could find among your friends. They are here every day and their association is good for all of them."

"Zeno," Caesar said, "you mention the children of my friends?"

"Yes, Caesar?" replied a puzzled Zeno.

"Zeno," Caesar said, "my friends, as dear as they are to me, do not have any special hold on precocious children. Please broaden your net. Look to those whom you assume are not my friends. I want Caesarion to see and live with the best progeny of Rome, not just the best of my friends."

Zeno shook his head and rolled his eyes. "My Caesar, is there no end to your wisdom. I should have thought of that. Of course. I will see to it."

"Thank you, Zeno. He has not spoken yet, but when he does, remember that I . . ."

What really happened?

Zeno this time interrupted. "Yes. Yes. I know. He is to speak like a Roman; also as a Greek; then also as an Egyptian—all without an accent from any of the other. We all remember your instructions. And we are dedicated to that. But of course he has not yet spoken a word."

Caesar smiled and knew that he had put young Caesarion's education in the right hands.

"Good, and thank you," he said.

Zeno and his entourage, with Caesarion tottering along, soon departed for some more play and lessons.

When Caesar and Cleopatra were alone again, Caesar asked: "I understand, Cleo, that you have been impatient with the sculptors."

"Oh Gaius, what a nuisance they are. Showing up at all hours and insisting that I sit still or stand forever like a statue."

"Well, you are modeling for a statue."

"Gaius, don't try to be funny. I wish you would put an end to it."

"I'll talk to them. Any news from Agatha?"

Cleopatra had left Alexandria in the trusted and capable hands of Agatha and Apollonios who coordinated easily with Ruffio and the Roman legions stationed there by Caesar.

"Gaius," she replied in faked exasperation: "Why do you always pretend not to know anything! Ruffio must be sending you reports almost every day."

"Not every day," was his dry comment.

"Very well. Of course you are most interested in the metal fabrications. She tells me that they have been able to send regular shipments of arrows, helmets, shields and swords up to your people in Apollonia. She cannot tell me what happens there, but then you must be hearing from your legates. The factories still seem to have been unnoticed by the Alexandrians, or at least the purpose of the factories. The Parthians have been true to their word

What really happened?

and have been delivering to "King Juba's" agent regular amounts of ore, though they have recently increased the price. I hope word of his demise in the African wars from which you have just returned does not reach them very soon. Agatha says we'll need a couple more shipments before your requirements have been met."

At this point their conversation had to end as young Caesar came toddling into the room, followed by Zeno and some women slaves.

"My apologies," said Zeno, "but he seems to think he is a Caesar. He goes where he wants."

"Well, I see so little of him as it is," Caesar said as he picked up his son. "Perhaps he is right. We need to be together more often. Why don't we all go into the garden and have some lunch. Zeno, please join us and give us the gossip from your friends."

Cleopatra was just beginning to get used to the absence of visits from the sculptors when in the following week Kassandra

"Yes," Caesar replied. "Word from Apollonia is that shipments have been arriving regularly. For the time being everything is being stored in out-of-the-way warehouses. No need to let the world know about this until we have to. The story is different with the crossbows, however. As soon as Balbus' friends in Epirus deliver a batch of crossbows to my legates in Apollonia, they are immediately distributed to the archers for training. We have to risk their being discovered by spies because the weapon is so unusual that it takes a lot of practice to utilize its full, and mighty, potential. Heavens, do I owe so much to Liang. By the way, Cleo, are he and Bao being kept safe and happy?"

"Of course, Gaius. I love them as much as you do. In addition, they offer such an unusual and valuable perspective to the academy. They are also very well liked and respected by the other scholars in the academy. Ever since I had that Chinese soldier executed, I have had

What really happened?

bodyguards watching out for them discretely. But the priest in charge of the academy and the director of the library already have pretty strict screening as to who can get into those buildings.

"And Agatha tells me that Liang and Bao are getting along famously with Varro and that armada of scholars, scribblers and architects he has brought from Rome on your project. Though both the priest at the academy and the library's director have bitterly complained about the noisy intrusion of this army. But I have promised them some special rewards for being patient with our guests until they finish their task. But the one thing I have backed them up on, otherwise I would have a revolution on my hands, is that Varro and his people will not be allowed to remove any original scrolls. They can copy all they please, even our most ancient and treasured manuscripts, but always under the eyes of our people. They are not to remove as much as a single original sheet. Varro has commented on the physical searches his people have to go through when they both enter and leave the Library, but Agatha says he understands and has been very cooperative.

"By the way, Gaius, speaking of original manuscripts, I must tell you later about that strange friend of yours, Cicero."

"Ah, I hear he has been here often," said Caesar. "I hope he has not made a nuisance of himself. He does get carried away sometimes."

"Yes, but the story is so amusing I must save it for dinner. Will you be staying for dinner?"

"Yes, tonight I will."

"Gaius, while on the subject of your library project, let me ask you a question that I have been curious about. Most of the slaves Varro brought with him to Alexandria are Greek teachers and scholars. Aren't you afraid that they will just walk out of the library and into Alexandria and disappear among the Greeks of my city? They of

What really happened?

course will be impossible to find after that. Not the least of all because of the assistance they would undoubtedly receive from the Greeks of Alexandria."

"Naturally," Caesar responded, "that was expected to happen with a number of them. But, so what? They most likely in the near future would have been given their freedom in any event and could walk off at that time if they so desired. This may just accelerate the process for some of them. But Varro tells me the Greek slaves are happy to be working in the most fabulous Greek library in the world and very few would even dream of taking off. They also know that their own personal freedom is not far off. In addition, he says that most of them believe in the project I have envisioned for Rome and they want to be part of bringing it to fruition.

"Varro, by the way, seems to have taken up his task with gusto. I am very pleased and frankly amazed at the old man's stamina. Were you still in Alexandria when he arrived?"

"Yes," Cleopatra answered, "I was. He immediately asked for an audience and he sat down with me for some time explaining what he needed. He has such an organized way of thinking. No wonder he has produced countless books. I called in the director and the priest and issued instructions to them while Varro was there. He was very pleased. He commented about how different things were now for him compared to when he first visited the library as a young student. A charming man, and so knowledgeable. I think we must have talked about every subject under the sun for the short time both of us were in Alexandria. You picked the right man for the job, Gaius, provided he lives long enough."

"Ah, provided we all live long enough."

"Now, Gaius, please stop saying things like that. You know how I hate such fatalism."
"Sorry."

CAESAR, CICERO & CLEOPATRA

What really happened?

XLII

Rome celebrated an unprecedented four triumphs for Caesar. After those triumphs in which all his veterans legions had marched, he discharged nearly all of them. They finally received their long-promised bonuses and plots of land, either in Rome or the provinces, sufficient to start a new life.

Agriculture was still the basis of the Roman economy. In addition, the farmers and their sons were still the primary recruiting ground for Rome's armies, though since Marius's time more use was made of the urban poor. Much of what Caesar did in this whirlwind of legislative activity was directed at strengthening and broadening these elements of Roman society.

It was about that time that Caesar's father-in-law, Piso, at a regular meeting of the Senate, raised the issue of recalling Marcellus from exile. This Marcellus had been the consul of 51 who had, perhaps as much as any other individual helped precipitate the civil war. He had demanded that Caesar immediately be replaced as governor in Gaul, thus immediately losing his immunities as an official and exposing Caesar to legal prosecution by his enemies, who were waiting for such an event. Then he

What really happened?

had publicly flogged an official of the Roman colony of Novum Comum that had been founded by Caesar in Transalpine Gaul. This flogging was contrary to a fundamental Roman custom protecting people with citizenship. It was intended as a very public insult to Caesar who was known as the protector of Transalpine Gaul.

Upon Calpurnia's father's motion, Caesar stood up and carefully laid out the offences thus committed by Marcellus and vowed never to let that scoundrel back into Rome.

"Marcellus," said Caesar, "and his family have immense estates in Greece. I am sure he is living in luxury and comfort, though in exile. So let it be and I do not begrudge him his luxury. But he has done enough damage to Rome and I will not allow him to come back here."

Now Cicero, to the surprise of many, rose from his seat and asked to be heard. This was unusual. For the past six years Cicero had been silent in the Senate, understanding that his side had lost and that it was best to be silent. But now, roused by the emotions of the Marcelli family, and the fate of this exiled Metellus, whom he truly admired, he asked to be heard on the subject.

Caesar looked at him for a moment and then said, "Dear Cicero, when would any rational person refuse the opportunity to listen to the voice of the most eloquent man in Rome? Please, let us hear from you."

Cicero then delivered an impassioned plea in defense of Marcellus, begging that he be allowed to return to his home and family in Rome.

Caesar had closed his eyes and listened with pleasure to the voice of Cicero. He followed his arguments, his modulations of voice, his subtle and not so subtle arguments. It was a pleasure to listen to such an eloquence which surpassed anything he had read or heard in Latin before.

What really happened?

Caesar was still lost in the eloquence of Cicero's voice when he realized that the senators around him were beseeching him to respond. He recovered quickly and decided just as quickly. He will do this for Cicero, he thought.

The Dictator stood. Then after a moment, he nodded his head, indicating assent to the motion to recall Marcellus.

The entire Senate, as much persuaded by the eloquence of Cicero as Caesar had been, erupted into a chorus of cheers and applause.

Cicero, moved, stood and said: "For such exceptional kindness, such unprecedented and unheard of clemency, such extraordinary moderation in someone who has attained absolute power over everything, and such astonishing and, one might almost say, superhuman wisdom— these are things I cannot possibly pass over in silence.... So what you have done for me, Gaius Caesar, is to open up my former way of life from which I had become debarred, and for all the others here present, to raise a standard, as it were, for optimism regarding the future of our country.

"As for your own deeds, Gaius Caesar, no genius could be abundant enough, no pen or tongue sufficiently eloquent and fluent, to embellish them or even to describe them. . . . I am continually aware, and I constantly tell others, that all the exploits of Roman generals and foreign powers combined, all the achievements of the most potent nations and illustrious monarchs in the world, fall short of what you have achieved: so enormous was the magnitude of your enterprises, and the number of your battles, and the lightning rapidity with which you acted, and the immense diversity of the military operations involved. No one else upon this earth could have traversed all those widely separated lands with the amazing speed with which you marched—or rather, I should say, with which you

What really happened?

conquered. But to conquer one's own heart, to curb one's anger, to show restraint in victory, to raise up a prostrate enemy . . . the hero who acts in this way I do not venture to compare to the greatest of mankind, because he seems to me to resemble a god.

"Your fame in war, Gaius Caesar, will be celebrated by the literature and eloquence of our own country and, one may safely add, of every nation in the world. There will never be a time when your praises are no longer sung.

"You had already outdone all previous conquerors in civil war by your fairness and leniency; and today you have outdone even yourself. It seems to me that what you have done is to vanquish Victory, since everything that Victory had placed in your hand you have let the vanquished have back. By the law of conquest, we on the losing side could well have perished. But by your mercy you have deliberately saved us. You are therefore invincible in the most accurate sense of the word, since you have conquered the savage law of Victory itself."

Cicero then made reference to the many rumors going about Rome about plots to assassinate Caesar and Caesar's often quoted remark that he did not worry as he had lived long enough.

"That is why," Cicero continued, "I was so distressed to hear your remark, sage and splendid though it is, 'Whether for nature or for glory, I have lived long enough.'

"Certainly not long enough for your country, and that is the most important point of all! Do not, by being wise yourself, imperil us! The welfare of every Roman citizen and the whole state has become dependent on what you do.

"And consequently all those of us who are devoted to the welfare of our country urge and entreat you to take good care of your life and your personal safety. Moreover, I know I am speaking for my colleagues when I add a further conviction of my own. Since you feel there is some

What really happened?

hidden danger to guard against, we promise you sentinels and bodyguards. And we swear we will protect you ourselves with our own breasts and bodies."
Caesar did not mean to be unkind, but he could only wonder about the effectiveness of these feeble "breasts and bodies" that would be arrayed in his defense.

XLIII

A month later, October, 46 BC, Caesar presided at the consecration of the magnificent Forum Iulius and the Temple of Venus Genetrix that he had been constructing for several years. These buildings, even more magnificent than Pompey's theater, until then the greatest building in Rome, would foreshadow the grand and monumental style into which Rome would grow under Augustus.

For the first time ever in Rome a golden statue of the familiar Venus, by legend an ancestor of the founders of Rome, as well as of the Julii family of Caesar, stood only several feet away from a golden statue of the Egyptian goddess, Isis. Caesar was by this extraordinary gesture preparing his fellow Romans for the evolution of the Roman Republic as he envisioned it. The Republic was now much more than Rome, or Italy, or even the Mediterranean, but would extend to lands to the east as yet unheard of.

Here, literally, the West met the East and lived in peace together. This was Caesar's message to the people of Rome, and the fact that Isis bore a remarkable resemblance to Cleopatra did not diminish that message.

That evening Caesar sought a respite from all the

What really happened?

ceremonies by taking a light meal by himself in his garden. When he saw his friend Balbus approaching, he was surprised but not disturbed even though he had given instructions that he was to be left alone. Balbus was almost family and was always welcome.

Balbus seemed to be uneasy as he approached Caesar and did not sit in the chair proffered by Caesar. He took a deep breath and then spoke.

"My friend, I am the bearer of bad news. I am sorry. Yesterday we received dispatches from Asia, but I wanted to wait until after the ceremonies to inform you. Forgive me for that decision, but I thought it best."

Caesar looked up and gazed at Balbus. His silent stare told Balbus that he had to continue, and so he did.

"Your cousin, the legate Sextus in Antioch, has been assassinated. He was killed during a mutiny of his troops. The first word is that the mutiny was led by a former Pompeian officer who had had infiltrated Sextus' legion. He is called Caecilius Bassus and he has been hiding out since Pharsalus in the free city of Tyre.

"It seems that many of Sextus' troops would routinely vacation in Tyre on their off. This Bassus made it his business to spend time with them. He knew many of them as he had served with them under Pompey. Apparently, after Pharsalus he has been operating more or less as a bandit out of Tyre with a small force of other former Pompeian soldiers. Somehow he succeeded in turning Sextus' legion against him with all sorts of lies, bribery and claims on former friendships."

Balbus fell silent and watched Caesar.

But Caesar only continued to stare at him without showing any emotion. Balbus forced himself to continue, for he had more bad news to deliver. "At the same time, Caesar, the dispatches also informed us that our ally Mithridates has been killed. There was an uprising in his capital and a usurper sits now on his throne."

What really happened?

Caesar at this point did raise his eyebrows, though ever so slightly. The two cornerstones of my eastern frontier, he thought. Both gone so suddenly. And my beloved Sextus. . . Sextus. . . Fortune, I do not protest, but you are so fickle . . . and cruel.

XLIV

"They are being transported by sea to Italy. They will be given enough money to enable them to set themselves up comfortably in Rome and begin their campaign."

"How many are there?" Peng Tao asked his agent Li Long.

"There are forty-three of them. Each one is healthy and has not only withstood the rigors of our brainwashing but totally absorbed every one of our suggestions as if they were their own."

"There are only forty-three left of the thousand?" asked a surprised Tao. There was skepticism sounding in his question, and Long knew he was being challenged.

"Yes," Long nevertheless answered with confidence. "The rest o them, over the almost two years we have had them, have either been executed when they realized what was happening to them; or became so crazed from our indoctrination that we had to kill them. But as I said, these forty-three are healthy and will be vigorous promoters. That will be enough for my program to work."

Tao said nothing in reply, but looked hard at Long.

XLV

When Caesar's legates in Spain sent him urgent messages in March of 45 BC that they could not any longer contain Pompey's two sons, Gnaeus—or as he was more popularly known, Young Pompey — and Sextus, Caesar was forced to leave Rome and go to a theater of war that he had thought had already been closed.

As was his wont, Caesar, though mostly with only raw recruits since by now he had discharged most of his veterans, aggressively pursued the sons of Pompey, trying to force them into a pitched battle between their forces and end this.

But Pompey's sons, having witnessed the horrors of Pharsalus, were not at all anxious to meet Caesar face to face. Thus it took months of maneuvering through the hills and towns of Further Spain and numerous inconclusive skirmishes between small individual elements of the armies, before Caesar finally was able to force Young Pompey to stand and fight.

Gnaeus had been heading south to the sea with his forces, where he intended to join his large fleet and escape Caesar's pursuit, at least for the time being. But Caesar was able to move swiftly, recognizing what Pompey was

What really happened?

attempting, and got between Pompey and the sea. This compelled Pompey to entrench himself before the town of Munda, but on most favorable conditions.

Pompey set up camp in front of the friendly town of Munda, itself situated at the top of a hill, so that his camp looked down on a slope that eventually leveled out after some distance and ended at a brook. Caesar would have to cross that brook and then come uphill to get at him, a very formidable position to attack.

Though Pompey's position was strong, Caesar judged that he could not let this opportunity pass. Rarely had he allowed his army to commence a battle in such an unfavorable position, fighting uphill, but here he had to chance it. He had had enough of chasing these people.

At dawn the two sides drew up in battle formation and the fighting commenced.

The line of battle stretched over a mile and a quarter, three lines of troops on each side. The formations looked quite similar as both sides had been trained as Roman soldiers and were led by Roman officers. Caesar had been moving along the course, urging his men on and encouraging them.

The opposing sides had been clashing bitterly, front line against front line, for hours. The three lines had already been rotated on both sides and their first lines were again on the front. Whatever reserves either side had were already committed. Only Caesar's cavalry had had little activity. The battle could easily go either way. If there was a break anywhere along the mile and a quarter line, the entire front would immediately collapse and the retreating army would be slaughtered.

What was left of Caesar's veterans, after their wholesale discharge following the African campaign, was with the Tenth and Fifth Legions, with barely five hundred in each legion from their 4,800 full strength. He had put them on the right wing of his line along with recently recruited

What really happened?

legions and they had been holding their own. But in the center he had placed more raw recruits.

Thus it was while he was at the far left wing of the line when officers rushed up to announce that the center of the line was faltering. If they broke, it was all over. Hence he charged at full gallop to the center.

The enemy troops in the center had heard, coming from the other side, the distinctive sounds of the cornet above the clamor of shouts, screams and the clashing of swords upon swords and shields upon shields. Roman soldiers on both sides of the battle line in this civil war all knew what it meant. Caesar had arrived and was among them.

The soldiers in the battling front line could only see the opposing soldiers in their own front line, thrusting their swords over, under and to the sides of their shields. But the Pompeian officers, on horses behind their lines, were able to look down the slope, over their own lines, and see that Caesar's front line was about to break. It was at that moment that they heard the horns' sounds.

At the announcement that Caesar was among them, both opposing lines instinctively began to firm up. Finally the Pompeian officers were able to distinguish, through the clouds of dust over the battle line, the purple cloak of the Commander, billowing behind a fast-charging Caesar. He was on his familiar great white stallion and surrounded by officers and horn players.

But to the astonishment of the Pompeian officers Caesar came to an abrupt stop at the very center of his line, dismounted from his rearing horse and threw off his cloak. Taking a shield from one of his soldiers and brandishing his own sword above his head, Caesar ran to the front of the line, shouting about him as he moved forward.

The Pompeian officers could not believe their good luck. This madman was now actually in front of his own

What really happened?

line and alone. They sounded their own trumpets to direct javelins at Caesar and urged their men to move forward to surround him.

Caesar, shielding himself from the dozens of falling missiles, shouted to the men behind him:

"Will your children say only of you that you abandoned your commander to the enemy?"

No one moved, so he just pushed on upward.

So, this is how you die, Caesar, he thought to himself, as dozens of javelins continued to fall upon him. Nevertheless he continued to inch his way up the incline, with his shield, already festooned with broken missiles, over his head. Curious, but I feel nothing. It is all very simple. We are to take the enemy. He is up there. Therefore we go up. Those who follow me, follow me. Those who don't, don't. If I die, I die . . . so it is.

First it was his own staff officers, once recovered from their surprise, who likewise quickly dismounted, grabbed shields and followed Caesar. He was soon no longer alone. The cornets kept blaring, now joined by the trumpets and bucina sounding the charge. Startled and then roused by their commander's extraordinary actions, even the rawest recruits among his soldiers recovered their courage with a vengeance and with one shout moved up to join him and then move ahead of him, first pushing their commander between and then finally behind them as they clashed with the enemy. Finally the entire center moved forward.

Moving to the back of the three lines, the Commander retrieved his purple cloak and remounted his while stallion. He had thus halted the wavering center and brought it even again with his lines on the right and left. The threat of an imminent collapse and catastrophe had been avoided.

He was again mounted on his horse but still at the center of the mile and a quarter line when he learned that his veterans in the Tenth and Fifth on his right wing had

What really happened?

been able to drag their comrades forward and were now about to break the enemy's left.

At the same time, in the distance Caesar could now hear the enemy's trumpets sounding orders for a movement He knew immediately that young Pompey was ordering some troops from his own right wing to disengage, circle behind their lines and then go over to support his struggling left wing. Sure enough, within minutes a cloud of dust rose from the enemy's right, indicating a reverse movement as some of its forces were rushing to their left.

Though Caesar knew that Pompey was just transferring troops from one side to support another side, he immediately shouted to his staff that the enemy was retreating. He ordered his staff to go up and down the line and announce that the enemy was retreating and to urge the men forward. Again the trumpets sounded the charge.

The enemy soldiers on the front line also noticed the movement in their rear and at the same time heard their opponents yelling something about a retreat. In the confusion the false report quickly spread that their side was indeed in retreat. Soon the Pompeian line began to falter at various points as groups of soldiers joined in what they thought was a retreat.

Caesar then sent his cavalry, fresh and eager to fight, into both the right and left flanks of the enemy to hasten their collapse. The enemy lines buckled and disintegrated, it seemed as if in an instant. Panic now ruled in the enemy's ranks. A stampede and slaughter quickly ensued. At the end of the battle, the enemy left thirty thousand soldiers dead on the field; Caesar had lost a thousand.

For these enemy Roman officers and soldiers, who had already twice defected on him, he would show no mercy. He ordered a relentless pursuit of the retreating army and that no quarter be given. The men on the other side also knew they were doomed if they could not escape. Most of

What really happened?

the remaining twenty thousand Pompeians found temporary refuge in the allied towns of Munda and Cordoba. Caesar ordered a siege of one, and then of the other. Within weeks each one fell and Caesar allowed his troops to loot both towns, slaughtering the remaining Pompeian troop sheltering in them. He had had enough of these people.

Yet it would still take him a few more months to subdue the remaining parts of Further Spain and to reorganize its local governments. This time he wanted to make sure there were no more mutinies and betrayals. He emptied the treasuries of the cities that had opposed him, and rewarded those that had supported him. He promoted loyal people in each town and made sure that they were adequately protected.

In these activities after the battle of Munda, he had been joined for the first time by his nineteen-year-old grandnephew, Octavian. As he did with other relatives in the past, he took this enthusiastic youth with him and kept him close. On the long march back to Rome, Caesar introduced him to the leaders of various towns and cities while he made his dispositions. Recent allies to Rome he granted the Latin Rights, a precursor to Roman citizenship once certain criterion of Romaness had been achieved, such as the number of elite who spoke Latin, the reorganization of the civil and criminal courts, etc.. To others who had some time previously already been granted the Latin Rights and had become sufficiently Romanized, he granted citizenship.

Caesar was pleased to find his nephew as precocious and wise as he had heard the boy was. During parts of the journey he had himself carried in a litter with only Octavian with him. Caesar had always been a quick judge of men and it was during this journey that he decided that Octavian was worthy of cultivation, especially now that his beloved cousin, Sextus, was no longer alive. They spoke of

What really happened?

Rome and what Caesar perceived would be the future of the Roman Republic.

Caesar promised Octavian that he would play a major role in his campaign on the Danube and then in Parthia. For that reason he would soon transfer Octavian to Apollonia for further military training with the troops who were already in training for the campaigns. For the first time in a long time, Caesar felt he again had a relative competent enough to be with him in governing the Republic.

XLVI

Caesar, usually a marvel of speedy movements, now unaccountably took his time to return to Rome. Perhaps he was truly tired; perhaps he needed time alone to think; perhaps he was losing interest.

He stayed for a while in the familiar province of Transalpine Gaul where he had spent so many years, passing time as a guest of various friends. Then, upon approaching Rome he sent his forces ahead, along with most of his staff, including Octavian, while he lingered by himself with his bodyguards, now Spaniards from Balbus' hometown of Gades, at his villa in Lavicum, just outside Rome. There he prepared a new will.

While Caesar was deciding on the allocation of his estate among his relatives in the event of his death, not far away at the port of Ostia there arrived an unusual group of forty-three Roman soldiers with an extraordinary tale.

"You see the brand on our foreheads?" said the leader, Marius. "It says that we are the slaves of Parthia. You see this," he added, pointing to the opening on the right side of his head. "They removed our right ears to further brand us."

Marius was trying to explain to the confused Roman

What really happened?

port officials who they were.

"We were in the legions of the great Crassus which fought in Parthia. After Crassus was defeated at Carrhae, many of us, perhaps ten thousand, were made prisoners of the Parthians. We were herded like cattle to the farthest reach of the Parthian empire, a city called Antiochia. There we were branded and our right ears were cut off so that if we escaped it would be impossible to travel in Parthia.

"We had been working in Antiochia for some time," Marius continued, "building bridges, roads, aqueducts, and the other things that we Roman soldiers have learned to do, when the camp we were in was attacked by some nomads from the east. The guards were overwhelmed and a large number of us were taken prisoner by the nomads. We were forced to march many miles before we reached a seaport. At that seaport the prisoners were separated into several groups and the forty-three of us boarded one ship. As it happened it was captained by a Syrian merchantman on contract with the nomads.

"Heavens knows where the nomads had intended to take us, but the Syrian, on seeing that we were Roman soldiers, took pity on us and decided to betray his employers. Thus when we were out at sea he changed course. His ship had been well provisioned and we sailed for many days. How many, I do not know, but it seemed to go on forever. We stopped at various ports for provisions and water. During the voyage we recovered our wits and our strength. Finally, the ship arrived at Rhodes. The Syrian captain seemed to know his way around Rhodes and soon came back with an Italian merchant. I do not know what arrangements he made with the Italian merchant, but soon all forty-three of us were escorted to another ship, captained by this Italian merchant, and taken to sea. Thus we have arrived in Ostia."

By this time all the members of the city council had gathered about the new arrivals and had heard their story.

What really happened?

"If all you say is true," their leader said to Marius, "then you should be welcomed back to Rome with celebrations. I will send a message to Caesar's Master of Horse and ask for instructions. Meanwhile you all will be guests of the city. You will stay in our homes and spend time in the baths and the theater, getting used once again to being Romans."

"Thank you," Marius answered for the group. "But we are anxious to return to Rome and see our relatives and friends who must have thought we were dead. We also want to pay our respects to King Caesar."

"Now hold on here," the council leader said. "I understand that you may had gone through a great deal, but we have no king here in Rome. If you were a true Roman you would know how loathsome the idea of a king is to us."

Marius was taken aback and seemed confused. He thought it best to say nothing.

"In any event," the council leader, now more composed, said, "your story is so extraordinary that I must inform Rome and await instructions. I will send ahead each of your names so that your relatives will be alerted and I am sure an announcement of your remarkable escape will also be posted in the Forum. In that way you will be properly greeted when you get to Rome. So now, permit me to escort you to our city center. So much has to be done. You need to be fed; new garments have to be made; you need to learn what has happened in the Republic during the past eight years. Much has changed, and you should know these things. So please come along."

XLVII

"That friend of yours, Cicero, is such an intolerable bore," Cleopatra commented to Caesar over dinner soon after his return. "You will not believe what he asked of me, or I should say, 'demanded' of me, the other day."

"Cleo, dearest, " Caesar said, "you need to be particularly sensitive to that great man. He has been through a great deal. His decades-long marriage collapsed in anger last year and then his beloved and beautiful daughter Tullia died just this past February. She was the whole world to him."

"Gaius, don't be so foolish. He divorced Terentia to get his filthy old man's hands on his eighteen-year-old ward and her fortune. His marrying that child Publilia made him the laughingstock of Rome."

"As to the child's fortune," Caesar dryly responded, "perhaps it will mean that Cicero will repay me the loan I made to him. But tell me, what was it that so bothered you?"

"You were in Alexandria, Gaius," Cleopatra said, "and you spent much time in the library."

"Yes?" Caesar said.

"Then you understand how sacred those scrolls are to

What really happened?

Egypt. They were collected by my ancestors and we have made Alexandria the intellectual capital of the world. The older the scroll, the more jealously we guard it. Well, would you believe that that child predator friend of yours is not satisfied with just getting his hands on an eighteen-year-old but wants to get his hands on some of the oldest and most precious scrolls we have in our library. He want me to send him the original writings of Aristotle, and then of Plato! If I even though of doing such a thing my own court ladies would hang me from the balcony."

"I understand," said an amused, but not surprised, Caesar. "Such a request is truly insensitive. But then again I have heard that Cicero is not himself as of late. You must remember that he is already sixty-one years old, and was very much affected by his daughter Tulia's death. They say he is a changed man."

"Oh, Gaius, always making excuses for your friends. He is only six years older than you. Would you use your age as an excuse for anything?"

Caesar smiled and thought it best not to respond to that. Perhaps he might confess to Calpurnia that indeed he was beginning to feel a bit tired of these endless wars, betrayals and disappointments, but he was not going to say this to the Queen of Egypt. Instead he said: "I came close to the end at the battle in front of Munda. It made me think that I should set my affairs in order."

Cleopatra had heard of his close call from some members of his staff. That was who Caesar was and she would have to learn to accept it. She saw him do the same thing in Egypt. It was part of the magic that made him beloved by his men. But it also meant that those who loved him could never tell whether he would return.

"The Will that I have had for years leaves everything to Pompey," Caesar continued. "It was made when he was both my son-in-law and ally. Aside from everything else, of course, he is no longer with us. So I have rewritten it. This

What really happened?

is a copy." He handed her a scroll.

Cleopatra took the scroll and proceeded to read it. Caesar noticed that her eyebrows went up at a certain point. Finally, when she finished reading it she said simply: "Nothing about our son?"

Caesar looked directly at her, as he knew that this was an extremely important matter for both of them. "Cleo, as things are now, neither the great families of Rome nor the common people will accept the Queen of Egypt's son as the heir to Rome's Dictator. There will only be chaos and revolution. Perhaps circumstances will change in the future. Much depends on how long I live and how Caesarion develops as a Roman. But now, it would be dangerous for everybody and a disaster for Rome if I named him as my heir, as much as I would like to. Let some time go by and let us see if the future will allow me to do that."
Cleopatra said nothing but just stared into the distance. Caesar could only hope that she would understand.

XLVIII

"My dear Callie, why do you always cry when I return?" Caesar said as they embraced.

"The news from Spain for so many months," Calpurnia responded, "had been so frightening. Sometimes I wish that I could travel with you on these campaigns. It would be easier on my nerves."

"So now my wife wants to be a warrior. There were many great generals among your ancestors, but they were all men." No sooner had Caesar said this then he knew it was a mistake.

" 'All men'," Calpurnia said very slowly, mocking his words. "Would you dare say that to the Queen of Egypt?"

His dear Callie was so much more than she appeared to be, he thought. He wished for a moment for her that she had been born in the east where women had greater freedom and rights.

Caesar had been away for so long that he had almost forgotten how intelligent and swift Calpurnia was. That was in fact why he had courted and married her in the first place, aside from her distinguished family. But he understood that this conversation really was about his relationship with Cleopatra. His wife had shown no

What really happened?

resentment, notwithstanding all the gossip and the obvious attention Caesar paid to Cleopatra, not to speak of the existence of Caesarion. Indeed he heard that Calpurnia and Cleopatra had developed a form of friendship, seeing each other at least weekly since Cleopatra had arrived in Rome. Some kind of understanding must have developed between these two women. For that Caesar was thankful.

Calpurnia was not only intelligent, but also kind. She would not let Caesar feel uncomfortable for more than a moment. So she swiftly changed the subject. "What was all that commotion in the Forum today? I noticed that you were there with a group of soldiers, but I could not get close enough to see much or hear anything."

"Extraordinary thing. Remember I told you about those ten thousand prisoners in Parthia, survivors of Crassus's army?"

"Yes, I do. Those poor men. What city was it where you found them?"

"It was on the far side of Parthia in a city called Antiochia. Well, a little while ago a group of those men arrived in Italy. They had been slaves of the Parthians and so branded. I saw the terrible branding when I was there so I recognized it. There is no doubt they are from Crassus's army. But they managed to escape after some raiders had kidnapped them in turn from the Parthians."

"This is unbelievable. Such great distances, and a handful from ten thousand," commented Calpurnia.

"That ten thousand is one of the reasons I am planning to campaign in Parthia. I promised those men there that I would come back. I managed to free them and supply them with money. But I have had no information about them since. So when I first heard about this group that arrived in Ostia, I was sure they were part of the prisoners that I had freed. But apparently these men had been sold off to some people in the east before I arrived in Antiochia."

What really happened?

"Do you have any plans for them?" Calpurnia asked.

"These men have served Rome well. I have provided generous pensions and asked them where they would like to live. I will purchase land for them where they choose and they can begin life again as prosperous farmers somewhere."

"Do you think," Calpurnia asked with a furrow in her brow, "that such men could settle down and be farmers now? Couldn't you make use of them in your government? You are always saying how you need more qualified people to run the Republic."

"Interesting you should say that, my dear. You are indeed wise," Caesar responded. "Men of such experience would normally be useful to me. But after spending some time with them I question whether they would be very helpful as government officials. They seem to be missing something. It seems that their awful experience has left them not only with disfigured faces, but also with disfigured spirits and minds as well. There is something amiss about them and I would not want them trying to carry out important matters, or giving orders to people."

"That is very sad," Calpurnia commented.

"And one more thing about them that disturbs me. They greeted me, when I received them, in a very strange way."

"How is that?" she asked.

"They completely prostrated themselves on the floor like they do before kings in the east and kept hailing me as their 'king.' I cringed when I heard that and everyone around me looked dumbfounded. You know how Romans despise the concept of a king. It was very embarrassing and it took me some time to get them to stop addressing me as such. For that reason, the sooner they are out of Rome, the better. I don't need to have any other enemies created over such nonsense."

"So you will not see them again?" she asked.

What really happened?

"I wish that were so. But it would be unfair just to send them away after all that they have been through. I need to give them time to settle down, get used again to their families. get this idea of 'king' out of their minds and then decide for themselves where they want to go. They are free to do as they wish. In fact their leader, Marius, has asked to see me in private. I like this Marius, and I have a vague recollection that I remember him as a favorite centurion of Crassus. In any event I feel compelled to consent to a private meeting. I have invited him to dinner tonight with Octavian at Balbus' house. Would you like to come?"

"Thank you, Gaius, but I am not sure I would enjoy that? May I pass on it?"

"Certainly, Callie, I understand."

"There is something else I am curious about," added Calpurnia. "You seem to be spending a lot of time with your grandnephew, Octavian? Do you like him?"

"Yes, I do. Very much. I think he can be a leader of men. He is very quick to pick up on things; knows when to say something, and even better, when just to observe. I will be sending him to join the troops preparing for Parthia in Apollonia where the young man can toughen up a bit before our campaign."

"Yes," Calpurnia remarked, "he does seem to be somewhat tender. Perhaps it is just that he is so young."

"My niece and her husband," Caesar responded, "were hoping, I suspect, to keep him away from Rome and all its dangers. They were urging a more rural or at least academic way of life for him. But I sense in him a lust for politics and governing. You should have seen how enthusiastic he was when we met with different town elders on our journey back to Rome. He seemed to soak up every nuance of what are very complicated relationships. But we will see. There is time enough, at least I hope, to determine what he is capable of. For now it is just a pleasure to have an intelligent and handsome

What really happened?

youth about us."
"Gaius, I missed you so. Hold me."

XLIX

"Marius, it is an honor to have you and the others in my house," Cicero said to the Carrhae survivor as he embraced him. "Cassius has told me about your miraculous escape. I wish I were at the Forum to greet you when you and your comrades arrived."

"Thank you, great Tullius Cicero," Marius responded. "It is our honor to be in your home. As soldiers we are not much for reading literature, but we all know about your worldwide fame. I would venture that if we had been allowed into the home of the Parthian princes, we would have found copies of your works."

"You could not please Cicero more," Cassius, with a sly smile at Cicero, could not help commenting, "than saying such things."

Decimus Brutus intervened before the irritated Cicero could speak. "But it is about you and your comrades that we want to hear. Tell us about the battle at Carrhae and your life as a Parthian slave."

Marius seemed not to have heard Decimus' question. "We all believe that it is vital for the Roman people to acknowledge Julius Caesar as their king," he responded. "Unless that is done the rest of the kingdoms in the east

What really happened?

will never pledge allegiance to Rome."

All the men in the room, other than the Crassus veterans, were startled by this incongruous reply. Yet they were not at all displeased.

Earlier in the day Cassius had quickly gathered them at Cicero's expansive villa on the Palatine Hill, previously owned by the wealthy Crassus. The idea had occurred to Cassius that morning during the reception in the Forum for the forty-three former Parthian slaves. Caesar, upon hearing of their exploits, had immediately put together a formal receiving party for the soldiers. Cassius could not believe the insistence these soldiers showed in hailing Caesar as "king" at the reception. Nor did he miss the great discomfort that this caused to Caesar and the crowd greeting them. It seemed to him that these strange men had been sent from heaven to further their plans to get rid of Caesar.

Before the Crassus veterans arrived at Cicero's villa the conspirators discussed their good fortune. Both Decimus Brutus and Marcus Brutus agreed that it would be to the cause's benefit to ally itself with these people. What could better assist them in damaging Caesar in the eyes of the public than these forty-three fools yelling that he should be their king? In agreement were all the conspirators that managed to get to Cicero's house on short notice, including Gaius Casca, his brother Publius, Tillius Cimber, and Trebonius.

To Marius's statement Marcus Brutus responded: "Indeed, we do agree with you, Marius, but you do know, do you not, that Romans do not like to hear about any person being their king."

"Yes," answered Marius, "unfortunately we have learned that in the last few days. The people are very ignorant. But this belief among the people can and must be changed. We can do it. It is preventing Rome from gaining the support of the people in the east. Please

What really happened?

understand that we have spent years among the enemy in the east. From that experience we have become convinced that only a king could defeat them. The eastern people respect no leader who is not a king."

None of the conspirators could understand the logic or passion of Marius and the rest of the soldiers. Nor were they in the slightest convinced by Marius' argument. But it did not matter. What they saw immediately in this campaign of these strange people to make Caesar a king was the perfect vehicle to bring down the Dictator.

"We would like to help you in your efforts to have Caesar recognized as our king," Cicero said with all the sincerity he could muster. "But our involvement in your efforts must be kept secret. Many of us are officials in Caesar's government, and we would not want our great leader to feel we were compelling him to do something he was not inclined to do. He still takes seriously the old Roman diastase for kingship. You see, it is not every Roman who would like to acknowledge that Caesar is their king. Some even may oppose it violently. So your campaign must proceed with a little caution, and perhaps secrecy."

"'Caution and secrecy,'" exclaimed Marius. "With all due respect, great Cicero, what is there to be cautious or secretive about? Caesar should be king and that's all there is to it. We will talk to the Romans on the street. We will attend meetings of the Senate. We will make everyone understand the vital importance of this measure."

The conspirators glanced at one another. These bizarre survivors, they thought almost as one, might not be easy to control. Their minds certainly had been damaged by their experience. They were liable to self-destruct with their fanaticism before they could be made use of.

Cicero tried to get a handle on things. "Yes, Marius," he said, "now that I think of it, I agree that caution and secrecy have no place in the road to making Caesar our

What really happened?

King."

Marius and the other soldiers nodded vigorously in agreement.

"But here in Rome," Cicero continued, "our Constitution is considered very sacred and is much protected by all classes of Romans. Even the slightest change in our Constitution is immediately met with fierce resistance, only for the reason that it is a change. So it is not wise to join together as a group and publicly propose changes in our Constitution. It would be a great change in our Constitution to have Caesar declared as a king. So things have to be done with some degree of care, particularly as Caesar has many enemies. It would be better to go about your task more indirectly if you want to be helpful to our great leader Caesar."

"Indirectly?" asked a skeptical but curious Marius.

"Yes. I believe we can get the public to become more accustomed to our cause if we let them know of it a little at a time. For instance, we can have little booklets made up to be circulated. We could post anonymous signs in the Forum. We could put signs urging kingship on statues of Caesar or even crown them with laurels signifying kingship. All these small things will help prepare the Roman people over a period, say two or three months, to understand and accept your kingship proposals."

"Let me make a suggestion," Marcus Brutus spoke up for the first time. "There will be a festival that comes up in February called the Lupercalia. We celebrate then the suckling of Rome's founders, the twins Romulus and Remus, by a she-wolf in a cave. There will be great gatherings in Rome and people will be thinking about the foundations of Rome itself. That is the time you can move among the crowds and push for going back to the early days of Rome and elevating Caesar to a kingship."

Cicero and Decimus Brutus smiled at the ingenuity of Marcus's idea.

What really happened?

"I have some ideas," Marcus Brutus continued, "about doing such things as crowning his statues with laurels, signifying kingship. Also, we may try actually to crown him with laurels, as he will be siting as the chief priest along the route of the course. Let us discuss these things, my friends."

After the veterans left for their own homes late that night, the conspirators could not contain their delight.

"By Jupiter," exclaimed Cicero, "heaven has sent us our deliverance. With these fools loose in Rome, I guarantee that within a few weeks all of Rome will be demanding that Caesar be either exiled or executed."

"That, Cicero, sounds a little too optimistic," replied Tillius Cimber. "They could yell 'king' all day, but I do not think anyone will take them seriously. They all seem to be in some kind of daze. People will write them off as screwballs."

"I tend to agree with Tillius," said Gaius Casca. "Unless something else occurs, or if Caesar hesitates in the slightest in renouncing such a title, I think they will make little headway."

"Then," added Decimus Brutus, "what can we do ourselves that will assist them?"

"We certainly cannot join their little party," said Marcus Brutus. "No one would believe us sincere if we started calling Caesar 'King.' Everyone knows that we, and especially my family, are Republican to the core and despise kingship."

"But perhaps," added Cicero, who had been lost in thought for some time, "just perhaps, we might add fuel to the fire and still stay safely within the confines of our Republican constitution."

"How is that?" asked Decimus.

"Caesar now is serving a five-year term as dictator. In the past the Senate has often appointed a person as a dictator to deal with some emergency. But the protection

What really happened?

of the constitution lay in the fact that the term of dictator was always strictly limited. Either it was to last the length of the emergency or for a specified time, whichever was shorter. What if we have the Senate, in the guise of granting Caesar even more honors, vote to make Caesar dictator for life? In fact he is dictator for life already, since he could obtain a renewal of his term whenever he wishes. But if we make him dictator for life officially, a position never held by any Roman in history, people will begin to wonder how that is much different from being a king."

"I like that," Cassius said. "It will begin to trouble a lot of people. Then on top of that these veterans will be prancing about calling Caesar a king. It might be enough to ignite the flame that we need."

"This is getting a little too bold," said a nervous-looking Publius Casca. "Caesar will suspect that something is amiss if we propose in effect to make him a king. He may begin to question some of the other things that we do to embarrass him. And what if he also discovers our encouragement to these soldiers?

"Why don't we just let him leave for the Parthian campaign that he is so intent on and for which he has been emptying the treasury. This time he is taking on more than even Caesar could handle. He most likely will never return. He is already a fifty-five-year-old man. And look at who he has proposed to hold most of the important offices while he is away for the next three years? Us! We will be governing Rome. So why take any unnecessary risks?"

"Publius," said Trebonius, "you do not know this man as well as we do. I have served him for many years, as had Cassius before he joined Pompey. Caesar simply does not lose in war. Whatever it is: Fortune, genius, accident, brilliance . . . he just always wins. We cannot count on his not coming back from Parthia. What's more, he is not just going to secure our border on the Danube and push back the Dacians. I have heard that he has secretly made

What really happened?

arrangements for a five-year absence, not just the three years publicly announced. He has provided for officials in secret documents to run the government for those two additional years. Contractors in Asia say that he has paid for five years of various supplies. To me this means he will not stop at Dacia or Parthia, but go on at least to fulfill the dreams of his friend Crassus. He will go on to Bactria and then beyond even Alexander the Great and take India. When he returns in five years he will come back as the dictator of a Roman empire, something twice or three times as large as the Republic is now. Then do you think there will be any chance of overthrowing him? The people will be ready to make him god, much less a king."

"I agree with Trebonius, though he does go on a bit much," commented Cassius. "I have heard nothing of a five-year plan. But I do not doubt your information. The point is that Caesar just does not lose at war. We have to get at him away from his veterans, off the battlefield and before he leaves for Parthia."

There was a general murmur of agreement.

"I like Cicero's idea," continued Cassius, "of an inflammatory decree making Caesar Dictator for life. Added to the kingship blabbering of those soldiers, it may start enough unrest to either curtail Caesar or push him into exile."

"And if that fails?" asked Decimus.

"Then we will have to consider other paths to freedom for Rome," Cassius said with what sounded like menace.

L

In the early part of each year the Italians celebrated the ancient festival of the Latin League. It honored Jupiter but it also had a political purpose in that it reaffirmed the allegiance among all the Latin cities of Italy. It had taken hundreds of years of battles and complicated negotiations to unify the cities under Rome's hegemony and this festival celebrated that achievement. It was usually held on the Alban Mount outside Rome and presided over by the consul of Rome. So it was on January 26, in the year 44 BC.

So it happened that after the Latin Festival activities on the Alban Mount had concluded, Caesar, who as consul had presided over the Festival, was returning to Rome with the other Roman officials when a group of men along the route started shouting: 'Hail, King of Rome!' over and over again. The rest of the crowd about them murmured their disgust and Caesar frowned, trying to ignore them. But when this group kept addressing him as "King," to the obvious anger of the rest of the spectators, he asked his entourage to stop. He rode over to the group that had been so addressing him and stopped just before them. He was not surprised to see that the cheering group consisted

What really happened?

of Marius and most of the other forty-three Crassus veterans. Caesar took a deep breath.

"My comrades," he said, "I thank you for your spirit and loyalty, but my name is Caesar, not king. It does not please me, or other citizens, that you address me as king. Please cease and desist."

The rest of the crowd cheered at hearing these words from Caesar, but Marius and his friends were startled by Caesar's rebuke and stood in chastised confusion. At that moment two Tribunes rode up with a group of soldiers. The Tribunes, Epidius Marullus and Caesetius Flavius, were well known to Caesar as close friends of Cassius and the other conservative members of the Senate.

The Tribunes shouted at Marius and his cohorts and accused them not only of hailing a citizen as king, which was illegal, but also of having festooned statues of Caesar with the royal insignia of a laurel crown, bound with white ribbons. Marius cried out loud that he did not deny the charges and was proud of them, as Caesar was their king. The Tribunes became even angrier and ordered their soldiers to arrest the demonstrators. Caesar showed no emotion but watched as the scene unfolded.

Caesar turned to his secretary Trogus and said quietly, "Please get Lepidus for me. He should be just behind the senators in the back."

Moments later Lepidus rode up beside Caesar. Lepidus had replaced Mark Antony as Caesar's second in command in Rome, the Master of the Horse. Aside from Caesar, he had complete authority over the governmental forces in Rome.

"Lepidus," Caesar said, "please ride along with those Tribunes and their prisoners. When you are well away from us will you see to it that all of the prisoners are released. I want no harm or injury of any kind done to these men. Explain to the Tribunes that it is my wish."

LI

"But in all the history of Rome," exclaimed Cicero, who was now debating a measure he had just introduced in the Senate, "has there ever been a leader like our own great Gaius Julius Caesar? He has vanquished the barbarians in Gaul, Germany, Britain, the upstarts in the east, and the riotous Egyptians, when others have failed in these tasks. Yet he has shown miraculous clemency to his enemies and has even appointed them to great offices. This man, descended it is said from the gods, is indeed himself a god among us."

The few senators who were in on the charade being played out by Cicero were concerned that he might be overdoing it. But the clamorous reception to this panegyric from many of the other Senators quieted their fears.

Cicero and his friends were hoping that appointing Caesar, who already was an absolute ruler as dictator for a term of ten years, itself extraordinary, as "Dictator for Life" would be the tipping point in turning the populace against him. With the crazy Crassus veterans annoying all of Rome with their constant insistence on calling Caesar their "king," this new measure might very well do the trick. They were convinced that the people of Rome would find

What really happened?

the combination of these titles and honors so repugnant that they would run Caesar out of town, or even kill him.

"My proposal," continued Cicero, in an attempt to make this extraordinary measure seem normal, "to appoint the great Caesar as dictator for life is not contrary to our constitution. You know that I am an avid student of the constitution. I assure you that it is merely a refinement of this office of dictator as we have known it over the centuries. The Republic is in a perpetual emergency, and only Caesar can deal with it."

Caesar had expanded the Senate from six hundred, a number that had been set by his uncle Marius when he was consul some years earlier, to nine hundred members. Together with the vacancies caused by the civil war, this expansion gave Caesar the opportunity to reshape the Senate, as one of his powers as dictator was to fill vacancies in that body. He appointed his friends, aides, and others whom he though competent, whether of noble birth or not, and even freedmen. Among his appointees were Gauls, Germans, Britons, Greeks from Naples and Sicily and the provinces in the east, Spaniards from Nearer and Further Spain, several centurions, and a number of other officers who had served with him. Thus into the Senate came his German bodyguards Aldric and Waldo, his advisors Balbus and Oppius, the centurion Cassius Scaeva, and such others.

These men were slyly ridiculed and despised by the old guard, including Cicero, even though he himself was a "new man," the first of his clan to have made it into the Senate. Nevertheless these people appointed by Caesar were senators and now under the law were equal to them. A most nauseating situation that they planned to correct once Caesar was out of the picture, one way or another.
The measure was passed on February 13, 44 BC by a resounding voice vote. Then the senators adjourned to prepare for the purification Festival of Lupercalia, which

What really happened?

would be celebrated the next day.

LII

All of Rome was alight with flags and banners. It was the Feast of Lupercalia, one of the many festivals that intentionally interrupted the routine of life in Rome, though this one was closer to the heart of Romans than many of the others.

The Feast was held under the supervision of a special group of priests called the Luperci. The Luperci counted among its members many young men from the most distinguished families in Rome, and this year it even had the co-consul Antony among them.

Some questioned the propriety of a consul running around Rome naked, as the Luperci would do during the feast, but Antony as usual could care less about what others thought. For him this was yet another excuse, and happily an official one, for drinking and carousing. He had been received back into the good graces of Caesar after a two-year term in the doghouse for his mismanagement of Rome while Caesar was in Alexandria. Among other penalties for this revival was the requirement imposed by Caesar that he pay full market price to the state for the house of Pompey that he had obtained at auction. Antony at the auction had agreed to pay that price but never did

What really happened?

so. Being in charge of Rome there was no one in Rome at that time who would confront him, until Caesar returned from Alexandria.

Caesar, as co-consul and dictator, was seated on a chair in the Forum as one of the dignitaries reviewing the feast. Before them would run the naked (except for loincloths) Luperci. Women would jump into the street at the approach of the Luperci and hold out their hands to be stuck by the thongs made from the skins of the scarified animals waved by the Luperci, a ritual that supposedly increased their fertility.

Antony had been drinking before dawn in anticipation of a whole day of officially sanctioned drunkenness. Caesar could not possibly reprimand him for participating in a feast! While the two goats and dog were being scarified and skinned, Cassius approached the already drunken Antony.

"Hey, Antony, how go things?"

"Ah, my good friend Cassius. Greetings. Will you be running with us today?" asked Antony.

"No, I'm a bit too old for that," replied Cassius, not afraid that he would offend the inebriated Antony, who was his own age.

"But," he continued, "I have an idea that would cause people during this feast much amusement."

"What more do we need than drink and running naked about the city? Is that not enough amusement?" responded Antony.

Cassius did not expect Antony to be already so far gone. Just as well, he would not suspect the trap.

"I was just thinking," said Cassius, "that we could play with Caesar a bit. He has been in a somber mood as of late, and buried in his plans for the Parthian campaign. Perhaps we can lighten his spirits."

"Now be careful, my friend," said Antony. "I have just gotten back into his good graces. I would not want to

What really happened?

jeopardize that with any foolishness. "

"No, no," said Cassius, now worried that perhaps Antony was not as drunk as he thought. "We all know that there is a party of men, those crazy Carrhae survivors, who have been tormenting Caesar with their cries of 'King' whenever they see him in the streets."

"Yes," said Antony. "I have met them. They do seem truly demented. Is that what happens to people when they become slaves and then are freed? Jupiter save us from that fate."

"Well," continued Cassius, "I just think it would be hilarious for Caesar to be confronted with a good friend of his who appears to have joined that party."

"How so?"

"Look here, Antony, I have a diadem which to everyone is a symbol of a king. What if you would crown Caesar with it as you pass the reviewing stand? That would cause such an uproar of laughter."

"Good heavens!" responded Antony, "Caesar would be truly pissed. But the spectators will laugh their heads off. Yes, yes! I will take the risk. It is too much to resist!"

What a fool, thought Cassius. No wonder Caesar is asking even his enemies to take part in governing Rome.

So it was that three times an ever-angrier Caesar had to reject the diadem offered by Antony. It did not help that all the Crassus survivors where yelling themselves hoarse in cheering Antony on, though most of the crowd was sneering and booing. What was it about Antony, thought Caesar, that makes him so blind sometimes?

To Caesar's dismay, the Tribunes Marullus and Flavius again rode up, accompanied by some guards. They demanded that the Crassus veterans cease and desist from their cheering or face arrest. The men just laughed at them. Being so challenged, the tribunes went into a rage and fell upon the men with their clubs, followed by their guards who did the same. Eventually the veterans were subdued

What really happened?

and put into chains.

Caesar was disturbed but made no move to interfere, as the Tribunes were sacred officers and represented the people of Rome. But he turned to his secretary Trogus and asked him to find Lepidus. He was not easy to find during the chaos of the festival, and it was some time before he appeared before Caesar. Again Caesar gave him instructions to go to the jail and have the Crassus veterans released.

Later that day while Caesar was dining with Cleopatra, Lepidus arrived.

"Caesar, I have some unhappy news to report."

"Well, go ahead, Lepidus," Caesar responded without changing his expression.

"By the time I got to the jail I found Marius and his comrades barely alive. They had been beaten and tortured on orders of the two tribunes. I immediately had the tribunes arrested and the best Greek doctors attend to the prisoners. They will all survive, but are in much pain right now."

Caesar's face tightened. It was never allowed that citizens, much less such honorable veterans as these men, should be tortured. This outrage was directed against him.

"Excuse me, Queen, but I must attend to this immediately," he said and left quickly with Lepidus.

He brought the two Tribunes before the Senate.

"For what they have done," Caesar declared, "they deserve to be put to death. They have tortured Roman citizens, something that is absolutely prohibited by our most ancient customs. What's more, these were honorable veterans who have already suffered much on behalf of Rome. I demand that the Senate vote to strip these men of their offices and that they be exiled."

The Senate so voted.

After Caesar was assassinated, this was one of the examples that Cicero would always raise as justification for

What really happened?

the murder. It was proof, he would argue, that Caesar had become an intolerable tyrant.

LIII

"It has not worked," said an exasperated Cassius. "Not many have been disturbed by Cicero's 'Dictator for Life' scheme or that farce we put on during the Lupercalia. Caesar is as much loved by the populace as he ever was. I believe we will have to take more direct action before he leaves for Parthia."

There were eight men gathered in Cassius's house late at night. They had been meeting periodically in different houses and in the dark of the night to avoid observation. These men hated Caesar and were consumed with a passion to destroy him. Some of them were ostensibly his best friends. Others felt compelled to pretend friendship. Most held important positions given to them by Caesar. But for one or another reason—some rational, some irrational—they wanted to put an end to Caesar.

Trebonius spoke. "Then we must kill him. It would be easy. He has given up his bodyguards and arrogantly roams about the city just with his two secretaries. We can kill him at any time in any number of narrow streets or alleys."

The room fell silent. They all knew in their hearts that this was what they wanted, but upon hearing it said so baldly, they were chilled to the bone.

What really happened?

Finally, Marcus Brutus spoke: "Yes, it is clear that is the only way. But the people will celebrate our deed once they are freed of the tyrant. Now they are under his sway because of ignorance or fear. They need first to be freed from him. Only then will they understand how necessary it was to kill him and they will celebrate us as liberators."

The stark reality of their becoming murderers, and of the foremost man in the world, settled upon the group as a dark cloud. Again, no one spoke for a long time.

"He will be leaving for the Parthian campaign in a few days, said Decimus Brutus, breaking the silence, "we must do it now. Once he leaves and joins his troops, we will never have the opportunity again."

The group began to discuss the risks and advantages of various places to attempt the assassination. Finally, over some mild objections from Trebonius, they settled on the meeting of the Senate that was planned for the Ides of March. Caesar was to make his final appointments and settle some other matters before leaving. It was agreed that the Senate meeting would be the most opportune occasion, particularly as no senator was allowed to carry arms into a meeting.

Decimus Brutus then explained how he planned to ensure their own safety during the assassination.

"As you know," Decimus said, "I am in charge of the gladiators in Rome for this month. I will have two hundred of the fiercest human beings at my command. There are games to be played in Pompey's theater during the week that the Senate is to meet. We can have Cicero call for the meeting to be held in Pompey's ante-theater, the Great Hall, so I will have my gladiators nearby and no one would question that. We won't tell Cicero why, except perhaps that we wanted to be away from the common people and the lower classes that tend to hang out at the Forum. As usual Lepidus has his Legion stationed outside of Rome, so they will not be able to interfere. Pompey's theater is

What really happened?

somewhat isolated and will be easy to defend if for some reason anyone attempts to interfere. I will have under my control the only armed group in Rome. By the time the deed is done, it will be too late for the legionaries to get to Rome and do anything."

"Speaking of Cicero," said Trebonius, "he has been pestering me to find out what we are doing. He knows we have been planning something, and he wants to be part of it. One of the things he keeps repeating is that it would not be enough to be rid of just the Dictator, that we must also eliminate his lieutenants, particularly Mark Antony. Doing away with the Dictator, he insists, will only be half the job. What should I tell him?"

"Oh, for heavens sake," said Decimus. "We really can't have that old blabbermouth at our meetings. First, he's incapable of keeping his mouth shut. He will immediately write off to his friend Atticus every detail of our plans and they will be known shortly from Athens to Further Spain. Then, try to get him to decide anything. Remember how it took him forever to cross the Adriatic and join Pompey? And you know how he hates the sight of blood. What's more, he will be asking questions forever. He will insist on looking at this and then that. He is just not a man of action. For his sake, and ours, let us leave him out of it."

"What's more," said Marcus Brutus, "we have all agreed that it is only the Dictator who is to be taken down. That will be the best way to make clear to the people of Rome that we are fighting tyranny, to rid ourselves of an oppressor, and nothing more."
There was a general murmur of agreement among the eight.

LIV

The conspirators met again in the late evening a few days later at the house of Cassius. This time there were twenty-three of them.

"Our whole group numbers about sixty," Cassius announced, "but most of our fainthearted associates have refused to take part in the actual killing. They want it to happen, but don't want the great man's blood on their hands. So at this point there will be only twenty-three of us next week going into the Senate meeting and carrying daggers under our cloaks or in our writing boxes.

"Sixty out of nine hundred is why our choice of doing it at this Senate meeting," Trebonius commented, "has always given me some pause. I would prefer an alley or behind a building—somewhere away from the public. We all know that some time ago he foolishly dismissed his Spanish bodyguards and travels about the city with only his slaves, friends and secretaries, none of whom would be any problem. But in a meeting of the Senate? How will the rest of the nine hundred Senators react? A great number of them are his close friends, some of them hardened veterans. Will they cheer us on? Or will they rush down and tear us apart? You know that a good part of the Senate

What really happened?

will hate this deed."

"Yes, Trebonius," said Decimus Brutus. "I recognize that many of the senators may at first pose a problem. When Caesar increased the size of the Senate he placed in it people totally loyal to him—including, disgustingly, centurions, knights, Gauls, Germans, and even freedmen and the sons of freedmen. Many of these are tough individuals who could cause us some difficulties.

"But I have anticipated this. I feel confident that with the arrangements I have made that we can control the situation."

Naso added, "We do not know how many senators will actually turn out for this session. There may be only our own sixty associates, or at most perhaps just a few hundred. That has been the average turnout for the last several meetings. But what if there are more?"

"Let's think about this," Gaius Casca suggested. "It will be Caesar's last appearance before his departure to the east. That's why we were compelled to set the Ides of March as our date. Everyone will want to show his face to the great Caesar before he marches off. So I feel that we should expect that at this particular session, unlike so many others, there will be a big turnout. We must be prepared for that eventuality. "

Cimber agreed. "Yes, this indeed is Caesar's last meeting with us before he takes off in a few days on his Dacian and Parthian campaigns. You have seen his preparations these past few months. Now everyone will be anxious to have himself seen by Caesar just before he leaves. I agree with Casca. There may very well be a big turnout. That could be a problem."

Basilus stood up and said nervously, "Which brings me to the point I have been trying to make for the past few weeks. Why do we need to kill Caesar at all? He is about to kill himself in this new war he is planning. Wasn't Crassus also totally prepared with an unheard number of legions

What really happened?

when he invaded Parthia but then found himself outwitted and cut down like a dog? You, Cassius, more than any of us, can certainly speak to that. You were there. The same will happen to Caesar, particularly since I hear that he intends not only to battle the Parthians, but then to go on further—perhaps to India and the Outer Ocean. I declare that Caesar will never return."

Trebonius let out a cry of exasperation. "No! No! Basilus. You still do not understand! We have been over this ground a dozen times already. We have agreed that our message must be clear—that the Roman people will not tolerate a tyrant—today, tomorrow, or ever. We are by this deed telling the Roman people that it is tyranny that we are eradicating, not just a man with a policy or not just a man in any event who may or not be with us much longer. This deed must go down in our history in the same way as the deeds of Brutus' ancestors—we are rising up against tyranny."

"Yes, Trebonius, all well and good," said Basilus, "but without Caesar, no matter how he disappears from this world, his movement will just wither and die."

"Basilus," Cassius loudly interjected, "I disagree with your complacent attitude and most vehemently agree with Trbonius. We have been through this god-dammed discussion numerous times and this argument has to end—we have all agreed on this. We cannot now go back and rethink our entire strategy. This is the very reason we have not brought Cicero into our group, as anxious as he would be to join us. This back and forth must end. Caesar must die! That is the beginning and the end of it all! If you don't want to kill Caesar, Basilus, then get the hell out of here and go hide in your house."

Marcus Brutus raised both his arms in a soothing gesture. "Take it easy Cassius. I'm sure Basilus is just thinking out loud and is not wavering in his decision."

"Absolutely correct, Brutus," Basilus replied with a

What really happened?

stern look at Cassius. "And thank you. But you Cassius, I do wish you would calm down. These days are difficult enough."

"Okay, everyone, relax" Marcus Brutus continued. "Let me review what we have already discussed. It seems clear to me that if Caesar is allowed to leave on his campaigns the people of Rome will still be looking to the great Caesar as their leader. Any proposals in Rome that go against what he has laid down will be defeated, and might even be considered treasonable. What's more, he has left his agents in charge. Lepidus is his main agent as Master of the Horse, with a legion just outside our gates to enforce his orders. There are no other legions anywhere near us upon whom we could rely to oppose Lepidus. In addition, Antony will remain as the sole consul until Caesar's replacement, another Caesarian, Dolabella, is put in place as the second consul. Thus, so long as Caesar remains alive, no matter where he is, his laws and policies will continue to be implemented—against the interest of our families and that of the traditions of Rome. So we have no choice. He must die at our hands and with that deed all that he has stood for will die also."

"Ye gods," said an highly irritated Cassius. "I hope we have finally settled that! Then let me now get back to the original question, Decimus. How do we control the scene at the Senate meeting? I know we will be the only armed senators there, but there may be hundreds of angry men raining down on us."

"More likely, Cassius, there will be hundreds of delighted men cheering their new-found freedom!" Marcus Brutus interjected. "But wait, wait. Don't get excited again. I agree with you that we should prepare for any eventuality, however remote. Go ahead Decimus."

Decimus Brutus this time stood and faced the group: "First of all there will be the rest of our associates scattered among the senators. They will be urging everyone

What really happened?

to stay in their places and hear what we have to say after the tyrant is dead."

Cimber interjected: "I hope you have something in addition to our timid friends."

Casca remarked: "Indeed!"

"If I may continue?" said Decimus with some annoyance. "I have explained my plans earlier to some of you, but since each one here is taking the same risk, each of you is entitled to know what my arrangements I have made for your safety.

"As you know Cicero has prepared it so that this meeting of the Senate will be held in the Great Hall in front of Pompey's theater.

Casca commented: "Irony of ironies . . ."

"Please Casca, stop with the interruptions!" Decimus demanded. "As I was saying, we will be meeting in the Great Hall of the theater complex. At the same time all week there will be games and performances by gladiators in the theater itself. Very conveniently I am in charge this month of all the gladiators present in Rome. So the appearance of armed gladiators in and around the theater will not raise an eyebrow, nor will the sight of my meeting with them from time to time to give them instructions raise any suspicions.

"Caesar's golden consul's chair for the meeting will have its back facing the many doors from the hall into the theater, while the senators will be facing Caesar and those doors. After the session begins and Caesar has taken his seat, with his back to those doors, the doors will open quietly and a host of heavily armed gladiators will silently emerge. They will not have their swords drawn just yet and will not be moving in any threatening manner, but they will be seen by all the senators. At the very moment the senators are stunned by the sight of this menacing host, we will be dispatching the Dictator to Hades."

The conspirators absorbed this for a short while, but

What really happened?

then Casca spoke with some mockery in his voice.

"Please, Decimus, don't tell me that you will be depending on slaves and criminals for our safety. Even gladiators know of the great Caesar and probably love him. What makes you think we could rely on them in an enterprise against Caesar?"

"Ah, for once, good point, Casca," Decimus said with a sly smile. "But these are not just your ordinary gladiators. I have chosen these men very carefully. These are slaves who have no idea of who this man is, or barely even of where Rome was until I brought them here last week.

"I have recruited the most brutal and depraved criminals from our salt and silver mines in Spain and Sicily. They are mostly men who had been condemned to death for despicable crimes and have been sentenced to the mines for the rest of their lives—however short that may be.

"From among these unlucky brutes I have chosen three hundred of the strongest and most savage. To them I have offered something they had never expected: freedom and a generous bounty to enable them to set off on their own. They will be divided into squads of twenty and each squad under the careful watch of a real gladiator who I have also selected for his loyalty to me personally—and who will receive his own freedom and a substantial bonus after the Ides of March.

"These, then, are the 'gladiators' that I will have stationed inside Pompey's theater. I will have them located in groups just inside the doors to the theater and they will appear, and be seen by the senators, just as we are killing the tyrant. If any of the senators attempt to descend to help Caesar, my gladiators have been instructed to surge out of those doorways toward the senators with their swords drawn.

"I am hoping that such a confrontation will stop the senators in their tracks. If not, many of them will die also.

What really happened?

There is no other way to deal with it. But I am sure that no senator will move an inch further after seeing such menacing brutes.

"That is how I have arranged things to keep the senators in place, even the bravest and rashest of them. I have to assume that all of them will opt for life rather than death, particularly when they realize that Caesar is already dead and their protestations would be meaningless except for their own deaths."

Cassius, Brutus, Trebonius, almost at the same time said in chorus: "Well done, Decimus!"

Even the more skeptical Basilus and Casca seemed satisfied.

"One more thing, comrades," said Cassius, "at the end, each of us must have Caesar's blood on his dagger. We must do this together, all of us."

There were vigorous nods, some less vigorous nods and some nodded not at all.

LV

"Caesarion looks and sounds like a Roman already," exclaimed Caesar. "Thank you and your friends Zeno. I knew you could do it."

Zeno, though unaccountably somber, was nevertheless pleased at the compliment and smiled along with Cleopatra. But he seemed to be preoccupied.

"Tell me," Caesar said, "what is troubling you? Is Caesarion disappointing you in any way that I have not noticed?"

"Caesar," said Zeno, "may I have a word with you in private?"

Caesar looked about and noticed that not only Cleopatra but also a number of servants, slaves, and friends of Zeno were in the garden with them. Cleopatra frowned on hearing this and looked at Caesar.

Caesar bent over and whispered to her: "Cleo, would you find a reason to have everyone leave so that you and I can speak to Zeno alone."

Soon the three were seated around a small table in the garden.

"Caesar," Zeno began, "you know that I was once the tutor of Marcus Brutus. I have also recommended tutors

What really happened?

for his children. In addition, many of my friends that I ask to bring their charges here are tutors of some very important people in Rome."

"Yes, Zeno," Caesar responded. "Your contacts in Rome among the Greeks was one of the reasons I wanted you to tutor Caesarion. Is there something you have learned from them that you wish to tell me?"

"For weeks," Zeno said, "I have been hearing disturbing rumors. These are rumors heard frequently in Rome so I had paid no special attention to them."

"Rumors?" Cleopatra asked. "What kind of rumors?"

Zeno breathed deeply. "Rumors about assassinating Caesar."

Cleopatra looked alarmed, but Caesar's gaze did not change. "Go on," he said.

"But today a dear friend of mine took me aside when he brought his charges to join us. He is tutor to the children of Gaius Casca. He wanted to speak to me privately. With much trembling he told me things that I am sure he wanted me to convey to you. You are much beloved among the Greek community in Rome."

Caesar nodded.

"He told me," Zeno continued, "that yesterday while he was with the children in one room, he overheard his master speaking to someone in the adjacent room, unaware that he was being overheard. Casca laid out plans to murder you at the meeting of the Senate on the Ides of March." Zeno then told Caesar the names Casca had given him of the senators involved in the plot.

"Caesar. You do not seem surprised to hear this."

"I have long become accustomed to the murder I see in their eyes, though frankly some of the names you mention do surprise me. I suspect there have been numerous such plots, each one disappearing when it came time for someone to pick up a dagger."

"Caesar, I beseech you," said Zeno. "I do not notice

What really happened?

any soldiers in the city. At least have Lepidus bring in a cohort from the Legion stationed outside Rome."

"Now, Zeno, how would I look showing up in my own senate with 500 armed men? The senators will feel like prisoners, not senators. One cannot govern that way."

"But you have always traveled with a large bodyguard. In Gaul, Asia, Alexandria, you were surrounded by hundreds of Guards – German, Gauls, and Spaniards. Why is it different now?"

"The times and circumstances are different today, Zeno. First of all this is Rome, not Gaul. If I cannot walk about my own city unarmed and alone, then I have failed as a leader and don't deserve to live."

"Good Jupiter! Caesar, have you gone mad? Forgive me my friend, but I must speak frankly. You have powerful enemies everywhere in Rome who desire nothing less than your death."

"I know that, and I often hear of plots to kill me, though none as detailed and credible as the one you have just laid out. But think, Zeno, just think about it for a while.

"I have expanded our Republic and fought my own people to become their absolute leader. But now I must govern a state whose responsibilities extend across the world. It is my judgment that I cannot govern without the cooperation of those whom I govern. Otherwise my orders would become empty words; my plans would gather dust. There will be no enthusiasm, no spirit in our world. Think of what a General, guarding a frontier far away from Rome, would do with difficult orders he receives from a man in Rome he does not believe in. Think of the farmer in Puglia who is asked to give up his sons for 16 years to serve a man in Rome he did not like.

"Unless the leading families of Rome as well as the men who do the work of war and building approve of me, then all my efforts to maintain a peaceful and prosperous

What really happened?

Republic will bear no fruit. Bread will not be delivered to where it is supposed to go; taxes from the provinces would not find their way to Rome; water from the aqueducts will fail to reach our fountains.

"No, Zeno, I cannot both govern effectively and at the same time rule by fear. They are incompatible. So long as the people believe I am more valuable alive than dead, I will live. When they feel otherwise, then I will die."
Zeno and Cleopatra were stunned and could just stare at the composed and confident face of Caesar, wondering how such a brilliant man, whom they loved, could believe the things he was saying. A sense of foreboding swept over them. Zeno dropped his head and closed his eyes, so as not to show the tears welling up in them. Cleopatra found herself able only to place a hand on Caesar's and whisper: "Gaius, oh my Gaius."

LVI

"My dear Callie," Caesar said in the most calming voice he could muster, "I am the leader of a great state. I cannot succumb to fears generated by the dreams of my wife. I love you and respect you, but please don't ask me to govern my actions by your dreams."

"Gaius, dearest," said Calpurnia, "you know that I have never tried to influence you in your activities. You are Caesar and I have always accepted that. But I have not ever felt so fearful for your life. The dreams I had last night were more than just dreams, they seemed like voices from the gods warning me about the Ides of March. I beseech you not to go to the Senate. There are evil people there who wish you dead. Tell them that you are not well or whatever. Then in a few days you will take your men to the east and be among your own loyal troops. Here in Rome there is nothing but hatred and enemies."

"Callie, it is one thing to want me dead, but another thing to kill me," said Caesar. "How often in the past have there been warriors on horseback, commanders at sea or generals in their tents who have planned my death. My demise has been much anticipated. Yet Fortune has in each instance swept them away, for it intended that I live.

What really happened?

So it is now. Your dreams and the stories of Zeno tell me the same thing: that many wish me dead. But none of that counts for anything if it is not also the wish of Fortune."

At that moment a slave entered to report that Decimus Brutus and Mark Antony were at the door. They had arrived to escort Caesar to the Senate.

"You see, Callie, they come to my door. It was I who called for this meeting of the Senate and I would seem foolish and weak if I failed to appear. I need to put in place the remainder of the officials who will govern in my absence. I will be gone for a long time, and the Senators must understand and accept my government by proxy. This meeting is to symbolize that transition. I will not be able to continue to govern this country if it is even suspected that I fear to die. Until the hand of the murderer actually plunges his dagger into me, his own fear of the resulting chaos, or the intervention of Fortune, may stay that hand. I am Caesar and I must act that way.

"I will return around noon, dear. We can have a pleasant lunch and then I will meet with my staff to finalize our departure for the east. Just relax and I will be back shortly."

They embraced and Caesar could not avoid noticing Calpurnia's tears. Women! he said to himself.

As he emerged from his house he was greeted by a great crowd of well-wishers and supplicants. With difficulty he got into his litter and the entourage moved toward Pompey's theater where the Senate was to hold its meeting. Decimus Brutus walked on the left of the litter and Mark Antony on the right.

"Decimus," Caesar remarked when they were about halfway to the meeting place, "why are all these gladiators about? I see so many of them."

"Yes, Caesar, you will remember that there will be special gladiatorial games this week. One important exhibition is to be performed in Pompey's theater, so the

What really happened?

gladiators are all heading that way. Though the Senate is meeting in the antechamber to the theater, there is ample enough room to hold us all, so there should be no conflict in the events."

Caesar recalled Zeno's report that Decimus was to make use of the gladiators in the scheme to murder him. But he remarked only, "It is you this month who is in charge of the gladiators, is it not?"

"I am, but most of the job is being managed by my lieutenants," answered Decimus quickly, while glancing away from Caesar.

Ah, Caesar said to himself, Zeno's information was right about Decimus. His guilt is stamped on his face, though he avoids my eyes. "Well," said Caesar aloud. "It is never displeasing to see such mighty men prepared to entertain us."

Decimus flinched at these remarks, as he was not sure whether Caesar for some reason was being sarcastic. He was so on edge that he jumped at the slightest suggestion of suspicion. On the other side of the litter Mark Antony kept up the quick pace and seemed oblivious to everything, perhaps hung over again.

When they reached the street where Pompey's theater was located, the crowds became denser and the gladiators became more evident. Even Antony for a quick second wondered about this. True, he thought, the gladiators were scheduled to perform in Pompey's theater, but they should be inside the theater or its wings, not out on the streets like this. But then just as quickly he shrugged off whatever uneasiness this odd situation may have caused him.

Caesar's litter and the entire entourage finally reached the doors of the Great Hall of Pompey's theater. Caesar alighted and was quickly joined by his two secretaries, Faberius and Trogus. As they walked up the stairway they were approached by Trebonius.

"Caesar! I am happy that you have finally made it here.

What really happened?

There were rumors that you were indisposed and would not come."

"Yes, Trebonius, my friend, when will there be no rumors of contrary movements, whether on heaven or on earth?" said Caesar, who felt another pain in his heart at the betrayal of yet another intimate. Zeno's report had included him in the plot, and here he was. Had he not done so much for this man?

Everyone laughed at this, while Trebonius took Antony's elbow and motioned him aside.

Upon entering the building Caesar noticed that the senators who were seated in the huge oval chamber had risen to their feet in a sign of respect to him. But there was a group of about twenty senators in the well of the chamber that caught his attention. Again the names of the clique named by Zeno as his assassins flashed in his mind, and there they were: Cassius, Marcus Brutus, Gaius Casca, Publius Casca, Tillius Cimber, Bacilianus, and even his beloved veteran legate, Servius Galbo.

Caesar hesitated at this point, trying to give himself more time to think. But Decimus Brutus urged him on, saying that the Senate had been waiting a long time for his arrival.

"So, you too Brutus, urge me on to my fate," said Caesar.

A nervous and confused Decimus could only reply: "Your fate, Caesar? No, it is just that we need to move on."

Caesar's face did not seem to show any expression. But if Calpurnia or Cleopatra could see him now, they would know that he had made his decision. He turned to his two secretaries.

"Trogus and Faberius, it is unnecessary for you to accompany me any further. Why don't you two go up there where I see Aldric and Waldo are standing, and some other friends of mine? Stay with them and then we will

What really happened?

meet again after this session."

"But Caesar," said Trogus, "we will need to be near you to record the events of this session."

"No, Trogus, just give me a couple of tablets and a stylus. I will take whatever notes are necessary and then you can fill in the rest from what you see and hear from up there."

Reluctantly Trogus gave Caesar three wax tablets and a stylus, and then joined Faberius as they climbed up to where Aldric and Waldo were standing.

Caesar was now alone, being escorted by Decimus Brutus. A quick glance back told him that Antony was still in discussion with Trebonius at the door. Ahead were the two dozen men surrounding his chair, acting as if they constituted an official greeting party.

Well, Caesar, he thought to himself as he moved into their midst, I am still not sure that this is your end. None of them will look me in the eye, each quickly glancing away as I try to read his soul. Will they now abandon their madness? Or will they dare to propel Rome into chaos and mayhem? How often have I faced death, only to have Fortune swoop down and intercede? Will this be one of those times?

But the murderers knew they could not hesitate at this point. They quickly drew the daggers hidden under their cloaks. As one they leaped upon him, almost inflicting as much injury upon each other as they did on Caesar. Some yelled: "Die tyrant!" Others: "The Republic is alive!"

Caesar said nothing, though his stylus found a home in the arm of Gaius Casca, the first to strike. Above all the shouts of the assassins could be heard the piercing wail of Casca. Caesar, in his final act to maintain his dignity, pulled his cloak up over his head and down over his legs as he slumped to the floor.

The rest of the Senate stood in shock at the fury in the well of the chamber. It ended as suddenly as it had begun.

What really happened?

Then, recovering their wits, many began to descend from their seats to go to the aid of Caesar. But as if by magic there appeared between them and the scene of the murder hundreds of gladiators with swords drawn.

Even the most loyal of Caesar's friends knew that it was fruitless at this point to lay down their lives. Friends who realized this held back others who did not care about their own lives and wanted to charge into the gladiators' swords. But Caesar was already dead. Even before they knew what was happening, Caesar had been killed. To now charge, unarmed, into the swords and daggers of these gladiators, would mean a pointless death. Thus Aldric held back a sobbing Faberius who wanted desperately to reach Caesar. Waldo was doing the same with Trogus.

There was no movement any longer down in the well. It was all over in no more than a minute. The killers now seemed themselves to be in shock at their own deed as they stared down at the bloody bundle of cloth that had once been Caesar.

It was curious, thought Caesar, that he no longer felt the pain of the stab wounds. What he did feel was the rushing wind as he galloped at a furious pace on his great white stallion. They had passed through Antiochia an hour earlier.

That woman by the road, he said to himself. By Jupiter! It is my mother Aurelia; and the lady next to her, Cornelia! But we cannot stop. We have to keep going. The veterans must have heard about the battles and I am sure they will be coming to meet us. They cannot be much farther away.

Riding next to Caesar was his cousin Sextus, and just behind them was Mithridates. As they came up to the ridge of a hill they could hear, above the shrill sound of the cornet announcing the presence of the General, the thunder of other horses. Finally they reached the top, and halted.

"Ah, yes," said Caesar, "there they are." He now rested

What really happened?

on his panting stallion and smiled, as did Sextus and
Mithridates. They had reached their goal.
Lead by Cinna, thousands of Crassus's veterans were
riding hard over the desert sands toward them, all cheering
as with one voice: "Caesar!" The brands on their foreheads
seem to have disappeared and their ears bore no
disfigurement. What could possibly disfigure such ecstatic
faces, thought a blissful and satisfied Gaius Julius Caesar.

EPILOGUE

THE REACTION

Contrary to the delusions of the conspirators, the people of Rome did not rise up to thank them as 'Liberators,' as Cicero gleefully proclaimed them. Instead, they were incensed by the murder of their beloved Caesar. So crowds immediately roamed the street to find the murderers and burn down their houses. The killers had shortly to run out of town for their lives to escape the angry citizenry. Antony, who was looking to take over Rome himself as Caesar's successor, was happy to give them safe exit out of town. But that accommodation did not last very long as eventually Caesar's furious veterans and loyalists would force Octavian and Antony to track down and kill nearly all of them, the rest taking their own lives.

Cicero.
While Caesar was alive, Cicero had nothing to fear, notwithstanding his treachery. It was only after Caesar's

What really happened?

death, so much longed for by Cicero, that he himself, as well as his brother Quintus and Quintus' son, found themselves on Antony and Octavian's Proscription List. They were hunted down and killed, a little more than a year and a half after Caesar' murder.

Caesarion.
Some years later, after Octavian had defeated Antony and Cleopatra, yet still fearing competition to his rule, he had Caesar and Cleopatra's son, the teenager Caesarion, tracked down and executed. He also executed, as potential competitors, the older children of Antony and Cleopatra. Only their infant children were spared, to grow up in the house of Caesar Augustus.

Octavian and Rome
Caesar, in his Last Will and Testament, gave his extensive gardens in Rome to the public and divided the rest of his vast estate among two of his nephews who had served with him and a grand-nephew, Octavian, who received a larger share and was also adopted posthumously.

The young Octavian proved to be remarkably adept politically, catering to Caesar's veterans, opposing Antony at first while enlisting Cicero as an ally, then joining with Antony, pursuing the conspirators until their destruction, agreeing to the murder of Cicero at Antony's insistence, and then finally crushing Antony and Cleopatra. He presided as Caesar Augustus over a peaceful and prosperous Empire for forty years, the Pax Romana.

There followed centuries of Roman rule in a large part of the world, but never an opening to China. Then mismanagement by successors weakened the Empire which found itself unable to resist the hoards of barbarians

What really happened?

that had always been pressing on its borders. The sophisticated and efficient organization that had maintained a vast and disciplined army on its borders eventually found itself unable to supply and support those armies. The barbarians then swarmed over the Empire time and time again until their looting and destruction gave us the Dark Ages.

Would our civilization have gone down that same path to darkness, destruction, ignorance and feudalism had Julius Caesar lived?

APPENDIX
SOME CULTURAL AND HISTORICAL BACKGROUND

SLAVERY

Slavery was a universally accepted fact of life by people living in the ancient world. Even the philosophers were satisfied that it was the way of the world. Both Plato and Aristotle argued that slavery was a rule of nature: some were born slaves and others non-slaves, and that both were happier that way. If a slave were freed, he should be returned to slavery. If a free man were enslaved (as in war or kidnapping), in a just world he should be freed. But a natural slave was like a tame animal or a useful tool, though he had some qualities of a human being and should be treated fairly.

Roman writers followed suit and further developed rules for the treatment of slaves — again it was best to treat them fairly and avoid harsh or arbitrary measures or abuse, not necessarily out of kindness but as the most

What really happened?

effective way to get more work and loyalty out of them. But the slave was property and the owner (master, lord) could do with him as he pleased. Over time peer pressure forced owners to avoid unusual treatment of their slaves, particularly household slaves.

Slaves were obtained 1) primarily as prisoners in war; 2) others were kidnapped by pirates or slave hunters;, and 3) others were born to slaves. The wealthier people who were kidnapped by pirates were more likely to be held for ransom rather than for slavery. Most slaves in the ancient world originated as prisoners in war as the "rules of war" at that time gave the conqueror complete control over the conquered — men, woman and children.

Rome's first wars of expansion were in Italy, including old and flourishing Greek colonies in southern Italy and Sicily, and then east along the Mediterranean into other Greek colonies and Greek-speaking territories and islands. Later there were Gauls and Germans taken as prisoners. The expansion into the Hellenized areas of the Mediterranean, such as most of the coastal towns in southern Italy, Sicily, along the Adriatic and north African coasts brought the Romans into more civilized and sophisticated societies. These the Romans admired and imitated — in their education, particularly of the "classics" in literature, philosophy, science and in rhetoric, and in language, art, dress, architecture, music, and other ways of life. By the time of Caesar the educated Romans were bi-lingual, Latin and Greek, with Greek being the preferred language among scholars and writers and those in the elite trying to show their sophistication. No Roman family of any wealth was without a Greek slave or former slave who tutored their children. The best teachers, doctors, craftsmen in Rome at this time were Greek or Greek-speaking slaves or former slaves."

During Caesar's day it is estimated that one-third of the population of Italy were slaves. Their masters had

What really happened?

freed many more. These "freedmen" would have obtained their freedom by purchasing it (slaves could earn money and own property), or were freed by grateful masters for years of loyal work , or freed out of respect for their great talent, intellect or scholarship or were freed in wills. Others had just walked to their freedom as for slaves in the city they could easily disappear into a society which could not distinguish them from free men or freedmen — as they looked like Italians or Gauls or Greeks or Thracian or Namibians or Syrians or Palestinians living in Rome. Indeed, it is said that at one time a Senator proposed a law requiring slaves to dress in a fashion so as to be recognized as such. The bill, however, was defeated when the debate made the Senators realize the danger of such a measure — the slaves would look about and see how many of them there were.

Since there was a general contempt in Roman culture for ordinary work, trades or careers (only agriculture — owning and operating one's own farm, or military service was honorable work), most tradesmen and skilled workers in mid and late Republican Rome, i.e., Rome of the Third, Second and First Centuries b.c., (doctors, teachers, innkeepers, retail merchants, millers, barbers, scribes, etc.) were either slaves or freedmen. One theory as to why Romans looked with contempt on the usual type of work or careers was that so many of these trades and professions were occupied by slaves — particularly the trained and educated prisoners of war taken from the Hellenized world. Further, since slavery was such an integral part of Roman life, it was thought beneath a free man to take "orders" from another man, except in the military. Likewise, the notion of spending a life at one occupation, again excepting the military, seemed very much like the life of a slave.

The private slaves, those owned by individuals, were either household slaves or rustic slaves. The household

What really happened?

slaves were the most integrated into Roman society; were those who more frequently received their freedom while still viable from grateful owners. These freed slaves might remain in the household doing the same work, or in the master's business as managers or overseers. Many household slaves might handle the financial business of the master, even representing him at land closings or merchandise purchasing. The freed slaves were expected to maintain a lifelong obligation of respect for their former master and remain among that masters " liens   that master's clients - prepared at any time to do a service requested by the former master or to accompany him on his walks about town to show the master's status and wealth. Those who were born into a household as slaves were the most cherished: educated and raised in the household and as much a part of the family as the children of the master and mistress — who were their playmates while growing up. Some were even adopted; or freed with enough money to start a business.

The rustic slaves were of two kinds. The more fortunate group attended to the master's villa or country estates and were similar in many ways to the household slaves, with duties of housekeeping and maintenance of the landscape. The other kind were agricultural workers. Those on small farms owned by an individual could find a degree of sufficiency and family. But those on the huge estates owned by absentee landlords were treated very much like tools and worked to their limit and are most similar to the slaves that worked in the American and Caribbean plantation system.

Then there were public slaves — owned by the government. Again, there were classes among these. Some were assistants and administrators for municipal officials or governors and were more influential and powerful than most free Romans. For instance, under a freedman or free Roman they were the experts who managed Rome's

What really happened?

massive and complicated aqueduct system. Slaves and freedmen filled the staffs of the magistrates and governors, as even that type of labor was looked down upon by Romans (agriculture — owning and operating your own farm, and military service, were the accepted forms of labor for a real Roman). But then there were the slaves who were sent along with the criminals to work themselves to death in the mines or to be entered into the gladiator schools where most ended up dead in the end.

In all ancient Roman history there were three slave rebellions, all within a period of 70 years: two in Sicily, one from 139 to 132 and the second from 104 to 100 b.c. Both originated with the rustic slaves, and did not extend to the household slaves. Both arose from cruel treatment by some owners and both were completely crushed. The third and most famous was in Italy, lead by Spartacus and originating from a gladiator school where the owner had been treating the gladiators harshly and unreasonably confining them,. Spartacus defeated some smaller Roman armies and then was totally defeated by a large force led by Marcus Crassus, with the six thousand survivors crucified along the Appian Road from Capua (near modern Naples), where it had started, to Rome as a lesson to would-be rebels. Slaves knew thereafter that any rebellion was pointless and doomed to failure.
(I used various sources for the above, particularly Don Nardo's Life of a Roman Slave (1998: Lucent Books, San Diego.))

THE MILITARY

Until just before Caesar's birth in 100, Rome did not have a professional military establishment. It relied on citizen-soldiers who were raised at the time any crises would so require. Consequently inexperienced consuls would often lead poorly trained men into battle with disastrous results. This was what was happening just before Marius began the first of his extraordinary five consulships in 107, when Rome had lost battle after battle and immense numbers of men in trying to stop mass migrations of German tribes into Roman territories. In addition, until the appearance of Marius only those citizens who owned a minimum amount of property were eligible to serve in the military.

This practice was fundamentally and permanently changed by Gaius Marius, an uncle of Caesar's by marriage. Marius for the first time raised men from the poorest citizens who were without property. Thereafter, most of Rome's military came from the poor. A recruit of volunteer once he joined was committed to 16 years of service or 16 campaigns. Thus there developed skilled warriors, particularly among the centurions, men who led about 100 men each. The centurions rose in rank over the

What really happened?

years and moved from the back of the legion to the front.

Rome relied primarily on foot soldiers to win its wars. What cavalry it had would be recruited from a wealthier class as the men had to bring their own horses, at least in the beginning. In addition, fighting on a horse was considered more honorable, so the aristocrats preferred to serve in the cavalry. However most of Rome's cavalry in its wars was supplied by its allies whose people utilized horses in their lifestyles much more than the Romans did. Likewise with any navy. Fleets were gathered from allies with histories of naval warfare.

A Roman legion consisted of 4,800 men divided into 10 cohorts of 480 men. This would be the original or paper strength of a legion, whose actual numbers would be reduced over time by death and sickness.

ROME BEFORE CAESAR

Rome had grown over the centuries from a town on some hills to the dominant force on the Italian peninsular. By the time of Caesar most of communities on the Italian peninsular were either Roman citizens or had the Latin Rights, a status just before citizenship, which was granted after Rome determined that the community had become sufficiently Romanized (Latin language; an educated elite; a systematic municipal government, etc.). Rome traditionally would freely grant citizenship to recently conquered peoples and attempt to incorporate them into the Roman state. This had mutual benefits, as the new citizens were now subject to recruitment into the army when necessary. One of the main sources of social unrest in the years just before Caesar was the growing conservatism of Rome's leading families who became more and more reluctant to extend citizenship to its allies or newly conquered people.

Aside from the issue of citizenship, the other main political issue roiling Roman life during Caesar's youth and just before was the question of the landless poor. Together with discharged soldiers, Rome and some of the other cities of Italy were accumulating large numbers of poor

What really happened?

and landless men and woman. Various reformers attempted to distribute land to these people, either by confiscation from the large estates, or grants from public land or by the state purchasing land, but most of the reformers were defeated and even killed by the old guard in the Senate. Senators were the greatest landowners in Italy and any threat to their possessions was frequently met with violence.

Rome at Caesar's time extended from the Iberian peninsular to the near east and included North Africa so that the Mediterranean was a Roman sea. Much of the area was Hellenized over the centuries by a succession of Greek colonists, and not only Southern Italy but Sicily and the northern coast of Africa was studded with Greek cities. Rome governed through a mixture of directly controlled provinces or associations with allies of various sorts, some in effect subject kingdoms and others ostensibly friendly allies.

ROMAN GOVERNMENT

Rome was ostensibly a Republic at the birth of Caesar, but was in fact controlled with a jealous and iron hand by several ancient families. The nobles presided in the Senate and ostensible governed with the knight or equestrian, the business class, and the rest of the citizens who would form the Assemblies. In practice, though, a faction of the Senate in effect controlled the equestrians and the Assemblies through a complicated system of connections, patronage, bribes and when necessary, violence.

There were 300 Senators for a very long time, then raised by Sulla and Marius to 600. Their final number, raised by Caesar, was 900. The lowest office which entitled one to enter the Senate was that of Quaestor, eight traditionally, raised to 20 by Sulla and then to 40 by Caesar. Then came the Praetors, 61 and then 8, the tribunes, 10, and finally at the top two consuls who ruled as co-equals. Each of these offices hand one year terms. This in itself led to much instability by the time of Caesar, with elections bitterly contested and often corrupted by money.

LIST OF SOME NAMES

A number of my friends, particularly Ann, who enjoyed reading an earlier edition of my book, have nevertheless commented on the difficulty of getting a handle on the names of these Romans. For one thing, they found it a struggle to run thru the two, three or four unfamiliar names of individuals in the story as they read along.

So I have revised the book to give most characters just one name, usually the one by which his contemporary colleagues would normally have called him or her. Exceptions are where two individuals would have the same name, a frequent occurrence in Rome, so I have either used two of their names or one different from what he would usually be called. For instance, there are two men called Brutus in this story. The more well-know Marcus Brutus, and the lesser-known Decimus Brutus. So in this case I call Marcus just Brutus, and the other, Decimus or Decimus Brutus. So as with Caesar's cousin, Sextus Julius Caesar, I call him just Sextus.

In an additional attempt to help with these names, I have put together a list with the full names of many of the

What really happened?

characters.

But first I think my readers would appreciate parts of "A Note on Roman Names" which appears as Appendix 2 to James S. Ruebel's Caesar and the Crisis of the Roman Aristocracy (1994, University of Oklahoma Press, Norman).
"A Roman male's name consisted of the praenomen . . . [of which there were a very limited number, like Aulus, Gaius, Gnaeus, Decimus, Lucius, Marcus, Sextus, Quintus, Tiberius], the nomen proper (the gens name that corresponds to our surname), and any official or unofficial cognomen or agnomina that are either traditional to that branch of the family or that have become a regular part of the individual's official identity. The nomen was of course hereditary; it identifies the person as a member of his gens. Most friends and associates, however, would call a man by his cognomen, if he had one. Hence, Romans who had three names are usually known by a version of their third name: Cicero, Crassus, Cato, Gracchus, [Caesar], and so on. If a Roman did not have a cognomen, he would be known by his nomen, such as Pompey (Pompeius), Livy (Liviuis), Sertorius, and the like."

I might add that as adult adoption was a common practice in Rome for various reasons, often dynastic, many adults would have their names changed or have another family name added. Likewise, slaves who were freed or provincials who were granted citizenship often adopted part or all of their former masters' or benefactors' names (for example, Marcus Tullius Tiro, former slave of Marcus Tullius Cicero; or the Spaniard Lucius Cornelius Balbus who received Roman citizenship through Lucius Cornelius Lentulus Crus).

For female Romans the rules were somewhat similar, but

What really happened?

the confusion for historians was magnified by the tradition of naming all the females in the same family with the same name.

Except where noted I have used the sources listed in the Acknowledgements for construction of this list, and in particular the Penguin Classics: Caesar, The Civil War (Jane F. Gardner); and Cicero, Selected Letters (D.R. Shackleton Bailey).

Titus Pomponius Atticus: born Titus Pomponius (110 –32 BC), came from an old but not strictly noble Roman family of the equestrian class and the Gens Pomponia. (Equestrians or Knights as a class just below Patricians and Senators. They consisted mostly of wealthy individuals involved in commerce such landlords, bankers, exporters and importers, merchants, individuals with large government contracts, tax collectors, owners of large factories, and the like.)

Atticus was a celebrated editor, banker, and patron of letters with major residences in both Rome and Athens, and country homes in Greece and Italy. He is best remembered as the closest friend of Marcus Tullius Cicero as well a friend of leading contemporaries of upper class Roman society. Atticus was known for his elegant taste, sound judgment and financial acumen.

Cicero's and Atticus' correspondence, often surprisingly frank, is preserved in Letters to Atticus compiled after Cicero's death by Cicero's freedman and personal secretary, Marcus Tullius Tiro, Atticus and Cicero's son. The letters are the source of much of the information we

What really happened?

have about the politics and society of the Late Republic.
(Primarily from Wikipedia)

Marcus Antonius (Mark Antony): Caesar's Questor (the
first elected public office in the political ladder and usually
served as an aide to a higher official) in 52 and one of his
principal, though flawed, lieutenants in the Civil War.
Tribune in 49 when he unsuccessfully tried to present
Caesar's compromise proposals to the Senate. Consul with
Caesar in 44, and after Caesar's death he eventually formed
the Triumvirate of 43 along with Octavian and Lepidus.
Later quarreled with Octavian and committed suicide after
defeat at Attium in 31.

Balbus (Lucius Cornelius Balbus): Prosperous native of
Gades (Cadiz, Spain), received Roman citizenship in 72
through Pompey's Lieutenant or Legate, Lucius Cornelius
Lentulus Crus, for his help in raising at his own expense a
cavalry force to fight the rebel Roman General Sertorius
on behalf of Pompey. Adopted the Cornelius family name
upon citizenship. Attached himself to Caesar during
Caesar's service in various posts in Spain, eventually
becoming one of his closest confidential agents and
financial adviser, loyal to the very end.

Balbus (Young Balbus): a nephew of the above, fought
with Caesar in the Civil War and was wounded in battle,
but continued with Caesar and served him well in Egypt.
Became a Questor in 44 on Caesar's nomination and
served under Asinius Pollio in Spain.

Bibulus (Marcus Calpurnius Bibulus). Scion of a patrician
family (families who could trace their origin to the
beginnings of Rome) and born the same year as Caesar so
went up the political ladder (cursus honorum) at the same
time, always unfortunately falling under the brilliant and

What really happened?

charismatic Caesar's shadow. Became his bitter enemy. As Co-Consul in 59 (the Constitution provided for two Consuls who acted together as the top executives in the Roman Republic) opposed Caesar's reform legislation, and after some violence in the Forum shutting himself in his house, sending out vile and slanderous pamphlets against Caesar. While shut in his house he also used what had become only a ceremonial power to read the auguries, seeing evil omens in the heavens each time Caesar was about to have votes on his legislation (hoping to run out Caesar's one year term of office) and according to tradition should have cancelled the votes, but simply ignored by Caesar who went on to exercise the office of Consul by himself. (Cicero years latter cited these votes as blasphemous and thus the resulting legislation illegitimate.) Married Cato's daughter Porcia, later wife of Marcus Brutus. Governor of Syria 51-50 and joined Pompey against Caesar in the Civil War. Died from exposure and pneumonia while stubbornly commanding Pompey's fleet in 48 trying to prevent Caesar's movement across the Adriatic in pursuit of Pompey.

Brutus (Marcus Junius Brutus). Sometimes called Caepio Brutus after adoption by his uncle Quintus Servilius Caepio. A Senator and usurious moneylender who reluctantly joined Pompey's side in the Civil War as the lesser of two evils, even though Pompey had had his father executed as a rebel years earlier. Brutus managed to avoid any military role in the Civil War though on the scene of some of the great battles; was forgiven by Caesar on account of Brutus' mother, Servilia, who had been Caesar's lover, and given many important posts in Caesar's government. Encouraged by Cicero, Cassius and others to follow his ancestors' examples and expel the tyrant (Caesar).
Decimus Junius Brutus Albinus (Decimus or Brutus).

What really happened?

Perhaps a distant relative of the more famous Marcus Brutus, above. Served honorably and courageously under Caesar in Gaul and in the Civil War; much favored by Caesar and richly rewarded with money, lands and governmental posts. Caesar so trusted him that he named Decimus as an alternate designee in his final will. But Decimus felt he deserved more at a time Caesar was bestowing rewards and high positions to freedmen and provincials. Further he, along with many representatives of the old ruling families, feared Caesar's evolving practice of governing the growing Roman state with the assistance of equestrians, freedmen, provincials and even slaves was a fundamental threat to the ancient powers of their families. He thus became, like the other Brutus, an avid conspirator and murderer of Caesar.

Gaius Cassius Longinus: Served as Questor under Crassus in campaign in Parthia. Took charge of Syria after Crassus' death at Carrhae in 53, somehow managing to escape with some cavalry from that catastrophe. Claimed in letters to Senate that he was defeating Parthian attempted invasions of Syrian when there were no such attempt, such claims questioned even by his ally, Cicero, who was in the area on his own governorship and familiar with events. Married to Brutus' half-sister, Junia Tertulla.

As Tribune in 49 joined Pompey in Civil War and served effectively as leader of sections of Pompey's great fleet. After defeat of Pompey at Pharsalus he was pardoned by Caesar and favored by him with important posts and monetary rewards. Became one of the leading conspirators against Caesar's life. Perished with Brutus at Philippi in 42.

Marcus Porcius Cato: somber, inflexible and ascetic leader of Senatorial conservative opposition to the First Triumvirate (Crassus, Pompey and Caesar); later made use of Pompey against Caesar, and after Pompey's death became the life and soul of the Senate's war with Caesar.

What really happened?

Committed suicide at Utica after the Republican defeat at Thapsus in Africa in 46.

Marcus Licinius Crassus: Counsel in 70 and 55. Joined Pompey and Caesar in 60 to form the so-called First Triumvirate. Left for Syria late in 55. Defeated and killed at the disastrous battle of Carrhae in 53 while leading an invasion of Parthia.

Publius Licinius Crassus (Young Crassus or Publius): son of the Triumvir. Admired Cicero in his early years and served brilliantly under Caesar in Gaul. Much loved by Caesar. Caesar allowed him to leave his service in Gaul with some cavalry to join his father in Syria. Was killed at Carrhae with his father.

Gnaeus Domitius Calvinus: loyal and effective officer of Caesar who served in the Civil War in Macedonia in 48; commanded the center at Pharsalus; supplied vital troops and material to Caesar while Caesar was trapped in Alexandria; Fought inconclusively against Pharnaces in Asia Minor; consul 53 and 42, Governor of Spain 39 – 36.

Aulus Gabinius: Military lieutenant and political supporter of Pompey. As Consul in 58 backed Clodius against Cicero. As governor of Syria in 55 upon Pompey's instructions had restored by force Ptolemy XII "Auletes" (flute player) to his throne in Egypt. Left some of his troops, the "Gabinians," in Alexandria to protect Ptolemy. Went into exile in 54 after conviction on charges of extortion, including taking large amounts from Ptolemy for his restoration. Recalled by Caesar and served him courageously in Illyria 48-47, but died of an illness there.

Lucius Cornelius Lentulus Crus: Praetor in 58; friend and correspondent to Cicero. Consul in 49; opposed Caesar

What really happened?

and joined Pompey in Civil War; followed Pompey to Egypt after defeated by Caesar at Pharsalus and was murdered in an Egyptian prison on orders of the young king Ptolemy and his advisers.

Marcus Aemilius Lepidus: Son of the Consul of 78 by the same name. As praetor in 49 had Caesar proclaimed dictator; governor in Further Spain 48-47; Consul with Caesar 46; governor of Gallia Narbonensis; Consul in 46 with Caesar. Joined Antony and Octavian in Triumvirate after Caesar's death.

Gaius Asinius Pollio: Born about 76, Praetor in 45, Consul in 40. Soldier, orator, dramatist, and historian. Governor of Further Spain at the time of Caesar's death, he joined Antony in 43 and remained his supporter, but lived on under Augustus until AD 5. Wrote a multi-volume history of the Civil War.

Gaius Rabirius Postumus: Roman banker who administered financial affairs of Ptolemy XII, primarily to recover payment for loans made by Roman bankers and Senators to Ptolemy in his efforts to recover his throne in Egypt. Caesar recruited him to his side in the Civil War and Postumus loyally served with him, including in Alexandria.

Quintus Caecilius Metellus Pius Scipio: A Scipio Nascia adopted by a Metellus. Considered corrupt and debauched in his way of life by later historians. Became Pompey's father-in-law and colleague in the Consulship of 52 after Pompey's wife, Julia, Caesar's daughter, had died. Joined Pompey in the Civil War. Escaped defeat at Pharsalus and sailed to Africa with Cato and the remainder of Pompey's army to continue war against Caesar on behalf of the Senatorial party. Defeated at Thapsus and committed

What really happened?

suicide.

Sextus Julius Caesar, grandson of the Consul of 91 who was Julius Caesar's uncle. Young Sextus was a loyal and courageous lieutenant of Caesar's in the Civil War and in Egypt. Placed in charge of Syria after they left Egypt, part of Caesar's preparations for an invasion of Parthia. Was assassinated the following year by troops under leadership of Caecilius Bassus who had fought under Pompey, escaped from the defeat at Pharsalus and had set up a gang of bandits in Tyre from among other former Pompeian soldiers.

Marcus Terentius Varro. From Italian town of Reate, born in 116. More of a scholar than a military man, he not very effectively headed Pompey troops in Spain in Civil War with Caesar. Surrendered to Sextus after Caesar defeated the Pompeians in Spain. Forgiven and released. Later recruited by Caesar to create a library system in Rome modeled on that in Alexandria. Not favored by Caesar's successor, Octavian, but continued to write prolifically on an encyclopedic scale. Died peacefully in very old age.

Lucius Vibullius Rufus: Pompey's "Prefect of Engineers" and fought with him against Caesar in the Civil War. Was captured twice by Caesar and forgiven each time. Became aide and lieutenant to Caesar after defeat of Pompey in Pharsalus. I have fictionalized his activity with Caesar in Egypt.

Zeno Artemidorus: what we know of Zeno is primarily from an anecdote repeated by the Greek writer Plutarch in his Life of Caesar written about 150 years after Caesar's death:

"Artemidorus the orator, originally from Cnidos, whose

What really happened?

work teaching Greek had made him a close enough friend of Brutus to know most of his affairs, wrote down what he wanted Caesar to know on a petition scroll and brought it to him. . . . [H]e approached him [Caesar] and said, 'Read this one yourself, Caesar, and read it soon. The matters it mentions are urgent and concern you personally.' Caesar took the scroll and although he repeatedly tried to read it there were too many people crowding around for him to have a chance to do so. But it was the only scroll he kept hold of, and he was still holding it when he entered the senate."

I have created a fictional role for Zeno as a confidant of Caesar's in order to tell some history while he and Caesar conversed. As for Plutarch's dramatic "almost got to him" story quoted above, I do not sense authenticity in it. It sounds too neat and a made-up tragedy of "what could have been if only" etc.

What really happened?

ACKNOWLEDGEMENTS

Gaius Julius Caesar's own Commentaries are recognized as
the first and foremost source.
A person cannot easily escape insights into his soul when
he writes. His choices of topics, words, views, treatments,
reveal to us as much about him as he does about what he
writes. His words in the Commentaries tell us who this
Gaius Julius Caesar was as a person.
I have used the 1960 translation by Rex Warner in the
Mentor Classic collection for the Gallic Wars; the 1967
translation by Jane F. Garner in the Penguin Classics
collection for the Civil War. At times I transcribed almost
word for word Caesar's commentary as translated by
Garner and Warner.
Next in importance of the sources I relied upon were the
ancient writers: Plutarch, Appian, Suetonius and Dio
Cassius.
Of the numerous books on Caesar that I have read as
sources, I list those that I have most heavily relied on,
particularly for their insights and judgments on the
character of Caesar, and I list them in order of my reliance:

What really happened?

Parenti, Michael, The Assassination of Julius Caesar (The New Press, 2003).
Billows, Richard A., Julius Caesar, The Colossus of Rome (Routledge, 2009).
Goldsworthy, Adrian, Caesar, Life of a Colossus (Yale University Press, 2006).
Canfora, Luciano, Julius Caesar, The Life and Times of the People's Dictator (University of California Press, 1999).
Dodge, Theodore Ayrault, Caesar, A History of the Art of War (Greenhill Books, 1995; first published 1892).
Freeman, Phillip, Julius Caesar (Simon & Schuster, 2008).
Gelzer, Matthias, Caesar: Politician and Statesman (Harvard University Press, 1968)
Meier, Christian, Caesar (Basic Books, 1982)
Walter, Gerard, Caesar, a Biography (Charles Scribner's Sons, 1952).
The Notes of Giles Lauren in the Latin Text of the Gallic Wars (Sophron Imprimit, 2012).
I have borrowed some ideas about Parthia from the delightful novels of Peter Darman.
For Cicero I have used his letters, political speeches and numerous works, all available in various publications and on the internet. In one chapter I quoted extensively from a speech given by Cicero, which he himself published, utilizing the translation of D.H. Berry found in Cicero, Political Speeches (Oxford World's Classics, 2006).

In addition I employed:
Carcopino, Jerome, Cicero, the Secrets of his Correspondence (Two volumes, Routledge & Kegan Paul, 1951).
Rawson, Elizabeth, Cicero, A Portrait (Penguin Books, 1975).
Everitt, Anthony, Cicero, The Life and Times of Rome's Greatest Politician (Random House, 2001).

CAESAR, CICERO & CLEOPATRA

What really happened?

For Cleopatra, about whom much less is known, I have
used, among others, the works of Joann Fletcher, Michael
Grant, Joyce Tyldesley, Ernle Bradford, Prudence J. Jones,
Stacy Schiff and Stephen Dando-Collins.

The maps in this book are original works of Canadian
cartographer Julie Witner (jewelcartografx@gmail.com)
whom I found through freelancers.com.

The cover image was primarily created by Vook through
Bowker Identifier Services, as modified by me.

The photo of the author on the back cover: Nick Pinto,
Xavier '57.

Editing services performed by Kirkus Editorial.

CAESAR, CICERO & CLEOPATRA

What really happened?